MARGARET ALLISON

Promise Me

POCKET BOOKS

New York London Toronto Sydney Tokyo Singapore

This book is a work of fiction. Names, characters, places and incidents are products of the author's imagination or are used fictitiously. Any resemblance to actual events or locales or persons, living or dead, is entirely coincidental.

An *Original* Publication of POCKET BOOKS

 POCKET BOOKS, a division of Simon & Schuster Inc.
1230 Avenue of the Americas, New York, NY 10020

Copyright © 1997 by Cheryl Klam

ISBN: 978-1-4767-1599-5

First Pocket Books printing July 1997

10 9 8 7 6 5 4 3 2 1

POCKET and colophon are registered trademarks of Simon & Schuster Inc.

Cover art by Sue Rother

Printed in the U.S.A.

To my grandmother,
Melva Patterson Coles

"Do you believe in angels, Alex?"

Steve ran his fingers softly through her long hair.

Alex shrugged her shoulders. "I don't know. . . ."

"I never did before. But now I do. You're an angel, Alex. Mine and Ollie's. You're here to help us."

Alex opened her mouth but no words came out.

"I had given up hope of ever finding anyone like you." He shook his head in disbelief. "You're so beautiful," he continued. "Beautiful inside and out. I've never met anyone like you. Intelligent . . . kind. When you're with Ollie, I can see the caring in your eyes." He paused, listening to the music. "I'm not quite sure what's happening to us right now. I just know that it's different for me. You're different," he said, as Aretha Franklin began to sing "I Say a Little Prayer." He held out his arms, inviting her to dance. "It's been a long time," he said. "But perhaps you can teach me, too."

Their bodies began to move together, melting into one form. "Sometimes you look so sad, Alex. So lonely." He held her to him, whispering in her ear. "I understand pain, Alex. You can trust me." She looked up at him, her eyes welling with tears. *This wasn't supposed to be happening.*

Praise for *Indiscretion* By Margaret Allison

Books by Margaret Allison

Promise Me
Indiscretion

Published by POCKET BOOKS

Acknowledgments

Thanks to all my family and friends who provided suggestions and encouragement . . . my husband Brian, Julie Anbender, Lisa Mitchell, and Michelle Ronsaville Morrow.

Thanks to Corinne Russell and Severn Sandt for their tips on reporter techniques.

Also thanks to the three people who helped make my dream a reality: Amanda Beesley, Linda Marrow, and Esther Newberg.

Promise Me

One

Alexandra Webster opened her eyes. She had been having another nightmare. The same nightmare that had plagued her sleep for the past six months.

The digital numbers from her small, portable alarm clock glowed in the cramped, dark room. Five A.M. The unofficial beginning of morning. It was late enough to justify getting up, but still early enough to go back to sleep.

Alex sighed as she closed her eyes, pulling the heavy winter quilt up to her nose. Outside it was another steamy July morning, but her apartment was a frigid fifty-seven degrees, because of a central air conditioner that refused to turn off.

The phone rang, causing her to jump. She flicked on the bedside light as she picked up the receiver.

"Hello?"

"Alex!" A female voice on the other end of the line was breathless with excitement. "Turn on the TV!"

There was no need for introductions. Alex recognized the slight Spanish accent as belonging to Conchita Juesualo Bernstein, a fellow reporter and just about the only friend Alex had left in the newsroom. "Chita?" Alex asked, referring to her by the nickname she had given her. "What is it? What's going on?" Alex asked, concerned.

"Channel Forty-two. CNN," was Conchita's reply.

Alex threw off the covers as she searched around her bed for the remote. She pulled it out from underneath some pillows and pointed it at the small TV on

1

her dresser. The TV flicked on, casting an eerie whitish-gray light around the room. Alex pushed in the number forty-two. A split second later, she saw why Conchita had been so excited.

Alex recognized the man on the clip immediately. He was Steve Chapman, the darling of the boxing world in the mid-seventies. The station was running an old news clip of the fight that won him an Olympic gold medal almost two decades before. Sweat ran down his powerful body as he smiled his shy, famous grin for the camera and raised his hands over his head in victory.

"Mmm, *él es muy guapo,*" Conchita murmured, referring to the boxer's swarthy good looks and powerful physique.

"What?" Alex asked.

"I said he's very handsome . . . you know? Sexy."

"What's going on?" Alex asked, ignoring Conchita's comment. "Did he die or something?"

"No. Although he probably wishes it was that simple," Conchita said as a newscaster came back on the air. "I'm working the graveyard shift. About an hour ago, a report came in that Chapman's wife had been found dead and Steve Chapman was being brought in for questioning."

This was big news, not only for Alex but for the entire city of New York. Steve Chapman was popular gossip fodder for the local newspapers. Unlike other professional athletes who had quit before they reached their prime, Chapman had not faded from the public eye when he quit boxing more than fifteen years earlier. The media had been fascinated with this intelligent, talented man who had given up a successful career as an athlete to pursue an education and make his fortune in the business world. When he married Leslie Anson, a society beauty and daughter of Gordon Anson, a powerful New York tycoon, the media's fascination with this handsome former athlete only intensified.

Alex muted the TV as she concentrated on what Conchita was saying. "How did she die?"

"Supposedly, she jumped."

"Supposedly?" Alex asked. She got out of bed and began to pace.

"That's right, There's no suicide note. Friends are already saying she wasn't depressed."

"Where was she?"

"At a house they were building on their own private island in the Keys somewhere." Conchita laughed her hoarse, sexy laugh. "I'll tell you one thing, if I had a husband that looked like Steve Chapman and my own island in Florida, I sure wouldn't be killing myself."

"Who found her?" Alex said, all business.

"Stevie boy did. And get this. She and her kid were the only people on the island."

"So?"

"So now the kid's not talking."

"What do you mean?" Alex asked. She was getting frustrated. She was half tempted to go into work and read the wire report herself.

"Supposedly, the kid saw the whole thing. Whatever it was."

"But if he's not talking, why do they think that Steve killed her?"

"Rumor has it that Leslie had asked him for a divorce and he didn't want to give it to her."

Alex's eyes glanced back at the TV instinctively. The newscaster had vanished, and "LIVE" was printed at the bottom of the screen. Alex watched, speechless, as an older version of the same proud boxer she had seen just moments before walked out of what appeared to be a government building in Miami, surrounded by a hoard of reporters. He looked more like a corporate executive on his way to a board meeting than a man who had just been interrogated by the police.

"Oh my God," Conchita said. "He *is* gorgeous. But he sure looks guilty to me."

"Humph," Alex said, pretending not to be impressed by Steve Chapman's dark, alluring features. She paused. What was she doing? This was not her story. Nor would it ever be. And Conchita should've known that. "Conchita. Why did you call me?" Alex asked, even though she already had a hunch. About a year ago, Alex's cousin had killed himself after he lost his company in a takeover coup by a corporate raider firm headed by Steve Chapman. Everyone in the newsroom knew that Alex was collecting news articles about Chapman. Her now ex-boyfriend, Tim Barnes, also a reporter at the *Times,* had even begun to tease her about her obsession, referring to Steve Chapman as her "boyfriend."

"Because," Conchita said, "you've got to cover this. It's your story, Alex. It's got your name written all over it. You've already got background on Chapman. This is perfect for you."

"No way," Alex said, flicking off the TV. She sighed. "There's a lot of reporters who'll be hot for this story. Besides, Dick wouldn't give this story to me if I was the last investigative journalist on the planet," she said, referring to the editor in chief of the paper.

"Ask Tim to talk to him for you. He's his right-hand boy now."

"Oh, right," Alex said sarcastically. She sincerely doubted Tim would be all that anxious to have her cover a story about a man who had once inspired jealousy.

"You've got to do something, Alex. I can't stand seeing you this way. You've always been such a fighter . . ."

"Okay, Conchita," Alex said cutting her off. "Thanks for calling. It's just . . . look," she said reasonably. "I've got a lot on my plate right now."

"You've got nothing on your plate right now, and that's your problem. If I were you, I would try my damnedest to get this story. This could be just what you need to get back on top."

Alex said good-bye and hung up the phone. Conchita's words were harsh but true. *Just what you need to get back on top.* Because everyone knew that she, Alex Webster, was most definitely not on top anymore. She was on the bottom, with neither a relationship nor a career. Both had dramatically crashed and burned within a single month.

Alex sighed. Without the TV and Conchita's low, husky voice blasting in her ear, the room seemed small and quiet again.

Alex stood up and went to the bathroom, splashing some cold water on her face. She was turning thirty this year, and suddenly she had little, if nothing, to show for it. She had a cold, tiny, dark studio apartment and about five thousand dollars in her savings account. She wasn't married, nor was she even dating anyone.

Of course, her life hadn't always been like this.

Until recently, she had been pleased with her life and what she was accomplishing, convinced that she had chosen the perfect career. She was an investigative journalist for the *New York Times,* and her job was challenging and exciting. Her job had been a dream come true for a woman who had grown up fantasizing about being a detective. While other kids were watching *The Brady Bunch,* she was reading Raymond Chandler and Dashiell Hammett. She had originally planned on attending the police academy, but instead she went to the University of Michigan and earned her undergraduate degree and began writing for the college newspaper. After graduating, she went to work for the *Detroit Free Press* and continued her studies in journalism at U of M, earning a graduate degree in journalism two years later. She worked the crime beat at the *Free Press,* and she thrived there. She left the *Free Press* to move to New York and work at the *Times.*

Within a year, she had developed a style that was as unique as it was unorthodox. Once assigned a story, she would do everything she could to get information on whoever or whatever was the ultimate subject of her investigation. She went far beyond the usual reporter tactics of following the paper trail and begging people for interviews. Alex would involve herself in her subject's world, going "undercover" if need be, taking on an assumed name and profession.

Of course, her once-promising investigative career was now over. It had been buried with one little boy: Lennie.

Just thinking about him was still enough to make her cry. It was no mystery why he haunted her sleep. After all, it was her story about children who were drug runners that put him in his grave. Although it had not been proven, nor had his killer ever been caught, Alex was convinced that Lennie was killed by an angry drug lord because he was the seven-year-old anonymous source for Alex's article.

After Lennie was killed, her editor discreetly transferred her to a position as a reporter for the Living Arts section. And although he had publicly assured Alex that Lennie's death was no fault of hers, by forcing her to retire from investigative journalism he had effectively extinguished the only fire that had inspired her, the only thing that had a chance of rescuing her from the enormous feeling of guilt that was consuming her.

Without her investigative career to distract her, she had been forced to face the personal life she had neglected for years. Alex glanced at the fluffy, unslept-on pillows she had piled on the "guest" side of the bed. The demise of her relationship with Tim had been one of the first casualties.

Not that breaking up with Tim had been a bad thing, she quickly reminded herself. On the contrary, he had been fooling around on her for years, and she had often told friends that if she hadn't been so busy and exhausted all the time from her work, she definitely would have given him the boot. But she never seemed to find the energy, and he always appeared so contrite and desperate for her love after his episodes of infidelity that she accepted the situation simply because it was easier than changing it. And besides, he, too, was an investigative journalist, working alongside her at the *Times*. If they had broken up earlier, she would've had to see him every day, flaunting his love affairs in front of her. Tim had supposedly been devastated when she broke it off with him, and although she was sure that his angst hadn't hindered his escapades, she still found it somewhat comforting.

And they *had* developed a sort of "friendship." She knew he regretted his actions and felt sorry for the pain he had caused her. But how far was he willing to go to help her? Alex reached for the phone. She was about to find out.

Despite the early hour, she dialed Tim's number. She knew she would wake him up, but if she was going to try to cover the Chapman story, she needed to move fast.

"Hello?" A groggy voice answered.

Alex sat on the bed, suddenly encouraged. He would help her. He had to. "Are you awake?"

"Alex? What's the matter? What time is it?"

"Too early to call anybody else." Of course, she could always call her mother in Japan, where it was already evening, but that was more trouble than it was worth. There was silence as she gave Tim a minute to wake up. She imagined him lying there with some unfortunate woman pretending to sleep beside him. Pretending that she didn't really care if he talked to his old girlfriend or not. Or, if the woman didn't know him that well, maybe she was trying to make herself believe that "Alex" was a guy.

"Well, I'm glad you called."

"Yeah. Right. Especially at five in the morning." She was in the mood for sympathy.

"I don't care about that, honey." *Honey?* This meant two things. The first was that he definitely wasn't alone. He never called her *honey*. The second point she could infer from his use of the word was that either he didn't care about his overnight guest or he was making sure the woman knew that he was already spoken for. A man with baggage who probably wouldn't be sending flowers the next day. "What's the matter?" he continued.

"I need your help with something."

"Hmm?"

"Conchita just called. Chapman's wife is dead, and it looks like it might be murder."

"What? Steve Chapman? *The* Steve Chapman?" he asked, suddenly awake.

"The one and only. Look, Tim, Conchita thinks this story is perfect for me, and I think she's right. I need you to talk to Dick for me."

"Sweetheart, I don't want you running off after this guy . . ." he began in a patronizing tone.

Alex thought she heard a voice in the background. A female voice. And it wasn't happy.

"Look, um, honey," Tim said, practically whispering into the phone. "I've got a little problem here. I'll call you later. I love you." Before Alex could hang up the phone, she thought she could hear a door slam through the line. Apparently, Tim's guest had gotten the message.

Alex sat down on the bed. She felt strange, as if she were still in a dream. Steve Chapman's wife. Dead. She always had a sixth sense for stories, and you only needed one to sense the story lurking there. She wondered how the police knew that Chapman's kid was a witness if he wasn't talking. Had someone else seen him at the crime scene?

She thought back to her dossier on Chapman. She knew he had a child, Ollie, but she couldn't remember exactly how old he was. She seemed to recall that he was about six or so. But she had no trouble remembering the photographs of Steve Chapman's wife, Leslie. She had been extremely beautiful. The type of girl who goes sailing through a life cushioned with Jaguars and expensive trips to exotic islands. She had grown up on New York's Upper East Side with a father who had made millions before she was even born. It was his company that Steve Chapman had inherited.

Steve Chapman, unlike his wife, had not grown up wealthy. He had been born in a poor part of the city, to parents who were struggling to pay the rent each month. After his parents were killed in a car accident, Steve went to live with his uncle, a crusty old character who, in between drinks, managed to eke out a living as a boxing manager. Although most of his boxers barely managed to turn professional, it was enough to get Steve interested in the sport. He became a Golden Gloves finalist when he was only fifteen; at the age of seventeen, he won the middleweight title. After winning a gold medal at the Olympics, he turned pro almost immediately and defeated the number three contender in the sport. After another successful year, he stunned the boxing world by passing up a chance to fight for the U.S. title, quitting boxing and using his earnings to pay for college. He went to Columbia, where he was an honor student. By the time he went to Harvard Law School, he had lost all trace of his Bronx accent and had traded in his T-shirts for starched shirts. He graduated from law school third in his class and was hired at the Anson Investment Group by Leslie Anson's father. Rumor had it that Leslie fell hard for her father's handsome young lawyer, and after a whirlwind courtship they married, having known each other for only three months.

Steve and Leslie Chapman had possessed New York City. People were fascinated by them. He was handsome, charming, and determined. She was beautiful and elegant. But shortly after the birth of their child and the death of her father, rumors began to surface of a rift in their marriage. The Chapmans spent more and more time away from the city. While he worked in Manhattan, Leslie focused on her horses and her child, spending quite a bit of time vacationing on their private island in Florida. Steve Chapman, known for his workaholic tendencies, focused his energies on his job, taking an already successful company and turning it into an empire. He bought businesses and sold them as though he were playing an easy game of Monopoly.

Alex's heart raced with excitement as she jumped off the bed and threw open her closet. She always felt this way when starting a big story. But, she sternly reminded herself, this was not her story. These days, she covered fluffy, feel-good, neighborhood stories, like how to buy inexpensive chintz for dimestore pillows and make a meat loaf the whole family will love.

The telephone rang, and she checked her watch. It was almost six. She crossed her fingers that it was Tim calling back to offer his support.

"Ciao, darling. Am I calling too early?" The static cleared, and Alex could hear the tinkle of ice cubes in her mother's evening cocktail. Her mother and Lou started their cocktail hour the minute Lou, her mother's fifth husband, returned from work. Lou was a successful executive for a chemical manufacturer based in Japan, where they had been living since they were married seven years ago. Her mother had been a society beauty who viewed marriage as she did her dentist appointments: a necessary evil. And as husbands go, Lou wasn't that bad. Although she'd had to move halfway around the world, her latest marriage allowed her to maintain her country club lifestyle.

Unlike Steve Chapman, Alex had grown up wealthy, if not happy. Her mother had come from money and had increased her net worth several times over by marrying rich old men who left her hefty inheritances. The only husband she referred to as a bad investment was Alex's father, who had been a perpetual student until he drifted off to Arizona, never to be heard from again. Alex was only five when he left, and although she always claimed that she had her hands full with one parent to manage, she secretly held her father's desertion responsible for the fact that she was continually drawn to men who could not commit.

Concerned about her daughter's safety, her mother had been appalled by Alex's career choice. Once Alex started winning awards, she quickly changed her tune, bragging about how she had always encouraged Alex to write and to persevere, no matter what the cost.

Still, Alex had a strained relationship with her mother and hardly felt like starting off her day with the slamming of phones, the inevitable result of their mother-daughter conversations. Especially when her mother had already had a few scotches. "Hi, Mom," Alex said.

"Alex, I've just received the most wonderful news. Whitney Coals is engaged! Apparently, her fiancé is extremely well-to-do . . . his family is very well connected in Chicago. Old, old money. They met at that party at the yacht club last summer. You know, the one I absolutely begged you to attend."

Alex pulled a short black skirt and a cream-colored blouse out of her closet. "That's why you're calling me at six in the morning? To tell me that some girl I barely remember is engaged?"

"Barely remember? You two were quite close in high school. You even took riding lessons together."

"Well that certainly *is* marvelous news, Mother," Alex said, hurrying into the bathroom and turning on the shower. "Thanks for calling."

"You don't have to get so testy, Alex. You could be getting married, too, you know."

"Mother, I don't want to be married. I don't even want a boyfriend. I have a wonderful, full life," she lied, trying not to look around her cramped, dim bathroom as she stuck her hand in the shower. It usually took a solid five minutes for the water to warm up. "I don't need a man to be happy," Alex said.

"Whaaaaat is it, Lou?" her mother interrupted, yelling away from the phone. "Oh, Alex, before I forget. Lou said he saw on the news that the same man who killed your cousin just killed his wife."

Alex furrowed her eyebrows as she ran back into her bedroom. She picked up her remote and flicked her TV back on. "Is that what it said? That he killed her?"

"Of course not. But we know he did. Of course, they'll never get him. It'll be another O.J."

Alex rolled her eyes impatiently. "Mother, I have to shower and get dressed for work."

"Why don't you go after him, Alexandra? It's not like you have a husband or children to stay home and take care of."

"Mother," Alex said, her eyes firmly planted on the TV, "I'm not doing that kind of work anymore. Remember? I was demoted."

"Your cousin Jerzy was a fine boy, Bunny's only child. She still blames Steve Chapman for his death. You know, Bunny knew Leslie Chapman when she was still Leslie Anson. Apparently, she was an absolutely beautiful girl. Simply charming. A marvelous tennis player. Everyone always knew she was making a terrible mistake when she married that hoodlum. That's what he was. A hoodlum. Oh, he tried to pretend he was well bred, but quite frankly, Alex . . ."

"Uh-oh, Mother. That's the other line. I won't keep you. Tell Lou I said hello. 'Bye!" Alex said, delicately hanging up the phone.

She sighed with relief. She found it too distasteful to hear her mother continue her drunken diatribe which, no matter what the subject, always led back to why one should always marry a fellow social registrar—which would inevitably lead her to a discussion of Alex's father, who, coincidentally, had not been in the social register. But Alex tried not to take it personally. After all, it was obvious her mother was suffering from some sort of dementia. Everyone knew that Jerzy had never really been a fine boy, although he was her aunt Bunny's only child.

Alex stopped thinking as her eyes focused back on the TV. It was another clip from Steve Chapman's boxing days. Alex studied the expression of confidence, of power, that radiated from the man. He looked as though he could possess the world if he wanted.

Alex stood up and turned off the TV. For once her mother was right. This was a story that she couldn't pass up.

Two

Obsessions are funny things. An idea or thought gets stuck in the mind, and, like a record player that skips, it just keeps getting replayed over and over again. And so the video of Steve Chapman walking confidently out of the government building kept replaying in Alex's head. She was intrigued by the dichotomy evident in his handsome features. His mouth seemed to be frozen in a sort of smirk directed at the mass of reporters that surrounded him. It was as though he were taunting them, promising them that regardless of the questions they shouted, he would never reveal the truth.

His eyes, on the other hand, reflected little of the confidence evident in his mouth. They were a soul-searching deep brown, bloodshot and tired. They were the eyes of a man who has seen something he can't escape. A man who has something to hide.

Alex sat at her desk, staring into her computer

screen as though she were searching for inspiration. She glanced around the gray-carpeted walls of her cubicle, desperate for a distraction. But the barren walls provided little inspiration. Unlike her coworkers' cubicles, hers was not decorated with pictures of a loving family and pets. The only thing on her wall was an ugly recipe calendar she had gotten as a gift when she opened up an account at her bank. Until now she had liked it that way. No reminders of the past. Nothing from the present.

Alex looked down at the computer disk in her hands. After the entire Lennie incident, her mind had been dulled with pain and guilt. When she had lost her old job, she was almost relieved. She couldn't think anymore. She didn't argue her demotion because she had lost her fighting instincts. She was tired. She didn't want to be a hard-hitting journalist anymore. She wanted to be something else. Someone else.

"Good morning, Alex." Alex looked up from her desk. Conchita was peeking over the top of her cubicle. She walked around the side and set a stack of Xerox paper down on Alex's desk.

Alex glanced up at her. Conchita was wearing a tight black sweater and a small black miniskirt with tennis shoes. Her curly brown hair framed her pretty tan skin and large brown eyes. "Why are you still here?" Alex asked. "I thought you were working the graveyard shift."

"I am," Conchita said. She nodded toward the black and white clock hanging against the far cement-block wall. "I don't know if you noticed, but you're alone on the floor. It's not even seven o'clock yet."

"Oh," Alex said, suddenly embarrassed. "I thought it was later than that."

"I knew you couldn't resist this story," Conchita said smugly. "So I made these copies for you."

"You made copies for me? Suddenly you've got all this free time? Or is it just writer's block?"

"It's just that I'm trying to help you with this story."

"I don't have this story . . ." Alex began.

"These are wire reports. Computer reports. On Chapman," Conchita said, whispering in a conspiratorial tone.

Alex glanced at her. "I told you, Conchita, I don't think I can convince Dick . . ."

"Alex, I know what you said," Conchita replied matter-of-factly. "But as your friend, I've got to tell you that I think it's just pathetic the way you've been crawling around here lately. You've got to do something. Move on. You can't do anything to help Lennie anymore."

"I don't want to talk about Lennie."

"Or Tim. Tim's beyond help."

"I don't want to talk about Tim, either. My relationship with Tim is over."

"Then act like it. Maybe you should fight for your old job. Or even, God forbid, go on a date. You've got to do something, Alex."

Alex sighed. She glanced down at the stack of papers in front of her. The top page contained a picture of Steve Chapman attempting to get into his car.

Conchita smiled as she followed Alex's eyes to the photograph. "He kind of looks like a movie star," she said.

Alex shrugged. He was, by all standards, a remarkably good-looking man. Tall and muscular, with a strong, yet not bulky, boxer's body. Graying dark brown hair complemented his dark eyes. But she wasn't typically attracted to the storybook good-looking type. In fact, her friends had a tough time understanding her choice of men. Alex's boyfriends always seemed to be the slightly unattractive, physically unimposing type who, despite Alex's achievements in her career, would forever refer to her as "my-girlfriend-the-one-who-looks-like-a-model." They were all extremely intelligent super-achievers who were surprised and flattered that someone with Alex's beauty would be interested in them. They had grown up not attractive but smart.

Alex, on the other hand, who had always been the "pretty girl," picked intellectual men as though someone might evaluate her intelligence on the basis of her dates. She was five-foot-nine, with silky black hair and blue eyes framed with dark black lashes. But she was not the type to spend a lot of time dwelling on her beauty. With the exception of an occasional splash of lipstick, she rarely wore makeup. When she wasn't working, she just yanked her hair off her face in a ponytail.

"I guess he's attractive," Alex admitted.

Conchita rested her weight on her hands as she leaned over Alex's desk. "Is he innocent or guilty?"

"For Pete's sake, I'm not a mind reader."

"Alex, you've always had an instinct about these things. Always. And I'm curious. What do you think?"

Alex shook her head. "I haven't even given it any thought."

Conchita stood up straight as she crossed her arms. A sly smile slid across her lips. "Guilty! You think he's guilty, don't you?"

Alex pushed the stack of papers back toward her. "Why don't you take this story? You seem to be fascinated by it."

"If I were you, I'd talk to Tim the moment he came in. Ask him for help."

Alex shrugged her shoulders. "I already did."

Conchita smiled proudly. "And?"

"He was . . . busy."

Conchita made a face. "That snake doesn't believe in sleeping alone, does he? Not even for a night."

"I don't care," Alex said, a little suspicious about the venom in Conchita's reaction. She had suspected that her friend had become prey to Tim's affable charm more than once. "Look, Chita," she said. "I'm not sure what went on between you and Tim . . ."

16

"Nothing while you guys were together," Conchita protested quickly.

"Chita," Alex said sincerely, "if you like him, you have my blessing. It's not Tim that I want."

"What *do* you want, Alex?" Conchita asked.

Alex shrugged her shoulders. "I don't know. I just . . ." She paused. She couldn't pretend in front of her friend any longer. "Oh, Conchita. What am I going to do? How can I convince Dick I'm ready to handle this story?"

Conchita thought for a moment. "What have you got going on today?"

Alex glanced at her computer. "Some story about a deli that attracts a lot of tourists."

"That won't take you longer than an hour tops, interview and story. So read up," Conchita said, motioning to the stack of papers she had put on Alex's desk, "and when Dick comes in, go and talk to him. Beg, plead . . . cry. Whatever. He likes you, Alex. And he doesn't want you to quit. You were nominated for a Pulitzer, for God's sake."

"What if I haven't got it anymore?" Alex interrupted. "What if I just can't handle it?"

"I know how you feel, Alex. I do. But you are capable. You just have to fight."

Alex shook her head. "Alex," Conchita said, leaning toward her. "You know what they say. Just what you always told me. Just do it."

Conchita spun on her rubber heels and walked away.

Alex sighed as she turned back to the mountain of paper on her desk. She knew why Conchita was being so helpful. And, although Alex knew that Conchita felt a little guilty about her relationship with Tim, Alex knew her friend's kindness had little to do with guilt. Conchita had been through a divorce two years ago (which explained her full name: Conchita Juesualo Bernstein), and Alex had helped her through it as much as she could. Several times she had even written

17

Conchita's stories for her when Conchita felt as though she didn't have the strength to come to work. But Conchita had recovered, and as fate would have it, just in time to watch Alex's career crumble.

Alex picked up the stack and sorted through the papers.

There were several reports to choose from. She selected the most recent and read it carefully, searching for anything that might clue her in on what really happened. Steve Chapman appeared to be sticking to his original story. He was claiming that on the day of Leslie's death, he had flown his own helicopter to Rye Island, planning to spend the weekend with his family. Leslie and Ollie were already there, having taken an earlier flight that same day from New York, where the Chapman family owned an apartment. When he arrived at the house, he found Ollie alone in his room. When Leslie still hadn't come back to the house hours later, Steve began to search the island for her, concerned that perhaps she had "sprained an ankle and was unable to walk back." Finding no sign of her in the stables or down at the beach, he checked the house that they were building on a cliff about a mile away from the main house.

According to the report, he discovered her body on the jagged rocks below the balcony off the master bedroom. The article didn't mention any reason why Leslie Chapman might have committed suicide. Nor was there any mention of a suicide note.

Alex picked up the phone and dialed Tim's extension. She knew that chances were pretty good that after his date had left, he had decided to come into work early. And she was right. He picked up on the second ring.

"Have you heard anything?" Alex asked. She didn't bother with a greeting.

"Hey," he said. He sounded as if he was rushed. "About?"

"The Chapman case."

"Oh, right. Your boyfriend," he added, somewhat immaturely. "Your boyfriend's in trouble."

"Tell me."

"Big trouble." He suddenly slowed down, as though he was in no hurry to supply her with any information. He was enjoying keeping her in suspense. "So did you get lonely last night? Is that why you called?"

"Look, I'm sorry I bothered you. I apologize."

"Normally I wouldn't have minded. But I had a friend over."

Alex rolled her eyes. It was obvious that he wanted her to be jealous. Tim was still hurting from their breakup, and although fidelity wasn't his strong suit, he still claimed that he loved her.

"A friend?" she asked, trying to play jealous. She glanced at her watch. She wondered how long they would have to banter before he gave her the scoop.

"Nothing serious."

"Okay. So what have you got on Chapman?" she asked a little too quickly.

"You don't give a damn, do you? You wouldn't give a damn if I slept with your mother."

"I'd be worried about you if you slept with my mother. She's a viper with men. We call her the black widow." It was true. "But that's another story."

Tim cleared his throat. "I just got off the phone with Matt," he said, referring to Matt Charles, the Miami bureau chief. "There's no suicide note. Rumors are flying around, but they're hard to confirm. People are saying that on the day of the murder, Leslie told Steve she was divorcing him and taking the kid. Steve got pissed, beat her up, and threw her off the balcony."

"What about the son?"

"He was on the island with his mother when it happened."

"What about the nanny?"

"Amazingly enough, considering their money, they didn't have one."

"Any construction workers around the site?"

"That's one of the weird things. They had been called off the job a week earlier. In the middle of construction."

"For what reason?"

"The lead contractor has given a statement already. Said they were simply told that the project was being 'put on hold indefinitely.'"

"Hmm," Alex said, thinking. "Anybody else around at the time of the death?"

"Some ranch hand who works for Chapman backs him up. He says Leslie Chapman and her kid were the only ones on the island. And that leads into my second rumor. The kid saw his mother die."

"But he's not talking?"

"He hasn't said a word since the accident."

Alex leaned back in her chair, thinking. "How old is he?"

"Hold on, let me look . . . seven. Skinny little kid. Oh, and one more thing. Her body's on its way back to New York. She's going to be buried tomorrow. Next to her parents."

Alex could feel her heart drop. Something was terribly wrong with this case. She could sense it. "What? What about an autopsy?"

"He claims that for religious reasons, he prefers not to have an autopsy done. And it looks like the police aren't going to press charges because they're not going to make him do the autopsy."

"My God," she said quietly.

"Apparently, Leslie Chapman had tried to commit suicide before. Twice. I guess that was the nail in her coffin, no pun intended."

"Just tell me one thing. Who's in charge of investigating the case?"

"Sheriff Woford Mulney. As luck would have it, a close personal friend of Mr. Chapman."

"Tim," she said, almost breathlessly. "I was wondering if, well, maybe . . ."

"No way, Alex," he interrupted, anticipating what she was going to ask. "You're not getting involved in this."

She paused. "Look, Tim, I'm trying to get my life back. At least what I can still salvage. You and I have been through a lot together. And . . . well, quite frankly, I need your help."

There was silence on the other end of the line. Finally, he asked, "Do you really think chasing this story is going to get you back on track?"

"I have to do something, Tim. My life is investigative journalism, not restaurant reviews. I need this, Tim. Please just talk with Dick for me," she pleaded, hating herself for begging.

"All right. But just for the record, I'm not going to help you go off to Florida to go after some good-looking former athlete who has half the women in this nation lusting after him," he said.

"Speaking of which," she said, putting a momentary end to his jealous rambling. "What do you think of the information that I e-mailed you?"

Tim pulled up her e-mail on his computer. "Whoa," he said, scanning through her memo. "Looks like the Chapmans were living the good life." He glanced over the information. Besides their own private island south of Miami with its horse ranch and partially built mansion, the Chapmans owned a 130-foot yacht and a penthouse in New York City.

"So is Chapman staying on the island?" he asked.

"You got it. He and the kid and I think one employee. He let two other employees go this morning."

"That's strange," he said. "Why would he get rid of everybody?"

"Afraid they might talk," Alex announced.

"But wouldn't that make them want to talk more?"

"Maybe."

"He probably fired them because he doesn't need them anymore. He's probably planning on unloading the place as soon as he can."

"I'm not so sure. He announced that he's taking a leave of absence from his company to spend some time with his son. And guess where he plans to spend this time? Secluded on the very island where his wife died."

"Why?" Tim asked, surprised. "I'd think he'd want to get out of there."

"I would, too. But in any case, I'd like to go down there and find out."

"Alex," Tim interrupted.

"Please, Tim. Dick will listen to you. Just warm him up for me . . . drop a hint that you think I'm the reporter who should cover the story. He listens to you. He respects you."

She could almost imagine Tim shaking his head as he said, "Alex . . ."

"Tim," she interrupted. "Please?"

He sighed. "All right. I'll do my best."

She smiled. "Thank you, thank you."

"Good-bye, Alex."

She hung up the phone. Somehow . . . somehow she knew that Leslie Chapman had been murdered. And Conchita was right. She was just the woman to prove it.

Three

The man stood at the window, looking out. A slight breeze blew into the room, causing the sheer beige curtains to billow around him. It was a glorious view of the sea from where he was standing. A view straight out of a postcard. Lush, bright tropical flowers framed a sandy path which led to a grassy bank towering over the bright blue waters of the Gulf of Mexico.

But Steve Chapman was not interested in gazing at the water. Nor did he even notice that the sun was shining so brightly that the sea looked almost luminescent. Instead, his attention was focused on the little boy sitting on the grass below the window. The child was hugging his knees to his chest, rocking back and forth as he chanted the same words over and over.

Ollie was a beautiful child, with blond hair he had inherited from his mother and large blue eyes. But if one were to get closer and look into those eyes, one would see that the person inside was millions of miles away. They were vacant, as though no one was ever coming home.

Steve stepped away from the window and looked around him. He was standing in Leslie's bedroom, the largest and grandest room in the house. It took up almost a third of the upstairs, with windows that overlooked not only the water but the barn and the stable as well. This was the only room that Leslie had bothered to renovate.

Unlike the rest of the house, her bedroom was professionally decorated, with new furniture, drapes, wallpaper, and paint. When Leslie had informed him that she had decided to renovate the house, he had been thrilled. After all, he had always loved the old house, and Leslie knew that. But as soon as she was finished with her room, she announced that she hated this house and a renovation wouldn't change her mind. The only way she would consider staying on the island was if they built a different house. A modern mansion.

Steve had often thought that she hated the house simply because he had loved it.

He walked over to Leslie's unmade bed, picking up a picture from her bedside table as he sat down. It was a picture of him with Leslie, taken shortly after they had announced their engagement. He had loved her then, at least he had thought he did. Leslie was like a pretty, delicate flower that demanded constant attention and affection. There was something inherently sad about her, something that made him want to protect her from the world. For a while, at least, Steve thought they were happy. But for two people from opposite extremes with nothing in common to bind them together, a collision was inevitable. And their collision occurred shortly after the death of her father.

Gordon Anson, Leslie's father, had a reputation as a coldhearted, ruthless businessman who had been born into poverty and made millions without an education. When he was fifty-five years old, he gained entrance into the social circle that had long ignored him by marrying the most eligible debutante in New York City, a young woman named Dominic Niles. Shortly after the birth of Leslie, Dominic died after taking an overdose of sleeping pills. Her death left Leslie alone with a father who had no desire to be a parent. He demonstrated his lack of affection by immediately enrolling five-year-old Leslie in so many boarding schools and camps that she quickly forgot that she had ever lived in a real home.

Gordon Anson wanted little to do with his daughter . . . at least until he met Steve Chapman. He had followed Steve's boxing career and had offered him a job before Steve was even finished with undergraduate school. Steve had deferred the offer until he finished his graduate work, at which point he accepted a job with Anson Industries. Anson, long aware of his failing health and the need to find a successor, embraced Steve as the son he never had, showering him with the praise and affection his daughter longed for. He encouraged Steve to court Leslie and then encouraged them to marry. Several months after Ollie was born, Anson died, leaving an immense estate. But instead of leaving it to Leslie or to Ollie, Anson had shocked everyone by leaving the company and all of his money to his son-in-law, Steve.

Leslie, who had married Steve to please her father, blamed Steve for her father's will, accusing him of turning her father against her. Never a particularly warm person, she became even more cold and distant, withdrawing completely from her husband. When it became clear that Leslie's attitude was not going to change, even years after her father's death, Steve offered her a divorce, but that only made things worse. Leslie was convinced he was trying to leave her penniless. She began to use Ollie to threaten him and promised that if he were to try and leave her, she would take Ollie away from him. Steve did everything he could to assuage her fears that he would leave her destitute, offering to give her anything she wanted, if only she would guarantee that he would have joint custody of Ollie, but she refused. She had no intention of giving him anything, especially their child. She hated him too much.

Steve stood up and walked toward the door. Still, he couldn't say that Leslie had been a bad mother. Quite the opposite. That's why her actions on the day she died had been so surprising. But it was inevitable that Ollie eventually would have felt the repercussions of the hatred she felt for Steve.

Steve shook his head as he ran a hand over his forehead, soothing the pounding headache that wouldn't go away. He had planned on packing up Leslie's things, but he simply didn't have the energy. And there was no one left to help him besides Roger, and Roger was busy taking care of the horses and the property. Steve had fired the rest of the staff. He didn't want anyone gossiping any more than they already had. The tabloids were already full of horror stories about his life with Leslie.

Steve paused. From the doorway, he could hear his little boy still chanting the same words. Steve had no doubt that he was still curled up in the same position, a position he would keep until his legs were so cramped he could barely walk. Steve shook his head.

He would take care of his son and protect him. He would get help for him. He wouldn't let anything or anyone come between them.

Four

Alex stood in front of the deli counter. The deli was a popular stomping ground for tourists, and the editor of the Living Arts section wanted a story on why. So far, she was having trouble understanding it herself. She smiled as a big, burly man in a white apron piled corned beef on two large pieces of rye bread. "This is what makes this place stand out," the man yelled at her, almost screaming to be heard above the chatter in the restaurant. "You can't get your mouth around the sandwich," he said, picking it up and waving it around in the air. He put it in front of his large, wide-open mouth to demonstrate. "See? And I've got a big mouth!" he said, spraying saliva over the sandwich as he spoke.

Alex nodded politely as she dutifully wrote down what he was saying. "You got all that?" he asked, nodding over the counter at her notebook.

Alex looked up. She nodded. "I'm afraid so."

"Here," he said, throwing the sandwich on a plate and pushing it toward her. "You try."

"That's all right," she said politely. "Really." She pointed to her watch. "It's not even noon yet."

"I'll wrap it up for you. It's on the house."

She managed a grin. "Thank you."

"When's the story going to run? You sending out a

photographer?" the man asked, wiping some sweat off his nose with the back of his big, beefy arm.

"Maybe. I need to write it up first. If they like it, they'll send someone out to take a few photos."

"Hey!" the man bellowed. "I'll tell you what. If it doesn't run, you owe me six-fifty for the sandwich. If it does run, come back, and I'll give you another one. For free!" The man hooted and slapped his knee as though that was the funniest thing he ever heard. "I'm just foolin' with you, little lady. Don't be a stranger, got it?"

Alex practically ran out of the deli. But by the time she stepped back into her office, she was smiling again. She had spotted Dick's car in the parking lot, which meant he was in the office.

Alex sat down at her desk and pulled out a thick manila folder that contained all the information about Steve Chapman that she had gathered over the past year. She put on her glasses and picked up the phone, dialing Tim's extension with the eraser tip of her pencil.

"Yeah," Tim answered. He sounded harried, and Alex's hopes dropped as she waited to hear his excuse of being too busy to speak with Dick.

"I'm back!" she said, almost cheerily.

"Alex?" he said curiously. "Back from where?"

"From the deli story. There's a corned beef sandwich in it for you if you've got any news."

Tim sighed. "Alex, come on. I'm so busy up here, I'm barely meeting my deadlines. Can we talk about this later?" he asked crankily.

"Okay. How about a late lunch?"

"I think you're missing the point."

"Look, I just want to know if you had a chance to talk to Dick about what we discussed this morning," she said.

Tim paused. He had been hoping to get some sleep before they had this conversation. "He doesn't want you investigating Chapman," he said slowly.

"How did he say that?" Alex asked. "Did he emphasize *Alex* or *investigating Chapman?*"

"What?"

"Is it me he objects to or the story line?"

"C'mon, Alex. He loves you, you know that."

"Yea. So much that he fired me."

"He didn't fire you," Tim replied.

"He demoted me. That's the same thing. I belong in the field, not writing about fatty sandwiches."

There was a confused pause on the other end of the line. "What?"

"C'mon, Tim. I thought you could help get Dick to send me. Give it another try."

"C'mon yourself. We've been over this before. He wants you back eventually. He just thinks you need a break."

"I've had one. For the past six months. And now I want to get back. To a real story."

She paused. Tim was silent.

"I don't think so, Alex," Tim said in a tired voice.

"What's the problem?" Alex asked, despite the fact that she knew all too well what the problem was. "He's always trusted my sense of a good story before. I know there's something weird with her death. I can sense trouble."

"No, Alex," Tim said, lecturing her like a strict parent. "If you go, you go on your own. If you dig anything up, you'll have to try to sell the piece by yourself. The paper doesn't want it."

"Dick said that?"

"In so many words, yes."

"He doesn't know what I have to report yet. Perhaps he should wait to see what I turn up."

"What you turn up? So you *are* going?"

"In so many words, yes."

He paused. "I see." He cleared his throat. "You're crazy to go after Chapman," he said. "Without the paper's connections, you won't even get on the island.

No one's going to talk to you. You're not the police, you're not . . ."

"A reporter?"

"You *were* a reporter."

"Pardon me, my snooty friend, but according to my business cards, I still am."

"Right. Gaye," he said, referring to the editor of the Living Arts section, "is going to send you to a private island in Florida to report on how Steve Chapman likes his steaks cooked?"

"I'm going freelance."

"God damn it, Alex. This is ridiculous." He paused. "You've gone too far," he said. "And I've encouraged you. I can't believe it. I didn't think you'd let your obsession carry you so deep into insanity."

"Thanks for your help, Tim. I'll talk to Dick myself." She hung up the phone.

She sat back in her chair and sighed. She hadn't really been planning on going to Rye Island. At least, not until Tim tempted her. Now she knew she wanted to go. Why shouldn't she? She had nothing keeping her here. She hated her new job, and she still had five thousand dollars left in her savings. She could live off that for a while.

Still, she thought, it would make it much easier if the paper was behind her. *If* she could persuade Dick to let her go.

She opened her lower desk drawer and pulled out her road atlas. She flipped to the map of Florida. Rye Island was part of a small cluster of privately owned islands sandwiched in between the Florida Keys and the Ten Thousand Islands. Besides the Chapmans, who traveled to the mainland either by private plane or boat, the island was uninhabited.

To get there, Alex would need to fly into Miami and rent a car. She lightly touched the map and outlined the route she would take, running her finger along Highway 41 across the southern tip of Florida, through the Everglades. Once she reached Everglades City, she could drop off the rental car and charter a boat to take her to the island.

She closed up the map. She wondered what kind of a horse ranch Steve Chapman had. She gave a silent prayer of thanks for her mother's insistence that she take horseback riding lessons. For the first time, she was also thankful for her mother's rich friends who spent their weekend afternoons at polo matches and summered in Virginia horse country. If nothing else, her mother knew how to be rich, and she'd unwillingly absorbed some of that knowledge herself. For the world Alex was about to try to enter, that knowledge was going to come in handy.

Alex checked her watch. It was lunchtime. She eyed the white bag containing the corned beef sandwich. Perhaps a little lunch might help to persuade Dick to let her go. Alex smiled as she grabbed the bag. It sure couldn't hurt. Besides, after today, she didn't think she'd be able to touch another corned beef sandwich again.

Five

The wind picked up an old Coke can and sent it rolling down the dirty city street. Alex kept her gaze firmly planted in front of her, ignoring the leering stares and catcalls from a group of boys who looked like they were still in elementary school. They were children who were advanced beyond their years, solely because they lived in an environment that had no place for youth.

It was Saturday, August twentieth, a hot, humid,

sunny afternoon. But even the bright, sunny rays beaming down on the garbage didn't mask the gloom and dank darkness of this street. Alex used to love New York. But the story that had brought her investigative career to a screeching halt had changed all that. Now when she thought of New York, she thought of the New York Lennie had known. A city full of streets much like the one she was on right now, similar to the street in her dreams, the street where Lennie lived.

It was on this street that her contact, Ray Caldoni, had his office.

It had taken a large, slightly soggy sandwich and the threat of quitting and going to the *Washington Post* to get Dick to send her to Florida. He had given her three weeks, which was barely enough time to get there and unpack, and he knew it. He didn't want her to go, but he didn't want to lose her to a rival paper, either. Alex knew that her talent was not in question. What Dick had objected to was some of the risks that she continued to take while on assignment. He wanted her to stay put for a while and not make waves, until he could decide what to do with her . . . or, rather, her career. But Alex had made it clear that she would no longer stay put. So he had compromised, trying to pacify her yet still keep her out of trouble and her byline off the front page.

Alex paused outside a Gothic-looking apartment building. Even though she was wearing dark sunglasses, the sun was so bright she still had to squint to read the apartment number outside the building. She pressed the buzzer.

"Identify oneself," the booming voice said intimidatingly.

"Long time no see," Alex said into the voice box. The buzzer sounded, and Alex opened the door. Ray was standing at the top of the stairs. He was a handsome man. His gray hair was neatly combed, and he was wearing pleated khakis and a crisp white collarless shirt that was buttoned all the way up. He did not look like a guy who specialized in making fake identification papers.

"You look beeeeautiful," he said, holding out his arms. Alex climbed up the stairs and gave him a hug. Ray ushered her into his small but lavishly furnished apartment.

"You look almost as beautiful as these," he said, picking up a stack of documents. "I've got everything you requested. First-prize ribbons, a couple of trophies, certificates . . . Alexandra Rowe," he said, using her new name, "is quite an equestrian."

"Alexandra Rowe" Alex said wistfully as she smiled. "Certainly has a nice ring to it." Alex picked up a first-place ribbon and admired it. "And the license and passport?" she asked.

"Right here," he said, holding up an envelope. "You've been to England five times over the past three years."

Alex checked inside. The driver's license looked as real as the one she carried in her wallet, and the passport seemed equally authentic. Behind the passport was a package of checks from a bank in Virginia printed with the name "Alexandra Rowe" on them, various check-cashing cards, and receipts from stores.

Alex glanced from the envelope toward Ray. He was great at what he did. You could tell him what you needed, and he would deliver, no questions asked. It was rumored that the reason the police allowed him to operate was that the CIA was his biggest customer. "You are simply the best, Ray."

Ray smiled. "I can't tell you how many women have told me just that."

Alex laughed before checking her watch. "I've got to run. Thanks again for getting this for me so quickly."

"No problem. Come again when you can stay for a while," Ray said, opening the door. "And Alex," he called after her, suddenly serious, "be careful."

Alex gave him a quick wave as she dashed down the steps.

Tim was waiting for her when she arrived. He stood up and smiled. He was wearing jeans, tennis shoes, and a bomber jacket made from distressed black leather. Because of his baby face and the fact that he was only about five-foot-six, he could almost pass for a high school student who was desperately trying to look cool. Alex gave him a small kiss on the cheek. He wasn't unattractive, but he wasn't the kind of guy who would inspire women to swoon on the street, either. Still, he had no problem dating women. He was funny and quick-witted, and his sarcastic sense of humor was as potent an aphrodisiac as a muscular physique.

"What's in the bag?" he asked, sitting back down.

"ID stuff," Alex said, sitting at the table.

Tim shook his head. "You just love to pretend you're James Bond, don't you?"

She flashed him a smirk.

"I ordered this for you," he said, pushing a large Styrofoam cup toward her.

"What is it?" she inquired, looking inside the cup.

"Your favorite. Tall, iced, decaf, nonfat, vanilla latte."

She smiled at him. "After all this time. You finally got it right."

"No small feat." He paused as he watched her take a sip of the frothy liquid. "So," he began, "Dick tells me that you leave tomorrow."

Alex nodded as she glanced around for a napkin to wipe the rim of white foam off her upper lip. "What else does he tell you?"

"Not much. He was late for a meeting. Alex," he said, shaking his head as he handed her his napkin, "how can I talk you out of this?"

Alex dubiously inspected the crumpled napkin before she delicately began to dab off her foam mustache. "You can't," she said in between dabs.

"Cracking this story won't just be a professional victory, it will be a personal one as well."

"Why? Because of that cousin that you never even met?" he asked.

"You got it. The Websters may not be a close family, but we're a loyal one," she joked. "My mom has even helped me quite a bit with this story."

"Pray tell," Tim said with a touch of sarcasm.

Alex smiled proudly. Tim had been on assignment the past two weeks and had missed one of the most dramatic coups Alex had ever pulled off in her illustrious career. Even Dick had been grudgingly impressed.

Alex leaned forward and said, "I'm in."

All trace of humor vanished from Tim's face. "What?"

"I'm in," Alex repeated. "On the island. They needed a horse trainer, and they hired me."

"You've got to be kidding," Tim said.

Alex laughed. "Afraid not. I'm surprised Dick didn't mention it."

Tim shook his head, obviously impressed. "How did you do it?"

"My mom got the ball rolling. She called this big ranch owner friend of hers and told him that a sweet little friend of hers, Alexandra Rowe, a friend of her daughter's from school, was an accomplished equestrian living in Middleburg, Virginia, who was trying to move to Florida. She asked him if he knew of anyone who might be able to help her. Well, he called someone, and so on, and so on . . ."

"And miraculously, you ended up at the Chapman ranch."

"I put an ad in the horse paper down there. And guess who calls? Roger Merrick himself."

"Who's he?"

"Steve Chapman's right-hand guy. He lives on the ranch with Chapman and his kid."

"What do you mean, he called you? Where?"

"I mean he called the number I had listed. A number connected to an answering machine."

"Sounds like Ray Caldoni's work."

Alex smiled and laughed. "Very sophisticated, huh? When I called him back, he told me that Chapman was a bit premature in firing the entire staff. That they needed some help with the horses."

Tim frowned. "And he hired you."

"Well, kind of."

"Kind of?"

"He seemed really uncomfortable. Like he didn't want to talk on the phone. He asked me a few questions, but it was like he didn't want to talk to me. He said he wanted me to come to the ranch for two weeks." Her eyes focused on her latte. "If it doesn't work out, I have to leave. I don't have much more time than that anyway. Dick only gave me three weeks to get the story."

Tim paused, thinking. "I don't know, Alex. It seems weird to me. Too easy."

Alex shrugged her shoulders. It hadn't seemed that easy to her.

Tim asked, "But won't he be able to find out in a split second if you're a phony?"

"You don't know Ray Caldoni," Alex said mischievously.

"I'm not talking about shady reference checks," Tim said, growing more irritated by the second. "Isn't the horse world pretty cliquey? What if this horse guy . . ."

"Roger Merrick."

"What if Merrick knows people in Middleburg?"

"He's not a horse person, so he's not connected with the horse community there," she replied, shrugging her shoulders. "He does a lot of stuff for Chapman, but he's trained as a pilot. He doesn't have any horse connections at all . . . which is why I advertised in the paper," she added. "I figured he'd look there if he needed someone. And apparently, I was right."

"What about this Chapman guy?"

"He's not a horse person, either. His wife was." She took another sip of her drink. "It *will* work," she said, slightly irritated.

"As long as he doesn't get suspicious and trace back the referral to a guy in Virginia who never even met you."

Alex looked away, staring absentmindedly into the street. "There's always a risk."

Tim leaned back in his chair. He crossed his arms. "I don't like it, Alex. There are just too many holes in the setup. Quite frankly, I'm surprised Dick signed off. I think you're getting in over your head."

Alex wasn't fazed by Tim's concern. "You're not going to talk me out of this."

Tim leaned over the table, peering at her suspiciously. "Do you even know how to ride a goddamn horse?"

"No, Tim, I don't," she said sarcastically. "Gee whiz, silly me. I forgot about that. And I went to so much trouble to pose as a trainer."

Tim was silent for a moment. "That will get you in there, sure. But do you know enough to pull off the charade day after day under the watchful eyes of Steve Chapman himself? He's an intelligent man, you know." Tim stopped himself. He looked at her suspiciously, as if an evil thought had just entered his mind. "Or perhaps it's not the horses you're planning to ride. Perhaps you have an alternative plan up your sleeve?"

Alex shot him an annoyed glance. "What's that supposed to mean?"

"It's supposed to mean that it's obvious you've always been interested in the guy. And he *is* single now. Perhaps being a trainer is just a short-term goal."

Alex stood up. "Thanks for the coffee," she said coldly. "I'll be in touch."

Tim crossed his arms in front of him as he watched her turn and storm angrily out of the coffee shop. The door slammed shut. He shook his head. He couldn't let her leave like this. He threw some money on the table and made his way toward the door.

By the time he caught up with her, she was already a block away. "Wait a minute," he said, grabbing her arm and stopping her. "I'm sorry, Alex. I still get a little jealous, that's all."

Alex frowned, glancing back toward the light. The pedestrian "walk" sign flashed on.

"Look," Tim said, putting his arm through hers and walking her across the street. "Why don't you come home with me? We'll blast the air conditioning, open a nice bottle of wine . . ."

"No thanks," Alex said. She had had enough of blasting air conditioners. And she had also had enough of his jealousy. She glanced down at him. "I'm meeting Conchita for an early dinner. And then I'm going home and going to sleep. I'm taking an early train to Middleburg tomorrow. I've got a flight out of Dulles at eight in the morning on Wednesday."

They stepped back up on the sidewalk. Tim looked at her as if trying to read her expression. She was incredibly stubborn, and once she had made up her mind, detractors would at best be dismissed.

Tim nodded. "Are you bringing your computer?" he asked almost sheepishly.

Alex nodded. "Of course."

"You might as well know that when Dick talked to me today, he asked me to help you out on this."

Alex stiffened. "I thought you said he didn't have time to talk."

"He didn't. He just asked me to help you out . . . he didn't give me any details."

Alex nodded, not sure whether to believe him.

Tim continued, "I'm not supervising you or anything . . . I'll just be your contact at the paper. Here to help you out. Do some background checks, confirm sources, that kind of thing."

Alex glanced down the street. Obviously, Dick was

washing his hands of her. If he thought she had a chance to really turn up something, he would have managed her himself. But then again, she thought, Tim was an old friend. And she would probably have a little bit more leeway working with Tim. "Is this a trial run for a job as a deputy managing editor?"

"Nah. I'll always be a simple reporter."

Alex shook her head as she laughed, "Right," The smile faded from her lips. "I'll keep you posted."

"Even if you don't need anything. Send me an e-mail every now and then to let me know how you're doing?"

Alex gave him a quick hug. "You can count on it."

"Oh . . . and tell Conchita I said hello."

Alex shook her head. He really was incorrigible.

Six

Alex stepped out of the airport rental car building and drew in her breath. She liked hot, sunny weather and had always felt, if given a choice, she would rather be hot than cold, but the scorching sun and thick, muggy air were enough to cause her to reconsider her choice. She walked toward the small economy car she had rented, struggling to manage her awkward load. Her right arm was weighted down by her computer bag, which she wore across her shoulder like a purse. Her backpack was dangling on the same arm, hanging heavily around her elbow. She carried a large weather-beaten duffle bag under her left arm like a football.

She reached the bright red economy car that she had rented and carefully set down her load before unlocking the car. She threw her duffle bag and backpack carelessly in the back, and then, utilizing all the care she neglected with her other luggage, she gingerly picked up her laptop and set it on the passenger seat floor. Sometime before she reached the island, she would be forced to tuck it discreetly inside her duffle bag and take her chances, but until then, she planned to treat it with as much tender loving care as she always did.

Alex sped down the highway, periodically glancing at the map spread out on the seat beside her. She was not nervous. She never was before she began an assignment. As a matter of fact, it was usually a calm, quiet period in which she was filled with an almost eerie sense of inner peace. And this assignment was no different. Even her nightmares had abated. At the beginning of an assignment, she was usually so prepared, and so determined, that her focus on the difficult charade distracted her from any anxiety. It was the calm before the storm, for after a few days under cover, the anxiety began to creep in. But because she typically chose her own assignments, and her stories were ones that she really wanted, the anxiety never really overwhelmed her. It was during the quiet periods, like after an assignment was finished, that she had a hard time dealing with life.

Alex looked around, admiring her surroundings. She was driving through the heart of the Everglades, and at one-thirty in the afternoon in the middle of the week, there wasn't a lot of traffic on this small two-lane highway. Both sides of the road were surrounded by stretches of wild marshland that continued as far as the eye could see. She thought about pulling the car over to the side of the road to see if she might be able to spot an alligator wading through the murky, algae-covered waters, but she realized that chances were slim that she would actually see something, and besides, she was on a mission.

She coolly went over the details of her new identity.

Alexandra Rowe, twenty-nine years old. Born on a farm in Michigan, where she lived with her mother. Never knew her father. In a lonely childhood, horses were her only constant friends.

Not too far from the truth, Alex thought to herself as she glanced down at the map once again. She was ready for this assignment. She felt more comfortable with her role than with any other she had taken on so far. And it had been surprisingly easy getting into the secluded and remote Chapman estate. It was obviously meant to be.

She only hoped that things would continue to proceed as smoothly when she arrived. Her goal was pure and simple: gather information that either confirmed Chapman's guilt or exonerated him. She had already done as much background work as she could, including the typical paper trail research which entailed looking up anything that was covered by the Freedom of Information Act. In researching Chapman, she had spent hours at a courthouse in New York, where she had searched for anything that might give her inside information on Steve Chapman and his family.

She also reviewed court papers, wills, real estate holdings, taxes . . . basically anything and everything she could get her hands on. And her research had paid off. So far, she had discovered several interesting tidbits about Steve and Leslie Chapman, the first involving Gordon Anson's will.

Alex had been rather surprised to see that it was Steve, not Leslie, who had been the main beneficiary. Although Gordon Anson had given no reason in his will to explain why he was leaving all of his money to his son-in-law, Alex found it extremely strange that he would exclude his daughter from his money. Either he felt she would not handle it properly, or he simply preferred his son-in-law to his own flesh and blood, but in any case, it hinted at deep, underlying family problems.

The second piece of information (which Alex had

discovered by looking up every single society column for the past eight years) was an unsubstantiated but recurring rumor that the Chapmans were getting a divorce. However unhappy their marriage might have been, Alex had determined from her research that neither Leslie nor Steve had ever legally filed for divorce.

Those two tidbits together told Alex that although Steve obviously didn't kill Leslie for her money, she might have threatened him with divorce, and he might have killed her because he didn't want her getting *his* money.

Alex glanced up at the clouds that had started to accumulate above her. She hoped she would pinpoint a substantiated motive during the second half of her investigation, the half she was beginning today. At this stage in the game, a reporter usually had several options. She could call friends and acquaintances of the subject and try to arrange interviews. Or she could plan a stakeout, where she sat in a dark, windowless van for hours, discreetly spying on her subjects and watching their movements. Another famed technique was the ambush, where the reporter surprises the subjects when they're least expecting it and throws questions in their faces machine-gun style.

But none of the traditional options suited Alex. Her style, if it could be called that, was not so simple. It was more time-consuming, although ultimately more effective. She hoped to gain the confidence of perhaps not Chapman but those who were close to him. Like the man who managed the ranch and even Chapman's son. *And if that doesn't work* . . . Alex bit her lower lip. If that didn't work, then she had to resort to the least desirable tactic. She would need to search for hard evidence, that is, search the house. Any personal space, such as bedrooms and bathroom medicine cabinets, gave important clues to what the owners were truly like. Desks were another ideal item to search. And computers . . . a computer could be a godsend.

But first, Alex reminded herself, before she went

breaking into their house, she would try to befriend everyone and anyone she could.

And considering the population of the island, there were only three choices. Roger Merrick, Ollie Chapman, and the suspect himself, Stephen Chapman.

Alex heard the roll of thunder and glanced out the window as dark clouds continued to accumulate. She hoped her luck would hold up.

The small speedboat carrying Alex crossed the rough sea of the Gulf of Mexico with effort. She swallowed back her nausea as the boat bounced over the waves as if it might capsize any moment. Alex stood beside the driver, having given her duffle bag, which was carrying her much-beloved computer, the more protected passenger seat.

"It's not as bad as I expected," the man driving the boat yelled over the noise of the engine. Alex nodded. "You're lucky," he continued. "This sea can get pretty rough sometimes."

Alex glanced worriedly at the man.

"What part of the island are you going to?" he asked.

Alex leaned toward him, as though she hadn't heard him. "What?"

"East, south, north."

Alex shook her head. She didn't know. It was a detail she had overlooked. She was confident it wouldn't be the last.

The man screwed his bushy eyebrows together suspiciously. "You work for Chapman's business or something?"

"As of today I do," she replied. "I just got a job on the estate."

The man glanced at her, alarmed. "You don't say," he said, practically shouting to be heard above the sound of the engine. "I thought he just sent everybody packing."

"Well he sent one too many," she yelled back.

The man raised his eyebrows curiously. "A job, huh? I didn't think there was too much activity on Rye Island these days. When Leslie Chapman was still around, I used to take her back and forth to the mainland every now and then."

"You knew her?" Alex shouted, holding her hair back off her face.

The man shrugged. "Well enough. It was a real shame what happened to her. She was an absolutely beautiful woman. No one would've guessed that she had anything to kill herself over."

Alex focused back on the water. "When was the last time you saw her?" she asked.

The man looked at her warily as he slowed the boat down. "You sound like a reporter. If you are, we might as well turn back right now. I've driven a couple of them over there, and I'm telling you, he won't talk to you. And there ain't no Holiday Inn on Rye, either. No sooner do I get back and put my boat away than they're calling me on their fancy phones begging me to come back and get them."

Alex laughed. "I'm sorry if I seem nosy. I'm just curious. You see, I'm the new horse trainer. I've been hired to take care of Leslie Chapman's horses."

Alex checked her watch. Roger had told her that he would expect her sometime in the early afternoon. It was already three. She had tried to call the number he had given her before leaving the mainland, but there was no answer. Nor was there any machine.

"I saw him once," the man said.

"Pardon me?"

"I saw him fight. In Las Vegas. Actually made some money off him," he added with a smile.

Alex nodded.

"He beat the crap outta that guy. It wasn't even a match. That kid could throw a punch, I'll tell you. And then he goes and tosses it away like that. Up and quits . . . all that talent . . ." he said somberly. "A damn shame."

"He's been successful, though," Alex added cheerfully.

"He's got money, if that's what you call it. For damn sure. He's got money." The man pointed straight ahead. "There you go," he said, slowing down as he pointed to a structure on the side of the island. "That's the building where Leslie Chapman killed herself."

From the distance, the unfinished house looked as if it had been victim to a severe fire, burning out the insides. The structure was perched on a cliff overlooking the rocky beach where Leslie Chapman's body was found.

"I can't drop you off there," he said. "Too rocky. And too windy. I'm going to drop you off on the north side."

Alex nodded. She wondered how long a walk she would have from the dropoff point.

The driver pulled the boat over to a small dock. "This is it," he said, turning off the motor as he jumped up and grabbed the dock. He pulled the boat in and threw a rope around a post.

Alex looked around her. Not a person, or even a building, was in sight.

"Is this the Chapmans' private dock?" she asked.

"Nah. It's kind of a community dock," the man said. "It's the Chapman community. He owns the island. And everything and everyone on it."

Alex grimaced. She appreciated a sense of humor, but the timing had to be right. "I know that he owns the island. I meant, is there more than one dock? Is it possible they might be expecting me at another dock?"

"This is the dock that I use," he said simply, not answering her question.

Alex set her duffle bag down on the dock. She hopped up. The man stared at her expectantly. Alex looked at him, expecting him to say something else. She suddenly realized he was just waiting to be paid.

She took out two twenties and a ten and handed the money to him.

"Thank you kindly," he said, turning on his own brand of grizzled Southern charm. "Call me whenever you want to get off the island, and I'll come and pick you up," he said.

"Thanks," Alex said. "For your help," she added, glancing down a path that looked as if it hadn't been used in twenty years.

She turned back as the man pulled the boat away, churning up mud as he went. Alex sighed as she looked back toward the quiet, desolate path. She glanced down at her leather sandals and heavy jeans, made damp by the splashing of the boat through the waves. She was already wet and tired. She pulled a pair of sneakers out of her duffle bag and changed her shoes. She heaved her duffle bag over her shoulder as she began to walk in a direction that she hoped would lead her to the house. If she could find it.

Considering the size of the island, she was surprised that no one had come to the dock to meet her. She had just assumed Roger would. After all, he had arranged her flight. He knew what time to expect her.

She looked into the jungle-like, leafy green flora that surrounded the path. Although she had known that the island, with the exception of the Chapman entourage, was uninhabited, she hadn't expected to feel so isolated so soon after setting foot on it. Her instincts told her to start screaming, to call back the boat before it got too far away.

She wondered how Leslie Chapman, long one of New York's most prominent socialites, could have stood being so far away from civilization. Although the island would have made a wonderful vacation destination, she could hardly imagine wanting to stay there for very long. After all, even in the most exotic vacation locales, life has a way of finding you again.

Alex trudged down the dirt path. She stopped again to pull a large straw hat out of her duffle bag and tied it under her chin. She felt as if she was on safari. And she might as well have been. She couldn't have felt more lost if she were in the jungles of Africa.

Alex was on the path for a good ten minutes before it dumped her out on a well-worn dirt road. *Aha!* she thought. She had to be getting close. She heard what sounded like a drum roll, and she peered up at the sky. The dark, ominous-looking clouds that had appeared as soon as she drove out of the Miami city limits were multiplying by the minute.

Alex checked her watch. Wouldn't they begin to wonder where she was and come looking for her? She felt the weight of the computer on her arm. Or would they leave her stranded in the rain, tramping through the mud in her sneakers?

She picked up her pace to just short of a jog and continued on, swatting at the occasional mosquito.

She heard the truck before she saw it. She stopped, watching as the truck navigated the narrow road, kicking up dust as it went. It pulled in front of her and stopped. A tall, thin man wearing a baseball cap opened the door and jumped out. "Alexandra Rowe?" he inquired politely. Shaggy blond hair was peeking out from under the cap.

"Yes," Alex replied.

"Hop in," he said. Holding her duffle bag in front of her, she climbed into the cabin.

"Just toss that in the back," the man instructed her.

"If it's okay, I'd rather hang on to it. I've got some stuff in here that has a lot of sentimental value. I'm afraid it might get wet back there."

"I can guarantee you it would get wet," the man said, starting the truck and making a harsh right turn into the field beside them before Alex had a chance to fasten her seat belt. She slid into him, bumping up against his arm.

"Sorry," she said, moving back over to the passenger side. The man held back a grin.

"Are you Mr. Chapman?" she asked, pretending

naïveté. Of course, she knew what Steve Chapman looked like. And this man was definitely not Steve Chapman.

"Roger Merrick," the man announced. "I heard the boat circling the island, and when you didn't show up, I figured you'd taken the long way to the ranch," he said.

"The long way?" Alex asked as the truck plowed through the field.

The man nodded silently.

Alex nodded. "So, you manage the ranch?" she asked, again pretending naïveté. Roger started to laugh.

"Wrong on both counts," he replied. "I'm a pilot by trade."

"A pilot?"

"I had my own business chartering small private planes out of New York."

"How did you end up here?"

"Steve needed some help. And my company went belly up after the boom of the late 'eighties. So I came here."

"I assumed when you called me that you worked with the horses on the ranch."

"Well, as you'll soon see," he said, making a sharp right turn, "that would be the second count. This isn't any ranch. So if that's what you're expecting, you're in for a disappointment."

Alex secretly breathed a sigh of relief. She really must have a guardian angel. "How many horses do you have?"

"We have about seven. I just don't have time to look after them with everything else I do around the place. So we had to hire somebody. The only other option was to get rid of them, since neither Steve nor Ollie even rides."

"Why did they decide to keep them?"

"They were Steve's wife's horses. I don't think he's

ready to part with them. Look, I'm sure you know this already, but Steve lost his wife recently. Leslie."

"Yes," she said. "I heard."

"Well, let me give you a tip. Don't ever mention her here. Not to me, not to anyone."

"Sure," Alex said.

Roger glanced at her sideways. "Don't worry about the horses," he said. "I've ridden almost my entire life, so I'll be around to help you."

"Thanks," she said.

"I guess now's a good time to go over a few rules. I don't know what you've heard about Mr. Chapman, and quite frankly, I don't care. Just keep your mouth shut and mind your own business, and leave him and his son to theirs. You're not allowed within a hundred feet of the main house. And you're not allowed to go in or around the house that's under construction. If you have any doubts about whether or not you should be in an area," he said, yanking the truck on to what appeared to be a dirt driveway, "get the hell out. Got it?"

"Yes," she said.

"This is not a job for the inquisitive or the easily bored," he continued authoritatively. "You'll be expected to work long and hard. At the end of the day, there's not much going on here. No bars or dance halls. And Mr. Chapman didn't want a satellite dish on the island, so there's no TV. But you'll probably be too tired to watch TV anyway."

Alex listened attentively to his quiet, calm instructions. She had expected him to have a loud, booming voice. Instead, he sounded like a polite, well-educated, kindly uncle. She guessed him to be in his early forties. It was possible that he was younger, but his weathered, bronzed skin aged his attractive features.

They were approaching the Chapman estate, although it barely qualified as an estate. An old, elegant stucco house that resembled a Southern mansion sat at the end of the dirt road, overlooking the Gulf of

Mexico. Despite the fact that the pink paint was faded and peeling, there was an air of grandeur to the house. The roof appeared to be held up by the six marble columns across the front. Three small windows were spaced out on either side of the large, imposing front door. The second floor offered six floor-length windows, equally spaced as well. There didn't seem to be any glass or screens covering the windows. Instead, giant white wooden blinds were pulled back to let in the cool sea air as much as possible.

The grounds surrounding the house were unruly and wild. Masses of wild flowers and weeds lay tangled in what Alex guessed had once been elaborate gardens. Gigantic old palm trees surrounded the house as if in a weak attempt to protect the fragile building from the tropical sun's fierce rays.

Off to the right of the house was a red barn with white, peeling shutters that appeared to be in only slightly better condition than the house.

Just beyond the barn was the riding arena, and behind that, several horses were calmly grazing in a buttercup-covered field.

"I've had a tough time of it the past few weeks trying to take care of the horses and keep up the place and all," he said. "I told Steve that I needed someone to help take care of the horses. Like I told you on the phone, when I saw your ad, I thought you seemed just right for the job," he said. He pulled the truck next to the barn. "You're going to be sleeping in there," he said, motioning his head toward the barn.

Alex tried to appear nonchalant. "With the horses?" she asked casually. At the very least, she thought sarcastically, she hoped for a private stall. Or maybe Steve Chapman was too cheap to provide that.

"Oh, no," Roger said, chuckling softly. "You're staying above the barn."

Alex nodded, relieved.

"You've got your own room, with a kitchenette and a bath," he said.

Alex grabbed her duffle bag and followed him out of the truck and over to the side of the barn. He walked up some old wooden steps and pushed open a door. He held the door open and motioned for Alex to enter.

Home sweet home, Alex thought, looking around her. Well, not exactly. But it would do. It would do just fine.

It was a small room, with windows on either side. The room was simply yet comfortably furnished. On the far side was the kitchenette and a small table and two chairs. On the other side of the room, a colorful quilt covered a double bed. A plump old green chair that was fraying slightly on the armrests sat in the corner, and a wooden dresser with a mirror on top was shoved up against a wall.

Alex set her duffle down on the bed. There was a slight breeze blowing through the old wooden blinds.

"If you need any supplies, like groceries and stuff, you can write them down, and I'll give the list to the man who brings in all of our supplies. He comes once a week. In the meantime," he said, opening her small refrigerator, "I've taken the liberty of ordering you a few items to last you until Friday."

"Thank you," Alex said graciously. "I certainly appreciate it."

"You'll be eating your meals in here, or if you want, you can take a picnic to the beach."

Alex simply nodded. She felt as though she had stepped back in time. Everything seemed so old-fashioned here. At least, she thought, they had electricity. If she got too hot, she could just sleep in the fridge.

Roger shut the refrigerator door. "Well," he said, glancing at his watch. "It's getting late. Why don't you put on your riding gear, and we'll get the horses in the barn?" He opened the door and paused. "Oh, yeah, there's a fan in the closet if you need it. Steve offered to put an air-conditioning unit in here, but I said I didn't think it needed it. There's a nice breeze here at night. Not to mention, the room's not insulated all that well," he said, motioning toward the blinds. "The cool air would just go right through." He shrugged his shoulders amiably and added, "If you want one, let me know, and I'll talk to Steve about it."

Alex nodded. After freezing her fanny off all summer in her previous apartment, she didn't think she'd mind a little heat. "Do you live in that pink house?" she asked.

He shook his head. "No. I've got a little bungalow by the water. Down the drive a little bit."

"Is that where the Chapmans live?" she asked, nodding her head in the direction of the house.

"That's the main house where you're . . ."

"Not allowed," she said, finishing his command. "Just wanted to make sure." She smiled at him, putting him at ease. "Thanks for showing me to my room," she said. "I'll change and be down in a minute."

Roger pursed his lips as though he was about to say something. He quickly changed his mind, and, with a nod in her direction, he left the room, closing the door behind him.

Alex shook her head. She had withstood a lot of tough assignments, but she had a sneaky suspicion this was going to top them all. Well, she thought wryly, the man did offer to put air conditioning in her room. Maybe she had pegged this Chapman guy all wrong.

Alex took out her computer and inspected it for obvious damage. After assuring herself that it had survived the journey, she tucked it safely away in the bottom drawer of her dresser. She walked over to the window nearest the dresser and paused to admire the view. It was a remarkable vision of lush tropical flora surrounded by a pine forest. Something caught Alex's eye, and she paused, taking the time to lean forward and peer intently over the scenery. The makeshift roof of the house where Leslie Chapman had died was clearly visible.

Alex shut the blinds and began to unbutton her blouse as she turned toward the window that over-looked the Chapman house.

Despite the peeling paint and overgrown weeds that surrounded it, it still possessed the symmetry and elegance typical of the tropical residences built by millionaires in the late 1800s. It was easy to imagine what it must have looked like in its heyday. It wouldn't take much to make a serious improvement. A new coat of paint would work wonders.

She forced herself to shut the blinds, and she continued to change her clothes, her mind already overwhelmed by questions. How could a wealthy socialite like Leslie Chapman spend a night in a run-down house like that, let alone live in it? Why hadn't the Chapmans bothered to fix it up? Weren't millionaires supposed to be choosy about their surroundings?

Apparently not these millionaires. She wondered where Steve Chapman was at that very moment. Was he inside the house, reading to his son like a dutiful, patient father, or was he busy managing his business empire by phone?

Alex finished taking off her damp clothes before unzipping her duffle and pulling out a clean, dry pair of jeans, her riding boots, and a waterproof hooded windbreaker.

She was about to begin her career as a horse trainer.

Seven

Alex walked up the steps to her apartment, wincing in pain with each step. It had been a long day, made longer by the fact that the rain had turned into a blustery thunderstorm, scaring horses that were already skittish around their new trainer. She had hauled, pulled, and yanked more than she had ever thought possible. She shook her head. It was only eight-thirty at night, but it felt like midnight. It was difficult to believe that she had only arrived at the ranch six hours earlier.

During those six hours, she had not seen any sign of Steve or his son. She was beginning to believe that they must have been off the island, although Roger had not made any reference one way or the other. But Roger seemed to be the quiet type, speaking only to give instructions or to ask for her assistance.

She opened up the door and breathed a sigh of relief. She was alone. She had survived her first day, and although it really hadn't been good, it hadn't qualified as bad, either. She turned on the light by her bed, and the room was immediately cast in a soft, warm glow. The rain had blown in through the windows, leaving small puddles on the floor. She closed the wooden blinds, temporarily cutting off her only air supply. She figured she would close them only when she was undressing; otherwise, she would leave them open, even if the rain did blow in. She didn't have much choice.

She walked into the small bathroom and turned on

the water in the old-fashioned cast-iron tub. She then yanked her windbreaker over her head and undid the buttons on her light cotton blouse.

Her eyes fell on the closet as she pulled out her ponytail and ran her fingers through her wet hair. She wiped the sweat and rain off her brow, remembering what Roger had said about the fan. She walked over to the closet and opened the door.

Suddenly, something jumped at her, almost knocking her down. Alex screamed as she instinctively held her hands out in front of her for protection.

It was not an animal, though, that jumped out at her, but a small boy. He seemed just as startled as she was, if not more so. He ran silently toward the door, slipping out before she could stop him.

"Wait!" Alex said, quickly regaining self-control. But the boy kept running, as if he hadn't even heard her.

Alex ran into the rain after him, almost breaking her neck on the slippery stairs.

"Wait!" Alex yelled again, just before slipping in the mud at the base of the stairs. She pushed herself up, all the more determined to catch the little rascal. The child was fast, but not fast enough. She caught up with him just before he reached the front door.

Alex grabbed onto his small shoulders and turned him around. The child stopped struggling as he focused his big blue eyes on her. He looked so terrified that Alex was momentarily taken aback.

The light outside the front door of the house flicked on, and the front door was thrown open. "Take your hands off him!" a tall, handsome, muscular man yelled as he stormed out of the house. Alex recognized Steve Chapman immediately.

"Ollie," he said, speaking in a calm, quiet voice as he placed his hands on the boy's shoulders. "It's all right. Go back in the house."

The child glanced up at his father. "Promise me," he said. "Promise me, promise me, promise me," he began yelling over and over again. He shrugged off his father's hands and ran into the house, leaving a trail of muddy footprints behind him.

Steve stood in front of Alex, his eyes glinting coldly like polished steel. Alex stood her ground bravely, as she suddenly realized that her wet blouse was hanging open, exposing her bra. She indignantly yanked her blouse shut with her muddy hands as she calmly met Steve's gaze. She hadn't planned on meeting him soaking wet and half naked, but she would just have to make the best of it.

"I know this looks terrible," she began quickly. "I'm Alex . . ."

"I know who you are," Chapman said. Although he had only been in the rain a short while, his T-shirt and jeans were already soaked.

Alex's eyes briefly focused on the firm, taut muscles that Steve Chapman's T-shirt so prominently displayed. Although it was a well-known fact that he was an extremely handsome man, she hadn't been prepared for the brute sexual appeal of his muscular form.

"Your son . . ." she began, staring down at his bare feet.

He cut her off, not giving her a chance to finish. "Stay away from my son," he said in a low, threatening voice.

"I will," Alex said defensively, returning his stare. "It's just that . . ."

"No," he said, interrupting her. "Stay away." And with that, he turned and stormed back into the house, leaving a stunned Alex to stand in the rain watching him. It was only after the outdoor light was turned back off and she was surrounded by darkness again that she moved.

Steve slammed the door behind him, a bit winded and confused by the beautiful woman he had just encountered. Although he knew that Roger had hired a woman to help out with the horses, he had not expected her to be so attractive. Nor had he expected her to show up on his doorstep soaking wet and half naked.

He looked toward the stairs. If he had any question about where his son had escaped to, he would have been able to find him by following the small, muddy footprints that led up the stairs. But he already knew where he would find Ollie. He would be in his favorite hiding place—in his closet, tucked into a little ball in the corner.

Steve began to stride up the stairs, taking them two at a time, as he thought back to the woman in the rain. He had not wanted anyone else on the island, but Roger had convinced him that a horse trainer was necessary. When Roger originally told Steve about Alex, or, more specifically, her qualifications, Steve had made it clear that he didn't want this woman interfering with his or Ollie's life. Roger had reassured him the woman would be so unobtrusive that Steve wouldn't even notice she was around. Obviously, Steve thought, Roger hadn't seen her when he made that prediction. It would be difficult, if not impossible, to ignore a tall, raven-haired beauty wandering around the island.

Steve shook his head, frustrated. He would have to have a talk with Roger in the morning. He wanted that woman to stay away from him. And away from his son.

Steve opened the door to Ollie's room.

"Ollie," he called out gently. He walked to the closet and opened the door. "It's okay, Ollie. She's gone." Steve peered inside at the small figure before him. Ollie didn't look at him. He kept his head down, **rock**ing back and forth.

Steve sighed. Ollie had been a normal little boy until his mother died. But Leslie's death had turned the healthy, rambunctious boy into a mere shadow of his former self. Steve could feel him slipping away, each day a little more. He knew Ollie needed medical attention, but he couldn't risk that right now. He didn't dare.

Steve crawled into the cramped, dark closet and sat next to his son. He put his arms around him in an attempt to comfort him. "It's okay, sport," he said. "Dad's here, right here with you. And he's not going to let anyone hurt you." *At least never again,* Steve thought.

Alex shut the door to her room and leaned up against it, crossing her arms. She was covered in mud. She stripped in the doorway, leaving her wet, dirty clothes piled in a heap at her feet. She was angry. How dare Steve Chapman treat her like that? After all, the incident had hardly been her fault. *His* child had been in *her* room, hiding in her closet. And after the long day she had had, the last thing she was prepared for was a little boy to jump out at her when she opened the closet door.

Her mind raced with questions about Ollie Chapman's odd behavior. What was he doing in her closet? Why did he keep repeating the words "promise me" over and over? And what on earth had put the look of terror into the boy's eyes?

Alex saw something out of the corner of her eye toward the other end of the room. Water was beginning to seep under the closed bathroom door.

She ran into the bathroom and turned off the faucet, throwing her only towel down on the floor to soak up the water. She shook her head as she stood in her bra and panties in the middle of her small, wet bathroom. Her first day on the island had quickly turned into an unqualified disaster.

Steve Chapman waited until daylight to call Roger and arrange for an emergency meeting. As he waited for Roger, he took refuge in the library, a small room that functioned as his home office. He liked it there.

It was a mishmash of furniture, none contemporary and all comfortable. Scores of rather musty old books lined the walls. The desk was a large mahogany monstrosity that had been built by craftsmen right in the library more than seventy years ago. A fat, overstuffed couch that had been in the house when he bought it was placed against the wall, facing a fireplace that he couldn't imagine ever needing to use.

A large ceiling fan twirled above his head, and the hardwood floors creaked with age as Steve paced back and forth, his mind still focused on the woman he had met the night before.

Roger knocked on the open door. "You rang," he said sarcastically.

Steve glanced up. "We had an incident last night," he said simply.

"An incident?" Roger asked. He plopped down comfortably in one of the big chairs that faced the couch.

"That woman you hired. She chased Ollie into the house last night."

"What?" Roger asked with disbelief.

"My guess is that he was hiding in her room and he scared her or something. But still . . . I didn't like it."

"What do you want me to do?" Roger asked in a tired voice. "We tried to get by without any help, and it didn't work."

"Did she tell you anything else yesterday? About herself?"

"Goddammit, Steve. I told you I checked her out. And she checked out fine. But if you don't like her, we'll just send her packing. She'll be gone today. But I warn you, it's not that easy finding someone who's willing to move out here and look after a few lousy horses."

"I'm not saying get rid of her. I just want to know if she seems interested in more than just the horses." He paused, focusing his cold, deep eyes on Roger.

Roger looked away. Steve Chapman had a way of looking at people that reminded them of his virile strength, intellectual as well as physical.

"I'm asking you to keep an eye on her," Steve continued.

Roger stood up, his confidence back. "Why didn't you say so?" He tipped his cowboy hat forward and put on his mirrored sunglasses. "It'll be my pleasure," he said, a smile creeping up his lips as he thought of Alex's physical beauty.

Steve understood the look in Roger's eyes. "Roger," Steve reprimanded him. "Just keep an eye on her. You can keep your hands to yourself."

"As I said," Roger cockily informed him, "it will be my pleasure." Roger gave him a nod as he left the room.

Roger walked toward the barn, thinking about what Steve had said. Unfortunately, he had lied when he told Steve that he had checked Alex's references. He had meant to, but he was more interested in filling the position quickly.

He shook his head. If she turned out to be a reporter out to get Steve, he knew his ass would be on the line. And that was a risk he couldn't afford to take. At least not right now.

Alex was standing outside the barn, brushing down a horse. Her long, sleek black hair was pulled back in a ponytail. She looked beautiful, Roger thought silently. *Almost too beautiful for a trainer.*

When Alex spotted Roger, she stopped brushing the horse and waved to him. "Hey," she said, smiling pleasantly.

He tipped his hat. "'Morning," he replied. He sat on the fence railing. He thought for a moment, watching her. "I was thinking that maybe this morning we might go for a little ride," he said casually.

"Sure," she said, shrugging her shoulders.

"We got this horse a while back that I've been having a tough time with. Seems she doesn't like anyone sitting on her. I was thinking maybe you might give her a try."

Alex looked at him. Was this supposed to be some sort of test? Roger sat on the railing, his arms crossed in front of him, his face revealing nothing.

"I'd be happy to," she said.

Roger jumped off the railing. "I'll bring her out."

Steve recognized the neighing of the horse immediately. He put down his papers and glanced out the window. The obstinate sound emanated from Leslie's horse, Rosie. Rosie was a $50,000 prize-winning champion who had refused to let anyone else mount her, let alone ride her, since her mistress died.

He watched as Roger led a stomping Rosie into the arena, toward Alex. The muscles in Steve's jaw began to tighten as he pondered the consequences. But surely, he reassured himself, surely Roger wouldn't ask this woman to ride Rosie.

Steve watched carefully as Roger tried to soothe the horse. Alex walked around to the side of Rosie.

Steve stood up. What was Roger doing? He knew what would happen if that woman attempted to ride Rosie. Was this some sort of test Roger had rigged up to see if Alex Rowe was as good as her résumé said she was?

Panic rushed through him as he dashed out of the house, running for the arena. He had to stop her before she got hurt.

"Wait!" he yelled, too late. Alex was on top of the horse, and obviously out of control. She struggled to stay on as the horse reared and kicked, doing everything in its power to throw her. Alex held on to the reins tightly, digging her knees and heels into the horse's side.

Steve ran toward the arena. "Roger!" he yelled. Roger turned and looked at him. "What the hell are you doing?"

Roger calmly raised an eyebrow and turned back toward Alex. "She's giving Rosie a lesson," he said.

Alex's brow was furrowed in concentration as she focused her entire being on the horse. She dug her lower legs into the animal, not relaxing until she could feel the horse calm down. She glanced at the jump to the right. If this was a test, she didn't plan on taking it again. She galloped the horse toward the jump.

"Stop her!" Steve commanded, watching Alex gallop toward the jump.

Roger shook his head. "She's got it," he whispered to himself, not taking his eyes off her. The horse flew over the jump, landing smoothly on the other side.

Roger ran into the arena to help Alex stop the horse.

Steve shook his head. He was surprised. And impressed. Leslie had been an excellent rider, but even she had been unable to jump with Rosie.

Roger grabbed the reins as Alex slid down the side. "That was a nice piece of riding."

"Thanks," she said, glancing over at Steve just as he turned back toward the house. She had seen him running out to stop her, and the fact that he had been watching her had given her even more incentive to take control of Rosie.

"So, you ride English," Roger said, referring to her style of riding.

"I'm trained in both English and Western," she said. "I just prefer English. Does he ride?" she asked Roger, nodding toward Steve.

Roger shook his head. "Nope," he said as he began to lead Rosie back into the barn. "But you obviously do. That was an excellent bit of riding out there," he said.

"Thanks," she replied, hiding her shaking hands as she followed Roger into the cool, dark building. She had surprised herself. She was sure that her mother would feel vindicated knowing that the money she had spent giving her daughter riding lessons had finally paid off.

"Who usually rides her?" Alex asked as she breathed in the distinctive, slightly sweet smell of wood chips and straw.

"She was Leslie's horse," he said, undoing the latch on her stall. The horse whinnied as though responding to the mention of her mistress.

Alex looked at the horse with dismay.

"She doesn't like going back in her stall," he said, yanking on the horse's reins. "C'mon, goddammit," Roger yelled, yanking hard on the reins.

Alex shook her head. "Try talking to her calmly," she said.

Roger gave the reins another yank, and Rosie resentfully stepped into her stall.

"I prefer to use the reins," he said, glancing over at Alex. "Can you clean her off now? Or did you need to rest for a minute?"

"No. I'm fine," she said, forcing a smile.

"Great," Roger said, smiling. "Afterwards maybe we'll take a ride down to the water with Sarah and Max," he said, nodding toward two horses at the other end of the stable. "Give them their exercise today."

Alex nodded. "Sure." She hesitated. She might as well take advantage of this brief moment of closeness. "By the way, I had kind of a strange experience last night. I got back to my room, and when I opened my closet, a child came running out. It scared the hell out of me."

Roger looked at her. "I'll bet."

"Was that Mr. Chapman's child?"

Roger hesitated. He nodded.

"Is he all right?" she continued. "I mean, he didn't say anything, he just . . ."

"Look, Miss Rowe," he interrupted, becoming cold and distant. "Like I already said, I wouldn't ask too many questions if I were you."

Alex innocently shrugged her shoulders. "I was just curious," she said defensively.

"You know what they say," he said quickly. "Curiosity killed the cat."

Alex watched him walk out of the barn as his words echoed in her mind.

Eight

Alex rolled up her sleeves and swatted a fly away from her face. It had been a long day. But then again, in the week since she had arrived, every day had been long. The weather had been hot, humid, and muggy, with showers almost every afternoon. Her days typically began at six in the morning and ended at seven at night. It was not the hours or the weather that was causing her to grow weary of her self-induced assignment, however. It was the slow, sorry pace of her investigation. Besides the initial incident, she had not seen Chapman or his child in the week she had been on the island. But at this point, she wasn't hoping for another personal encounter. She needed access to the house. And she needed it fast. Time was running out.

Of course, she hadn't quite figured out how she was going to get inside. Not only did she have to sneak past Steve Chapman himself, but she had to escape Roger, who rarely let her out of his sight. Even her hope to visit the construction site where Leslie had died had been dashed by her watchdog overseer. Of course, Alex thought, she wouldn't tell Tim about the snags she was encountering in her investigation. In fact, although she religiously checked her e-mail each day, she had avoided communication with Tim. She wanted to wait until she had something to tell him besides how to brush a horse.

Alex pushed her straw hat back on her head as she wiped the sweat off her brow. The air was even heavier than usual because of the thick storm clouds that were quickly covering the sky over the island. She knew horses didn't like thunder, and she wasn't sure how much time she had before the storm broke.

She walked up to Rosie and grabbed the horse by her bit. Alex smiled. She was beginning to act and feel like a real cowgirl. Her white skin had turned a healthy bronze, and her manicured nails were nonexistent. The insides of her legs were so sore it took all of her energy not to walk with a limp.

"Hey, Alex!" Roger called out. He was galloping toward her on Max, a sleek, beautiful stallion. With his cowboy hat and the red bandanna tied around his forehead, he looked handsome in a Marlboro Man sort of way. Although he had been pleasant enough, she had been unable to have any real conversation with him, despite the hours they had spent together. He reminded Alex of the quiet, shy type who lets loose once he's had a drink or two.

"We better get these horses inside. Why don't you grab Rosie and bring her in. I'm gonna clean off Max, and then I'll grab Tootsie," he said, referring to the miniature horse that she assumed had been bought for the Chapmans' son.

Alex turned away from him as she rolled her eyes. Roger seemed to thoroughly enjoy having an underling to boss around. He sometimes treated her as though she had little, if any, common sense. Rather than point out that she had been preparing the horses for the storm for the past hour, she gave him a quick, courteous nod as she continued to lead Rosie back into the barn. "Here you go," she said softly as she pulled a carrot out of her pocket and handed it to the horse. She had decided that the key to handling Rosie was always to remind her of who was boss, and constantly to soothe her and sweet-talk her. It was a fine line one needed to walk, but so far she had managed it. Despite his cavalier attitude, she knew that Roger had been impressed with the way she was able to handle Rosie. If he had had any doubts about her, she knew that Rosie had laid them to rest. Since Rosie had accepted her, Roger seemed to accept her as well.

She opened up the door to the stall and quickly turned back toward the horse. Rosie had made it clear that she did not like going back into her stall, and the whole maneuver had to be performed with absolute precision. Alex grabbed Rosie's reins with both hands as she began to back into the stall, gently pulling Rosie as she sweet-talked her into compliance.

A sudden crash of thunder caught her unaware, and before she had a chance to react, the horse reared.

Alex instinctively yanked the reins, pulling the horse into her and away from the door. Rosie reared again, causing Alex to scream as she was knocked to the ground.

"Alex!" Roger shouted, running inside the barn. Rosie was rearing outside her stall, and Alex was nowhere in sight. "Alex!" he yelled again, lunging toward Rosie. He grabbed her reins and maneuvered her into Max's stall. He turned back toward Rosie's stall.

Alex was inside the stall, lying on the ground. "Are you all right?" he asked, kneeling beside her.

Alex looked at him as the tears began to well in her eyes. She knew that if she opened her mouth to answer she would begin to sob.

"Oh my God," Roger said, panicking as he saw the tears in her eyes. "You're hurt."

Alex nodded as she began to cry. It wasn't that she was in terrible pain. At worst, she had sprained her ankle. It was just that the accident was the final straw. It was all she needed to send her over the edge. She had worked hard since she had been there, and she had discovered nothing. She was in over her head. With life.

"Where?" Roger asked, confused. "Where does it hurt?" he asked.

She had trouble getting the words out between her sobs. "My ankle. I hurt my ankle."

"Can you sit up?" Roger asked.

Alex nodded, embarrassed that she was crying. "I think so," she said. She began to sit up, but the simple effort of changing her position caused her to wince in pain.

"Don't move," Steve commanded from behind Roger. Roger stepped aside as Steve took his place beside Alex's crumpled form.

He knelt down beside her and took her hands. The stern visage he had presented the other evening had disappeared. He seemed genuinely concerned. "What happened?" he asked tenderly.

"She screamed, and the horse reared . . ." Roger began, making it sound as if she had screamed for no reason whatsoever.

She would've liked to say something in her defense, but the best she could do was shake her head. Oh God, she thought. This was terrible. She was hurt and crying like a baby in front of the man she had come to investigate. It didn't get much worse than this. "The thunder scared the horse . . ." she spat out between sobs.

"Okay," Chapman said quietly, brushing the hair away from her damp forehead. "Just lie still for a minute."

Alex watched Steve as he gently ran his fingers over her shoulders. For some reason, she felt better now that he was there. He had a take-charge charisma that made it seem everything was going to be all right.

"Roger," Steve commanded, "go check on Ollie."

Roger nodded. He half ran, half walked out of the barn.

Steve turned back toward Alex. He ran his hands down her arms. "Does this hurt?" he asked. Alex was mesmerized by the sound of his soothing, tender voice. It was a soft baritone that for some reason made her think of thick honey. Substantial yet sweet. Alex shook her head, wincing again. "Don't move, just answer," he said. "Does this hurt?" he repeated, running his hands down her legs, checking for broken bones.

"My ankle," she said.

Steve nodded. "Your neck and shoulders feel all right?" he asked, reaching his hands inside the neckline of her shirt as he touched her bare neck gently.

"Yes," Alex whispered.

"Just your ankle?" he asked again, already untying her shoes and pulling them off. He took off her sock and rolled up her jeans to expose her ankles. "Your right ankle is swollen." His eyes locked on hers. "I'm going to take you into the house. It will be easier to take care of you there. Do you feel like you can walk if I help you in?"

Alex nodded, attempting to push herself up by her elbows. She quickly decided to milk this accident for all it was worth. A little pain was worth the price of admission into the main house.

"We'll lay you down inside where you'll be more comfortable until we get the doctor out here," Steve said, leaning over her as he helped her up. Alex felt a wave of dizziness, and she instinctually grabbed onto Steve to balance herself. Steve responded by swooping her into his arms.

"I can walk," she protested weakly.

"Why walk when you can ride?" Steve replied, carrying her out of the barn. Alex could feel the power in his strong arms as he held her to him. She allowed her head to fall against his shoulder. She had never been carried by a man before, and she had to admit, she was kind of enjoying it, despite her pain. He seemed so sweet, so kind and gentle. Not at all like the handsome demon she had expected.

For a quick second, she almost felt attracted to him, but fortunately she had her wits about her enough to remind herself of why she was on the island. Although she had made some unwise choices in her past regarding the men she dated, as of yet, at least, she had avoided dating anyone who may have committed murder.

Steve kicked the front door open with his foot and carried her inside the house. Alex gazed up at the dusty chandelier drooping in the unexpectedly large entranceway. A grandfather clock stood against a faded mossy green wall.

Roger appeared at the top of the grand circular staircase and peered down. When he saw that Steve was carrying Alex, he rushed down the stairs.

"Let me help you," he said.

"I've got her," Steve said, pulling her into him. Alex was afraid to look into his eyes.

Roger stood aside, allowing them to pass. "Ollie's in his room. Where are you taking her?"

"To the guest room," Steve replied as he began to carry her up the stairs. "Call the doctor. Tell her you'll be by to pick her up."

"Is she that bad?" Roger asked.

"I think she should get checked out by someone," Steve replied.

"I'm all right. Really," Alex said, piping up.

Steve shook his head as he reached the top of the stairs. "Your ankle is swollen. We should find out if it's broken. And you look like you're going to be covered in bruises."

"I'm just dirty," she replied.

Steve smiled. "We'll see," he said, opening the door to a room. He laid her down gently on the bed. "Roger's taking the helicopter, so the doctor should be here soon."

"The helicopter?" Alex asked.

"In addition to his talents on the ranch, Roger is

also an accomplished pilot. He'll have her here in no time."

"Oh my God," Alex began. "Please. I'm fine. Really. Don't go to any trouble," she said, wiping her nose with the back of her hand.

Steve shook his head. "You should have a doctor look you over." He sat down next to her on the bed. Alex couldn't help but be suspicious of his sudden caring. Was he worried that she might sue him? "Do you want some water?" he continued. "Something to drink? A shot of whiskey, perhaps?"

Alex studied his face. He had the strong, chiseled features of a man who was an athlete in peak condition, although even in the darkness she could see the gray that was beginning to creep into his dark hair, something she thought made him even more attractive. He was wearing blue jeans with a loose, wrinkled linen shirt that only had three of its buttons buttoned, as though he had dressed so hurriedly he hadn't had time to close it properly.

"Maybe some water," she said. "And some aspirin."

"You got it. I'll even throw in some ice for your ankle," he said, standing up. "By the way," he said. "I don't think we've been properly introduced. I'm Steve Chapman."

Alex gave him a weak smile. "And I'm . . ."

"Alex Rowe," he said. Steve hesitated. "I've been meaning to talk to you about the other night. Roger told me that Ollie was in your room and surprised you." He paused. "I'm sorry if my son scared you. Ollie's only seven, and I think he gets bored here all day with me. It's been a long summer . . . for all of us."

Before Alex could respond, he gave her a quick, courteous nod and left the room, leaving her to stare after him.

Nine

Alex's eyes snapped open. She smiled when she saw where she was. *I've made it,* she thought to herself. She was in the main house.

She turned her head toward the tiny rays of sun that were peeking in through the closed blinds. As she raised a hand to her forehead, she noticed the sheer, gauzy material of her nightgown. She pushed down the crisp white sheets as she glanced curiously at her attire. She was dressed in a nightgown that looked as if it needed a tiara to be complete. It was a light blue satin empire-waist gown with layers of sheer silky panels draped over the sleeves and skirt.

Alex scooted up in bed, groaning as she moved. She felt as if she had been trampled on by wild elephants, an analogy that wasn't far from the truth.

She heard a noise. She leaned forward, wincing in pain. She heard it again. A groan. An echo of her groan.

She peeked around the other side of the bed.

The child, Ollie, sat on the floor in the corner of her room. He was smiling.

"Hello there," she said. "What's your name?"

The smile faded from the boy's face as he stared at her.

"Can you tell me your name?" she asked, peering at him intently. He was a beautiful child, with long, lush lashes that framed big blue eyes.

"Ollie," Steve interrupted, appearing in the doorway. "I asked you to stay away from Miss Rowe," he said sternly to his son.

The boy stared at him.

"That's all right," Alex said. "I don't mind."

"Go to your room, please," Steve said, looking at his son. Ollie stood up and backed away, as though frightened. When he hit the wall, he jumped and ran quickly out of the room, dashing past his father. Steve looked after him, and for a quick second a brief wave of sadness flashed over his face. But it was gone by the time he had turned back toward Alex. "He seems to be fascinated with you, Miss Rowe."

Alex shrugged her shoulders uncomfortably. She was mortified by her hysterics the night before. Nothing like having a nervous breakdown in front of your employer.

"So. How are you feeling this morning?" he asked charmingly as he focused his deep brown eyes on her. He sat down at the edge of her bed. He was dressed casually in a short-sleeved rugby shirt and jeans. His brown hair was thick and tousled.

"Fine. I guess," she replied, scooting over. "I'm really sorry about last night."

"Sorry? About what?"

"I was tired . . . I think I overreacted."

"You've got a bad sprain. I've had them myself. And I've cried every time I got one," he said, his eyes twinkling mischievously.

Alex smiled. "I doubt that," she said.

"How did you sleep?" he inquired politely.

"Great," she said sincerely.

Steve nodded. "The doctor gave you a painkiller that knocked you out," he informed her.

She motioned to her attire. "I don't even remember getting dressed in my party outfit."

"That was my wife's," he said.

"Not that it's not lovely," she continued, slightly embarrassed.

"I didn't want to go rummaging through your room

looking for your pajamas, so I simply asked the doctor to dress you in one of my wife's old nightgowns."

Alex tried not to grimace. There was something about wearing his dead wife's clothes that left a little to be desired. Although it was a good sign. If he had her nightgowns lying around, perhaps he hadn't packed up her personal items yet. "Thank you," she managed. "So what did the doctor say?"

"No broken bones. No concussion, although she did recommend that you stay off your feet for about a week."

"A week?" she repeated.

He nodded as he stared at her intently. Alex looked away, aware that she was blushing.

"Which is why," he said, "I've decided that it would probably be best if you returned to your home."

She looked back at him, surprised. She was aware she had overreacted, but wasn't that kind of a harsh punishment?

"I'll fly you back home today, if you want. Besides the helicopters on the island, we keep a private plane at the Miami airport. Roger will take you. You can just stretch out and sleep all the way there."

Of course, Alex realized. He was trying to be charming so that she wouldn't cause any problems. He was trying to smooth-talk his way out of a lawsuit. "That's not necessary. I'm quite happy here. Really. I won't be a bother. I can go back to my room above the barn and wait it out there. I can't imagine I'll need to stay in bed for an entire week. I'm already feeling so much better," she said, wincing with pain as she tried to sit up straight.

"Let's see how that ankle looks this morning," he said, noticing her wince.

Alex slowly pulled her leg out from under the covers. Steve picked up her foot and inspected her swollen blue ankle by running his fingers gently around her bruises.

"Do you have any family, Miss Rowe?" he asked, gently holding her leg as he focused on her ankle.

"I have a mother," she replied. "And a stepfather."

Steve nodded. "And how do they feel having you isolated out here with two men and a boy?" he asked, glancing up at her.

"I'm more than capable of making my own decisions. Perhaps you didn't notice, Mr. Chapman, but I am an adult," she said. She paused. She sure didn't sound like one.

Steve gently set down her leg and smiled at her with a soft twinkle in his eye. "I assure you," he said softly, "I noticed."

Alex glanced away. *Remember your role,* she reminded herself. *He's trying to test you. To determine if you really are who you say you are. Play it like an ingenue.*

"I'm sorry," she replied quickly. "It's just that, well, my mother had a very difficult time when I decided I would rather work with horses than with people. She had hoped that at the very least I would become a veterinarian, but I'm afraid I disappointed her there as well. My mother and I have been estranged for some time now, and the only family I've ever really felt attached to have been the horses I've worked with. So . . ."

Steve stood up and walked over to the window as he spoke. "So you ended up here. And you don't really care about the fact that you're young and single and the chances of meeting eligible men are negligible indeed."

Alex stared at him. He knew damn well that those types of questions were not only inappropriate but illegal as well. "I'm not looking for a husband, Mr. Chapman. I'm looking for a job," she said simply. Steve turned back toward her. A grin appeared on his face. She knew then she had passed the test.

"Well," he said, suddenly focused back on her,

"you'll stay here in the house with us until you're well enough to go back to work."

Alex nodded, trying to hide a smile. She couldn't have handled this better if she had planned it.

"We'll bring your meals up to you while you're here," Steve continued. "Let me know if I can get you anything else."

"I would like to take a shower, if I could," she said.

"Sure. There's a shower right at the end of the hall," he said. "And Roger brought you some crutches." He nodded toward the crutches leaning against the wall. "Tell me where your clothes are, and I'll go and get them for you."

Alex paused. Her computer . . . where had she left it? She was sure she had tucked it away in her drawer, but she still didn't want Steve or anyone else rummaging around inside her room. "That won't be necessary," she replied quickly.

He looked at her suspiciously. "You don't want your own pajamas?"

She shook her head. "You see," she said calmly, thinking quickly, "I usually sleep in the nude."

He raised his eyebrows, surprised and slightly bemused by her admission. "I see."

Roger tapped on the open door. "I hope I'm not interrupting anything."

Steve stood up quickly, immediately reverting back to a cold, professional tone of voice. "Not at all." Steve glanced at Alex. "I was just leaving," he said.

Roger nodded at him as Steve walked past. Roger waited in the doorway as he watched Steve walk toward the stairs. He then turned back toward Alex as he stepped inside the room.

"Holy shit," Roger said, half under his breath. He smiled at Alex. "You certainly gave us a scare."

"I'm sorry about that," she replied sweetly.

"I kind of feel responsible in a way. I should've warned you about Rosie," he whispered.

"She's done that before?" she asked.

"Once or twice. She hates loud noises."

"Most horses do," she said honestly. "It was my fault."

He walked over to the window and opened her blinds. "You don't mind if I let a little air in here?" he asked.

"Thank you," Alex said, watching him carefully. There was something about Roger that made her uncomfortable.

He paused, looking out the window. "Beautiful day," he said. "Cool for around here. But I won't imagine it'll last long."

She shrugged.

"You comfortable here?" he asked, motioning around the sparse, white room. Besides an old dresser with a portable fan on top of it, the room was empty.

"Yes. Thanks."

"You need anything? I'm going to the store today," he said.

"I'd love some books," she said.

"What kind?" he asked.

"Anything. Suspense, adventure . . ."

He smiled. "I'll do my best. And I'll bring you back some lunch. How does junk food grab you?"

"I love it," she said, grinning.

"Coming right up," he said. And with a tip of his hat, she was alone again.

The afternoon passed uneventfully, remarkable only because of the eerie stillness of the house. Besides a brief appearance by Roger, who brought her some lunch and a stack of dusty westerns, she had been left alone. But her solitary afternoon had not been spent in vain. She had already learned that this was not the house of a typical, active little boy and a man who was running a multi-million-dollar corporation. There was no ringing phone, TV, radio, or washer to break the stillness. Every now and then, she would hear footsteps outside her door, but besides that, the house was quiet.

Alex lifted herself out of bed and stood up slowly, gingerly putting pressure on her sore ankle. She guessed that she could manage walking without her crutches if she wanted to. But she had no intention of doing that in front of anyone anytime soon. She would play the sick act as long as it was working in her best interest.

She stood up and limped toward the door. Sore ankle or not, she didn't have time to waste. She had to begin her search of her surroundings as soon as possible. She heard a noise outside the door and quickly hobbled back toward her bed. She pulled the covers back over her as she closed her eyes, pretending to sleep. Ollie pushed the door open, peeking in. When he saw that Alex's eyes were closed, he stepped inside and walked to the edge of her bed. He stood there staring at her, waiting for her to open her eyes.

Alex could sense his presence. Her eyes snapped open, and she smiled at him. She was lucky it was Ollie. Anyone else would've been able to tell she was faking.

Ollie held out a piece of a fern plant. She looked from the plant to him.

"What have you got there?" she asked. The boy stepped toward her, still holding the leaf out to her. "Is that for me?" she gently asked again.

The boy dropped the fern on her lap. She picked it up. "Thank you, Ollie. It's beautiful. I love it," she said, pretending enthusiasm for his gift. She glanced back at him and smiled. "Ollie is your name, isn't it?"

The boy nodded, his small, delicate face still not registering any emotion.

"Ollie is a fine name," she said. "As a matter of fact, I once had a parakeet that was named Ollie. He used to talk to me. To sing to me," she continued.

"Have you ever seen a parakeet, Ollie?" she asked. Ollie just stared at her blankly.

She sighed. It was obvious that she was not going to get him to talk today. Perhaps he was just shy. But, she reminded herself, he had approached her, not the other way around. And it wasn't the first time.

"Ollie!" she heard Steve call from downstairs. Ollie didn't move.

"Ollie," Alex said. "Your father's calling you."

She could hear Steve walking up the stairs. "Ollie!" he called again. She watched the boy curiously, trying to detect if he displayed any fear at the sound of his father's voice.

"Promise me," Ollie whispered, still staring at her. Then he turned and ran out the door.

"There you are, sport," she heard Steve say. "Where have you been?" Steve's voice sounded warm, teasing, even loving. "Come on. I want to show you something," he said. Alex heard the sound of footsteps going back down the stairs. She looked toward the window. *Promise me.* Those were the only words Ollie had spoken since she had been there. What did they mean? And why did he repeat them over and over?

Alex fluffed her pillow as she lay back down on her side. She had a feeling that the child had seen quite a lot with his innocent, big blue eyes. Something that had disturbed him so much, he couldn't speak.

She had seen some strange, dysfunctional homes and families in her lifetime. But she had never encountered anything quite so strange. If Steve Chapman had nothing to hide, then why was he hiding?

Ten

The stillness was deafening. So deafening that Alex couldn't sleep. She heard the grandfather clock toll twelve times, signifying the witching hour. She sat up, her eyes open wide. She glanced at the painkillers in the little brown bottle beside her bed, guaranteed to give her sleep. She had avoided taking any simply because she wanted to have her wits about her while she was in the house.

Through the window, the full moon reflected off the water that surrounded the island, illuminnating the sparse furniture in her room.

Alex swung her legs over the side of the bed. She couldn't stand lying there one second more. Especially when she was in a house loaded with evidence just waiting for her. She needed to take advantage of the sleeping household. She had had plenty of time to plot her strategy, and she had calculated that the best place to begin her investigation was Chapman's desk.

She lifted herself up and looked toward her crutches. As she grabbed the chiffon robe that was lying on the end of her bed, she made a quick decision to do without them. She threw the robe over her shoulders and hobbled toward the door.

The hall was dark. She smiled to herself as she tiptoed out of her room.

She walked over to the banister and peered down. A ray of light was visible under a closed door off to the right of the entranceway. She listened intently.

Nothing. But the light was not a good sign. Too

much of a chance that she would be discovered. Disappointed, she turned back toward her room. That was when she heard it.

Thump, thump, thump . . .

She stood still, listening. A chill ran down her spine. It was the sound of a fist making contact. It was the sound of a fight.

She crept back to the banister and leaned forward, peering toward the closed door.

Someone was getting beaten up, and whoever it was, he was taking his punishment quietly. *Ollie . . .*

Without a moment's hesitation, she hobbled to the huge staircase. Her anger and adrenaline fused, giving her the strength she needed to ease herself down the stairs.

She was convinced that Ollie was in trouble. Everything suddenly made sense. After all, Ollie Chapman had the symptoms of an abused child. He didn't speak because he had been beaten into silence.

But could Steve Chapman, the man who had seemed so sensitive, so warm and caring, be capable of hurting his own child? Had she been duped? Perhaps his display of warmth was an act meant to throw her off his track. And perhaps his warmth toward his son had been simply for her benefit. She had seen it a million times before. Parents who pretended to love their children in public only so that they could abuse them freely in private. Bruises, cuts, broken bones were all explained without questions. Lennie had been a boy like that.

She reached the bottom of the stairs and paused. The noise had stopped again. She remembered the way Ollie had stared at her that afternoon. Had he been trying to ask her for help?

She grabbed a small iron statue off the entrance table and slowly walked toward the door. She paused, ready to swing, with her hand on the doorknob. She heard the punching begin again, and she swung open the door.

The scene was not what she had expected. The large room was empty except for a punching bag hanging from the middle of the ceiling. Steve Chapman stood in front of it, wearing only a pair of jeans and standing in his bare feet. His strong, muscular torso was coated with sweat. He turned toward her with his fists raised, as though he were ready to go after an intruder.

She inhaled with surprise and dropped the statue.

Steve paused as he took a moment to catch his breath from his workout. His surprise changed to anger as he stood there, staring at her. The light in the room blazed through her sheer gown and robe, making the chiffon almost see-through.

"What are you doing?" he asked, dropping his fists. He approached her dangerously, slowly, like a panther stalking his prey.

Alex began to back out the door. She had made a grave error, allowing her emotions to get in the way of reason. She had been so convinced that a child was being abused that she hadn't bothered to think of the obvious: a boxer was working out. And now she was about to pay for her mistake. "I . . . I couldn't sleep. I heard a noise, and I thought maybe someone was breaking in . . ." she whispered. She knew she was in trouble. Her excuse was weak at best. She was like a fly that had unwittingly walked into the spider's trap.

Alex glanced behind her. One more step, and she'd be out of the room.

Before she could escape, Steve was in front of her. He reached behind her and slammed the door shut behind them, trapping her in the room.

Alex backed against the door as Steve's eyes wandered over her, drinking in the sight of a beautiful woman standing half naked in front of him. "That was very brave of you, to come down here all by yourself to catch a burglar," he whispered in a low, threatening voice as he fought for control of his desire. If he was any closer to her, his lips would have been touching her ear.

Alex nodded, shrugging slightly. She was beginning to feel as if she had stepped into an old Jekyll and Hyde movie. Caring, sweet Dr. Jekyll was gone, and in his place was a man whose entire body radiated raw, unrefined emotion. He was dangerous.

"Well," she said, turning her back toward him as she put her fingers on the doorknob. "I'm very glad to see that it's only you, Mr. Chapman. Good night," she said, as sweetly and innocently as she could manage. She turned the doorknob.

The spell was broken. Dr. Jekyll had returned. "Just a minute," Steve said, commanding her to stop. She glanced back over her shoulder. Steve crossed his arms in front of him as he walked toward the window, thinking.

"I thought you weren't supposed to be walking yet," he said finally.

"I, well, it hurts," she said, shrugging her shoulders. "I heard you . . . well, I heard a noise, and I just went to investigate . . ." she said, her voice drifting off.

He studied her carefully, as if evaluating her excuse for truthfulness. "I'm sorry if I scared you," he said finally. "I didn't expect to see you there when I turned around."

"I'm sorry I barged in on you and interrupted your workout, Mr. Chapman," she said.

He shook his head. "Don't do that," he said.

"Do what?" she asked sincerely.

"Please call me Steve. 'Mr. Chapman' makes me feel like I'm your guardian or something. And I'm not that old."

"Okay, Steve." She stepped back toward him as an offer of truce. She didn't want him to know that she was frightened of him. "Interesting room," she said, her eyes scanning the huge, empty space. "I like what you've done with it," she added, attempting a bit of weak humor.

Steve looked at her, slightly amused. "It's the dining room." He looked around him as he took off his boxing gloves. "My wife and I didn't do a lot of entertaining." He glanced back at her. "Together at least," he said.

Alex looked at him curiously. What was that supposed to mean?

He glanced at her. His eyes ran down her body, so visible underneath the sheer sheath of chiffon. Alex crossed her arms in front of her, aware of the effect her attire was having on him.

"Do you box every night?" she asked.

He hesitated. "When I can't sleep—which is almost every night." He glanced away. "As I'm sure you know, I recently lost my wife, Ollie's mother."

"Yes. I'm sorry," she said.

He nodded. "So am I," he said quietly.

She looked at him as if she might find the truth in his eyes. He turned away from her and sighed. "Good night, Alex," he said, with his back to her.

She felt awkward, as if he had just informed her that she had overstayed her welcome. "Good night," she replied, limping out of the room.

She reached the stairway and looked up. Somehow the stairs hadn't seemed so steep on the way down. She jumped up onto the first step. Despite the fact that she was holding on to the banister, she lost her balance slightly. A sigh of pain escaped her lips as she instinctively put weight on her hurt foot to steady herself. Suddenly, a strong arm shot out and lifted her off her sore ankle. Steve stood behind her, holding on to her. Before she had a chance to thank him, he spoke.

"Put your arm around me," he commanded. Alex obeyed quietly, and he easily whisked her off her feet. He carried her up the long, winding staircase with the same ease he had demonstrated the night before. His body was slightly sweaty from his workout, and her sheer nightgown clung to him as though he was magnetically pulling it off her. Her breast, bare underneath the layer of satin, rested up against his naked chest.

"This isn't necessary," she protested quietly.

He didn't look at her, choosing instead to focus on the steps ahead of him. When he reached the top of the stairs, he set her down carefully, gently, as if he were handling an extremely fragile porcelain statue.

"Thank you," she said, slowly removing her arms from around his neck. He glanced at her, and she thought for a moment that she saw the hint of a smile.

"Good night again," he said, turning and walking quickly back down the stairs.

She watched as he walked back into the dining room, shutting the door behind him.

"Good night," she whispered quietly to herself.

Eleven

Alex had been a virtual prisoner in the old, eerily quiet house for four days, and what had originally seemed like an excellent idea now seemed unbelievably stupid. She was beginning to despair of ever getting an opportunity to look around. During the day, Steve was always in or near the house. And the nights were no better. Steve was a chronic insomniac who appeared to work out and read until the sun rose. She knew he had to sleep sometime, but, unfortunately for her, so did she.

Alex sighed heavily, more out of frustration than pity for herself. She was tired of being confined to bed in her frilly gowns and dining on bachelor food. Steve had avoided her since the boxing "incident," arranging for Roger to bring her her meals, which he did quickly and efficiently, with a minimal amount of conversation. She suspected that Steve had instructed Roger not to talk to her any more than was necessary. It was as though Steve had decided he wanted her off the island. And rather than simply order her off, he planned on driving her away with boredom.

The only member of the household who had continued to show her any warmth was Ollie, who, despite his father's watchful eye, managed to visit her several times a day.

He liked to bring her little presents, pieces of plants or shells he had found in the sandy soil. He even brought in a turtle, which he unceremoniously dumped on her lap.

She always talked to the child, although he never responded. He wouldn't even answer yes or no to simple questions, yet she was fairly certain he understood her. If she pressed him for an answer, he would only repeat the same eerie phrase he had been chanting since she first met him: *Promise me.* When she questioned him about what it meant, he seemed to get even more upset and repeat it with even more frequency.

Alex was beginning to suspect that the boy might be autistic, although she had never been exposed to autism before. From the little she did know about the condition, the vacant stares that radiated from Ollie seemed symptomatic. But, she reminded herself, Ollie's stares were not always vacant. She knew the child was capable of emotion. Sometimes he would sit on the floor, rocking back and forth, and when she looked into his sweet blue eyes, it was easy to recognize the tears he was trying to so hard to blink away.

She understood why the child seemed so disturbed. After all, there was nothing to do in this depressing house except focus on the loss of his mother. There were no other children to play with and no school to escape to. There was nothing to break up the boring, heavy inertia made worse by the hot, humid days.

Alex began fanning herself with her hand. The portable fan on her dresser was directed straight toward her bed, but she could barely feel it. She'd gotten so uncomfortable that she'd pulled her hair up in a makeshift bun, securing it with some bobby pins she'd found in the top drawer of the bedside table. She thought it insane that a man as wealthy as Steve Chapman would choose to live in a decrepit house in the tropics that didn't even have air conditioning. But then again, the eccentric boxer who rarely slept bore little resemblance to the millionaire who wore Armani suits and was chauffeured around New York.

Alex was distracted from her thoughts by a light tapping on her door.

"Come in," she said, straightening her robe.

Steve stepped inside the room. He appeared stiff and uncomfortable. "Hello," he said.

"Hello," she replied, meeting his gaze directly. *Speak of the devil . . .*

"I'm taking Ollie to the mainland with me. I was wondering if you needed anything."

She shook her head as she motioned to the books on the floor. "Roger's got me all set up."

He raised his eyebrows as he quickly scanned the titles. "Westerns?"

She shrugged.

"Roger's down working on the helicopters, so you'll be on your own for a while. Think you can manage?"

Alex felt a bolt of adrenaline charge through her. This was the moment she had been waiting for. It took all of her willpower not to smile.

"Of course," she said calmly.

Steve nodded, looking at her. "Is your ankle feeling better?" he asked, after a moment's hesitation.

"A little," she said.

"Good." He paused. "See you in a bit."

He left the door open. Alex lay in bed impatiently,

waiting for him and Ollie to leave. She smiled when she heard the front door slam. She forced herself to wait a few minutes longer, to give them time to get into the car and down the driveway.

She went over the layout of the house in her mind. Where should she begin her search?

Alex stepped out of the bedroom and paused in the doorway, looking at either end of the upstairs hall. Her eyes settled on the door at the end of the hall that had been closed since her arrival. She didn't think that was the master bedroom, since Steve slept at the opposite end of the hall. A closet?

Alex walked over to the door and turned the knob. Locked.

She stepped backward, pondering the situation. She quickly said a prayer of thanks for the hot, sticky weather that had forced her to wear her hair up in a matronly bun. She pulled a bobby pin out of her hair and stuck it in the lock, wiggling it around until she heard a friendly-sounding click. She breathed in deeply as she pushed it wide open.

It was like seeing an oasis after being in the middle of the desert. Heavy, expensive antiques were professionally arranged on plush Oriental rugs. Large picture windows framed by sheer beige silk drapes wrapped around the room, giving an expansive view of the gulf as well as the stable and riding arena.

Alex stepped inside carefully and shut the door behind her. There was a scent to the room. A slight perfumed scent . . . of lilacs. It was a woman's scent.

She looked around her, breathing in the perfumed air as she tried to memorize each and every detail. This was a room that had been lived in, quite graciously at that. Had this been the master bedroom suite? Had Leslie and Steve once shared this room?

The room looked as though whoever lived there would be coming back at any moment. The bed had been slept in, but the covers were tousled on one side only, as if only one person had slept there. A long, cream-colored silk nightgown, similar to the one Alex was wearing, lay on the floor in front of the closet, as though the woman who had worn it had changed quickly, not bothering to hang it up. Fashion magazines were scattered about. The large oak vanity table had jars of expensive creams and perfumes scattered about. A silver-backed hairbrush full of strands of long blond hair was lying beside a tube of lipstick.

Alex walked to the closet and slid open the mirrored door. Racks of expensive-looking clothes lined the two tiered bars. She shut the closet doors and walked over to the dresser. She opened the top drawer slowly, quietly, as though she had not yet decided what she was looking for. The entire drawer was crammed full of delicate, handmade, silk bikini panties which had been tossed haphazardly inside. Alex shut the drawer and pulled out the one directly underneath. Inside were various colored silk stockings and garters which were tangled around all different types of swimsuits. Alex untangled a small, turquoise polkadot one-piece and held it up. It had obviously been worn by a woman who enjoyed showing off her figure.

Feeling like a voyeur, Alex shut the drawer and moved away from the dresser, focusing on the mirrored vanity table. She picked up an expensive-looking bottle of French perfume. She held it to her nose. Lilacs.

Alex set the perfume back on the vanity and leaned over, inspecting the framed pictures that were placed on top. She picked up a picture of a woman standing beside a horse. The woman was Leslie—Alex recognized her from news photos. In the picture, Leslie was wearing her equestrian outfit and holding a trophy in her hands. Her long blond hair was loose, hanging below her shoulders. She had big blue eyes and perfect straight white teeth. There was something unnatural about the picture that detracted from her beauty. It was the expression on Leslie's face. Her smile looked almost forced, but it was the eyes that held Alex's attention. She almost looked . . . frightened. It was the same expression she had seen in Ollie's eyes.

Alex set the photo back down and picked up the one that had been next to it. It was a black-and-white picture from the 'fifties of a couple with a baby. The woman held the infant up to the camera is if asking the photographer to focus on the child, rather than her.

Even if Alex hadn't recognized Gordon Anson, she would have known it was a photo of Leslie with her parents. Her mother looked so much like her. The same beautiful face with the same forced smile. The same haunted look in the eyes. Gordon Anson emanated little of his wife's fragility. He stood by his young wife like a fearless warrior, claiming his prize.

Alex carefully put the picture back down. She picked up a frame that had been facedown and looked at it. It was a picture of Leslie and Steve, standing arm in arm, with little Ollie looking out shyly from behind Leslie's skirt. They looked stiff and uncomfortable, as if posing together as a family was painful.

Alex placed the picture back facedown, the way it was. Someone had obviously not wanted to look at it. Was is Steve? Or Leslie?

Alex forced her attention away from the top of the vanity. She could think about her questions later. Right now, she needed to continue her investigation.

She opened the drawers of the vanity and began peeking inside. Everything that Leslie Chapman bought, from face creams to makeup, was either the very best on the market or the most expensive.

Alex turned back toward the unmade bed, noticing for the first time the night table. On top of the nightstand was a crystal decanter half filled with a golden liquid. Next to the decanter was a matching crystal glass and a picture of Steve and Leslie, which, from the looks of the clothes they were wearing, must have been taken at least ten years before. At least in this photo they looked happy, though there was still the same eerieness in Leslie's eyes.

Alex focused on the glass. There was still a little bit of liquid left in the bottom. She picked it up and held it to her nose. Scotch.

Suddenly, the downstairs door slammed shut. Alex's eyes calmly focused on the bedroom's open door as she set the glass down. Someone was in the house.

She limped toward the doorway, attempting to make as little noise as possible. She glanced into the hall. She could hear Steve downstairs, talking to Ollie.

Alex stepped into the hall and turned back toward Leslie's room to close the door. It was at that precise moment that she realized she had a problem. The lock.

She could lock it the same way she had opened it, with a bobby pin, but it might take a few minutes. Minutes she couldn't spare. She had no choice but simply to close the door and return at a later time to lock it. She would just have to hope no one noticed it wasn't locked before she had a chance to come back.

She held her breath as she limped back to her room, trying to avoid any creaking on the wood floor as she moved.

She had just slipped into her bed when Ollie burst into the room.

"Hello there," she said, as cheerfully as she could manage. "You're back early."

"I couldn't even get Ollie on the boat," Steve said, appearing in her doorway. "He was upset."

"He was?" she replied. She focused on the child. "Why were you upset, Ollie?"

Ollie stared back at her blankly.

"Because he didn't want to leave you," Steve said, looking at his son.

Alex raised her eyebrows, surprised. "What?"

"Ollie, why don't you go to your room for a while," Steve said. "Dad has some business that he needs to take care of with Miss Rowe." Ollie stood still, as though he hadn't heard his father's request.

"Ollie. Please." Ollie took a few steps backward, still staring at Alex. He then turned and ran out of the room. Steve shut the door.

"Is there a problem?" Alex asked.

Steve looked at her. "No," he said. "How are you feeling?" he asked awkwardly, even though he had asked her just that less than an hour earlier.

"Much better," she replied.

"Good," he said. "You know, I guess I'm surprised you haven't been up more and walking around. You must be getting pretty antsy."

She smiled. "I thought I was supposed to stay off my ankle in order for it to heal. And I want it to heal as quickly as possible. So I can get back to work," she added quickly.

He nodded, looking at her as though he didn't quite believe her.

She paused. Had he heard her walking around when he came in? She forced her eyes away as she pushed herself up. "So were you serious when you said that Ollie didn't want to leave me?" she asked.

He nodded again as he sat on the edge of her bed. She scooted over as far as she could, but her bare foot was still resting up against his back.

"I wasn't positive that was it until we drove back here and he jumped out of the car and ran straight up to your room. He's grown very attached to you over the past week. It's a little strange. I've never seen him like this. Usually he avoids people. Especially strangers," he said.

She shrugged her shoulders. "Maybe I remind him of someone."

"Perhaps," he said. He hesitated. "Alex . . . I'd like you to move back to your apartment this afternoon."

"Have I . . . is anything wrong?" she asked.

"No," he said, standing up. "I just think it's time, don't you?"

She thought about the door she had left unlocked. She would have to find a way to lock it before she left. "Yes. I, well, thank you. It was very nice of you to take care of me like this." He looked at her a moment, then glanced downward as he left the room, as if he was deep in thought.

Alex sat up straight. Why had he suffered such a sudden change of heart? Obviously, he was less than thrilled that his son had developed an affection for her. She looked at her clothes, folded neatly on the chair. Steve seemed aware that she was taking advantage of his hospitality, but she was fairly certain he had not figured out why. Perhaps he was even flattering himself that she wanted to stay in the house because she wanted to be closer to him. If that was the case, she intended on playing it for all it was worth.

Steve stepped heavily down the stairs. Ollie's behavior worried him. He didn't like the idea of Ollie becoming so attached to a woman who was only passing through, a woman he hoped would leave within the next couple of weeks. He wasn't comfortable around her. There was just something about her that made him uneasy. He had been wrong to allow Roger to bring her here.

He needed to get rid of her. Soon.

He went in his office and shut the door. Sitting down wearily at his desk, he opened up a file and glanced down at it. How much longer did he have to wait before he could move on with his life? After Leslie's death, his lawyers had instructed him to "lay low," to disappear from public life for a while. The island had been an obvious destination.

In the beginning, he didn't mind. Leslie's death had left him almost shell-shocked, worried about his son. He had looked forward to taking care of Ollie in solitude. To giving his son time to heal away from the public eye.

But unfortunately, he hadn't realized how severely

Leslie's death had affected Ollie. He was beginning to realize that he needed to take Ollie away from the island . . . away from the memories of his mother.

As soon as he could, as soon as it was safe, he would get Ollie the help he needed. He would take him to the best doctors, take him anywhere he needed to go. He would spend the rest of his life doing anything he could to take away the pain his son was suffering.

Alex paused at the top of the stairs. She was dressed in the clothes she was wearing the day of the accident. She slipped out of her room and peered over the railing. The library door was open, and she could hear Steve inside as he spoke softly into the phone.

She paused, waiting for her chance. She quickly glanced up and down the hallway, looking for Ollie. The door to Ollie's room was wide open. It was possible that he was inside. If so, he would surely hear her outside his mother's bedroom. She glanced back toward Leslie's room. It didn't matter. She had to take a chance.

She tiptoed down the hall, being careful of her sore ankle. She reached Leslie's door and pulled the bobby pin out of her pocket. She stuck it into the lock, smiling as she heard it click shut. She had succeeded.

"Ollie!" Steve called upstairs. Alex's breath quickened as she hastened back to her room.

She was halfway down the hall when she heard it. A quiet noise, just pitiful enough to stop her dead in her tracks.

She glanced back toward Leslie's room. She wasn't sure, but she thought the noise had emanated from behind Leslie's locked bedroom door.

She stood up against the hallway wall, waiting to hear if Steve was going to come upstairs. But the house was silent, which meant that either he had decided to look for Ollie elsewhere, or he, too, had heard the sound.

Suddenly, she heard the noise again. It was quiet, but she could still make it out. It was the unmistakable sound of a child crying.

Alex glanced back toward Leslie's room. The truth of the situation dawned on her as her breath quickened with fear.

Ollie is locked inside Leslie's room.

"Ollie!" she heard Steve yell out the front door.

Still hugging the wall, Alex backtracked quickly, fumbling nervously with the bobby pin. She dropped it on the floor and picked it up, her hands shaking as she jammed the bobby pin into the lock.

She held her breath as she felt the latch lift up. She opened the door partway, praying that it would open without a telltale creak. Successful, she peered around the door. Ollie was nowhere in sight.

"Ollie?" she whispered.

She listened. She heard the muffled whimper again. She walked to the closet and slid the mirrored door open. She squinted into the darkness. "Ollie?"

"Promise me," he whispered.

Alex bent down on her knees as she leaned inside. Ollie was in the back corner of the closet, rocking back and forth. She held out her arms. "Ollie," she whispered. "We have to go. Why don't you walk back to my room with me?"

Ollie didn't budge. Small beads of sweat began to break out on Alex's forehead. She had to get Ollie out of there. Steve could come up and find them at any moment. "Ollie," she said quietly, "if you don't come with me right now, your daddy will be very mad at me. So mad that he'll probably make me leave. Do you understand, Ollie?" she asked, feeling a little guilty about threatening an obviously disturbed child with desertion. But she didn't have any choice. Besides, it was true.

"Ollie!" she heard Steve call from the front yard. Good, she thought. Maybe he thought Ollie was down by the water.

"Ollie," she said, "that's your dad. He's looking for you. If he finds you in here, he's going to be very upset." She paused. "Please," she said, appealing to him with her arms outstretched. Ollie leaned forward and hugged her. She closed her eyes, as though she, too, might start to cry. But she couldn't allow herself the luxury. Not now, anyway. "Good boy," she said, pulling him to his feet.

She led him out the door. "Ollie," Steve called from back in the house. She grabbed the bobby pin out of her pocket and tried to lock the door. She could hear Steve start up the stairs. "Ollie?" he said.

She turned back toward Ollie. "Go to him. Run. Stall him," she whispered. She turned back toward the lock. She doubted Ollie even understood her.

She was wrong. Ollie ran to the steps, meeting his father halfway up. "What's going on?" Steve asked suspiciously. "Where have you been? Didn't you hear me calling you?" He picked the boy up, noticing his tears. He glanced up the stairs. He had a suspicion that somehow Alex was involved. He put Ollie down and ran up the stairs, taking them two at a time. He almost ran into Alex at the top.

"Steve!" she said. "What's the matter?"

He stopped. Alex slid the bobby pin into her hair. "It's just that . . . I couldn't find Ollie. He's been crying," he said, looking back toward his son. Ollie stood on the stairs exactly where Steve had put him down. He was staring at Alex.

"Oh," she said, shrugging her shoulders. "I explained to him that I was moving back to the apartment, and he got a little upset, I'm afraid."

Steve looked at her in disbelief. "Didn't you hear me calling him?"

"Just now?" she asked, shrugging her shoulders. She shook her head. "I'm sorry. Were you calling him long?"

Roger walked into the house. "Anybody home?" he called out, walking toward the stairs.

Alex breathed a sigh of relief. A distraction.

"Hey," Roger said, looking up the stairs at them. "What's going on?"

"I was just leaving," Alex said, squeezing past Steve. She leaned on the banister as she half walked, half hopped down the steps.

"Need any help?" Roger asked, leaping up the stairs to aid her.

"Thanks," she said, accepting his arm.

Steve followed Alex down the stairs, eyeing her suspiciously. He went to take Ollie's hand, but Ollie dashed on ahead, opening the front door and holding it for Alex. At the sight of the boy's chivalry, Steve grinned in spite of himself.

"Why, thank you, Ollie," Alex said, reaching the bottom of the stairs. She slipped her arm out of Roger's and turned back toward Steve. "And thank you for your hospitality," she said, smiling as sweetly as she could muster.

Steve nodded. "Of course," he said. "Do you think you'll need any help getting up the stairs to your apartment?" he asked.

Alex smiled. "No. No thanks," she said.

Steve nodded. "Send Ollie back to get one of us if you do," he said. Alex thanked him again before leaving.

Roger and Steve watched Alex and Ollie leave the house. When they were out of hearing distance, Roger said, "Little Ollie has certainly become attached to our horse friend."

Steve shrugged his shoulders, unable to take his eyes off Alex. Roger looked at him curiously. "Perhaps he's not the only one," he said.

Steve glanced at him. "What the hell is that supposed to mean?" he growled.

"Nothing," Roger said, shrugging his shoulders. "It's just that, well, I'm sure you didn't notice since you're still so broken up about Leslie's death," he said, with a hint of sarcasm, "but she is a beautiful woman."

Steve looked at him. "I don't like what you're implying," he said, his eyes glinting dangerously. "I'm not happy about Miss Rowe's presence on the ranch at all. I don't trust her," he added, walking back into his study.

"What are you saying?" Roger asked as he followed his boss. "You want me to fire her?"

Steve looked out the library window.

"I want her to give *you* a reason to fire her. A reason she won't question. I don't want her to think I'm forcing her out."

"Can I ask you why?" Roger asked. "Has she done anything? Given you any reason to mistrust her?"

Steve hesitated. "Instinct. There's something about her that doesn't quite jive." He turned back toward Roger.

Roger sighed. "Okay," he said, obviously not happy about his instructions. "I'll do my best," he added, turning to leave.

"That's all I ever ask," Steve said, sitting down behind his desk.

Roger stopped and turned back toward him. "No," he said, shaking his head. "You usually ask a lot more."

He walked out of the room, shutting the door behind him.

Alex sat on her bed, her laptop in front of her. She had about ten e-mail messages from Tim, the last one threatening to come down there and find her if she didn't reply within twenty-four hours. She outlined what had happened to her and then typed her request: "Please do what you can to research the child: Ollie Chapman. Any mention of autism in the files????"

Alex paused as she remembered the scotch she had found on Leslie's bedside table. She quickly typed:

"Also, please check the driving records of Leslie Chapman. Any DWIs?"

If Leslie had been picked up for drunk driving, it might not prove that she had killed herself, but it might lend credence to the rumor that she had a drinking problem. And alcoholism and depression often went hand in hand.

After she sent the message to Tim, she accessed the medical hot line, inviting anyone with experience with autism to join her. After a few hours, she signed off, still not convinced that Ollie was suffering from autism. But what else could it be? The shock of his mother's death? And why wasn't he in school? After all, most schools had started their fall session, yet Ollie remained on the island. Why? Alex had checked, and until Leslie's death, Ollie had been enrolled in school. Yet now it appeared his father had no intention of sending him away this fall.

Was Steve concerned about the media? Or was he worried that Ollie was not mentally fit to return to school? And if that was true, why wasn't Ollie under medical supervision? Alex could sense he was an intelligent boy. But she had no doubt that he was in need of serious psychiatric treatment.

Alex signed off. After she had tucked her computer back inside the dresser drawer, she stood in front of her bed and put her arms up over her head and yawned, indulging in a slow, lazy stretch toward the ceiling. For the first time since she had arrived on Rye Island, she was going to bed feeling somewhat encouraged. The four days she had spent inside the Chapman house had more than made up for the week she had wasted. Alex smiled confidently as she turned off the light. It was a clear night, and the full moon cast her entire room in a soft, warm glow. Alex pulled back the bed covers as she distractedly glanced out the window.

What she saw caught her attention immediately. She dropped the covers and stepped away from the window, a chill running down her spine. A man had been clearly visible in an upstairs window of the Chapman house. He had been standing in front of the window, looking out into her window, staring at Alex herself. She hadn't gotten a good look, but she felt certain it was Steve. It had to be. And the room he had been standing in was Leslie's room. She glanced at her bed, calculating its angle from the window. He would not have been able to see her working on her computer, but still . . .

Why was he staring in at her?

Alex stepped farther away from the window. Maybe she was jumping to conclusions. Maybe it just *appeared* that he was staring at her window. Maybe he was really looking beyond it . . . *at the building where Leslie was killed.*

Alex turned off the light. She peeked back out the window.

He was gone.

She paused, as she attempted to slow her breathing down. Questions spun in her mind. Why had he been in Leslie's room? Was he aware that she had been in that room, looking at Leslie's belongings? Rifling through her closets, studying her photos, smelling her perfume?

She quickly walked over to her door and locked it, even though it gave her little comfort. She crept back into bed and lay on top of the covers as she listened to the relaxing sound of the fan's whizzing blades.

She closed her eyes, unable to sleep. All she could think about was the lonely boy who refused to speak, and the sad, mysterious man who was watching her.

Twelve

By noon the following Friday, the temperature on Rye Island had reached a steamy one hundred degrees. And that was in the shade. In light of the heat, Alex took it easy on Rosie as she trotted the horse through the shady path.

It was the first day her ankle had not bothered her, and she intended to make the most of it. It had been two days since she left the main house. Two long days and long nights.

She felt that her investigation was proceeding fairly well, although she had to admit she was a little concerned about the lack of time she had left. It was September second, and she only had one more week to clinch her story. She had a sneaky suspicion she was going to have to ask Dick, or Tim, for an extension. She wasn't sure, however, that they would give it to her.

Alex stopped in the shade of lush, old palm trees and dismounted. According to Roger's directions, this was the spot of the original gardens. As Alex wrapped Rosie's reins around a tree, she noticed the thick, overgrown brush that sprouted in clumps around the trees. Although the gardens had long ago been consumed by the natural rhythm of nature, there were still elements of a former cultivated beauty. A rosebush with beautiful, soft peach-colored flowers bloomed in the middle of a patch of ferns. Off to her right, a statue of a headless mermaid appeared to jump out of the green, algae-covered water in a small lily pond.

Alex walked over to the statue and ran her fingers along the jagged edge where the unfortunate mermaid's head had been. She thought it a shame that the Chapmans hadn't bothered to renovate the gardens . . . or the house, for that matter. The island was so lush, so beautiful. It just needed a little tender loving care to restore the home and the gardens to their former glory.

"Hey."

Alex spun around. Roger was walking toward her. His sun-bleached blond hair was matted down with sweat. His dirty denim shirt was rolled up at the sleeves, exposing his tan, muscular arms. "You look like you've been working hard," she said, nodding toward the dirt padded on the knees of his jeans.

"You could say that," he said with a smile. "A tree fell down. I'm cutting it up."

"For firewood?"

Roger laughed. "Yeah, right. We're gonna have a bonfire. Roast some marshmallows. Are you up for it?"

She smiled. "Nothing would surprise me."

"You got that right," he agreed. He looked up at the sun, brushing his sweaty hair back with his forearm. "I can't imagine having a fire in this place. It's always hot as hell."

"But the house does have fireplaces," she reminded him.

He grinned, as though she had gotten a joke. "Just the library," he said.

She nodded. She turned back toward the pond.

"Just taking a rest?" he asked.

She shrugged. "It's so beautiful here." She patted Rosie as she got ready to jump back on. "But I guess I should be getting back."

"What's your hurry?" he asked, putting his hand on her arm. "I noticed you already did your chores."

She glanced down at his hand before looking back into his lonely eyes. "I guess I could wait a few minutes."

He removed his hand and smiled. Alex stared up at the blistering sun. "I was hoping to find a good place to swim."

"I've got the perfect place for you," he said. "There's a beach on the other side of the island. Leslie used to swim there all the time. It's not that big, but there aren't any rocks, and the waves aren't that rough."

"How do I get to it?"

"Head down the dirt drive to the side of the house. After about a quarter of a mile, you'll see a path on your left. It'll take you right to the beach."

"Great," she said. "Thanks."

"So," Roger said, sitting on the grass in front of the statue, "do you like modern art?" He laughed, pointing to the mermaid.

"What's the story?" she asked, petting the horse. "Where did all these weird statues come from?"

"The same place the house and the chapel came from."

"The chapel?"

"Otherwise known as my bungalow. Everything was built by this wacky guy who owned the island in the early nineteen hundreds. He was a former naval officer turned millionaire playboy who bought the island for his extremely beautiful, much younger mistress who just happened to be his wife's wealthy niece."

Alex's eyes lit up. She loved a good story. "This was their house? Their Xanadu?"

"For a while. It's kind of a sad story. You see, when the couple first fell in love, the girl told her family. They threatened to disown her unless she broke off the affair. But the millionaire begged the girl not to break up with him, promising her anything she ever desired."

"So he divorced his wife?"

"Except that. His wife wouldn't give him a divorce. The girl agreed to run away with him, so he took his young mistress and moved away from the scandal, setting her up on the island. Since he couldn't offer her marriage, he tried to give her everything else. He built her a house just like the house she had grown up in—which explains why someone would build a fireplace in the middle of hell. He made the estate into a showcase, with lush gardens and a swimming pool. He built a separate building just for parties, with a gazebo that overlooked the gulf and scores of beautiful gardens. They had servants to cater to her every need."

Alex smiled. "But?"

"There is always a *but,* isn't there? In every great romance."

Alex shrugged her shoulders.

"But apparently that wasn't enough," he continued. "After living on the island for only a month, her family relented and sent a letter to her stating that if she returned immediately, all would be forgiven. The millionaire turned almost despotic over the threat of losing the woman he loved and forbid her to leave the island. Fearful for her life, she escaped by boat one night, sailing it across the sea by herself." He paused, staring at the pond.

"What happened?"

"The millionaire never recovered, nor did he ever return to his wife. He fired all of his servants and let the place go. He died right here by this pond several years later. As he fell over, he grabbed onto the mermaid's head, knocking it right off. They found him right where you're standing, holding the head in his hands."

Alex stepped back from the pond. "My God," she said, dismayed. "Are you kidding?"

His gray eyes crinkled with mischief. "Yes. About how and where he died. He did die on the island a few years after she left. But I don't know the details."

Alex laughed. "Wow. That's still some story. Even without the mermaid ending."

"Yes, it is. This place has a long history of failed romances leading to death."

She paused. "What do you mean?"

He stood up and flashed her a patient, tired smile. "Nothing," he said. "I better get back to work. Have a good swim."

Alex waited for a while before riding back. She had been touched by Roger's story. Not so much *what* he said but *how* he said it. He had seemed to be hinting at something, although she wasn't quite sure what. His own despair? His own loneliness?

When she finally did leave the pond, she rode back slowly. She was dismayed to see Steve walking toward the stable when she arrived. He was dressed in a suit, looking more like the corporate executive she remembered from news photographs.

She lifted herself off the horse and led Rosie into the arena as Steve continued to walk toward her. She closed the gate and turned around.

Steve was heading up the steps to her apartment. She furrowed her brow worriedly. What was he doing? Surely he had seen her putting Rosie in the arena.

As soon as she rounded the corner of the barn, she saw where Steve was heading.

Ollie was sitting on the landing at the top of the stairs, waiting outside her apartment for her to return.

"Hello," she called out. Steve paused on the steps, glancing back toward her. Ollie stood up, but as usual, he did not smile or greet her back.

Steve gave her a quick nod as he proceeded to walk up the stairs. He stopped in front of Ollie.

Alex quickly followed him, taking the stairs two at a time. "What's the matter?" she asked from behind him.

Steve glanced down toward her impatiently. "Nothing is the matter. I've got to head to Miami, and Ollie is going to go with me."

Ollie grabbed onto the railing as if he was planning on staying.

"C'mon, Ollie," Steve said.

"If you want, I can watch him," she offered. "He could stay here."

Steve paused. "Thank you," he replied. "But that won't be necessary." He leaned toward Ollie. "C'mon, sport. It'll be fun."

Alex hesitated. She turned away and began walking back down the stairs.

"Promise me! Promise me!" Ollie began yelling at Alex as soon as she reached the bottom of the stairs. Alex stopped and turned back toward him.

"Ollie, please," Steve said, his face becoming flushed. Alex felt almost sorry for him. It was obvious he had no idea how to handle his son.

She focused on the child. "Ollie, what's the matter?" she asked soothingly as she faced him. But that just seemed to make things worse.

"Promise me," Ollie said, his blue eyes filling with tears.

"What's the matter?" Roger asked, appearing at the bottom of the stairs.

"Ollie doesn't want to go," Steve said, loosening his tie. "And I'm not going to make him."

"You go ahead and go," said Roger, who had appeared at the bottom of the stairs. "I'll look after him."

"You don't mind?" Steve asked, looking down toward him hopefully. Alex raised an eyebrow. Apparently he didn't trust her to watch his son.

Roger shook his head.

Steve hesitated. He checked his watch. He flashed Roger a forced smile. "I'll be back tonight," he said, kissing his son on the forehead. He stood up, hesitating slightly. He slowly walked down the steps, his eyes focused on the ground below as if he was already reconsidering Roger's offer. Alex leaned back against the rail so that Steve could pass her. He accidentally brushed up against her.

"Excuse me," he said, snapping to attention. He cleared his throat and picked up his pace, almost jumping down the rest of the stairs.

Alex and Roger were silent as they watched Steve get into his car. Steve gave them a quick wave before firing up the engine.

Alex turned toward Roger. "I'd be happy to take him swimming with me," she said, motioning toward Ollie.

"The kid can't swim," Roger said as Steve drove away, his car kicking up a cloud of dust behind it.

Alex glanced up at Ollie. He sat with his elbows on his knees, his little hands holding up his chin. He looked bored enough to sink into sleep. "I can teach him," she offered. Roger shook his head again as he climbed up the steps. "Thanks, but no thanks," he said. "I don't think Steve would like that too much. He's pretty protective." He paused, glancing back at Alex. "So, you know how to get there, right?"

"Yep. Down the road about a half mile. There's a little path on the left."

Roger nodded. "It's a quarter of a mile. Have a good time." He focused his attention back on Ollie. "C'mon," he said. "Alex has to get ready." Ollie's eyes flew open at the sound of Roger's voice. With a burst of energy, he ran down the steps, flying past Alex and Roger and disappearing into the forest.

Roger shook his head. "Goddamn," he said.

"I'll go and find him," Alex said.

Roger stopped her by grabbing her arm. "No. You go ahead. I'll take care of Ollie," he said in a voice that left no room for discussion.

Alex grabbed a quick bite before changing into her light blue one-piece bathing suit. She threw on a T-shirt and slipped on a pair of flip-flops she had bought at a drugstore in Miami. She grabbed a backpack overloaded with an old sweatshirt, a Walkman, a western novel, and a towel and set off to find the path.

If she didn't think she might run into Roger and Ollie, she would have tried to visit the construction site. But the thought of Roger and Ollie lurking in the forest was enough to deter her. And besides, her investigation had been proceeding so well, sneaking off to the construction site was a risk she didn't yet need to take.

Alex paused at a small clearing off to her left. Following Roger's directions, she slid down the grassy embankment and walked on a path that someone had carefully and recently cleared through some brush. It took her about twenty minutes to reach the beach, but it was worth the effort. The beach was an isolated area of white sand, surrounded by palm trees and brush. A small, new-looking dock jutted into the water.

She slipped off her T-shirt and stepped into the water. Unlike the opposite end of the island, it looked as if one could wade fairly far before hitting any rocks or going too deep. She ducked under the surface, feeling the cool, refreshing water rush around her tired, sore limbs. She began to kick slowly, swimming away from shore. She stared at the clear blue sky as she thought about what Roger had said to her in the garden.

She was intrigued by the island's past. But she disagreed with Roger. The island might be hot, but it was too beautiful to be hell. But its history didn't quite qualify it as paradise, either. She decided it was the devil's own version of Eden.

She lifted herself out of the water and onto the dock. Using the dock as a diving board, she dove back in and began to do some of the water ballet movements she had learned as a child. She awkwardly ran through the movements, giving herself directions just like her former swim instructor. *Leg bend, then straight up in the air, slowly sinking down in the water. Float perpen-*

dicular to the sky, then back flip into perpendicular position.

She was just beginning to convince herself that she really did have some water ballet talent, when she saw something move out of the corner of her eye. She shook the water out of her eyes and blinked. Ollie was standing on the shore.

She waved at him.

He stood motionless, watching her. She felt so sorry for him, standing out there by himself. Damn his parents, anyway. Why hadn't they ever bothered to teach him to swim? She thought it cruel to move to an island and never teach a child how to swim.

Alex swam toward shallower water and stood up, glancing toward the beach.

But Ollie wasn't there. She looked around, concerned. She quickly spotted him on the edge of the dock, bent over as if studying the water.

"Ollie!" she called out. "Don't move!"

Still looking at the water, he took a step, causing a small splash as he fell in.

"Ollie!" Alex yelled. She half ran, half swam over to where the boy was gasping for air, his little head bobbing up and down as his arms floundered about helplessly. Alex grabbed him from behind and started dragging him back toward shallower water. As soon as she could reach the bottom, she righted him and carried him back to shore. Ollie clung to her, his small frame heaving as he gasped for air. She set the child down on the sand and, after making sure that he was breathing all right, allowed herself a moment to catch her own breath as she loosely looped her arm around him protectively.

"What the hell happened?" Roger yelled, seemingly appearing out of nowhere as he ran onto the beach. He kneeled down next to Ollie, who was leaning against Alex.

She paused, still trying to catch her breath. "He fell in. Off the dock," she managed.

Roger shook his head. "When I couldn't find him, I knew he had to be here." His gray eyes focused on her accusingly. "Dammit, Alex. I told you not to take him swimming. I told you he didn't know how," he said angrily.

"I didn't take him. He must've followed me."

Roger shot her a cold glare as he stood up. He bent over and picked Ollie up. Ollie stared at him, not making any effort to resist. "C'mon," Roger said, holding on to Ollie as he looked down at Alex. "I've got the truck. I'll drive you both back to the house." Alex jumped up and wrapped the sandy towel around her slim waist. She grabbed her backpack as she hurried to catch up.

Roger put Ollie in the middle of the front seat. Alex jumped into the passenger seat, squeezing in next to Ollie. She unzipped her backpack and yanked out her old sweatshirt, which she gently wrapped around Ollie's shaking shoulders.

Roger pulled up in front of the house and turned off the truck. He took Ollie's hand as he moved to get out of the vehicle.

Ollie grabbed onto Alex, not letting her go.

"C'mon," Roger said impatiently, peeling Ollie's fingers off Alex. "We need to get you inside."

"I'll come in with you," Alex said to Ollie, trying to comfort him.

"No," Roger said, roughly lifting Ollie out of the truck. "I don't think that's a good idea." He pushed the door shut with his foot.

Alex grabbed her backpack and jumped out of the truck, running to catch up with Roger as he carried Ollie toward the house. She grabbed his arm, forcing him to stop walking and look at her.

"Roger, please. I'm telling you, he followed me there."

Roger looked at her. He shook his head disgustedly as he carried the silent child back into the house.

Alex looked after him, stunned. Why wouldn't he believe her?

With one final glance toward the house, she walked slowly back to her apartment. If Roger didn't believe her, she knew her chances were slim that Steve would.

Thirteen

Alex stood by her window sipping some homemade iced tea. The sun had set almost an hour ago, but Steve still wasn't home. She had been anxiously awaiting his return all day. She had the feeling he was not going to be happy about the beach incident, and she wanted a chance to explain herself. If there was going to be a scene, and she felt the chances of that were pretty good, she wanted to get it over with.

Of course, if Roger kept his mouth shut, there wouldn't be any scene at all. But after his behavior that afternoon, she seriously doubted that he would. Roger had surprised her. She had begun to think of him as a friend, and his behavior on the beach had confused her. Why had he so steadfastly refused to believe her assertion that Ollie had come there on his own volition? He obviously really believed that Ollie was so severely handicapped that he was incapable of finding his own way to the beach. But she knew otherwise. Ollie was intelligent. She could sense it. And he had followed her.

She sat down on her bed in front of the fan. She wondered how Ollie was faring. She hadn't seen any sign of either Roger or Ollie since the incident. She had knocked on the door several hours earlier to try

109

to talk some sense into Roger and to find out how Ollie was doing, but to no avail. Roger hadn't even come to the door.

She leaned back on her bed, not even bothering to take off her cheap flip-flops. Swimming always made her feel tired, and even the iced tea hadn't helped to wake her up. The heat made her tired as well. It seemed as if everything took so much more effort when it was hot. The evening had cooled the air a bit, but at eighty-five degrees, it was still pretty steamy. She was tempted to take off her light cotton shift and wait in her underwear, but she didn't want to risk Steve barging in on her half dressed. She set the iced tea down on her nightstand, promising herself that she would only close her eyes for a minute.

But she didn't keep her promise. In fact, by the time Steve returned an hour later, she was sleeping so soundly that she didn't hear his car.

It was not until he was running up the stairs to her apartment that she woke. And none too soon.

She jumped out of bed, instinctively straightening her dress. She opened the door as Steve reached the top step.

He didn't waste any time. "What the hell were you thinking?" he said angrily.

She paused, still half asleep. She blinked her eyes as she regained control of her faculties. "Perhaps you should listen to what really happened before you make accusations," she said, allowing him inside.

"Roger said . . ." he began.

"I can guess what Roger said," she said, cutting him off. She was awake now. Wide awake. "But I'm telling you, I didn't take him in the water."

"I would be much more understanding if you at least told me the truth."

"That is the truth," she said, facing him. She forced herself to slow down. She could understand why he was upset. He hadn't been there. And he had no reason not to believe Roger. "Look," she said reasonably.

"It's late. Maybe we should talk about this in the morning."

He stared at her curiously. It was as if he had suddenly noticed something about her, something that did not please him at all. He walked toward her slowly. "You seem very confident, Miss Rowe," he said.

She backed up. He was making her nervous. She shrugged. "I didn't do anything wrong."

He stopped. He shook his head, turning away. "I'm sorry, Miss Rowe. You may not have done anything wrong. But I still think it's best that you leave. As soon as possible."

She shook her head. "This whole place is so strange," she burst out, throwing her arms up in the air. She needed to play frustrated. She needed to turn the tables. "Why would I take a child who can't swim down to the beach without his parents? Why would I want that responsibility?"

Steve paused as he turned back around. He stared, unflinching, into her eyes. "I'm sorry, but there seems to be no other way to say this. You're fired," he said coolly. He began walking to the door.

Furious, Alex grabbed his arm to stop him. "You know I didn't take him down there, don't you?"

He glanced down at her hand on his arm. She pulled it back immediately. "Roger will fly you back to Miami tomorrow," he said softly, almost comfortingly. He opened the door.

"Why are you doing this?" Alex whispered.

Steve stopped, still facing outside.

"It's because Ollie cares about me, isn't it?" she continued. "And you can't stand that. You can't stand to make your child happy for one minute, can you? It just tears you apart that he's capable of feeling genuine emotion, unlike you."

He turned back toward her. "Are you basing that on your limited contact with me over the past few weeks, Miss Rowe, or do you know more about me than you let on?" he asked as though threatening her.

She stared back at him coldly.

"Pack your bags tonight. Roger will be here first thing in the morning," he said, stepping out of the room. He was finished with her.

"Damn," she said to the closed door. She couldn't believe she had let her emotions run away with her like that. She had lost her cool. And she had ended up fired. How could she, a seasoned pro, have let this happen?

Alex pulled her duffle out of the closet. She sighed. She knew how. She had let her emotions get in the way from the very beginning. She should have stayed away from Ollie instead of encouraging the friendship.

Well, she thought solemnly, Tim would certainly get a good laugh. She had gotten herself fired. Again. And it had taken her even less than the three weeks she had been allotted. She was quite a fast worker.

She took her clothes out of the drawer and began throwing them inside her duffle. She had blown it. Blown it before she had learned anything.

So what? she thought heatedly. She had her whole life in front of her. She didn't really need this story, she tried to convince herself. She could go anywhere.

Unfortunately, there was nowhere she wanted to go.

Shortly after dawn, Roger was knocking at her door.

"Ready?" he asked with an amiable smile, as though he were picking her up for a day at the beach. She grabbed her duffle bag and her backpack.

"Let's go," she muttered.

Roger tried to take her duffle bag from her, but she resisted. "I've got it," she said coldly. She was angry about yesterday. She blamed him for the misunderstanding.

"I see someone hasn't had her morning coffee yet."

"Excuse me, but I'm always a little out of sorts the day after I get fired," she replied testily, walking out of her apartment. Roger followed her down the stairs.

"Hey! You're not mad at me, are you?" he asked innocently.

She glanced over her shoulder. "Knock it off. You and I both know you're the reason I'm leaving."

"C'mon," he said, following her to the car. "I had to tell him what happened. The kid was all upset. And in the end, it wouldn't have made any difference anyway."

She ignored him as she carefully set her duffle in the back of the truck. She climbed into the passenger seat without looking at him. He pulled out of the driveway as she looked back toward the house.

"How's he doing this morning?" she asked quietly.

"The usual. I mean, the guy's a jerk," he said. It took her a minute to realize he was not referring to Ollie, as she had been, but to Steve.

She looked at him curiously. "I was referring to Ollie," she said. Roger raised his eyebrows, mildly embarrassed. "Oh." He paused. "I don't know. He was pretty calm this morning."

She sat there silently for a minute, not saying anything. "I thought you had a close relationship with Steve. Haven't you worked for him for a while?"

He laughed. "Hardly. He was never here until . . ." His voice drifted off.

"Leslie died?" she asked.

Roger nodded.

She paused. She had to move carefully. She needed information. And Roger was her last chance. He seemed to be looking for an opportunity to confide in her. She guessed that since Steve had just fired her, he thought that she would be a sympathetic soul. "I'm sorry I snapped at you yesterday," she said. "I was just frustrated."

Roger glanced at her. "You didn't snap," he said. "Look. I think you deserve to know that the whole accident thing . . . it's not the reason you got fired."

Alex looked at him, alarmed. "What do you mean? Steve said . . ."

"He's a liar. He told me to keep an eye on you. He wanted you off the island, one way or another. The accident just gave him a good excuse."

"But why?" she asked as the truck barreled down the one-lane dirt road, creating a cloud of dust behind it.

"I don't know." He paused for a moment. "He doesn't like his kid becoming too attached to anybody."

"What about you?"

He laughed. "That kid's not attached to me."

She hesitated, thinking. "You don't like Steve very much, do you?"

Roger stared in front of him. She could see the muscles tighten in his jaw. He didn't need to say anything. The answer was obvious.

"Why do you stay?" she asked softly.

He sighed. "I've known Steve for a long time. Besides that, I've got some business to take care of."

"What do you mean?" she asked curiously.

Roger made a sudden turn off the road that sent her crashing into the door. She rubbed her arm. She hoped he was a better pilot than driver.

"Sorry about that," Roger said. He pulled into a grassy lot that had two helicopters sitting on it. "Afraid the discussion is over. It's time to leave . . . Xanadu."

"Two helicopters?" she asked, nodding toward the bug-like aircraft.

"One was Leslie's. That's the one I flew. The other is Steve's. He flies himself."

She nodded. Roger jumped out of the car. He untied the rotary blades and motioned for her to get in. Alex shot a quick look back toward the truck, as if she was trying to think of anything she could do to stay there.

"C'mon," Roger called out. Tightly grasping her bag containing her computer, she walked quickly toward the helicopter as Roger helped her inside.

* * *

Steve was at his desk when he heard the helicopter leave. He went to the window and watched it fly overhead. He still had to explain to Ollie that Alex was no longer on the island, nor was she coming back. It was a discussion he was not looking forward to.

He sat back down behind his desk and rested his weary head in his hands. He hadn't been able to sleep at all the night before. All he could think about was Alex. It wasn't that he questioned his decision to let her go. He had had his concerns about her before Ollie's near drowning, but that had cemented it. He *had* to fire her, he reassured himself. And he was having regrets not because he was going to miss her but simply because he had grown accustomed to having someone else on the island, someone to break up the monotony.

But he couldn't kid himself. He had felt something for Alex. Something he had not felt for another woman for years. It was an attraction that threatened to cloud his usual clear judgment.

He shook his head, still justifying his decision. It was simply too risky to have Alex around. Ollie was becoming restless, more disturbed. Steve couldn't trust him to keep silent. Although Steve felt certain that Ollie had not said anything about Leslie's death to Alex, he knew that Alex had wondered why Ollie kept repeating "promise me."

Damn! He slammed his fist down on the table. This was not a life that he was living. He needed to get away, to escape from this damn house and all of the memories.

He stood up and walked to the window. He knew what he had to do. He had to take Ollie away. On the yacht. He would leave that afternoon. He would take a minimal amount of crew and risk Ollie talking. He had to. They couldn't stay in this ghost-ridden house one more day.

Alex was relieved when she saw the skyline of Miami. She glanced nervously at her pilot. Aside from the headset wrapped around his head, he looked just like he did on the ranch. Same bleached-blond hair. Same faded, slightly dirty jeans. She focused back on the pattern of the airport runways as she listened to Roger communicate with the terminal. If she hadn't actually seen him fly a helicopter, she would have had a hard time believing he was capable. He always seemed to strike her as a kind of laidback, reformed California surfer type. Not that she had anything against laidback individuals piloting aircraft. She just preferred her pilots to be the more uptight, obsessive, "checked this control a million times so I'm sure it's working" type.

She closed her eyes and focused on her breathing as the helicopter drifted toward the ground. "What's the matter?" Roger asked her. She began to answer but realized that he couldn't hear her. He motioned for her to push the button on her hand control which activated the microphone in her headset.

"Just a little tired," she replied.

He nodded and she forced herself to keep her eyes open as Roger skillfully brought the helicopter down on a narrow strip of concrete outside a small terminal. He leaned over and pulled off her headset. He then reached back and pulled her duffle bag and her backpack from behind their seats. "You enter the airport over there," he said, shouting above the rotary blades. She nodded as she opened the door.

She felt a hand on her arm and glanced over at him. He was pulling out a wad of bills from his pocket. "It's two thousand dollars. More than enough for a one-way ticket back to Virginia," he yelled, offering her the money.

She shook her head. "Forget it," she said. She didn't like the feeling of being paid off by Steve Chapman.

"Take it," he commanded. "Steve insisted. Consider it your pay. Anyway, you're going to need it. How will you get back without it?" he asked, sincerely concerned. She had to be careful. He was right. Alexandra Rowe would have needed it. Not that Alexandra Webster couldn't use it, too, but she wouldn't have taken it if she could have avoided it.

"You're right," she said, accepting the crisp hundred-dollar bills. "Hey," she said, pausing. She had an idea. It was a long shot but worth a try. "Do you want to go get something to eat? It's on me," she said, holding up the cash.

He shook his head. "Another time," he said.

She nodded. She wasn't surprised he didn't accept.

"Good luck to you," he said, giving her a nod good-bye.

She flashed him a quick wave before turning and walking toward the terminal. She would be in the airport only to pass through. She wasn't leaving Miami just yet.

Fourteen

Steve looked across the soft, green waters of the Caribbean. He had always felt slightly uncomfortable on the yacht. It had been his father-in-law's, bought at a time when he considered himself a rival of Aristotle Onassis. At one hundred thirty feet, the yacht was not nearly as big as the Onassis yacht; however, it was large enough to attract quite a bit of attention when docked in a tourist area. Steve liked it because, in spite of its size, he didn't need a large staff on board. In fact, his current crew consisted of only three men.

It had been only three days since he had left the Rye estate. Three very long days. His red, tired eyes focused back on the small cabin window behind him. Ollie lay in that room, his eyes open in a glassy stare, his small hands clutching a sweatshirt that Alex had left behind. He was muttering the same words over and over again. The words that only Steve understood.

Steve tightened his fists as he stared out into the water. He wanted so much to help his son. To save him. Yet he continued to make terrible mistakes. Mistakes that would resonate in Ollie the rest of his life. Like allowing Ollie to grow close to a stranger during a period in his young life when he was extremely vulnerable. When Alex had first come to the island, Steve had hoped to monitor their relationship. To keep them apart. He now realized that his efforts had failed terribly. Ollie had grown extremely attached to Alex, and her sudden dismissal, preceded as it was by the death of his mother, was too much pain for his young soul. And Steve had foolishly thought that a boat trip would get Ollie's mind off Alex. Instead, it seemed to make Ollie feel even worse. Each day, the rocking of the boat seemed to remind him that he was traveling farther away from Alex. And each day, he ate less and less, until he finally stopped eating altogether.

A small man with white hair wearing a bright, tropical print shirt appeared out of the hull. "Steve?"

Steve straightened as he turned around. He had known the man in front of him for years. Long enough to recognize the concern on the old doctor's face. "What's the matter with him, Randall?"

Dr. Randall Jacks shook his head. "He doesn't have a fever." He paused. "Steve, I . . . well," he said, stumbling over his words. "This isn't easy for me to say."

Steve turned away. He knew by the tone of the doctor's voice it had been a mistake to call him. He had only called him because he not only had an excellent reputation in internal medicine, but he also happened to be living in the nearby Bahamas. "I've examined Ollie carefully," he continued. "And there's nothing wrong with him—except what's in his mind."

"What are you saying?"

The doctor sighed. "Simply put, Ollie seems to be experiencing severe psychological trauma. I think you need to get him back to the States. Immediately. I think he needs to be hospitalized."

Steve walked toward an end table and picked up a warm, half-finished glass of iced tea. "In the psychiatric ward." Steve stated this as though it was a fact.

"For a while. I think he's suffering from posttraumatic stress disorder. You see it a lot with war veterans. It's not as common in children, although sometimes children who have been abused or been through an especially traumatic experience suffer from it."

"He just lost his mother."

"I understand, and that may indeed be the cause, but still . . ."

"But physically, he's fine," Steve said, not listening to him.

"I told you," the doctor said in a slow, patronizing tone. "His problem is not physiological but psychological. Now, I'm not a psychiatrist, so I can't make an absolute diagnosis from a simple examination . . ."

"Then don't," Steve said, cutting him off. He turned and faced him, his steely cold eyes focusing on the smaller man.

"Steve," the doctor continued, "you won't be able to put him back in school like this. Surely you know that."

"How much do I owe you?" Steve asked coldly, cutting him off.

The doctor looked at him and shook his head. It was pointless to argue with a man as stubborn as Steve Chapman. "Nothing," the man said, realizing that Steve had no intention of listening to his advice. He stepped up toward the dock. "He needs special care, Steve. Soon. Before it's too late."

"Thank you, Randall," Steve said, dismissing him. "Thank you . . . for your time."

He waited until the doctor was off the dock before going back to his son.

Ollie was curled up in as fetal position, holding on to Alex's sweatshirt as if it was his favorite blanket. Steve brushed the boy's damp, matted hair away from his face.

He knew what he had to do. He was just having trouble carrying it out. He gulped down the remainder of his warm iced tea and hesitated. He picked up his portable phone and dialed Roger's number. Roger answered on the second ring.

"Roger," he said, "I need you to find Alex and bring her back. Do whatever it takes. I don't care. Just find her. Bring her to the boat. And hurry." He paused. "If you have any trouble, let me know. I'll find her myself."

Roger stood up and gritted his teeth as he looked up at the ceiling. A day had passed since Steve's request, and he had gotten nowhere in his search for Alex. He knew that the phone would be ringing any minute with Steve asking him where she was.

Roger broke a pencil in half and threw it at the wall. He laughed at himself. He really needed to control his temper. Soon he'd be like Steve, beating up a stuffed bag every night to make himself feel a little better. His eyes focused on the neatly typed résumé Alex had sent him after he had seen her advertisement. He picked up the paper and looked it over carefully, as though he might have missed something. He had called the references at the bottom of her résumé, but no one seemed to know where she was. He had even checked the airlines, and as far as he could determine, she had not returned to Virginia. At least not by plane.

He plopped down in his chair, exhausted. He rubbed his hands over his eyes. She could be anywhere. And he didn't blame her. Maybe she had just taken the two thousand bucks and booked herself on a cruise or something.

He leaned forward, looking around the room. His eyes settled on the phone book. He smiled. Of course.

He was obviously not going to be able to find her himself. But that didn't mean he couldn't hire someone who could. He jumped up and grabbed the thick book. He flipped to the yellow pages and stopped at the D's. *D* for *detective*. He chose a company at random and picked up the phone. He knew Steve would not like what he was about to do, but he didn't care. Steve had given him a task, the first challenging assignment he had given him ever, and he was determined to prove that he was more than just a has-been, more than just Steve Chapman's charity case.

Fifteen

"**A**lex, I'm worried about you."

Alex's eyes shifted from her croissant to the man sitting across from her. "Why?"

Tim leaned forward. "You haven't had sex in ages. Do you know what that is doing to your anxiety level?"

"It seems to be having a bigger impact on you than on me," she replied, sipping her foamy, iced drink.

"How long has it been? A year?"

Alex looked around the air-conditioned café. Actually, it had been longer than a year, not that she would ever admit that to him. She should never have even called him.

She should have given herself a day or so first. Time to get her thoughts together. Instead, she had called him almost the moment she arrived at the Miami airport, still emotionally drained from her experience on Rye Island. And when he had insisted on flying down to spend the weekend with her, she hadn't had the strength to tell him not to. She hated to disappoint her old friend, but she was about to. Because she knew, right now, that she had absolutely no desire to sleep with him. And if he thought their present conversation was an aphrodisiac, he was mistaken.

"C'mon, Tim." She motioned toward his briefcase. "What's in there?"

He slumped in his chair resignedly. "I had hoped that maybe your little sojourn on Rye Island would have exorcised Chapman from your mind. Apparently not."

"I'm on a story," she said simply. "Just because my plan to get close to him . . ." She paused nervously. "Just because my job didn't work out, that doesn't mean I'm just going to forget about it."

"C'mon, Alex. It's over. You gave it your best shot. Let's just view this time together as a little vacation before we go back to New York."

"I can't vacation. I still have four days left."

Tim shook his head. "What are you going to do in four days?"

"I'm going to stay in Miami to . . . to do some research," Alex said evasively.

He looked at her curiously. "What are you thinking? That he's going to ask you back?"

She shook her head.

His eyes narrowed as he looked at her suspiciously. "How are you registered at the hotel?"

She swallowed. "What do you mean?"

He laughed. "I don't believe it. You're registered at the airport hotel under the name of Alexandra Rowe, aren't you?"

She looked toward the waitress. "Can we have the check, please?"

"You want him to be able to find you."

"I grew attached to his child. He's not well . . ."

"Right," he said, angry and frustrated.

"So you're not going to tell me what's in the briefcase?"

He raised his eyebrows. "I *was.*"

"Why are you acting like that? What is it? A negligee or something?" she asked, irritated.

"Something better. Something that is a surefire turn-on."

She smiled. "Information."

He picked up his worn leather briefcase. "Maybe."

"Quit teasing me," she said, with the first natural smile she had shown him since his arrival.

He leaned back in his chair. "Ah, power. What a wonderful feeling," he said sarcastically.

"Tim!"

He pulled a file out of his briefcase and opened it up. He waved a piece of paper in front of her. "Leslie Elizabeth Chapman. Motor vehicle driving record."

Alex leaned forward and attempted to yank the paper away from him. Tim held it out of her reach. She smiled. "What does it say?"

Tim laughingly gave in. "In the past five years, she has received two warnings for driving under the influence and one conviction. Her license was suspended for six months last year."

Alex nodded as the information registered. "So we're looking at a fairly serious problem."

Tim shrugged. "I would say so. Anyway, that little piece of info inspired me to do a little bit of checking up on her myself."

"And?"

"I know this will shock you, but the Chapmans weren't very happy together."

The smile faded. "What have you got?" she said, all business.

He pulled out a spiral pad and flipped it open. "Mrs. Leslie Chapman." He shook his head. "A rather tragic character. Born in nineteen fifty-eight. Mother took an overdose of sleeping pills and died shortly after Leslie was born. Grew up in boarding schools. Not close to her father . . . although it was her father who wanted her to marry Steve Chapman. But then again, rumor had it that he informed her that she would either marry Steve or be disinherited."

"So they both forced her to marry him."

"I don't know exactly what role Chapman played in this. I don't see why he'd want to force somebody to marry him. Unless, of course, he wanted the money."

"Bingo."

"Who knows?" he said, shrugging his shoulders. "And, like you wrote in one of your numerous memos before you left, the old guy played a nasty trick on her."

"What are you talking about?" Alex asked.

"Leaving everything to Steve when he died. Not to her. Everything he owned, the company, the apartments . . . everything except for . . ."

"One dollar. So she couldn't even contest the will." Alex shook her head. "The poor woman," she said.

"You got that right. At least she would have been, without Chapman."

"What about Ollie? Any info on whether or not he's autistic?"

Steve shrugged. "Nothing. Until last year he attended the Lowman School in New York City, an incredibly expensive private school for rich kids."

"Yeah, yeah. I know." She had reviewed all that information before she left. But just because he was in school, that didn't mean he wasn't suffering from autism.

"Any grades or teacher reports?"

He looked away sheepishly. "Unfortunately, no."

Alex frowned. "Any new info on Chapman himself?"

"There's no satisfying you, is there?" he said with a smirk.

"I've got to admit, your information leaves a little to be desired. You haven't really told me anything that might make me change my mind about Chapman's guilt . . . or innocence."

"And your mind is made up?"

"Not yet. But right now, it's looking like she killed herself," she said, thinking aloud. "If Steve killed her, where's the motive?"

"Steve?" he asked suspiciously.

She blushed, attempting to ignore him. "Chapman. Whatever."

"Who knows? Maybe it was a crime of passion. They got in a fight, and he threw her off a building."

She shook her head. "I just don't think so."

"And why is that?" Tim asked, leaning forward.

Alex paused. Her blue eyes settled back on Tim. "Because I just have a sense that he's not a murderer. He's too . . ." She paused, searching for the right word. "Gentle," she said finally.

"*Gentle?* You've got to be kidding me!" Tim said with a harsh burst of laughter. "The man was a damn boxer. He won a gold medal for beating the shit outta . . ."

"That's not the only reason," Alex interrupted defensively. "I had a chance to visit the local library yesterday."

"And what did you find out about this gentle man?"

"I found out what happened during one of her suicide attempts."

Tim pulled off a piece of her croissant and shoved it into his mouth. "Go on," he said.

"Two years ago, the Chapmans attended a party in a hotel here in Miami. Apparently, at this party, Leslie became convinced that Steve was flirting with a waitress. She threatened to jump off the balcony. She made quite a scene. It sounds pretty dramatic. The local magazine's society page was full of gory details."

"I don't remember hearing about this."

"Neither do I. But it was common knowledge around these parts that she was a little unstable."

"Maybe he was a jerk, and that was the only way she could get his attention."

"I can think of more productive ways she could deal with an unfaithful husband."

"Like that woman in Virginia . . . what's her name . . ."

"Don't be disgusting. I was thinking more in terms of filing for divorce."

Tim smiled and shrugged his shoulders.

She thought for a moment. "I want to find out if Leslie had an insurance policy on her life. And I want to know if either one of them has had any affairs."

"From the tone of your voice, one might think that it was me who was working for you."

Alex shook her head. Tim was joking, but it was obvious that he resented helping her with this story. Not that Alex cared. After all, she needed help, and he was supposed to be providing assistance. And so far, he was doing a lousy job.

She asked, "Were you able to track down any sources on those rumors of divorce?" She knew that Leslie hadn't officially filed for one. If she had, it would have turned up on the paper trail.

"Afraid not."

"Tim!" she said, irritated.

"Look," he said, raising his hands in frustration. "I said I'd help you because Dick wouldn't let you go otherwise. But I've got my own job to do, Alex. I don't have time to baby-sit you."

She stood up, eyeing him coldly. "I wasn't aware I needed a baby-sitter."

Tim shook his head. "Oh, God, here we go. I'm sorry, Alex," he said mechanically. "I didn't mean it."

"Forget it," Alex said, pretending not to be hurt.

"Shall we?" she said, grabbing her purse. "I want to take a shower and rest for a while before dinner."

"That sounds like a great idea," he said, raising his eyebrows expectantly as he followed her away from the table.

She turned back toward him, shooting a polite smile in his direction. "Great. Then we better check you into your room so you can do the same."

"I have to stay in my own room?" he asked, putting a hand on her back.

"I told you that was the way I wanted it."

"But I thought you might have changed your mind after you saw how good I was at information," he added, whispering in her ear.

She shook her head. "You'll have to do a little better than that."

As the cab pulled into the hotel drive, Tim spoke. "Ah," he said sarcastically, glancing around the concrete-block, nondescript hotel entranceway. "Charming. A regular home away from home."

Alex flashed him a look that told him to be quiet. "Maybe you shouldn't stay here if you find it so nasty," she said, paying the driver.

"Maybe I shouldn't," he replied, following her out of the cab. "As a matter of fact, I don't think I will. Mind if I use your phone to call for reservations downtown?"

"Since when did you get to be such a prima donna?" she asked, walking into a lobby that, although it was early evening, still smelled of bacon and eggs.

"You could come with me," he said. "I'll get a room with double beds."

She didn't even bother to answer him as she stepped into the elevator and pressed the button for the fourth floor.

She walked silently to her room, unlocking the door. She pointed to the phone. "There you go," she said.

She stopped. The message light was blinking. "There's a message," she said, surprised.

"Great," Tim said sarcastically as he set his luggage down. "Maybe it's from your *boyfriend.*" He stepped into the bathroom, locking the door behind him.

Alex walked over to the phone. She had just picked it up when she heard a knocking on the hotel room door. She hesitated for a second, then glanced through the peephole. Her heart sank. "Just a minute," she yelled, loud enough so that Tim would hear. She kicked Tim's expensive leather duffle bag under the bed.

She opened the door. "Roger!"

"Hello, Alex," he replied, looking at her suspiciously.

"What are you doing here?"

He hesitated. "Mind if I come in?"

"Of course not," she said as naturally as possible. "Please do," she said, opening the door wider. He walked past her. She glanced at Tim's briefcase, hoping that he wouldn't notice. *Stay in the bathroom, Tim,* she thought to herself, avoiding looking at the closed door.

"I called earlier and left a message for you . . ." he began.

She nodded toward the blinking light on her phone. "I just walked in this minute. I was about to retrieve my messages when you knocked."

"I'm sorry to just barge in on you like this, but Steve asked me to find you."

"What is going on?"

"Ollie's ill. He's refused to eat since you left. Steve wants me to take you to him."

"Oh my God," she said, sitting down on the edge of the bed. She had been worried about Ollie. But she had never thought that he would harm himself. "Back to the island?"

Roger shook his head. "No. They're on the yacht.

Off the coast of Mayaguna Island. Near the Bahamas."

She looked up at Roger. "How did you find me?" she asked.

He crossed his arms in front of him. "It wasn't easy. I had to hire a private detective to track you down."

Alex nodded. "I'm flattered. I don't think I've ever had a detective looking for me," she said.

"I guess, as a horse trainer," he said, emphasizing the words *horse trainer,* "you wouldn't."

She looked at him carefully. Had the investigator stumbled onto her true identity?

"Why don't you pack up?" he said. "Steve wanted us to leave tonight."

"Tonight? I . . ."

"There's money in it for you," Roger said. "Steve wanted me to make that clear."

She looked around. "I don't care about the money," she said, looking at him. "I just need a couple of minutes to throw my things together." She glanced toward the bathroom, sure that Tim was seething inside. "Do you mind waiting in the lobby, while I shower and change?" she asked.

He shook his head. "Of course not."

"Thanks," she said. As soon as Roger left, Tim stepped out of the bathroom. Alex held her index finger up to her lips to signal him to keep quiet. She grabbed him by the arm and pulled him back inside the bathroom, turning on the fan and starting the shower.

"Don't go, Alex," he whispered urgently.

"You heard him," she said. "Ollie is sick."

"That is not your problem anymore, is it?" he said, grabbing her by the shoulders.

"This is a break for me," she said. "A lucky break. And I have to take it."

"There's something weird about this whole situation. Why doesn't the guy take the kid to the hospital?

Get him in psychiatric treatment. Something. You're not a doctor!"

"No. I'm an investigative journalist."

"Don't do this, Alex. I have a bad feeling about it."

"And I have a bad feeling about returning to New York without a story."

"Your time is up!" Tim said. "You have to come back."

"Don't be a fool," she threatened. "This is a big break . . . worthy of an extension."

She shrugged away. She glanced at the bathroom door, avoiding his eyes.

Tim swore under his breath. Despite his hesitation, he knew that she was right. "I'll give you two more weeks."

She smiled. "I want you to wait here until I leave. Wait at least ten minutes before leaving this room."

He started to protest, but she shot him a look that he knew all too well. He couldn't say anything. Her mind was made up.

"I'm sorry about this, Tim." She paused. She put her hand on his cheek. "I really am," she said sincerely. He got her message. And she wasn't referring to the story. She didn't care about him the same way he cared about her.

He watched her walk out of the small, steamy room. "Sure you are," he said to himself. "Sure you are."

It was night when they arrived, but Roger had no trouble bringing the two-engine plane down on the slick, narrow landing strip and steering it over to the pint-sized airport. Roger unfastened his seat belt and stepped out of the plane, not even bothering to check on his passenger, who was scrambling to keep up with him.

Alex opened the door and hopped out. It had rained several hours earlier, and the humidity was fierce. She could almost feel her straight hair curl the minute she stepped into the hot, tropical night.

Roger handed Alex her baggage.

"Go into the airport. A driver will be there to greet you. He'll take you to the boat."

"Aren't you coming?" she asked, a little concerned at the thought of having to be alone with Steve.

He shook his head. "Have a good time," he said, with a ring of sarcasm coating his words. He walked back behind the plane.

Alex had no trouble finding the driver. He was waiting for her as promised, with a big sign that said "ALEX." He spoke a broken, cheery blend of island English. Even though she had quite a bit of trouble understanding him, she was able to determine that he was driving her to some dock, at which point she would board a water taxi that would take her out to Steve's yacht.

The cab's headlights illuminated the dirt road as they drove past dark clusters of bungalow-type houses. Alex rolled her window down and almost relaxed as a warm, floral-smelling breeze blew into the backseat. The driver pulled into a marina and rolled down his window to talk to a man wearing cutoff Bermuda shorts and a stained T-shirt with a big yellow happy face on the front. They gave each other a friendly greeting, and then the man standing outside the cab stuck his head in the window and introduced himself as her ride to the boat. He grabbed her duffle bag and backpack and helped her onto the boat with a big smile, as if she were a tourist on her way to see the dolphins.

The small boat jumped over the waves, bumping along, and Alex worried it might split in half at any moment. The night was dark, made even darker by the clouds floating lazily over the moon. She could see the hazy outline of a large ship in the distance. The driver motioned toward the ship and smiled. They had Steve's yacht in sight.

She swallowed as the driver pulled up alongside the

boat. She could see the silhouette of a man on the deck. A man who was waiting for her. Steve.

The driver said something and pointed toward the steps in front of them. Alex nodded and grabbed her duffle, but the man shook his head, taking the bag away from her. She understood. He was carrying her luggage. She climbed up the steps. As she reached the top step, she was aware of Steve's hand on her arm.

Steve lifted her onto the deck and handed the man some money as he took her bags from him. Steve turned back toward her.

"Hello," he said.

She attempted a smile. "Hi."

He sighed. "Thank you for coming," he said.

His hands brushed her fingers as he gallantly took her luggage.

"This way," he said, nodding toward a stairway. He led her down two flights of stairs and inside a room that looked like a plush parlor, complete with a fireplace.

He set down her luggage. They looked at each other awkwardly.

"I'm glad you came," he said.

She nodded, trying to hide her surprise at his appearance. The past several days had had an obvious impact on him. He looked disheveled and tired, with deep circles beneath his eyes. He was in dire of need of a shave, and his jeans and shirt looked as if they needed to be cleaned and thrown in the dryer on the permanent press cycle.

"I'll take you to Ollie," he said appreciatively. He led her through the room and down a hall paneled in dark, shiny mahogany. He opened up the last door on the left. "See if you can get him to eat something. I made him some soup, but he wouldn't touch it."

Alex walked into the dark room. Ollie was lying on his bed, curled up in a little ball. His eyes were closed tightly shut, and he was desperately clutching her sweatshirt in his hand.

Steve turned on the soft bedside lamp as Alex sat on the bed. The sight of Ollie holding on to her sweatshirt for comfort moved her to tears. "Ollie?" she whispered. Ollie opened his eyes. He stared at her.

"It's me. Alex. I've come to see you. We're going to have so much fun. I'm going to stay here with you and your dad."

He sat up in bed. He glanced over at his dad, wanting confirmation. Steve nodded. "That's right," he said. "Alex is going to stay here with us."

"I want you to eat some soup for me, Ollie."

Ollie looked at her blankly, but at least he was sitting up—an opportunity Steve was determined to take advantage of.

"I'll go get it," Steve said, looking at Alex.

Alex turned back toward Ollie as Steve left the room. "What's going on, kiddo?" she asked. "Have you been giving your dad a tough time?"

Ollie sat still, staring at her.

"I know you were angry at him, Ollie. I was, too, but you've got to promise me you're not going to hurt yourself because you're angry at him," she said.

"Promise me," he whispered. "Promise me."

Alex looked at him sadly. "Oh, Ollie," she said, brushing his hair away from his forehead. "What did you see that made you so sad? Can't you tell me?"

Ollie just stared at her.

She sighed. "Well, we don't need to worry about that right now. I want you to think good thoughts of all the fun things we're going to do. Your dad and I have a lot of plans for you. Fun, fun things."

Steve walked back in, carrying a tray with a bowl of chicken soup. "Here you go, sport," he said, putting the tray down. They sat in silence, watching as Ollie carefully sipped his soup. When he was finished, Steve took the tray away. "I'll bring this back up to the kitchen."

He leaned down and whispered in Alex's ear. "See if you can get him to fall asleep."

"Ollie," Alex said after Steve had shut the door. "I want you to lean back in bed and close your eyes. I'm going to tell you a story," she began, patting his head. He shook his head and started whimpering. He grabbed her arm. "I'm not going anyplace," she said. "I'm going to stay here with you. I'm going to tell you a story. A story about . . . the monkey and the bear," she said, making something up. She began to tell an impromptu silly tale with as many comforting details as possible about a monkey who wanted the bear's soup. She knew that her story was too juvenile for an intelligent seven-year-old, but it was the best she could do. And it seemed to be working, she thought as she watched his eyes close. She was boring him to sleep. As soon as she heard the regulated breath of a deep sleep, she kissed him gently on his forehead and tiptoed out of the room, closing the door behind her. She walked back into the parlor.

"How did it go?" Steve asked.

She shrugged. "He's sleeping."

He breathed a sigh of relief. "Thank you."

"What exactly happened?" she said.

He shook his head. "He's hardly eaten anything since you left. And he hasn't been sleeping. He doesn't want to leave his bed. It's been pretty bad."

"And you think it's because of me?"

"It started right after you left," he replied. He shook his head. "He's had a tough time of it the past few months. Losing his mother and all. You filled a void in his life. When you left, it was like losing his mother all over again."

She nodded. So Ollie had been close to his mother. So much for the abuse theory.

"Drink?" he asked, walking over to the bar.

She nodded.

He poured two glasses of wine. "Since we're in the tropics, we should really be having piña coladas, but I'm afraid I don't have any coconut milk."

Alex took the drink, refusing to return his smile.

He sat down on the couch. "Please," he said, motioning for her to sit facing him.

She stood still, ignoring his instructions as she sipped her drink.

He paused, aware that she was angry. "I owe you an apology," he said.

She looked back down at her wine. She had him where she wanted him, and she was enjoying the reversal of power. He needed her.

"I'm sorry I lost my temper the night I fired you. I realize now that I was wrong. I'm sure that Ollie *did* follow you down to the water. I had no idea he was so . . . infatuated with you."

She shook her head. "I wouldn't go that far. I think he's just a little kid who's sad and lonely. I played with him. Gave him some attention. That's all." She paused, turning back toward him. "What's wrong with Ollie? Why won't he speak?"

Steve shook his head as he shrugged his shoulders. "He was fine until Leslie died. Then . . . I don't really know. He hasn't spoken since."

"Except to say 'promise me.' "

Steve glanced up at her. "Right."

She paused. "Has he seen a counselor?"

He looked at her carefully, letting her know that she was on sensitive ground. "He's upset about his mother's death."

"That's understandable. But isn't this behavior a little extreme? I mean, not talking. Only saying 'promise . . .' "

"That's enough," he said quietly yet intensely. He paused, aware that he had startled her. He shook his head. "I'm sorry. I *will* get help for Ollie. Soon. I was just hoping to wait until this whole thing blew over. It would be too hard now. The media would be all over him. In the meantime, Ollie needs a friend. And he likes you." He shook his head as he sank into his seat, exhausted. "Look, I know you're not trained for this. I just . . . I thought you might be able to help."

Alex was surprised by her sudden urge to comfort him. "I'm sorry," she said simply.

He smiled at her as if he appreciated her apology. His gaze drifted over her, slowly absorbing the way her loose fitting T-shirt clung to all the right places and the way her jeans wrapped around her slender hips and long legs.

Alex brushed her hair away from her eyes as she looked away self-consciously. Steve snapped back to attention.

"We need to discuss payment," he said suddenly. "I realize that this type of work is not really what you want, so I'm going to compensate you generously for your efforts. I'll pay you seven hundred dollars a week. In cash."

"Well," she said, sitting down. "That certainly is generous."

"Good," he said, pulling an envelope out of his back pocket. "Here's two weeks. In advance."

She shook her head. "You just gave me two thousand for . . . airfare. Remember?"

"Take the money," he said sternly. He kept his eyes focused on hers as he picked up her hand and stretched out her fingers. He put the bills on her palm and curled her fingers around them.

"Thanks," she said, her eyes locked on his.

"So," he said, switching the subject as he pulled his hand away. "I was surprised to hear that you hadn't gone back to Virginia," he said. "What made you decide to stay in Miami?"

She leaned against the bar, facing him. She looked at him. "Ollie," she said simply. "I was worried about him. I was hoping that you would reconsider."

He leaned forward. "Well, we would have had an easier time finding you in Virginia. As it was, we had a hell of a time tracking you down. I was beginning to think that Alexandra Rowe had vanished from the earth," he said.

She shook her head. "Not at all."

"In any case, I'm glad we found you again," he said, staring at her intently. In fact, he had been anxiously awaiting her arrival ever since Roger had called him to say that she had agreed to come to the boat.

Alex looked away, blushing slightly.

Steve suddenly realized that he had embarrassed her. "Why don't I give you a little tour of the boat, show you where things are," he said as cheerfully as he could, putting down his drink. "I want you to feel comfortable here."

Alex nodded. She set her drink on the table and followed him down the hallway. He stopped outside a closed door. "You have your choice of rooms," he said. "This is one," he said, opening up a door and revealing a small but glamorous room with a double-size canopy bed. "This is another," he said, pushing open another door. "And this is yet another," he said, opening the third door. Alex walked into the third room and glanced around. This room was even more glamorous than the first two, with soft white carpeting and a queen-size bed.

"It's stunning," she said.

"My father-in-law built this boat. This room belonged to his wife," he said.

"They didn't share a room?"

He shrugged his shoulders. "Kind of. This one has a door that opens into the master bedroom," he added softly.

She glanced at him coldly. "So your room is on the other side of . . ." she began.

"My room is right through here," he said, opening a door. Alex nodded disdainfully as she peered around his arm. The master suite was decorated in varying shades of gold and blue. Above the king-size bed was a large modern painting that she could only assume was an original.

"Is that a Picasso?"

"Yes."

She turned back toward him. She had grown up

around a fair amount of money, but she had never seen anything that compared with this.

"The first room will be fine," she said, walking quickly back toward the front.

"I haven't finished the tour," he said, crossing his arms patiently. She turned back.

"You know where Ollie's room is," he said, pointing to the left. "And these stairs lead up to the dining room, kitchen, and sun deck," he said, walking up the stairs. "C'mon," he added, motioning for her to follow him. "There are four levels on the boat. The crew live in the bottom level. The first level is the one we're on right now. The level directly above us is more of a recreational area."

She followed him up a huge, winding wooden staircase. A staircase that she would expect to see in a Southern mansion. It opened into a large room, complete with fireplace, grand piano, and large picture windows that wrapped around the entire space. In the center of the room was a grouping of four rounded couches that faced each other, making a circle.

"The living room," he said. He walked through the room. He stopped to open two glass doors. "And this is the sun room," he said, pointing toward a smaller yet still impressive room, decorated in soft greens. "The sun deck is out through those doors. Beside the lap pool."

"The pool," she said, nodding her head knowingly. "Of course. What's a yacht without a pool?"

He smiled at her. "Don't get your hopes up. It's not that grand. I wouldn't dive in there. It's only five feet deep. My father-in-law built it so that he could swim laps. C'mon," he said. "See for yourself." He led her through the sun room and out onto the deck.

The pool's underwater lights were on, illuminating the smooth, black bottom. "I told you it was small," he said.

"I think it's perfect," she replied. She looked up from the pool, her eyes focusing on the cool dark water that surrounded the yacht. The lights of the island were barely visible in the distance.

"And this," he said, motioning toward a staircase outside the sun room, "leads to the upper deck. There are two main rooms up there," he said, pointing up the stairs. "A gambling room and a bar. I never use either."

He glanced back at her. She looked at him expectantly as her long black hair blew gently away from her face. He had a sudden, crazy urge to kiss her. Instead, he forced himself to look away as he spoke. "Let's walk around the deck to the kitchen," he said, leading her around the side of the boat.

As she followed him, Alex ran her fingers along the protective railing as if the ship might lurch at any moment. Not that she felt unsafe. It was so large, she couldn't even feel the gentle surge of the waves underneath them. In fact, despite the fact that they were surrounded by the Caribbean, the boat had the feel of an opulent, spacious hotel. "The kitchen is through here," he said, opening a glass door and motioning for her to go inside. She walked underneath his arm and into a large gourmet kitchen, loaded with sparkling new appliances and countertops. "If you have any food preferences, let me know. You're on your own for breakfast and lunch. But we have a local island chef bringing in dinners, and she's actually quite good."

"What do you do when you're cruising?"

"Cruising?"

"Whatever you call it. You know, what if you're in the middle of the sea?"

"One of the crew members is a pretty good cook. He fills in."

"Where are they?" she asked. She suddenly realized that she hadn't seen anyone else since she came on board.

"They're not here right now. When I dock, I like my privacy. I usually just put them up at a hotel on whatever island I'm near. That way, we're all happy. They get a vacation, and I get privacy. When I'm not using the boat, I keep it in Miami, and they live on board."

"You don't use it much?" she asked.

He shook his head. "Not that much," he said. "It's a little big for me. And a little grand." He moved through the kitchen. "The dining room is this way," he said, opening another door. Alex peeked around him. The room was large, with sliding glass doors on either side. A round mahogany table that seated twelve was in the middle of the room.

"It's nice when we open these up and let the breeze come in," he said, walking through the room and sliding the glass doors open. Alex could feel a light breeze almost immediately. Steve stepped back onto the deck and leaned up against the railing as he stared across the sea.

"Beautiful," she said, following him outside. She stood next to him, her hands clutching the railing. She looked up at him. "But there's so much furniture."

He looked at her curiously. "What do you mean?"

She smiled. "Where do you box?"

He grinned, looking back toward the water. His curly hair blew away from his eyes. "I don't box on the boat. Like I said, I've never spent much time here."

"Do you miss it?" she asked after a pause.

"For some reason, I've never had much of a desire to box when I'm on the water."

"No. I meant, do you miss boxing as a profession? I heard you used to be pretty good."

"Looking into my background?" he asked teasingly as he glanced sideways at her.

She blushed. "No. Someone mentioned that you . . ."

"I don't know," he interrupted, putting her out of her misery. He looked toward the water. "Sometimes

140

I guess I miss it. At least, I think I do. It's hard to say. My life was so much simpler then."

She paused. "What made you quit?"

"I saw boxing as a means to an end. It gave me money, which gave me power. The minute I made enough money to do what I really wanted to do, I quit."

"And what was that?"

"To go to school. A good school. That was my dream." He hesitated. "When you grow up poor, you never take your education for granted."

She looked at him suspiciously. "Yeah, I know."

"You do?" he asked, sincerely surprised.

Alex was irritated. Why was he so surprised that she should understand? "What's that supposed to mean? That you think I was a spoiled rich kid?"

"Weren't you?"

"No," she said indignantly, stiffening as she faced him.

He smiled. "I don't mean to be critical. It's just that I grew up poor. I can always pick out the people who grew up with money and the ones who didn't."

"Oh, really," she said, crossing her arms in front of her.

He faced her as well, leaning sideways on the balcony. He was sure of himself, and it showed. "You don't really care about money because you've always had it," he said, as if reeling off facts. "You probably didn't think twice about going into a field that didn't pay all that well, because you could always fall back on your trust fund."

"I don't have a trust fund," she said through her teeth.

"Rich parents?" he offered.

"No," she replied quickly. "At least not my father," she added truthfully.

He raised an eyebrow. "Your mother?" he asked teasingly.

"So what?" she said. "She hasn't supported me in a long time."

He nodded, but it wasn't in agreement. He had already made up his mind about her. He checked his watch. "It's getting late. You must be tired."

"I am," she said indifferently.

He paused for a second, waiting for her to leave. He pointed into the living room, toward the stairs. "Do you know how to get back to your room?"

She shot him a nasty look as she walked past him. "I'll manage. Good night, Mr. Chapman," she said coldly.

"Pleasant dreams, Miss Rowe," he replied with a touch of humor in his voice.

Damn him, she thought, walking toward the door. He always made her loose her cool. She glanced back at him. He stood there, staring at her curiously. She shut the glass door a little too loudly on her way in.

Sixteen

She opened her eyes. The slight rocking of the bed momentarily disoriented her. She glanced around the room. She wasn't in New York, Michigan . . .

No, she realized. It was worse than that. She was on Steve Chapman's boat in the middle of the Caribbean.

She had no idea how long she had tossed and turned the previous night before she finally fell asleep. But she did know that she had lain in the dark for several hours, feeling the slow rocking of the boat that she hadn't even noticed until she climbed into bed. After several hours, she was so seasick that she was tempted to jump overboard and swim toward dry land. By the time she finally drifted off, it was well past midnight, and Steve had not yet returned to his quarters.

Alex imagined him as she had left him, standing at the railing of the boat, staring off into the distance. She wondered if he ever really slept, or if his conscience refused to let him seek respite from the demons that plagued his daily existence.

She leaned up in bed, only to be welcomed by a familiar sight. She smiled at the child sitting in the corner. "Hello, Ollie," she said. "Are you waiting for me?"

He nodded.

Alex glanced toward her open door as she heard Steve call Ollie's name. She glanced back down at Ollie, who didn't seem to care that his father was looking for him. Within seconds, Steve appeared in the doorway, apparently no worse for wear from his sleepless night. His dark, curly hair was covered by a baseball cap. A rugby shirt and shorts revealed the muscular tone of his imposing physique.

Alex pulled her blanket up to cover her, even though she was wearing a T-shirt and shorts.

"Just like old times," Steve said, smiling. He looked at Ollie. "Time for breakfast. Are you ready?" he asked Alex.

"Sure. But I really just want coffee. And a shower. Not necessarily in that order."

Steve nodded. "C'mon, sport. Let's you and I go upstairs and have some cereal." He took Ollie by the hand and began to lead him out of the room. Steve glanced back at Alex as he shot her a smile. "Take your time," he said.

As soon as it was safe, Alex threw the covers off and sat up. She walked into her private, black marble bathroom and turned on the shower, thinking the whole time. Ollie had seemed much better this morning. So, for that matter, had Steve. She flinched as she remembered the nasty pot shot he had taken at her the night before, basically implying that she was spoiled.

Despite having more money than she had ever seen before, he still seemed to have a chip on his shoulder about being born on the wrong side of the tracks.

Or did he? Alex stepped into the warm, pulsating water and tilted her head down so that it massaged her stiff neck. She squirted out some shampoo and lathered up her hair, her mind focused on Steve. She rinsed out her hair as she tried to pinpoint exactly what it was about him that was nagging at her.

Her sixth sense was telling her that even though he had practically referred to her as a spoiled brat, his words had seemed shallow. It was as if he had been trying to find something out. He was goading her into revealing more information than she wanted, a tactic she had used herself more than once.

Alex stepped out of the shower. She grabbed an oversized fluffy towel and draped it around her. *Well, Mr. Chapman,* she thought silently. *Go ahead and try.* If she was correct about assuming that he, like her, was hunting for information, he was going to have a tough time getting it out of her.

She dressed quickly, slipping into her conservative, one-piece bathing suit and pulling a large T-shirt dress over her head. She ventured out into the hall and up the stairs. She breathed in with pleasure as she stepped into the living room.

It was a beautiful day, and the view was spectacular. The cool, turquoise water seemed to glisten all around the boat.

Alex walked through the living room and into the dining room.

Steve was sitting at the table, hunched over some papers. A small cellular phone was in front of him.

"You made it," he said, smiling at her. A nice, warm, friendly smile.

"Where's Ollie?" she asked.

He leaned under the table. "Ollie? Do you want to

144

come out and say hello?" Steve poked his head back up. "He'll be out in a minute. As soon as he's finished with his cereal."

She nodded, unsure whether to be amused or concerned that Steve let his child eat under the table. "Sit down," Steve said, standing up and pointing toward a chair. "I'll get you your coffee."

"I can get it," she said.

"No," he said. "Please. Allow me."

She smiled at him quickly as she obeyed, sitting down stiffly. She leaned underneath the table. "How's it going, Ollie?"

Ollie focused on his cereal, ignoring her.

Alex sat back up as she glanced at Steve. Tim had been right. This whole idea was crazy. Ollie didn't even seem to care that she was there.

"Here you go," Steve said, putting the coffee in front of her. He sat down beside her. "So," he said awkwardly.

"So," she continued. "I thought I might teach Ollie how to swim this morning."

His eyes narrowed.

"If it's all right with you, of course," she said.

He shook his head. "I don't know. He's still pretty weak."

"I used to be a lifeguard," she said. "We'll be right here in the pool. Nothing is going to happen."

He leaned under the table. "What do you say, sport?"

Ollie stared at him. Steve looked back up at Alex. "I think that's a definite yes." He paused, watching Alex sip her coffee. "I was very tired last night. I'm sorry if I upset you."

"You didn't," she said in a tone of voice that stopped all conversation.

He studied her as if he didn't really believe her. He shrugged. "Good." He stood up. "C'mon, sport," he said, bending down with his hands on his knees, focusing on the child under the table. "We've got to get you into your trunks." Ollie peeked out from under the table. He glanced at Alex. "We'll meet you by the pool."

When they came back, Alex was in the water, swimming laps. "This is strange," she said. "Swimming in a pool that's floating on the ocean."

"How do we begin?" Steve asked.

"You can go back to your work. Ollie and I will be as quiet as possible," she said, leaning against the edge of the pool. "Come here, Ollie," she said. "It's fun. I'm going to help you."

Ollie walked forward. He stopped just out of reach of her arms.

"I'm not going to make you," she said. She kicked away from the side of the pool. She began doing her water ballet, pretending not to notice as Ollie walked up to the edge. Suddenly, she heard a splash.

"Ollie!" Steve yelled, alarmed. Alex grabbed Ollie and held him up. Steve stood at the edge of the pool, looking at them worriedly.

She shot him an icy stare. The last thing Ollie needed when he was trying something new was to have his dad acting as if he was not capable.

"Ollie and I are having fun," she said, emphasizing the word fun. "I'm sorry if we're being too loud," she added.

Steve nodded. "Sorry," he said, walking sheepishly back to his chair.

"Okay," she said, focusing back on her pupil. She turned him onto his stomach, keeping him afloat by placing her hands underneath him. "The first stroke is called the doggy paddle."

Steve glanced at her over his papers. Catching his eye, she shrugged. "Got to start somewhere."

Steve watched his son splash in the water. He wanted so much for Ollie to experience some pleasure in life. To make up for some of the pain he had experienced. His gaze shifted to the woman who held his child in her arms. Her black hair was slicked back from the water, allowing him an unrestricted view of the naturally long black lashes that framed her soft blue eyes. Although he didn't think he had ever seen a suit that covered more skin than hers, even the suit couldn't hide the ample bosom that swelled underneath its shiny blue surface.

He swallowed as he forced himself to look away. What was he doing? After all, Alex had consented to be his son's nanny. And he already knew that as soon as his son was feeling better, or as soon as his lawyers agreed that he was free from the past, he would dismiss her and get proper medical care for Ollie. She was to be treated as a remedy for Ollie, a temporary salve to ease Ollie's pain.

But, Steve realized, Ollie was not the only one benefiting from Alex's company. Still, Steve argued as he continued his inner dialogue, he had to benefit from a distance. As tempted as he might be by Alex's obvious attributes, he knew better.

Alex leaned over the railing. She was alone on the deck. Steve was tucking his son into bed, and the cook had just left, motoring her little boat back toward shore.

The warm, tropical evening breeze blew Alex's hair away from her face as she breathed in deep, smelling the fragrant salty air of the Caribbean. Her first day as a nanny had been a success. Ollie was learning to swim. And more important, Steve was letting him. She smiled to herself. She had almost enjoyed herself today. Her smile faded as her mind drifted back toward Ollie.

He seemed to be holding so much pain inside his little body. She was convinced that he might not be speaking because he was afraid. Afraid that once he started talking, the barrier would be broken, and his pain would come spilling out.

But Alex felt that he needed to let the pain out, if

only just a little at a time. They needed time to bond, to learn how to trust each other.

It wasn't going to be easy, if today was any indication. Steve Chapman hadn't let her out of his sight. Whenever she was with Ollie, Steve was never far away. He was obviously suspicious of her ability to take care of Ollie, and she knew that Ollie was able to sense his father's hesitation. Not that she blamed Steve. He didn't know her, and therefore had no reason to assume that just because her son desired her company she had the ability to care for him. And, to be honest, she hadn't minded the closeness. It gave her an ample opportunity to observe Steve as well.

Alex focused on the water. She had to tread carefully. After all, she *had* come to help Ollie, but she had also come to investigate his father.

She thought over the day, trying to remember what she had observed. Steve had seemed much more relaxed and less formal than he had on the island. He truly enjoyed being on the water, and it was evident in his visage. He seemed to be a quiet man—and a serious one. When he wasn't with Ollie, he was either reading a stack of office papers or giving orders on his cellular phone. But for a man with such a high-powered position, Alex found it interesting that he was the only one placing the calls. It was a rare occasion when the phone actually rang.

"He's sleeping," Steve said, stepping out onto the deck. "He's absolutely exhausted, but happy. Thanks to you," he said. He sat on one of the couches, looking out at the water.

She smiled appreciatively. "Thank you for dinner," she replied politely. The three of them had eaten their evening meal out on the sun deck, where they had enjoyed an unobstructed view of the sun setting over the Caribbean.

"So," he said, his voice forcing her to face him again. "Do you have anything you'd like to do tomorrow?"

She smiled. "I would imagine my choices are limited."

"You imagine correctly."

"I'll probably get Ollie back in the water again." She looked at him as she hesitated. "Steve . . ." she began a little nervously. "Why doesn't Ollie go to school?"

He looked into the water, his voice breaking, betraying his pain. "How could I send him to school like this? Not talking. Repeating the same words over and over."

"What was he like before his mother died?"

Steve's eyes squinted at the moon as he fondly remembered the son he used to know. "He was full of energy . . . but pensive. He was always a sensitive kid. Sweet and smart."

"He should see a doctor," Alex began. "A good therapist could help him deal with the loss."

"Look," he said coldly. "I appreciate everything you're doing for him. But there are some things which . . . you don't understand."

"But surely you could have him tutored."

He turned toward her. "He's just missing a semester," he said defensively. "That's all. He'll be back in school for the winter term. When he's better."

"What if Ollie doesn't get better?" She wasn't sure if she had just thought it, or if she had actually been silly enough to say it.

He turned and looked at her. The look in his eyes told her she had not been thinking silently. "He *will* get better," he said, determined.

She looked back toward the water, breaking away from his stare. "I'm sorry," she said quickly. "I didn't mean to insinuate . . ."

"Insinuate what?"

She swallowed. Why couldn't she just keep quiet? "Nothing."

He looked at her, his demeanor softening at the

sight of her. "It's getting late. I think I'll retire," he said with forced formality. "Good night, Miss Rowe."

"Steve," she said, stopping him. "Please. Call me Alex."

He paused. "Good night, Alex."

But he didn't go to bed. At least, he wasn't in his room several minutes later when Alex passed it on the way to her cabin. His door was open, and she could see that his palatial suite was empty. She had shut the door to her room and locked it, as though she feared he might intrude on her at any time. She undressed and readied herself for bed, the whole while her mind replaying their conversation in her head. Had she really overstepped her bounds yet again? She slipped into bed, turning off the light as she peered out into the darkness. The ship was quiet. Eerily quiet. And still.

She forced herself to shut her eyes as she began to count. She didn't like to count sheep. Instead, she counted whatever she happened to be wishing for at the time. Sometimes, when she was really busy with work, she would count days off. But tonight she had reporting on her mind. The Pulitzer prize, to be more specific. One prize . . . she smiled. Two prizes . . . even better. Three prizes . . .

Steve sat in the dark, watching his sleeping child. He pulled the covers up around Ollie's small shoulders. Curled up on his side as he slept in the big bed, the child looked smaller than his age.

Steve sighed. Alex's words rang in his head. *What if Ollie doesn't get better?*

Steve closed his eyes briefly. He needed to focus, to concentrate. Ollie *would* get better. That was all there was to it. And when he did, he would understand why he must never, never speak of what happened the day Leslie died. Perhaps, Steve realized, Ollie refused to speak because he himself was afraid that he would not be able to keep his secret.

Steve bent down and lightly kissed the boy's forehead. Before Ollie was born, he had not thought it possible to love someone more than life itself. When Ollie was born, Steve had promised himself that he would give his son everything that he himself had lacked growing up. Steve had thrown himself into his business, working to provide the life that he had dreamed about when he was young. Summers at the cape, warm winter vacations, private schools . . . but somehow, once he and Leslie had accumulated their various possessions, once they had attained their goals, they lost their meaning as they quickly moved on toward other achievements, other goals and possessions. Soon it was not enough to stay at a glamorous hotel in the winter . . . anyone could do that. Instead, they had to own their own island. It was not enough to fly first class. Instead, they had to own their own plane and helicopters.

It was only after Leslie died that Steve realized he had not given his son the one thing that he himself had always wanted. A father. Someone who listened to him. Who played with him. Who put going to his son's soccer game ahead of a board meeting.

But life had given him another chance. And he intended to make the most of it. "You'll see, Ollie," he whispered. "Things will be different, I promise. We just need to get through this tough time, sport. And everything will be okay."

Ollie turned onto his back. With his eyes still closed, he whispered, "Promise me."

Mr. Pulitzer must have cooperated, because by the time Alex opened her eyes, it was morning. She pulled her watch off her bedside table. When she saw how late it was, she jumped out of bed. She grimaced the minute she saw the color of the sky. No wonder her room was so dark. Rain clouds threatened ominously overhead, and the boat, despite its size, was rocking slightly with the waves.

She showered, dressed quickly, and walked upstairs

to the living room. Ollie was sitting rather stiffly on the couch. She sat down next to him and smiled brightly. "Well," she said. "So much for our second swimming lesson."

Steve appeared from the kitchen just as it started to rain. "There's coffee if you want some," he said.

She shook her head. "I don't think I could stand anything right now."

He smiled. "Feeling a little seasick?"

"More than just a little," she said.

He nodded. "Do you want something for it?"

"I'll ride it out for a while."

"There are things you can do without taking medication," he said.

"Like voodoo?"

He walked in front of her. "Give me your hands." She looked at him.

"Let me show you something," he said. She offered him her hands.

He held on to them lightly, using his thumbs to apply pressure to the middle of her wrists. "Feel any better?" he asked.

"Well . . ." she said hesitantly.

"Give it a minute," he said.

She nodded, feeling slightly uncomfortable as she watched him hold her hands. "This is supposed to work?" she asked curiously.

He shrugged his shoulders. "I don't know. I read about it once. I figured it was worth a try," he said.

She looked at him, not sure if he was trying to be funny or not. She thought she could see the hint of a smile as he dropped her hands. "I guess not," he said as he walked toward the window.

She glanced back down at her wrists. She used her left hand to apply pressure to her right wrist, just as he had to her left. She thought that maybe she did feel a little better.

"Where are you going to be working today?" she asked.

"I don't know," he said. "Where are you guys going to be?"

She hadn't counted on rain. What in the world was she going to do with a seven-year-old boy all day long? She never thought she'd admit this, not even to herself, but she was wishing for a TV.

"I'm not sure yet. Where are Ollie's toys?" she asked. "In his room?"

He thought. "I don't think we brought too many of his toys. We did bring some books, though."

She glanced at Ollie. "Any crayons?"

Steve nodded. "In Ollie's room."

"Great. And we'll need some paper."

He opened his briefcase and pulled out a pad of paper. "Is it arts and crafts day?"

She looked at him curiously. "Why? Did you want to sign up?"

"Maybe."

She smiled. "We'll be at the kitchen table."

He watched her walk out of the room. "I'll be in here," he called out, suddenly feeling a little foolish. He forced himself to look back at the papers in front of him.

Alex sat down at the kitchen table. It was hard not to be distracted by the copy of the *Times* that was sitting on top. She unfolded it. Tim had a story on the front page. She looked at his familiar byline as a surge of professional jealousy ran through her. Her time would come, she reassured herself, when she would again have a story on the front page. And if her luck continued, it wouldn't be long.

"All right, Ollie," she said, smiling at the child beside her as she opened the box of crayons. "Which color do you like?"

The day passed uneventfully. It was not until evening that the rain finally stopped. Alex stood in the doorway, watching the final drops of rain drip onto the deck chairs. She turned back toward Steve and Ollie. She stood in the living-room doorway, watching them, cup of coffee in hand. Dinner had been served in the formal dining room and had been awkward but enjoyable. The cook had brought her niece in to serve, and between courses, she and Steve had done their best to make small talk with each other. Most of their conversation surrounded the dinner itself, which was delicious. There were several courses, and each one contained an "island delicacy," which, after the first few translations, she had decided she would enjoy more if she didn't know what it was.

Ollie had seemed content, almost happy, as he sat between them. And now he sat on Steve's lap, avidly listening to a rather interesting rendition of the Jules Verne classic, *20,000 Leagues under the Sea.* She had to hand it to Steve. He was really giving the story his all, doing his best to change his voice for different characters and make the story appealing to a seven-year-old child.

"But wouldn't that be endangering the lives of my men?" Steve read, giving the ship's captain a thick Irish accent.

Alex smiled just as Steve glanced up, catching her eye. He flashed her a bashful grin before focusing his attention back on the book.

Alex sat down on the couch, attempting to read a book she'd chosen from the packed shelves.

"Okay," Steve said, reverting to his own voice as he closed the book. "Time for bed," he announced. He stood up and took Ollie's hand. "I'll be back," he said, glancing at Alex.

Alex stopped pretending to read her book and glanced at Steve's back as he walked out of the room. The idea of being alone with him made her more uncomfortable than she liked to admit.

She was standing up to leave when he came back. "Are you leaving?" he asked.

"I was just thinking that I should probably go to bed," she said.

"Oh," he said, disappointed. "I was hoping we might . . . talk tonight."

She glanced at him, curious. "What did you want to talk about?"

He sat down on the couch. "It's just that . . . well, I don't really know you. That's all."

She faced him directly. "Do you know all of your employees?"

He smiled. "Not even close. But I like to make exceptions toward those employees I suddenly find myself living with."

"Should I write out a rough copy of my résumé to refer to?" she asked sarcastically.

He got up, walked over to the bar, and began fixing himself a drink. "Perhaps you *should* go to bed. Thank you for a lovely time at dinner," he said.

She hesitated. Why was she antagonizing him? She walked up to the bar. "I'll take one, too," she said, nodding toward his drink as she attempted to be pleasant.

He glanced up at her and nodded, displaying a hint of an amused smile.

"What's the weather supposed to be like tomorrow?" she asked. *The weather,* she thought. *Now, there's a good topic. So creative, too.*

He smiled at her. "Cabin fever?" he asked.

She shrugged her shoulders. "So . . . is it supposed to rain?"

He handed her a glass of brandy. "I didn't mean for this to be unpleasant," he said, smiling calmly. "I just wanted to get to know you. I really don't know anything about you. Roger handled the hiring."

"There's not much to know," she replied, sitting on the couch. She hoped she could pull this off. The trick was to tell him as little as possible. "I've spent my whole life working with horses."

"Roger said you grew up in upper Michigan."

"That's right," she said. "On a horse ranch."

"Kind of a strange place for a horse ranch."

"So is Florida."

"Good point. So," he said, sitting next to her. His arm was casually resting up against hers. "I guess you had a short riding season."

"Yes." She slid away from him.

"Did you go to college?"

She shook her head. *You see, Mr. Steve Chapman? I'm really not your type.* "I've always regretted that," she said, trying to sound sincere.

"It's never too late," he said. "You're still young."

She threw him a wry smile. "Thanks."

"No, really," he said.

"It's expensive," she replied, still stinging from his "rich girl" barb.

"And your mother wouldn't help you?"

"No," she said coldly. "As I've told you, we're estranged."

He paused, looking at her. "That's too bad."

"Is it? You don't know my mother."

He leaned back on the couch. "I'm sorry," he said, his index finger lightly touching the rim of his glass. "I didn't mean to bring up a painful subject."

"It's not painful," she said, unable to look at him.

"No one wants to be alone in this world, Alex," he said softly.

She forced herself to look at him. "You talk as if you speak from experience."

He nodded. "I do."

She suddenly felt sad. She raised an eyebrow. "You see?" she said, forcing herself to think of lighter issues. "You were wrong about the trust fund."

He gave her a patient smile. "Perhaps you could get a scholarship. I saw you ride Rosie. You're good. It's worth looking into."

She shrugged her shoulders. "Did you like college?" she asked.

He smiled. "Some of the happiest years of my life."

"And you never miss boxing? Wonder what might have been?" she asked, thinking about his reaction several nights ago when she had mentioned it.

He rolled his fist into a ball and looked at it. "I only boxed because I happened to be good at it. You had to fight to survive where I grew up. Or learn how to run like hell. I guess I could've been a track star, too," he said with a smile.

"You ran from kids trying to beat you up?"

"More than once. My uncle found out what was happening, and he had a fit. He said no kid related to him was going to be a coward. So he started giving me boxing lessons."

She shook her head. "Sounds like you grew up in quite a rough neighborhood."

Steve laughed. He looked at her mischievously. "Quite," he said. Alex had the feeling he was teasing her a bit. "Everybody had to watch their backs," he said, dropping his Ivy League tone and sliding into a heavy Rocky-like accent.

Alex laughed. "And you went to college to learn how to speak like a preppy easterner. You've succeeded beautifully."

He smiled.

"You mentioned your uncle. What about your parents?" she asked.

"Dead," he said, resuming his regular voice.

"I'm sorry," she said, immediately feeling bad for asking him a question to which she already knew the painful answer.

"They died when I was five. I lived with my uncle."

"The one who encouraged you to become a boxer?" she asked.

"That's the one. But I wouldn't say he wanted me to be a boxer. At least, not in the beginning. He just wanted me to defend myself. But once he taught me how to box, I was hooked. I became kind of a bad kid, always picking fights. When I wasn't fighting, I was spending my time at the gym with my uncle, watching him train his boxers."

"So he finally gave you a chance."

"Not exactly. One day when he wasn't looking, I purposely picked a fight with one of his top boxers."

"And you won the fight?"

"Hardly. I even lost a tooth," he said, laughing. "But my uncle said he didn't know how it happened, but somehow I got a lot of guts. So he started training me."

"What tooth did you lose?" Alex asked, looking at his seemingly perfect white teeth.

"This one," he said, leaning down and pointing toward his upper front right tooth. "This isn't real."

She studied it carefully. "They did a great job," she offered.

"Why, thank you," he said, smiling as though he found her comment very funny. "How's your brandy?"

"Strong," she replied. She paused. He was staring at her.

He suddenly broke his gaze away, as though he realized what he had been doing. "Well," he said, somewhat embarrassed as he stood up. "I guess I *can* still have a civilized conversation," he said, walking over to the bar.

"Is it over?" she asked, surprising herself. As much as she hated to admit it, she was enjoying herself. Steve Chapman was quite an interesting man.

"It doesn't have to be," he said quietly, setting his drink on the bar. He turned around and looked at her. Their eyes locked for a split second as sudden tension hung heavy in the air.

"Alex," Steve said a little hoarsely. "Surely you must have someone missing you right now."

Alex looked at him curiously. "What?"

"A boyfriend waiting for you back home?"

She laughed. "No."

"I find that hard to believe."

"Well, that's because you don't know me very well. If you did, it's really not all that surprising."

"You're twenty-nine. And you don't have a boyfriend? Never been married? Why?"

Alex shook her head. She laughed uncomfortably. "What is this? Twenty questions? Or is twenty-nine? And what makes you think I've never been married?"

Steve looked away. "I'm sorry."

Alex walked to the railing. The wind blew her hair back as she looked out onto the water. "Well, you're right. I never have been married. Although I did have a boyfriend. I even lived with him. But he wasn't faithful," she said, surprising herself with her candor.

He shook his head. "He was a fool," he said quietly. Alex opened her mouth to speak, but she was too surprised to think of anything to say. "And so you ended it."

She shrugged her shoulders. "More or less."

Steve nodded. "So you're still not quite over this man."

She shook her head. "No. Nothing like that. I cared about him. But I wasn't really in love with him. Not real love, at least."

Steve pulled back as he looked at her. "What's real love?"

She shrugged. "I don't really know," she said honestly. "I just know that I've never felt it."

He gazed at her. "But surely you have an idea of what you're looking for."

She shrugged her shoulders. "Not what but who. Someone who's strong . . . and sensitive. Good sense of humor. Someone who listens to me. Really listens. And someone who's crazy about me . . . and sweet . . . did I say crazy about me?"

Steve laughed as he leaned up against the deck railing. He held the glass between his fingers as he smiled. "Yes. Right after you said you wanted someone who really listens to you."

It might have been her imagination, but it seemed

he was leaning forward, almost as though he were going to kiss her. She glanced away as she looked toward the water. "Perhaps you're right. I guess I am feeling a little tired. And we don't want to rush things."

She immediately realized what she had said. *Rush things? Rush what?* Steve took a step toward her, his eyes gazing at her lustfully.

She backed away. "I meant . . . rush conversation. I think it's best if we start off slow in the conversation department. You don't want to pull a muscle . . . in your jaw or something," she said, rambling nervously.

He nodded. He turned away. "I know what you mean," he said quietly. Whatever desire she had heard in his voice was gone. "Good night, Alex," he said, smiling the same tired smile he always seemed to reserve for her.

She nodded, setting down her drink and walking to the doorway.

"Oh, and Alex," he said, turning back toward her as she left. "Thank you."

She paused for a moment, not sure how to respond. She left the deck silently, not looking back.

The spicy, lemony scent of Alex's perfume hung in the air as Steve focused his gaze back on the water. He had revealed more of himself than he had intended, but he had found it easy and natural to confide in Alex. There was something about her that made him *want* to confide in her.

He stared up at the starry sky. Although he hated to admit it, he had found himself looking forward to their evenings together. His mind replayed the sight of her walking away. The way her slender hips had moved beneath the simple cotton dress. The way her thick black hair had shimmered in the moonlight.

Despite his affection for Alex's obvious physical attributes, however, it was not his attraction to her that was worrying him. No. His attraction had little to do with her looks.

When he was boxing, he had had his pick of beautiful women. But not one of them had made him feel the way he felt around Alex. It was as if he was a schoolboy with a crush. Just seeing her smile made him happy. He wanted to talk to her, to confide in her. And he wanted her to tell him everything about herself, things she had never confided to another soul.

What was happening to him?

He shook his head. The only solution was to stay as far away from her as possible. If he could stand it.

Alex focused on the bright blue sky. The first thing she had done that morning was to look out the window to determine if she would have to spend the day indoors.

After the previous evening, she didn't want to be that close to Steve. Something was happening between them, something that was not meant to be. They had been thrown together, and whether that had been by fate or destiny, Alex was determined to prevent a mistake.

And so apparently was Steve. For shortly after she had come up on deck, he had mumbled some excuse about seeing some property on the island and, after giving her his pager number, had driven off in the motorboat that was anchored alongside the yacht. She was safe, for a while at least. There was no one to tempt her to danger.

Alex leaned on the mahogany table. She and Ollie were sitting in the dining room. She had opened the doors and turned off the air conditioning so that they could enjoy the cool Caribbean breeze.

Ollie tugged on her arm and pointed to the work he had just finished. She looked down at his brightly colored picture and smiled. He had spent the last few hours making different-colored versions of the same fish. She smiled as she watched him carefully choose the colors for his latest fish.

One needed only to look into Ollie's eyes to see that he was his father's child. The same distant expression. The same lonely pain.

Alex paused. She knew the expression well. It was the same thing she saw when *she* looked in the mirror.

"What do you want to do now?" she said, sitting up straight. He may be content to draw fish all day, but she needed to do something active. Something physical. She was driving herself crazy. "Do you want to go swimming?" Ollie ignored her, picking up the box of crayons and staring at the different colors. "I'll take that as a no," she muttered to herself.

Alex walked to the living-room doorway. Her eyes fell on the stereo system in the corner. Music. She hadn't even realized how much she had missed it.

Alex approached the stereo cautiously. It was the top of the line. She felt certain that Steve wouldn't mind.

She crossed her fingers as she looked for a decent CD to dance to. She thumbed through the neatly stacked discs on top of the player. All classical. She smiled as she leaned closer, her eyes focusing on the last CD in the bunch. Aretha Franklin.

She popped the disc into the machine. "C'mon, Ollie," she said as "Respect" started blaring out of the high-powered stereo system. "I'm going to teach you how to dance."

She began snapping her fingers and swinging around. Ollie looked up from his coloring and stared at her, his sweet face watching her blankly. "This is fun, Ollie. R-E-S-P-E-C-T," she half sang, half yelled. "Find out what it means to me," she called out. She kept dancing, swinging her hips and tapping her feet, doing her best to get into the music. She had been feeling so stifled, so uncomfortable. The tension was beginning to wear on her. At least with a child around, she had an excuse to dance. It was feeling pretty good to jump around and be silly.

She heard a steady clapping noise and was surprised to see Ollie clapping his hands together. "That's right," she said happily. "You got it, Ollie! You got it!"

She ran into the dining room and grabbed Ollie's hands, hoisting him up. She pulled him back into the living room with her. Still holding on to his hands, she began gently swinging them back and forth. "All right! You got it!"

She twirled him around. She was surprised to see a hint of a smile. She bent down and gave him a big hug. "Isn't this fun, Ollie?"

Ollie took two candles off the coffee table and began using them as make-believe drumsticks, pounding the air in front of him.

"Bravo!" she said.

She pressed the button to repeat the same song. "Get ready, Ollie . . . here we go!" she yelled. "All right! Let's move it!" She began to jump around, more like aerobics than dancing.

She spun around and grabbed Ollie's arms again. "C'mon, Ollie," she said, rocking him back and forth. They fell down together, and she smiled proudly at the small boy.

She stopped. Someone was clapping. Steve stood behind them, his handsome, tanned face grinning with amusement.

Alex stood up quickly, embarrassed. She ran over to the CD player and stopped the music. "I didn't hear you," she said sheepishly.

"Obviously," he said, looking at Ollie. He smiled. "Don't stop on my account."

"No . . . we were getting tired. Weren't we, Ollie?" She could feel Steve's eyes on her as she walked back toward Ollie. "Well, Ollie," she said, still out of breath. "Shall we get back to our coloring?"

Steve lightly touched her arm.

Alex glanced sideways at him. Was he aware that his hand was on her arm?

Looking at Ollie, he said, "I'll read Ollie a story. You look like you could use a break."

"No," she argued. "I'm fine. Really."

"It's all right, Alex," he said, speaking to her in a low, soothing voice. He dropped his hand. "Go for a swim. Read a book. Whatever. We'll see you at seven for dinner." He offered Ollie his hand. "C'mon, sport. Let's go out on deck." Alex watched them step outside, hand in hand.

Alex smoothed the wrinkles out of her white, light cotton dress with her hands. She had spent the first two hours of her afternoon siesta trying to read a book in her cabin. She had spent the last hour deciding what to wear to dinner.

She walked up the stairs slowly, as if at any moment she might give in to her desire to change her clothes. To put on something that hid her figure. For her current outfit left little to the imagination. It had almost seemed as if her conscience had been fighting with her body. Her conscience had told her to wear the most conservative outfit she could find, but her body hungered for Steve's approval. She had attempted to compromise, but if either side had been a victor, it had definitely been her body. For although on a hanger the simple shift had a long, straight, simple shape, on her body it transformed itself into a sexy dress that clung to her curves as if it had been designed just for her.

Despite a considerable amount of effort spent trying to keep herself focused on her investigation, she had found herself easing into a comfortable, natural flirtation with Steve. It was difficult not to—after all, the passion in his deep brown eyes was not exactly hidden. But it was the way he took care of Ollie that made her warm to his sometimes gruff ways. It was obvious that despite his tragic childhood and his years as a professional boxer, Steve Chapman was a cultured, sensitive man who was totally devoted to his son. After all, what other father took the time to read his child *20,000 Leagues under the Sea?* Although she still wondered why Steve refused to seek psychiatric help for his son, it was clear that his refusal was not because of a lack of caring. Steve's love for his son was so obvious and so touching, it made her question the priorities in her own life. She had always placed so much emphasis on her career, putting it above everyone and everything else. Even Lennie's death had made her question her ability, but not necessarily her priorities. But seeing Steve with Ollie made her long for a child, for a family. She was beginning to wonder if perhaps it was time to reevaluate her life. Perhaps it was time to make some changes.

But there was something else besides his love for his son that attracted her to Steve. It was a deep sense of understanding that only a shared experience can bring. For although she and Steve had come from very different backgrounds, they both had arrived at the same place. Not only did they share the same tough work ethic, but both seemed to have adopted it as a way of escaping their past.

Not that her childhood had been as difficult as Steve's. It wasn't. But she and Steve had one powerful tragedy in common: neither one of them had had a father. And although Alex did have a mother who continued to have various assorted husbands, as a child Alex had always longed for the nuclear family she assumed, incorrectly of course, that everyone else had.

Alex reached the top of the stairs and paused. Steve was standing in the living room, looking out the window with his back toward her. She glanced longingly back down the stairs, as though to set foot inside the room would be passing the point of no return.

Steve caught her reflection in the window. He

turned around, his eyes softening visibly as he admired her.

"Hi," she said almost shyly.

"Hi," he replied, giving her a small, appreciative smile that told her that her efforts had not been in vain. He swallowed and hesitated, as though he was having trouble concentrating. "Do you . . . ah, want something to drink?"

"Sure," she replied, walking toward him.

"Wine?"

She nodded.

"That's right," he said. "You like Chardonnay."

She smiled. He had obviously been paying more attention to her at their dinners than she had thought. "Right." She watched him take a bottle of wine out of the fridge behind the bar and uncork it.

"Where's Ollie?"

Just then, the cook stuck her head in the door. "Dinner is ready," she called out cheerfully. She had a very distinct accent, although Alex couldn't place it. "Mr. Ollie is already under the table."

Steve looked at Alex and grinned as he handed her a crystal goblet filled with wine. "It's a family tradition to sit *under* the table," he said jokingly.

"Doesn't everybody?"

"No. Some of us actually sit *on* the table."

She laughed. He smiled at her, motioning for her to go first. He followed her out to the deck, his eyes never leaving her.

Dinner, once Steve had persuaded Ollie to come out from under the table, was pleasant, although at times it was almost uncomfortable. She wasn't sure what was going on, what had changed between her and Steve, but something was different. It was evident in the way they looked at each other. In the tingle that she felt every time he smiled at her. It was as if they had begun an elaborate dance, a dance that begged for an equally elaborate finale.

After the dishes were cleared and the cook had

gone home, Steve asked Alex to wait for him on deck while he put Ollie to bed.

She sat on the couch trying to relax while she finished her second glass of wine. She sat up straight when Steve stepped onto the deck, holding two goblets in front of him. "I took the liberty of pouring you an after-dinner drink," he said, replacing her empty wine glass with the brandy snifter.

He sat in the chair next to the couch. "So," he said, taking a sip of brandy.

"So," she said, looking at him.

He smiled. "Ollie certainly seems to be responding to you," he said.

"I'm growing very attached to him," she replied.

He nodded, hesitating. "And he to you. You two had quite a party here today."

She stirred her drink with her finger. "We were just dancing," she said, a little defensively.

"I wasn't being critical. I think it's great," he said, gazing at her as if trying to read her mind.

Alex looked away. The way he was looking at her made her feel uncomfortable. There was something . . . sensual in his eyes.

Alex jumped up and walked over to the railing. She stared off at the distant lights of the island. "What's the island like?" she asked.

"It's beautiful. It doesn't have a lot of the tourist traps that you find on most of the other islands." He stood up and walked over to her. The wind whipped through his thin linen shirt, revealing his strong, muscular chest. Alex admired his outfit, wondering if he had dressed that way for her. Khaki pants, blue linen shirt, hair combed. She thought she could even smell cologne.

He leaned against the railing, his arm casually resting up against hers. She instinctively jerked away.

He glanced at her, and she thought she could see a bit of amusement ripple over his finely etched face.

"I like it there," he said, nodding toward the island.

"I like being removed from . . . society. The people are down-to-earth, real people. They don't seem to care about where you came from or how many companies you own. So I thought this might be a good place to live . . . eventually," he said, motioning back toward the island.

She nodded.

"Alex," he said, hesitating. "There's a reason why I asked you to wait for me tonight."

Alex swallowed. "Yes?"

"I know we can't expect you to stay with us forever, and I'd like to get Ollie back to Rye Island with enough time to get him situated before you leave. How long can you stay?"

She turned away, suddenly overcome with guilt. She had a desperate and sudden urge to confess her true identity.

"I don't know," she said, still not looking at him.

"I've upset you," he said, looking at her closely.

"Don't be ridiculous," she replied. She turned to face him. "What do you expect of me?" she asked.

"In terms of. . . ?"

"In terms of work. When we return to the island, will I be taking care of the horses again?"

"Is that what you want?" he asked.

She paused. *No,* she felt like saying. She wanted to tell him who she really was. She wanted him to . . . want her. "I'd like to be compensated for the additional workload," she said, realizing that her words sounded angry.

He paused. "I don't expect you to take care of the horses and look after Ollie as well," he said reasonably.

"Good," she said, forcing herself to eye him coldly. She needed to stop this obvious flirtation. While she still had enough willpower to do it.

He sat back on the sofa, giving her the distance her look desired. "Perhaps we could work out a compromise. If you like taking care of the horses and Ollie, perhaps you can do both. A couple of hours each day."

"And who is going to teach Ollie?" she asked.

"What?" he asked, trying to be patient.

"I'm not a teacher. And I'm certainly not a doctor. Ollie needs help, Steve. And he sure as hell isn't going to get it on that island."

Steve stood up. He swallowed. His demeanor had changed almost immediately. He was stiff, angry. The Steve she knew from the island. "You have overstepped your bounds," he said, his expression growing tight. "I appreciate your assistance with Ollie . . ."

"He needs help. Professional help," she repeated. She was fully aware she was antagonizing him, but she couldn't stop herself.

"If you're worried that I will rely on you to teach him as well, you need not. I don't expect that of you," he informed her crisply.

She simply looked at him.

"And if you're worried about not being compensated financially," he continued, "you are in an excellent position to ask for more money. I think you know that Ollie is attached to you. I also think you know that I'll pay you what you want. But I warn you, I don't like being taking advantage of."

"Neither do I," she said.

"Think about it, and let me know what you want," he said, setting down his drink. "Good night, Alex," he said coldly. Alex watched as he turned and walked toward the stairs.

"I'm not doing this for money," she blurted, before he was out of hearing distance.

He turned around to face her. He shook his head slowly, as if he was suddenly very tired. "There're things that you don't understand," he said, walking back toward her. "That doesn't make me a terrible parent. I love Ollie. I want what's best for him. He's going back to school as soon as he can. And I will get him help, I promise you." He hesitated as he stopped in front of her. "I don't want us to have this conversation again."

She nodded.

He flashed her a kind, exhausted smile. "Good night, Alex," he said, turning away again.

"Steve," she said, stopping him once more.

He paused.

"I'm sorry. I think you're great with Ollie. I really do. I've never seen a father so kind and sweet with his son."

"Thanks," he said quietly, standing still.

She walked up to him. "I mean it. I really do. I think Ollie is very lucky to have you."

Steve shrugged his shoulders. "I don't know. I'm not sure what a good father is. Hell, I don't even know what a father is."

"I don't know what a father is, either," Alex announced. "I'm not sure I know what a family is." She hesitated for a split second, surprised by her own candor. She looked down at her feet. "I just . . . I think it's difficult to be a single parent, especially under these circumstances, and . . . I think you're doing a fine job." She shrugged her shoulders as she glanced nervously toward the water. "For whatever that's worth."

He glanced at her. "It's worth quite a bit." He paused, standing in front of her. "Alex," he said softly. His hand reached out as his fingers gently ran around the outline of her face. He gently lifted her chin so that she was looking at him. His gaze seared through her. "I don't know what's happened to you that made you want to withdraw from life like you have. I just . . . I feel like you understand Ollie and me . . ."

She glanced away.

He continued, "I understand if you don't want to talk about it."

Alex nodded, convinced that Steve sensed her pain regarding Lennie. Was her sorrow so obvious? Or was it just that Steve was so perceptive?

"I'd like to take you and Ollie to the island tomorrow morning," he said in a voice that was almost a whisper.

She nodded, still unable to find her voice.

"We'll leave first thing." He took her free hand and held it to his chin as he paused for a moment, staring deep into her eyes. He smiled as he gently brought her hand back down. "Good night," he said, giving her hand a gentle squeeze before letting go.

Alex watched him leave the room before downing the remainder of her drink.

Seventeen

The sleek speedboat skidded across the smooth, clear water. The wind whipped through her T-shirt and the oversized scarf she'd wrapped around her waist. The water splashed onto the boat, soaking her white T-shirt and revealing the bright blue of the swimsuit she wore underneath. Ollie clung to her hand, his little neck sandwiched in a giant life jacket.

Steve slowed the boat down and approached a dock. "This belongs to the hotel," he said, nodding toward a row of rustic-looking stucco cabins. "But they let me park here. We can catch a taxi out front," he said, tying up the boat.

He untied Ollie's life jacket and picked him up, carrying him off the boat. He set him down and turned back toward Alex, offering her his hand.

"I'm fine," she said, making the jump by herself. She followed him around the cabins to the front of a large stucco building. A small sedan was sitting in front.

The man behind the wheel nodded as Alex, Ollie, and Steve slid in the back. "We're going to a house off Cova Road," Steve said to the driver. The driver smiled, revealing three missing front teeth.

"Okay, beautiful family," he said in broken English.

Alex rolled her eyes as she focused on a group of palm trees. The road was a dirt road and obviously not used by many cars.

"It will be better on the highway," the driver said. Alex looked down at Ollie and smiled. She smoothed his hair as he rested his head against her.

Steve smiled at her. "I want to show you some property."

Alex nodded. She focused her attention on Ollie as the car drove down a road that wrapped around a cove framed by the Caribbean. They had traveled about four miles when Steve spoke. "Make a left," he said to the driver, pointing toward a gravel-covered driveway.

The cab traveled up a long drive that seemed to wind itself around a tall, mountainous hill. There were evergreen forests on both sides of the drive. The foliage was so thick, the house wasn't visible until the cab reached the clearing at the end of the drive.

"Who owns this place?" Alex asked.

"We do."

"We do?"

"Ollie and I. As of yesterday. It was exactly what I was looking for. I knew it immediately." He paused, glancing at her. "Do you believe in love at first sight— or second, as the case may be?"

She shook her head quickly as she swallowed. She had the distinct impression he wasn't referring to the house.

"No. No, I don't," she replied quickly.

He smiled as he looked out the window. "I didn't use to. But I've recently changed my mind." She raised her eyebrows as she glanced back out the window. He seemed so casual about everything, so relaxed. It was making her a little nervous.

"Look at this place," he said enthusiastically. "This side is like a Midwest forest, but the other side is pure Bahamas. Sandy beaches and sunshine."

The cab stopped in front of a large, unusual-looking wood house with a thatched roof. Steve opened his door and helped Ollie out of the car.

Alex slammed her door as she looked around.

Steve said, "It's interesting, isn't it?" He unlocked the door and held it open, motioning for Alex to enter.

Alex had to agree with him there. It was interesting. It was unlike any house she had ever seen before. She nodded politely at Steve as she stepped inside.

She inhaled deeply with pleasure. The whole back of the house was open, so that one could walk straight through to the terrace without even opening a door. Steps off the side of the deck led down to the water. "Oh my," she murmured. "It's beautiful."

"At night you can hear the drums from the village. Played for the tourists, of course."

"There don't seem to be too many tourists around here."

Steve shrugged. "They're here. They're just hidden. But, like I mentioned last night, it's not like some of the other islands," he said.

"C'mon," he said, taking Ollie's hand as he grabbed some towels. "The beach is this way." He led them through the patio toward a steep set of stone stairs.

"Who could ever sell this place?" Alex asked, trying to make conversation as they walked down the stairs toward the beach.

"You really want to know?" he asked. "I'm not even sure I remember all the details. All I know is it's a long, sordid story."

"I love those kind," she said.

He laughed. "Okay, here it goes. It belonged to a TV director. The guy had an affair with the star of his TV show. He actually brought the woman here . . .

and the girlfriend found out. They're breaking up because of it."

"That's too bad," she said, trying to sound sincere. "So why is he selling it? Too many memories?" she said with a smirk.

"The girlfriend got it as part of the property settlement. But she didn't want it. She wants the money," he said, picking Ollie up and carrying him onto the beach.

"Property settlement?"

"California. They'd been living together for a while."

"Hmm," Alex said. "I can't say I blame her. Who is the guy? And what's the TV show?" she asked, trudging in the sand after him.

He shrugged his shoulders. "I don't know. I wasn't really interested in gossiping with a real estate agent. I'm sure she's telling someone about me as we speak."

"Well, I hate to disappoint you, but that really doesn't count as a long, sordid story. It's just very L.A."

He raised an eyebrow. "Is that so?" he said, putting Ollie down. He threw down a beach blanket. "Do you know about L.A.?" he asked, turning and facing her.

"No. I just know about long, sordid stories. And that definitely did not qualify," she said, her eyes focused on the turquoise water in front of her.

He laughed. It was a slow, deep, almost sensual sound. He looked at her as though he had just found himself in the presence of the greatest wit in the East. "Why don't you go for a swim?" he offered. "I'll stay here with Ollie. We need to get him lathered up with sun screen, anyway."

She looked down at the child. "Maybe he wants to come, too. Ollie, do you want to go swimming?"

Ollie shook his head. Alex nodded. She understood. The pool was one thing, the Caribbean quite another.

"Go ahead," Steve said, encouraging her.

Alex glanced toward the water nervously. Unlike

Ollie, however, it wasn't the water making her nervous but the idea of having to take off her shirt in front of Steve—even if she was wearing a bathing suit underneath.

She casually turned her back to him and pulled the damp shirt awkwardly over her head, throwing it to the ground. "I'll be back," she said, quickly glancing at him over her shoulder.

Normally, she liked to wade in the water for a few minutes to get acclimated to the temperature, but this time was different. This time she had an audience. And she didn't feel like performing. She ran into the water, quickly diving under. She swam for a good twenty minutes, every now and then casually glancing toward Steve and Ollie, who both appeared to be staring straight at her. She swam away from them, trying to focus on the clear green water. A school of fluorescent pink fish swam underneath her, their sleek bodies clearly visible above the smoky white sand. She flipped over onto her back and closed her eyes. She floated on the surface of the sea, her face pointed toward the hot tropical sun.

After a few minutes, she flipped over onto her stomach and dove under the water. She held her breath, swimming as fast as she could, as if exorcising a demon from her body. And although there was a demon she needed to exorcise—her attraction to Steve definitely qualified as a demon—she had a feeling it wasn't going to leave her body willingly.

In fact, her demon was growing in intensity by the minute—even though there was nowhere for it to go. After all, if she became involved with Steve, she might as well just kiss her career good-bye. She'd be the laughing stock of the media. First Lennie, then this. After all, word was sure to get out that she had come here to investigate him. Tim would see to that. Besides the havoc it would wreak on her career, what about her personal life? For all she knew, Steve might be, well, he just might be a murderer.

Maybe.

But maybe not. Perhaps Leslie Chapman had committed suicide. After all, it was well documented that the woman had been emotionally fragile. And she had tried to kill herself before.

It was a possibility that Alex needed to consider. It was a possibility that she *wanted* to consider.

Alex resurfaced and began doing her own version of the breast stroke, a combination doggy paddle and breast stroke that would make any swim instructor cringe.

She glanced back toward the sand, but Steve and Ollie were gone. Slightly relieved, Alex stood up in the waist-high water and dug her toes into the smooth, sandy bottom as she glanced down the beach. She could see father and son in the distance, walking hand in hand. It was a picture-perfect family scene.

She slowly walked out of the water and sat down on the beach towel as her mind focused on her interaction with Steve the previous evening. He had seemed so sweet, so perceptive. It was almost as if he could sense what she was thinking. Feel her pain. He had almost caused her to lose her control and burst into tears with a confession.

Alex shook the water out of her ear. She had to get control of herself. She had been taken by surprise. After all, she hadn't even expected to like Steve Chapman, let alone be attracted to him. But the Steve Chapman she was getting to know was not the Steve Chapman she had expected. Each day, he seemed to reveal a little more of himself to her. And the more she saw of him, the more caring and sensitive he appeared. He didn't seem like a man who would be capable of hurting anyone. Especially the mother of his child.

But, then again, she reminded herself, he once made money beating people up. True, the people he beat up were strong, muscular men who were trying to do the same to him, and it was under the guise of boxing, which she supposed qualified as a sport, but slugging away at someone is still slugging away at someone. Even if there *is* money involved.

The problem, Alex realized as she lay down on the towel, was that she had lost her objectivity. It wasn't that she was simply attracted to this man. She was becoming infatuated with him.

Alex closed her eyes as though she could blink her feelings away.

A few moments later, a shadow passed in front of her, blocking the sun. Steve stood over her, looking at her with a concerned, serious expression.

"Is there something wrong?" she asked. "Where's Ollie?" She leaned up on her elbows.

He nodded toward the water. "He's building a sandcastle."

She smiled. Ollie was bent over, with his back toward them. He was industriously scooping out sand.

Steve motioned toward her. "You're getting sunburned."

She glanced at her shoulders. "I'm fine," she said, a little too quickly.

He smiled at her. "Are you always like that?"

"Like what?"

"So stubborn . . . so frightened . . ."

"Frightened?" she asked, insulted. "I am the least fearful person I know," she boasted.

"Then come here," he said, picking up a bottle of lotion. "Let me put this on you."

She shook her head quickly. She didn't like the idea of Steve smearing lotion all over her.

"I won't hurt you," he said, smiling at her teasingly.

"I'm not worried," she said.

His smile vanished. "Then prove it," he whispered, his eyes locked on hers. He was daring her.

She swallowed. It was as if he was drawing her to him magnetically. She slid over to him, sitting with her back to him.

He squirted the lotion on his hand and began rubbing her bare back. He slid the straps off her shoulders as his fingers lightly massaged the tension out of her neck. She closed her eyes and slowly inhaled. There was something sensual about the way the cream made his fingers slide over her tired, sore, tense muscles.

He leaned forward, his hands resting against her upper back, his fingers almost touching the sides of her breasts. "There," he said, whispering in her ear. "That wasn't so bad, was it?"

"Thanks," she said, moving away. She looked at him. "I'd hate to get burnt." She stood up and wrapped a towel around her waist.

He handed her his shirt. "I don't want you to get burnt, either."

Alex looked away. She wished he'd stopped speaking in double meanings. She found it neither clever nor cute. But that time, she had to admit, she had walked right into it.

"You better put this on, too," he said.

She shook her head. "Don't be silly. I've got the lotion on now. I'll be fine."

"The sun is dangerous. And we've been out in it too long already."

"Perhaps I should go back up," she said, turning toward the stairs.

"Alex," Steve called out. "Do you want to stay here tonight?"

"What do you mean?" she asked.

"Stay here. In the house. There're plenty of bedrooms," he added quickly.

"I'll do whatever you want," she offered. "I'm flexible." She blushed as soon as she realized what she had said.

He smiled. "I'll keep that in mind."

"I'm just here to look after Ollie," she replied, ignoring him. "Don't worry about me."

"You don't mind not having packed an overnight bag?" He paused, looking at her with a hint of a smile.

"Oh, that's right," he said, his dark brown eyes focusing on her. "You don't wear pajamas, do you?"

She looked down at the sand, aware that she was still blushing. There was no denying it. He was flirting with her. And it was all her fault.

Ollie turned back toward them. He came bounding over as soon as he realized that Alex was leaving.

"What do you say, sport?" Steve asked, glancing at his son. "Do you want to stay here for a while?"

Ollie looked at him. He nodded.

Steve paused a moment, incredulous that Ollie had responded to a question instead of his usual blank stare. He had heard Steve. And he had replied. Steve glanced at Alex and smiled. He picked Ollie up and hugged him. "If you want it, you got it. We're staying here tonight." He laughed.

Alex shook her head, incredulous as well. In the month she had known Ollie, that was the first time she had ever seen him respond to a question. Alex smiled proudly as she ran and patted Ollie's back. Steve looked at her gratefully. "Perhaps we should call Tikky and tell her to bring dinner here instead of the boat," he said.

Alex just smiled.

Steve led the way back up to the house. "Okay," he said, walking into the spacious living room. "We need some showers and some bedrooms." He paused as if trying to remember where everything was. "Follow me," he said, putting Ollie down.

Alex looked around the living room. "This is magnificent," she said, admiring the bamboo furniture and window coverings.

"Distinctly Balinese," Steve said. "Everything is made out of bamboo. Even the ceiling," he said, pointing upward.

"What happens if there's a serious rainstorm?" she asked.

Steve smiled as he shrugged his shoulders. "You get wet?"

She nodded. "Good answer." She wandered through the living room and down the hall. "That's a bedroom in there," Steve said, motioning toward a door on the right. She pushed it open. The room was large but minimally furnished. A queen-size bamboo bed was set on a platform framed at each corner by thirteen-foot pine posts over which was draped sheer silk netting. A trio of double doors opened onto a view of the Caribbean.

Steve walked in behind her. "When you sleep at night, you drop the netting so that the bugs don't get in," he said, pointing toward the bed.

She shook her head. The house was unlike anything she had ever seen before. "It's absolutely magnificent."

"You can stay in here," he said to her. "The bathroom is through there."

He closed the door behind him. She turned back toward the room, suddenly realizing that this was probably the master bedroom suite. She opened the door. "Steve," she said. "Isn't this the master bedroom?"

Steve stopped. "What difference does it make?"

"Well, *you* should stay in here," she said.

He furrowed his eyebrows, confused. "Why?"

"Because . . ." She shrugged her shoulders. "Because it's your house."

He smiled. "I'd like you to take that room," he said simply. She looked at him curiously. She was a little embarrassed. And flattered.

"Thanks," she said, feeling herself beginning to blush again.

She shut the door and looked around, admiring the luscious, tropical view from the balcony.

She opened the door to the bath and stared in awe. The roofless, plant-filled shower was built with stones and paved with slate. Large, leafy ferns were placed in all the corners.

Alex let the cool water run down her back as she

stared up at the blue sky above her. When she was finished with her shower, she took advantage of one of the large terry robes that were folded up in the cupboard and slipped into the soft, inviting bed, carefully pulling the mosquito netting down around her. She lay down on the pillows and closed her eyes as she thought back to the dark, cold, tiny apartment she had left weeks ago. A few more days here in paradise, and she doubted she'd be able to return.

Steve scooped his small son up in his arms and began to climb the steep stairs that led to the house. He couldn't keep his thoughts away from Alex.

He glanced down at the silent child in his arms. Even Ollie had fallen in love with her. In fact, Alex seemed to be the missing link in their family. What they needed to become whole.

"You like Alex, too, don't you, son?" Steve asked quietly as he carried the boy inside the house. Ollie stared up at him. But Steve could read the expression in his eyes.

Steve smiled. "I thought so."

After he had settled Ollie into bed for an afternoon nap, he walked back out onto the balcony and leaned on the bamboo ledge.

His thoughts drifted back to the lovely woman sleeping in the other room. He found her to be a complete enigma. She was extremely beautiful, yet she didn't spend time worrying about her appearance. She was down-to-earth, comfortable in a T-shirt and jeans, yet there was something about her that radiated elegance, regardless of what she was wearing. She was smart, tough, and independent enough to move to an island with a man accused of murdering his wife, yet still vulnerable enough to cry.

And there was something else about her. Something he couldn't get out of his mind. A sadness in her eyes. Sometimes when he looked at her, he had to fight the urge to take her in his arms, to take away her pain. To make her happy.

Steve sighed. She needed to trust him before he could help her. And her trust was a gift he had not yet earned.

When Alex awoke, the sun was already beginning to set. She decided to forgo the T-shirt as she slipped back into her dry suit. As she wrapped the scarf around her waist, she opened the door and ventured back into the living room. Steve and Ollie were out on the balcony. Steve was leaning over his son, pointing toward the sunset.

She smiled at Steve as he glanced back toward her. "Well," he said, smiling at her teasingly as he turned to face her, "I'm not sure whether to offer you coffee or a cocktail."

She laughed. "How long did I sleep?"

"About two hours," he said. "We tried, but we're not very good at taking naps, are we, sport?" He took Ollie's hand. They walked back into the room, Ollie's somber expression frozen in place.

Steve walked over to the bar. "Martini?"

"A martini sounds lovely. Is this martini compliments of our friend the director?"

"Yes, indeed. He left this place fully stocked."

"Perfect," she said, laughing. She tousled Ollie's hair. "Do you like it here?" she asked the child.

Alex led Ollie over to the bar and helped him up onto a barstool.

"Cheers," Steve said, handing her the glass.

"Cheers," she said, sitting next to Ollie. She toasted them both with her drink. "My friend here will have a Shirley Temple," she said, nodding toward Ollie.

"One Shirley Temple coming up," Steve said, pouring some ginger ale into a small glass and stirring some grenadine into it. "Don't slug this down, my friend," he said, winking at his son.

Alex turned back toward the open view of the

water. "I've never seen anything so spectacular," she said.

"I'm glad you like it," he said seriously.

Alex looked at him and laughed. Steve just grinned as he toasted her with his glass.

That night, they ate on the balcony overlooking the sea, feasting on various island specialties cooked up by Tikky herself. Alex helped Tikky clear and wash the dishes while Steve put Ollie to bed, a routine he usually liked to do alone.

By the time Steve reappeared, Tikky was gone and Alex was alone on the balcony. He smiled when he saw her, pausing to admire the way her sheer makeshift skirt blew back in the warm evening breeze. She was leaning over the railing, her expression somber as she stared out at the sea, deep in thought. It was only the distinct sound of Aretha Franklin hovering in the air that broke her trance. Suddenly aware that she was no longer alone, she turned toward Steve. He stood leaning up against the door frame, his hands in the pockets of his loose linen pants. "Hi," she said, embarrassed. "How long have you been standing there?"

"Not long," he said with a hint of a smile as he walked toward her. He stood beside her, facing the water. "I chose some music for you," he said.

She glanced up at him and smiled. He leaned forward, not looking at the water anymore, just looking at her.

"The view is beautiful," she said.

"It certainly is," he replied, his eyes glancing down her body, focusing on the way the bathing suit silhouetted her tall, svelte figure.

She glanced at him quickly before looking back at the water. "I think Ollie is making real progress," she said nervously.

"Thanks to you," he said.

She shrugged her shoulders modestly.

"How's your sunburn?" he asked.

She glanced at him. "I didn't get burned," she replied a little defensively.

He looked at her tenderly. Slowly, he took a hand out of his pocket and gently brushed a strand of hair away from her face.

"Don't," she said, brushing away his hand.

He sighed. "I'm sorry. I just . . . I feel something for you." He shook his head. "It's been so long since I felt anything like this . . ." he said, his voice dwindling off.

"Please," she said, fighting for control. Her mind was in turmoil. She wanted him to touch her . . . to kiss her. Yet she didn't dare. There was too much to lose.

"There's something between us," he said. "Since the first moment I saw you . . ."

"Look, Steve," she said, breaking away and turning from him. It was easier to talk to him if she didn't have to look at him. "You're going through a difficult time right now. I understand that. Both you and Ollie," she said quickly. "You just lost your wife, your child's mother."

He stood silent. Listening to her. Studying her. "I'm sorry," he said finally, standing behind her so closely that she could feel his breath on her ear. "Perhaps I was assuming too much." He paused, as if waiting for her to say something. But she was silent. He sighed, backing away. "I certainly don't want to do anything to make you feel uncomfortable. Let's just forget that we even had this conversation."

She nodded her head. "Right," she said.

He paused. "If you'll excuse me, it's getting late. I think I'll go to bed."

She closed her eyes for a moment. He was so kind, so gentle. She could feel what it would be like to have his strong arms wrapped around her. "Wait," she said.

He turned and looked at her.

"I . . . I . . ." she began as he walked slowly toward

184

her. He stopped in front of her, his eyes gazing at her. "I'm just confused," she admitted quietly.

He placed his index finger on her lips to silence her. "It's all right," he said. He moved his finger around her lips. "Do you believe in angels, Alex?"

Alex shrugged her shoulders. "I don't know . . ."

"I never did before. But now I do. You're our angel, Alex. Mine and Ollie's. You're here to help us."

Alex opened her mouth, but no words came out.

"I had given up hope of ever finding anyone like you." He shook his head in disbelief. "You're so beautiful," he continued. "Beautiful inside and out. I've never met anyone like you. Intelligent . . . kind. When you're with Ollie, I can see the caring in your eyes." He paused, listening to the music. "I'm not quite sure what's happening to us right now. I just know that it's different for me. You're different," he said, as Aretha Franklin began to sing "Say a Little Prayer." He held out his arms, inviting her to dance. "It's been a long time," he said. "But perhaps you can teach me, too."

She laughed, accepting his invitation as she held on to his strong, callused hands. They began rocking back and forth, stiffly. His hands pressed against the back of her waist, gently pushing her into him. She could feel his body up against hers, strong and solid. Her mind was fighting for reason, but her body wasn't listening.

He ran his fingers softly through her long hair as their bodies began to move together, melting into one form. "It's good to hear you laugh," he said softly. "Sometimes you look so sad, Alex. So lonely." He held her to him, whispering in her ear. "I understand pain, Alex. You can trust me." She looked up at him, her eyes welling with tears. This wasn't supposed to happen.

He took her face gently in his hands, and, using his fingers, he began to wipe away her tears. He slowly leaned toward her, kissing her face softly, following the path of her tears. He pulled away slightly, studying her reaction. She kept her eyes closed, as if anticipating his next move. He smiled as he hugged her tightly, his fingers slipping inside the back of her swimsuit. He kissed her once again, this time with more passion. She leaned into him, pressing her body against him.

It was her body that was controlling her, daring her to explore her passion. His tongue swept inside her mouth, and she met it greedily, moaning softly as he delved inside her. She felt as if Steve had broken past her line of defenses, and now that he was in, she would never let him escape.

"Steve," she whispered, looking up at him longingly. It was the look he had been waiting for.

He picked her up and carried her into the master bedroom. He laid her down on the bed and dropped the netting around them. A warm, gentle breeze blew through the air as he leaned over her.

"Ollie," she said, shaking her head.

"He's sleeping," he said, drowning her protests with another kiss. She relaxed as she felt his arms encircle her. She felt protected and safe, in their own romantic world.

Alex pulled him to her as she slid her fingers inside his shirt and began to unbutton it. She found his nipple and squeezed.

Steve glanced down at her, his eyes heavy with temptation. He finished unbuttoning his shirt and pulled her to him, pressing her lips against his smooth chest.

She ran her tongue around his well-defined pectoral muscles until he gently pushed her away from him. He slowly pulled one swimsuit strap down off her shoulder. He then leaned forward and began to leave soft butterfly kisses trailing from her neck to her shoulder. He moved to the other shoulder, giving it the same tender treatment. He leaned back, pulling the straps down even farther so that her breasts were completely exposed. He gently laid her back down as he skillfully began touching her chest, running his fingers slowly around her breasts, dragging them playfully toward her nipples. He pinched her nipples lightly, watching them grow hard. He gently kissed her neck, running his tongue down toward her nipples.

She ran her fingers through his soft, wavy hair. She had never met a man who had made her feel so excited, so desired. She closed her eyes tightly as his mouth gently sucked on her nipples and then pulled away as he ran his tongue over her breast and down her stomach.

His hands slid down her legs, gently pulling up the scarf that was functioning as a skirt. His right hand slipped easily inside her swimsuit.

But the feel of his hand on her most sensitive part was enough to snap her out of the spell she had fallen under.

Her conscience, which had been mute the entire evening, suddenly regained its voice. And it wasn't happy.

Alex grabbed Steve's hand. "Wait." She slid back as she pulled her bathing suit back up. "I . . . I'm sorry. I can't."

He leaned forward and gently ran his fingers down the side of her face. "What's the matter?" he asked quietly.

"I . . . I just can't. I'm sorry."

"It's all right, Alex," he whispered. "I don't want you to feel bad," he said, taking her in his arms. "I want you to feel good."

"I'm just a little . . . nervous."

"Shhhh," he said, hugging her as he ran his fingers through her hair. "We'll take it as slow as you want. We don't have to do anything at all. I'm fine just being with you."

"Thanks," she replied a little awkwardly.

He pulled back and smiled at her, as though he found her response funny.

"No. Thank *you,*" he said. He laughed. "Do you want something to drink? Like water?"

"That would be great," she said, relieved.

"You've got to promise me, you won't move," he said. "Not an inch."

She smiled. "Then you'd better hurry."

She leaned back, resting against the soft pillows as she tried to relax and enjoy the warm breeze floating in the air. She was a little embarrassed that she had let things get so out of hand. She felt so uninhibited with him. She was so excited that she had lost control of her reason, something that didn't happen to her very often, especially when it concerned sex.

She glanced anxiously toward the doorway. Steve must think her quite a tease. But he didn't seem to be angry. Just the opposite. He seemed sweet and gentle. Not to mention patient. She sighed as she focused on the balcony. She had to calm down. After all, nothing really had happened. And she *had* utilized control.

She swallowed uncomfortably. She had controlled her actions. Her feelings, on the other hand, were another matter.

"I'm back." Steve was standing by the side of the bed, holding a glass of water in his hand. He sat down next to her and pulled her toward him so that she was resting against his chest. He held the glass to her lips, allowing her to swallow some of the cool liquid. "How does it taste?" he asked.

She smacked her lips. "Like water?" she said.

"No, no, no," he said teasingly. "Here. Taste again." He stuck his finger back in the glass and then put it in her mouth. She sucked on it gently. He closed his eyes, inhaling slightly with pleasure. She could feel him become hard with lust. "Very expensive water?" she said, smiling wickedly.

He laughed. "It's very fancy bottled water. It took me a few minutes just to figure out how to open it. But whatever they paid for it," he added, his voice growing husky, "it's worth it."

She took the water away from him and turned to face him. She held the glass to his lips. He swallowed some, causing it to splash on his chin. She pulled the glass away and began to lick it off.

"Alex," he murmured, fighting for control. "I think you better stop that. I'm doing my best to be patient . . ."

She smiled, pulling away. "I just wanted to give you a preview."

He raised his eyebrows. "I guarantee you I don't need a preview. I'm already excited for the show." Alex smiled, pleased at the effect she had on him.

He took the glass away from her and set it on the floor next to the bed. He turned back toward her as she cuddled in his arms. "Life is strange, isn't it?" he said, shaking his head.

"What do you mean?" she asked, resting her head against his chest as she gazed up at him.

"It's just that I've been all over the world. I've met all different types of women. It just seems strange that the one time in my life when I'm definitely not looking, isolated from all the world, you appear."

She glanced away. "Did you spend a lot of time looking when you were married?" she asked.

She could sense the change in him immediately. His muscles tightened slightly, and his voice sharpened. "No," he said, glancing away. He sighed as his muscles relaxed a bit, and his voice lost some of its edge. "Look, I know you've probably heard rumors about me and my wife. I just . . . well, don't believe what you read." He shook his head. "According to the papers, I married Leslie for her money and to raise my social standing in the world," he said acidly.

"That was bullshit," he continued. "I never gave a damn what people thought about me. And if I was just interested in money, I would've continued boxing, for chrissakes. Leslie's friends never thought I was good enough for her, simply because of where I was born. I was a blue-collar boy, orphaned and poor. A kid who grew up on the streets. I learned how to fight to protect myself, not because I was looking for an extracurricular activity. I just wasn't part of their old-money, elite world, nor would I ever be. I thought it was bullshit. I still think it's bullshit."

Alex thought back to what her mother had said when she found out that Leslie Chapman had died. "What about Leslie? She married you. She must not have cared about silly social registers."

"She cared about pleasing her father. And I mistook that for love. Her father may have thought I was good enough for Leslie, but I'm afraid Leslie didn't share his opinion." He looked down at her as he kissed her forehead. "I've said enough," he said abruptly. "More water?" he asked, moving her head gently as he leaned over and picked the glass up off the ground.

Aware of the uncomfortable element that she had introduced, Alex sat up and pulled her scarf around her. "Are you cold?" he asked, rubbing her back.

She shook her head.

"Alex," he said, smiling sadly. "The past is still a little too close for me to talk about it. I'm not proud of the situation I lived in for ten years."

She nodded, observing him carefully. "Did you love her?" she asked quietly.

He hesitated as though searching for the right words. "I loved her . . . as much as I could." He leaned in, kissing her softly on her cheek. "It's getting late," he said. "Perhaps I should go to bed." He stood up.

She grabbed his hand. "Stay with me," she said. "I mean, I know that Ollie shouldn't wake up in the morning and find us together. Just stay with me for a little while . . ." She wanted him near her. For as soon as he left, she knew the anxiety and doubts would come creeping back, and she wasn't ready for that. She felt so comforted in his arms. So relaxed.

He smiled at her gently as he slipped back onto the bed, lying next to her. He gathered her in his arms and curled his body around her, pulling her in close to him.

He softly kissed the top of her head. "Go to sleep, Alex," he said. "I'll be right here with you."

But Alex stayed awake for a long time, listening to the sound of the waves slamming against the shore.

Lennie was waiting for her on the roof of his old apartment building. She smiled at him, but he didn't smile back. He was angry at her.

He didn't look well. Dark circles underlined his dark brown eyes. Dirt was matted in his curly hair. He was wearing the same small black suit he was buried in. "Lennie," she murmured, stepping closer to him. He shook his head, backing away from her as if frightened. "Lennie. Lennie, it's me. Alex. I'm not going to hurt you."

She realized that she was wearing Leslie Chapman's blue chiffon nightgown. She glanced down at it, checking to make sure that she hadn't gotten it dirty. She looked back up at Lennie just as he began to cry. "Lennie," she said, trying to soothe him. He stopped crying.

"There. See? I'm sorry, Lennie. Just give me another chance. I promise you . . . I'll help you." She walked to the edge of the roof where Lennie was standing and stretched out her hand to him. "I'm here to help you. Just trust me," she whispered.

Lennie stared at her suspiciously. "Promise me?" he said, his little face brightening as he decided to give her another chance.

"I promise," Alex said. Lennie offered her his hands and smiled.

Alex reached toward Lennie, but instead of pulling him in to safety, she pushed him as hard as she could.

She saw Lennie's brief expression of disbelief and shock as he fought to maintain his balance. She stood still, watching him flail his arms unsuccessfully, almost floating off the roof.

She picked up her flouncy skirt as she coolly stood on the edge of the roof, watching Lennie's little body careen down the twenty-story drop toward the cold, unforgiving city street.

Someone was screaming. Alex opened her eyes, suddenly realizing that the scream was coming from her. Steve was beside her, shaking her gently.

"Alex!"

Alex breathed in. She ran her hands over her forehead. *Lennie.* She'd killed Lennie.

"You're having a nightmare. Everything's all right," he said, holding her close to him. "I'm here, Alex. Everything is all right."

Alex pushed him away. She sat up in bed, still trying to get her wits together. She didn't want him to see her like this.

"You were having a bad dream," he said, sitting up behind her.

She grabbed a blanket that had fallen off the bed and looped it around her shoulders to cover her nakedness. She stood up and walked over to the balcony.

"Tell me," he said gently.

Alex stood still, unable to answer. Although it wasn't cold, she was shivering.

"What is it?" he said softly, intently focused on her. "Do you want to talk about it?"

She turned back toward him. "There was a child . . . who I loved. He was killed. And I . . . I'm still having nightmares about it." She turned back to face the water.

Steve paused. It was a confession he hadn't been expecting. "Was he your child?" he asked.

She shook her head, brushing away a tear. She was surprised that she had revealed so much. But she hadn't been able to help herself. For some strange reason, she wanted him to know.

Steve stood up and walked behind her. He looped

his arms around her protectively. "I'm sorry," he whispered.

She looked up at him. "I felt responsible. He had been in trouble. I tried to help him. I hurt him instead."

"What happened?"

She shook her head. "I became close with a child who was involved with a gang," she said. "I tried to help him, to get him off the street. The head of the gang found out. He thought the child had betrayed him intentionally. He killed him for it. To make him an example to the other kids." She rested her head on his shoulder.

"How old was he?" he asked.

She looked up at him. "Seven," she barely managed to say.

Seven, he thought. *Ollie's age*. He brushed a tear away from her cheek. She looked so vulnerable, so torn with pain. His lips drifted toward hers as gently and naturally as if he was born to kiss her.

She closed her eyes as she felt his lips on hers. It was as if he was drawing the pain out of her. All the months of not sleeping, of guilt, of loneliness. She reached her arms around him and pulled him closer.

The next morning, Alex was awakened by the sound of voices outside her door. Her eyes snapped open. She jumped out of bed, pausing to blush slightly at the sight of the indentation in the bed where Steve had slept.

She walked into the living room. "Good morning," Steve said, looking at her tenderly.

She blushed. "Good morning," she said.

He nodded toward the table. "There're some muffins and coffee, if you're interested. Ollie and I were just going to go down for a swim."

"I'll be down in a minute," she said, avoiding looking at him. He took Ollie by the hand and began whistling as they walked down the path leading to the beach.

She looked after him, shaking her head slightly. There was no turning back now. She rolled her eyes, remembering how Steve had comforted her after her nightmare. What had she been thinking? How could she jeopardize her whole career like that? Confiding in a man like Steve Chapman. A man she was here to investigate.

Unfortunately for her, a shared confidence was not the worst mistake she had made last night. She had practically made love with Steve Chapman.

Alex glanced around her. She had a desperate urge to escape. To run away. To forget about this investigation before she made another dreadful mistake.

She sipped a half cup of coffee as she worked on calming herself down. By the time she made it down to the beach, she still was not totally convinced that she could stick it out.

Steve held Ollie up in the water. "I'm not sure how I'm supposed to teach him," he called out to her. She nodded as she pulled off her T-shirt, wading out to join them. He handed Ollie to her but continued standing beside her.

"Like this," she said, holding Ollie as he kicked. She tried to focus as Steve continued to stand beside her. After a few minutes, Ollie began to look winded, and Steve carried him out of the water.

They dried off in the sun, silent. Finally, Steve turned toward Alex. "I hate to say this . . ." he began.

She had been waiting for this. Expecting it. He wanted to tell her that he'd thought about it and the previous evening had been a mistake. "I totally agree," she said quickly.

"All right, let's go," he said.

"What?" she asked, confused.

He smiled. "Let's go."

"Where?" she asked, standing up.

"I was just going to say that we should get back to the boat. And you said you totally agreed."

"Oh, right," she said, mumbling almost incoherently.

"That is what you thought I was going to say, wasn't it?" he asked, looking at her suspiciously.

"Of course," she said.

Steve's desire to return to the yacht abated almost as soon as it was in sight. Alex was surprised to hear him swear under his breath.

"What?" she asked.

He nodded toward the yacht. A male figure was visible on the deck. "We have company," he said.

"Crew?" she asked.

"I'm afraid not," he said. She was about to ask him who the man was until she noticed Steve's expression. His features had hardened into a stony mask of control.

They were greeted on the yacht by a ruddy-looking man with hair the color of a used Brillo pad. He offered Alex a hand, assisting her onto the boat.

"Hello," she said, suddenly embarrassed, as she glanced back toward Steve for an introduction.

"Hello, Jay," Steve said, focusing his eyes on the man. "This is a surprise. What brings you out here?"

Jay smiled. "Business."

Steve nodded. "Jay, I'd like you to meet Alexandra Rowe. She's my son's . . . nanny," he said quickly.

Jay raised an eyebrow mischievously. "Of course. Pleased to meet you, Miss Rowe," he said, looking at her as though she was an impostor. He turned back toward Steve. "You didn't tell me you had hired a nanny for Ollie."

Steve shrugged as he lifted Ollie onto the yacht. "I didn't think it was any of your business."

"I'll take Ollie downstairs for a while," Alex said, interrupting their discourse before it got nasty. She grabbed Ollie's hand and led him inside.

*   *   *

"So," Jay continued, once the two men were alone. He looked at Steve.

Steve sat down as he pointed to a chair. "Have a seat."

Jay sat across from him.

"What is it?" Steve asked. "Am I being subpoenaed?"

The other man shook his head. "No. But the media trial is continuing. And it doesn't help to have the *New York Times* threatening to report that you've taken your girlfriend and your son to the Bahamas."

"Knock it off, Jay. She's not my girlfriend"

Jay raised an eyebrow. "I'm your lawyer, Steve. I'm on your side. Remember?"

Steve shook his head. "Alex was helping out at the ranch. She was taking care of Leslie's horses. Ollie grew attached to her. When Ollie and I decided to stay out on the boat awhile, he missed her. So I brought her out here. That's all."

Jay shrugged his shoulders. "I'm not here to interrogate you, Steve."

"Then lay off," Steve said quickly. "If that's why you came all the way out here, you've wasted your time."

Jay leaned back in his chair. He gave Steve a patient, cool stare. "Somehow, someone leaked this to the media," he said, pausing. "Did you check her out?"

"Of course," Steve replied, a little too quickly.

Jay shook his head. "You're not a very convincing liar, Steve. As your lawyer, I'm recommending you go back to the island now. If Ollie would rather be with this girl than with you, then leave him here. But you need to start acting like the bereaved husband. Or else you're going to be in serious shit."

"I thought I *was* in serious shit," he said.

"You're about to be," Jay replied, threatening.

Steve hesitated. "Alex," he called out, his eyes focused on Jay.

Alex appeared in the doorway. She smiled politely. "Yes?"

"Jay and I are going to the island. I don't know what time we'll be back." He glanced at her quickly. "If you have any trouble with Ollie, you can page me."

"Of course," she said, flashing him a professional smile as she turned and walked back into the living room.

Steve focused back on Jay. "Shall we?"

Alex had hoped that a day away from Steve would give her some perspective on the previous evening and allow her to talk herself out of caring for him, but instead she spent the day anticipating his return. She showered and dressed for dinner, surprising herself by putting on makeup and fixing her hair. But there was no sign of Steve. She and Ollie ate their meal in silence, her thoughts focused on the father of the child beside her. She couldn't help but wonder why Jay had surprised Steve by showing up on the boat. It was obvious that Steve hadn't been expecting him.

She felt so confused. Less than forty-eight hours earlier, she might have been able to handle a guilty confession from Steve. But now things were different. She wanted him to profess his innocence to her . . . to the world.

She could tell that Ollie wanted to stay up and wait for his father, but at about nine o'clock, she read him several pages of *20,000 Leagues under the Sea* and tucked him in. She sat with him until he fell asleep. Steve still wasn't back.

Alex walked up onto the sun deck and sat on the overstuffed couch. She wrapped her arms in front of her and shivered slightly. She felt a creeping sense of fear. Despite the boat's large size, it still seemed so small in the water . . . so unprotected.

Alex looked up toward the half moon. It was a cloudless night, and the stars were clearly visible against the black sky. She tried to distract herself by focusing on the constellations. Because of her limited knowledge of astronomy, she was able to pick out what looked to be about five big and small dippers.

She leaned back against the pillows of the soft couch. She knew she wouldn't be able to sleep until Steve returned, and she had no intention of returning to her cabin until he came back. She wanted . . . she needed to talk to him.

She snapped to attention when she heard the sound of a motorboat approaching. She stood up as Steve hooked the boat up to the yacht.

"Hello," she said into the darkness as soon as she heard him climb on board.

Steve reached over to the wall and switched on a soft halogen light. "I thought you'd be sleeping by now," he said.

"You mean you hoped I'd be asleep by now."

He sighed. She was right. He knew that he had to talk to her about what he had discussed with Jay; he was just hoping their discussion could wait until morning. He walked past her without touching her and sat on the chair. "Have a seat, Alex," he said, somewhat coldly.

She tugged down her short cotton sundress as she sat across from him. Her long black hair fell loose around her shoulders.

His eyes ran down her shapely legs, settling on her wrap sandals.

"Alex," he continued after a brief pause. "I went back to the island today because I needed time to think. Time away from you."

She swallowed. She had expected this conversation earlier. When it hadn't happened, she had mistakenly assumed that it wasn't going to.

"I think it's best that we not get involved right now," he continued. "With that in mind, I've decided that I should leave tomorrow. You and Ollie can stay on the island or on the boat without me."

She shook her head, distraught at the thought of Steve leaving. "Why?"

"Ollie seems to be more attached to you right now than to me. One of us has to go. I think it should be me."

"What are you talking about?" she asked.

"I don't want to get involved right now. Not with you. Not with anyone," he said, standing up straight.

She stood up to face him as the anger rose in her throat. "That's not what you said last night."

He looked at her sadly. "Last night was a mistake."

She shook her head. "You're lying."

He turned away from her. He couldn't bear to look at her. To hurt her. But it was unavoidable. "Alex, I think I should leave before we get carried away by loneliness," he said.

Alex nodded slowly. "I see," she managed, trying to maintain some dignity. "I understand. You're probably right." Even though she felt as if her heart was breaking, her words were even and calm. "I understand. If you'll excuse me, I think I'll go to bed. I'm feeling a little tired," she said quietly, moving toward the stairs.

Steve tightened his fists in an effort to restrain himself as he watched her walk away. He couldn't run after her. He had to let her go.

But he didn't want to rationalize. He couldn't. Not if it meant staying away from her.

"Wait a minute," he said, grabbing her arm just as she got to the stairway.

She shook off his hand. "You're right, Steve. Let's just forget it," she said, starting down the stairs.

"That man who was here today was my lawyer."

Alex stopped and turned back to face him.

"He informed me that I'm risking my freedom by being out here with you."

"What?" she asked, the tension tightening in her chest.

"He had some inquiries from the press, asking for

confirmation on a report that I was cruising the Bahamas with my son and a young woman." He shook his head. "It doesn't look good for me to be alone with you right now, for obvious reasons."

Alex felt ill. She hoped that those inquiries had not been from Tim. True, he had been angry at her when she left, but she couldn't believe he would take it out on her like this. She walked back to the couch and sat down. "I see," she managed, deep in thought.

Steve sat down next to her. "I tried to deny that you and I were involved, but he didn't buy it."

"So that's it?" she asked quietly, looking at him.

The moonlight caught her hair, casting a soft sheen to the silky strands. Steve reached out and touched her face. He shook his head. "We can't be together," he said softly, instinctively moving closer to her as their lips met. His body denied his words as his lips pressed down on hers.

He knotted his hands in her hair as he rubbed his lips over her cheek toward her ear. "What are you doing to me?" he whispered hoarsely.

Alex pulled his shirt out and slid her hands around his bare back, pulling him in closer to her.

He broke away and offered her his hand. "Come with me," he said. Alex stared into his eyes, almost hypnotized by her own desire. She accepted his hand and followed him down the stairs.

Steve paused outside the door to his room. Still holding her hand, he bent down and kissed her, deeply and passionately, as his free hand opened the door.

He motioned for her to enter the room as he turned on the dim halogen lights above the Picasso. Alex took a step inside and nervously looked toward the bed. The lights made it look like some sort of romantically lit stage.

She heard Steve shut the door. She closed her eyes as he put his hands on her bare shoulders and touched his lips to her neck. She instinctively relaxed, breathing a soft moan of desire. She couldn't reason. Her intellect had collided with her passion, and the result was chaos.

Steve turned her toward him as he cupped her face in his hands, forcing her to look at him. "I want you, Alex," he said, gazing into her eyes intensely. "I want you more than I've ever wanted any woman before in my life."

Alex closed her eyes as she tenderly placed her hand on top of his. He kissed her forehead. "If you're not ready . . . tell me now," he whispered.

She glanced up at him and smiled as her fingers moved toward his shirt. She began to unbutton it slowly, kissing his well-muscled chest as she went.

When he could bear it no longer, he took her hands, held them to his lips, and kissed them tenderly. "Get into bed," he commanded softly.

She looked toward the bed and then back to him again. He nodded as he took off his shirt. She slipped off her sandals and walked quickly toward the bed. She pulled down the covers and began crawling under them with her dress still on.

Steve threw his shirt on the chair. "Wait a minute," he said, looking at her mischievously. He crossed his arms in front of his bare, muscled chest. "Aren't you forgetting something?"

Alex looked down at her dress. She didn't think she had the nerve to take it off in front of him. "I'm embarrassed."

"Why?" he asked, curious.

"At least turn off the light," she said, motioning above her. He smiled as he walked over and sat on the edge of the bed. He trailed a finger lightly around the outline of her face. "I want to make love with you," he said. "But first, I want to see you. All of you."

She glanced at him hesitantly, and he gave her a slight nod of encouragement. She crawled out of the covers and got up on her knees, facing him. She lifted her dress over her head and threw it to the floor. He inhaled sharply, his breath getting shorter with excitement. "What about these?" he said hoarsely. He slipped his fingers inside the elastic of her underpants and ran them around her bikini line.

"What about them?" she managed.

"They have to go," he said teasingly.

"What about these?" she said, slipping her fingers inside the top of his jeans. "They have to go, too."

He smiled. "Ladies first," he said, gently pulling her down on the bed. She sighed slightly as she felt his fingers move deftly toward her most sensitive part. "Steve," she said, but he drowned her word with a heavy, passionate kiss as his finger slipped inside her. She felt she would lose control right then, but she fought back. He caressed her until she thought she would scream with desire. He was skillfully teasing her, playing with her until he was ready to let her release. He gently lifted her hips as he slowly pulled off her panties. "You are so beautiful," he whispered as his hand casually moved back in between her legs. Within seconds, she was shaking in his arms with pleasure.

She closed her eyes as he kissed her eyelids. He then took both of her hands gently in his and kissed them as well. She wrapped her legs around him as he pulled her on top of him, his tongue slipping inside her mouth.

He ran his fingers up and down her bare back. She reached toward the buttons of his jeans and undid them.

He kicked his pants off and leaned over her, his eyes gazing at her. "I want you," he whispered.

She closed her eyes, feeling the immediate surge of pleasure as their bodies united. She dug her fingers into his back. "Look at me," he commanded. She forced herself to meet his penetrating gaze.

He pushed deeper inside her, each thrust bringing her closer to complete release. She sighed as she felt her body letting go. She could feel his muscles tighten as he pushed deeper and deeper. It was not until she felt the waves of pleasure rock through her once again that he shuddered, his eyes closing briefly as a slight moan escaped his lips.

He opened his eyes and gazed down at her. He smiled slightly and began lightly nuzzling her neck. He took her hand and kissed it before curling his body around her, pulling her in tight. She closed her eyes, blissfully happy and peaceful. So that was what all the fuss was about, she thought happily. Up until now, she hadn't really understood.

Alex woke up. She was back in her own bed, where she had crept in the middle of the night. She hadn't wanted to confuse Ollie by sleeping in his father's bed.

She sat up when a momentary flash of doubt whipped through her. And why wouldn't the child be confused? Anyone would. After all, she had just made love with a man who may have killed his wife.

But he was innocent, she thought to herself. She knew it. Leslie was an alcoholic. She was unstable and depressed. And she had killed herself, just as she had tried to before. But this time she had succeeded. And so now, an innocent man who had done his best to protect his child was moving on with his life. And Alex was going to help him. If he would let her.

But what if he didn't? What if he still wanted to leave her? Just because they had slept together didn't necessarily guarantee that he would be staying. As a matter of fact, he might have already left.

She grabbed her robe as she opened the door. She was greeted by total silence. She walked past the empty bedrooms and crept upstairs. She looked around the living room. There was no sign of Steve or Ollie.

Practically running, she hurried outside and looked toward the spot where Steve had hooked up the motorboat. It was gone.

She felt two strong arms grab her from behind.

Steve slid his arms around her small waist and pulled her in close. "Good morning," he said as he nuzzled her ear. She breathed a sigh of relief.

He turned her around to face him. "What's the matter?" he asked curiously.

She smiled. "I thought . . . I thought you left."

He looked pensive for a moment. "Did that upset you?" he asked, looking into her eyes.

She broke away. "Yes," she said, swallowing. She looked around. "Where's the boat?" she asked.

"I sent most of the crew back to the island until we decide what we want to do. But, believe it or not, Ollie wanted to go for a boat ride. So one of them took him back to the island on the motorboat to help him pick up some supplies." He gave her a little squeeze. "All your hard work with Ollie is working wonders." *And he's not the only one you've helped,* he felt like adding.

She nodded, breaking away. "Good." She walked toward the railing. "So . . ." she said, as nonchalantly as she could manage. "Have you decided what you want to do?"

"I'm trying not to think about it," he said, standing beside her.

"I have an idea," she said, facing him. "Why don't we go back? All of us. I'll go back to my job on the ranch. It will be business as usual. Above suspicion. No one needs to know. Right now, anyway. Not even Roger."

He shook his head. "You think we can keep this from Roger?" he asked.

"Not forever. But maybe for a while," she said.

He paused for a moment. Then he smiled. "It's certainly worth a try. But right now, we've got more important things to discuss," he said, pulling her against him. "Like how we're going to spend our time this morning."

She shrugged her shoulders, looking at him mischievously. "I have *no* idea," she said as Steve undid the tie on her robe.

Eighteen

Roger closed the file and dropped it beside his bed. Not bothering to remove his boots, he sat down on the twin bed and kicked up his feet as he lit a cigarette. He watched the embers glow in the dark room as he removed his cowboy hat, flinging it haphazardly across the room. He chuckled silently to himself.

Alex Rowe . . . Alex, Alex, he hummed quietly to himself. He wasn't sure which name he like better. Alexandra Webster or Alexandra Rowe. Alexandra Webster had kind of an aristocratic sound to it. Whereas Alex Rowe sounded more down-to-earth. Less pretentious. It sounded like the name a horse trainer would have, which is exactly what she was pretending to be.

He glanced at the copies of the *New York Times* articles Alexandra Webster had authored that he had scattered around the room. Alex Rowe may have been a better name, but he was beginning to think that he preferred Alexandra Webster. Alex Rowe had been boring him, but Alexandra Webster . . . now, there was a very unusual woman. A very talented woman.

He understood now why she had fallen into their lap at the ranch. It was no accident. As a matter of fact, she had developed an extremely elaborate and risky plan. It was brilliant simply because it had counted on luck to succeed. And succeed she had, despite the controls that had been in place to prevent that very thing from happening.

She had played them all for fools. But now, he,

Roger, was the one with the upper hand. Over Steve. Over her. Over everyone. For once.

He sighed. She had almost gotten away with it. And she would have if he hadn't hired that detective. But the detective had unraveled her story by making a few calls to some contacts in Middleburg, Virginia. Apparently, no one had heard of an Alexandra Rowe.

After that, it was easy. If she had made up a fake identity, with a fake background, Roger knew she had to have some money behind her. He had known right then that she was a reporter. He had told the investigator to check around. Within hours, he had found Alex's real last name.

Now, he thought, he just had to decide how to proceed from there. He glanced over at the phone as he forced himself to sit up. He knew where to start.

"When do we arrive?" Alex asked. She was sitting on the deck of the boat, her tan legs peeking out from under her beach wrap.

He shrugged his shoulders. "Tomorrow afternoon," he said, his eyes focusing on his son. Ollie was in the pool, the life preserver making his little head bob above the water as his entire being focused on doing the doggy paddle, which he was managing quite well. He had become a fan of the water lately. Every morning, he woke up anxious for a swim and immediately put on his life preserver, still damp from the previous day. "If the weather holds up," Steve added.

Alex smiled as she leaned back and closed her eyes, basking in the warm sun.

It had been a week since they began their journey back toward Miami, and she had grown very accustomed to their easy, natural pace of life on the water. Warm, sunny days spent playing with Ollie. Quiet, romantic evenings and nights spent alone with Steve.

She opened her eyes, aware that Steve was staring at her. "What?" she asked.

He looked toward the water. "I'm going to miss being on this boat," he said.

She nodded. "I am, too."

He shook his head and laughed.

"What's so funny?" she asked.

He shrugged. "Us. You."

"What do you mean?" she asked.

"It's just . . . you're not at all like I expected."

"And what did you expect?"

"I don't know. I guess I'm realizing that I am who I am. It feels so good to be with someone who's content to just . . . be. The superficial perks in life just don't impress you."

She laughed. "Like what?"

"A big career, a lot of money, that type of thing doesn't seem to motivate you. And I like that."

She looked away. She had planned to tell him the truth about herself. But she hadn't been able to find the right time. Or at least that was what she had been telling herself.

"Steve . . . I . . . there's something I should tell you," she began, summoning up her courage.

She was interrupted by the low pulse of the phone. "Go ahead, get it," she said, relieved that she had a temporary reprieve.

Steve hesitated. "Go on," she said again.

"Yes," he said authoritatively, picking up the phone. "Hey." He paused, putting his hand over the mouth of the receiver. "It's Roger," he whispered. He listened for a moment. "Can it wait?" she heard him ask. "We'll arrive in Miami tomorrow." He paused. "Okay, great. See you then," he said, hanging up the phone.

"That was quick," she said.

"I want to enjoy my last day of . . . vacation. Before we go back to the dreary homestead."

"Why don't you fix that place up?" she asked.

He shrugged his shoulders. "I don't plan on staying there that long. And I really shouldn't be doing a lot of redecorating right now. It might look a little strange."

"Why don't you move or go away for a while?" she asked.

"Like where?" he asked.

She was thinking out loud, not paying too much attention to the words as they came out of her mouth. "The house you just bought."

"Ollie needs to be near a school. At least eventually."

"Europe?"

He sighed. "I've thought about it. But I was advised to stay in the States for a while."

She paused, the sadness of his words hanging over her. She flipped over onto her stomach. She balanced her elbows on the floor and rested her chin in her hands. "Do you ever miss her?" she asked quietly.

He didn't hesitate. "Her death was a tragedy. A tragic finale to a sad life."

"You didn't answer me," she insisted.

He looked at her. "What were you going to say before Roger called?"

"Nothing," she said, shrugging her shoulders.

He stood up.

"How could Leslie live in that place?" she asked, still focused on his relationship with Leslie. "I'm surprised she didn't try to fix it up."

His face began to tighten. "I don't think you'd be so surprised if you knew her. Actually, it was totally in character," he said rather coldly.

"What do you mean?"

"I mean it suited her needs." He paused, looking at her. After a split second, he glanced away. "She wanted to get away from me, and that island seemed like the obvious choice. She couldn't fix the house up because that would have been something that I would've liked."

"But what about you?" she continued. "Were you comfortable having Ollie live in a house like that when you could easily afford a place like this?" she asked, motioning around the boat.

"Ollie didn't live there," he said, his voice growing colder with every word. "Neither, really, did Leslie. It was our vacation home." He paused as he focused his attention back on her. "I don't like to talk about my life with Leslie. One of the things I like about you is that you appeared to respect that."

He stood up and walked back into the living room. She quickly followed him.

"I'm sorry," she said, keeping an eye focused on Ollie. "It's none of my business."

He glanced back at her as he shook his head. "My relationship with Leslie was complicated," he began. He spoke slowly, searching for the right words. "She never forgave me . . ." he said, his voice drifting off as he looked at his son.

"For what?" Alex asked, encouraging him to continue.

His brown eyes focused on her. "Leslie thought that I persuaded her father to betray her. Her father was a wealthy man, and he left me his money. After he died, she changed. I mean, things had never been great between us, but after that, they became almost unbearable. I offered her the money, anything she wanted . . ." He shrugged his shoulders as he leaned against the wall. "She knew I wanted a divorce. That just made things worse." He crossed his arms in front of him as he glanced down at the floor. "Our relationship became a marriage in name only. I suspected she was having affairs, but as long as she was discreet, I really didn't care. She had informed me that I was free to do as I pleased as well. So I focused on my work and my son while my life developed some sort of crazy rhythm as I racked up the frequent flier miles. And then she tried to kill herself. She took a bottle of sleeping pills, just like her mother."

"I'm sorry . . ." Alex began.

"So was I. Fortunately, unlike her mother, the maid

discovered her before it was too late. Leslie spent two months in the psychiatric ward. When she got out, I dedicated myself to making the marriage work. But the closeness seemed to make things worse."

"What do you mean?"

"One night, we were at a party, and Leslie had too much to drink—as usual. She became convinced that I was flirting with a waitress. She threatened to jump off the balcony. I thought she was going to do it."

"But I thought you just said that she didn't care if you had affairs."

"I wasn't having an affair with anyone," he said angrily. He paused as he collected his thoughts. "Affairs take time . . . and energy. I had plenty of opportunities, I just . . ." He shook his head as he remembered. "I think Leslie knew that I was faithful, but it didn't seem to matter. She was an alcoholic. She would say one thing one minute and do the opposite the next.

"The night she threatened to jump off the balcony, she just went crazy. It took me more than an hour to calm her down. And by then the police had arrived." His gaze shifted toward Alex. "I pleaded with her to get professional help. I was afraid that she would try and kill herself again. And I was right," he continued, his voice increasing in intensity. "In a way, I think I was responsible for her death," he said hoarsely.

Alex walked over to him and put her hands on his shoulders.

He turned toward her, the grief evident in his deep brown eyes. "I keep thinking that I should've tried to put her in an institution that could've helped her. I should've insisted on it . . ."

"Steve. Don't. Don't do this to yourself," Alex said, comforting him as she put her hands on his cheeks.

He paused, staring deep into her eyes. "No more questions," he said, almost pleading with her.

She nodded. She was not there as a reporter anymore. She reached for Steve's hand and squeezed it.

*　　*　　*

They arrived in Miami shortly before dusk. A car met them at the dock to take them to the airport, where Roger was waiting with the helicopter. Alex sat in the backseat with Ollie, holding his hand as the helicopter lifted into the air. They arrived on the island within an hour.

Alex carried her suitcase back to her apartment by herself. Although she and Steve had decided that in front of Roger they would act as if nothing were going on between them, she fully expected Steve to visit her tonight, if he could.

She got back to her room and flipped open her computer. She went on-line immediately and opened up the file containing her mail.

The first letter was from Tim: "Sorry you bungled our weekend. I had big plans. Behave yourself."

The second letter was a little more dramatic: "When the hell are you getting back? It's been over a week. I've thought a lot about this, and I've decided that this whole thing is ridiculous. Come back to New York. This guy could sue your ass off if he finds out who you are. Or worse."

But it was the third letter that concerned her: "I don't know when you'll get this, but I do know you're in trouble. Someone called the paper the other day inquiring about you. Wanted to know where you went . . . why you left. They talked to Elaine, and she put them through to me. When I asked who they were, they said they were a credit card company and you owed money. Ran a check on the company, and they don't exist. Watch your ass. P.S.: No life insurance. Working on the affairs."

She could feel her breath quicken as she instinctively looked toward the window. She had a sinking feeling in her stomach. Roger was on to her. She knew it. The detective must have found something out about her when they were looking for her in Miami. But if Roger knew, why didn't he tell Steve when he talked to him on the phone?

She opened up the last piece of mail from Tim: "Where the hell are you? I'm concerned. I called Steve's attorneys in a weak and desperate attempt to bring you back. I don't like this. And now some kids have come forward stating that they heard the wife screaming for her life before she fell to her death. Get out of there. By the way—your time is up. Haul ass back here before you're fired."

She heard a door slam and looked up. Roger was leaving the house. She watched him get into his truck and drive away. She knew that Steve would wait to put Ollie to bed before he came to see her. If he came. And she had a feeling he would.

She typed a quick note back to Tim: "I'm back at the ranch. What's this about the kids? Please give me details and an extension. Too dangerous to write more but am very close to getting proof. Thanks."

She tried to forgive herself for the little lie she wrote about being close to getting proof. But she had little choice—she needed an extension. She couldn't leave right now. Not when she was smack in the middle of . . . everything.

Alex closed up her computer and put it away. She thought about going to see Steve right then, to tell him the truth about who she was, if Roger hadn't told him already. But she decided against it. She would wait for him to come to her.

She readied herself for bed, taking her time. Once she had her nightshirt on, she pulled her paperback out of her suitcase and crawled into bed, fighting off panic.

She forced herself to lie in bed quietly as she looked around the dark, little room. She missed the plush comfort of the boat. She missed Steve.

At twelve-thirty, Alex got up and looked out the window. The dining-room light was on. Steve had to be boxing again. She paused, wondering what to do. She couldn't take the waiting anymore. It was obvious that Roger had told him. Otherwise, wouldn't he have come to see her by now?

She grabbed a robe and walked over to the main house. The window in the dining room was open, and she could hear the sound of his fists hitting the bag as she got closer to the house. She slipped inside the front door and walked quietly toward the dining room.

He stopped as soon as he saw her standing in the doorway. He walked up to her, not saying a word as he undid his glove.

She looked away from his sweat-covered torso and stared at the floor as she waited to be confronted. He pulled his right hand out of his glove and lifted her face. She felt his lips press down tightly as his bare hand pressed against her back, pushing her into him. His kiss was so intense it left her gasping for air.

She pulled back. "I was wondering why you didn't come over . . ." she began.

He smiled. "The night is still young."

She pulled away, confused. "I'm kind of surprised that you're boxing again."

He shrugged. "Stress reliever."

"Why so stressed?" she asked as casually as she could manage.

He looked at her and sighed. He began to take off his other glove as he said, "I have to go to Miami tomorrow."

Alex breathed an inaudible sigh of relief. Roger obviously hadn't told Steve that she was a reporter, which meant that Roger probably didn't know himself. "Why?"

"I have a meeting with Jay. Something's come up that needs my attention. By the way, I asked Roger to look after Ollie tomorrow. I figured you might need a break."

"I never mind watching Ollie," she said. "But what's this in Miami?" she asked, even though she assumed it had something to do with what Tim had written in his e-mail.

"Apparently," he said, hitting the punching bag lightly with his bare hand, "there were some boys on a boat the night Leslie died. They say they heard her pleading for her life."

"What?" she said, managing to sound surprised. "That's not possible."

He shook his head as he swung at the bag. "Of course not."

"What are they . . . why are they doing this?"

"I don't know. But I'll find out."

Alex paused, studying his reaction carefully. "You're not . . . concerned?"

"Why should I be?" he asked a little too quickly. He began to massage the knuckles of his right hand.

She shrugged her shoulders. "What if the police believe them?"

He walked over to her. He began running his fingers through her hair. "You have such beautiful hair," he said. "It's so thick. Beautiful black hair. The color of night." He leaned in and kissed her forehead. "I'm going to take a shower," he whispered. "Why don't you go back to your apartment? Take off all your clothes and get into bed. Wait for me."

Alex watched him walk out of the room. She felt a sick sense of fear well in her throat, as though the man she loved had just confessed his guilt. Of course, he hadn't. And he wouldn't, she told herself. Because he was innocent.

She looked up at the moon as she walked back to her apartment. On the boat, they had seemed so far away from all this. Everything had seemed so pure, so innocent. But now they were back. She was suddenly reminded of all the loose ends in this case. All the little details she had ignored, simply because she had found herself falling in love with her subject. And although she still wanted to believe that Steve had not killed Leslie, she could no longer ignore the unanswered questions that were nagging at her.

For instance, her instinctive distrust of men and human nature in general made it extremely difficult to swallow Steve's reassurance that, one, he had been faithful during his marriage, and, two, despite the fact that he was faithful, he had not been bothered by Leslie sleeping around.

A persistent, frightening scenario reminiscent of *Othello* began to unfold in Alex's imagination. Perhaps Steve really had loved Leslie . . . and because of that he had refused to give her a divorce, threatening to cut off the money if she divorced him. When he found out that she was planning on leaving him, for another man, he killed her.

After all, Leslie *had* had affairs. Steve had said as much when they were together on the boat. Perhaps her infidelity was his justification for murder.

She stepped into her apartment and shut the door behind her. She felt so guilty and confused. How could she suspect him of murder when she was falling in love with him? Alex realized that she had it backward. The question she should be asking herself was: How could she fall in love with a man she suspected of murder?

Backward or not, she had a problem. She couldn't sleep with him. Not now. Not with the doubts that were surfacing about his innocence.

She got into bed and stared at the ceiling. What had she done? What was she doing? She thought of Ollie. Sweet little Ollie. He was keeping something, too. A secret. *Promise me.*

She closed her eyes even tighter when she heard the door open.

Steve walked into the room, silently slipping into bed. He nuzzled his cheek against her neck as he wrapped his arms around her. Alex breathed in the fragrant smell of soap as she lay there as still as she could manage.

Satisfied that she was sleeping, Steve cuddled up against her. She lay awake until she heard his slow, regulated breath. She was alone once more.

"Why, hello."

Alex turned and smiled at Roger. "Good morning."

She was tired, and she was sure she looked it. After Steve had fallen asleep, she had lain in bed awake for hours. And now she needed to determine if Roger had discovered her true identity.

She turned back toward Rosie's stall and stepped inside, shutting the gate behind her.

"Good morning," he said as though he was imitating her. He peered at her through the bars of the gate. "It seems like Ollie isn't the only one who needs you around here."

"Oh?" she replied uncomfortably, patting Rosie on the side.

"Rosie's been acting up, too," he said, nodding toward the horse.

She laughed. "It must have been tough, having to look after all the horses when we were gone."

"I didn't," he said.

"Excuse me?"

"There's a nice young fellow I hire when I need some extra help around here. He lives on the mainland, though, so it's kind of tough for him to do this full-time." She nodded.

"Did you have a difficult time dealing with Chapman?" he asked.

Alex paused, growing more confident with each moment that Roger neglected to mention her blown cover. She shook her head. "Not really. I think he was appreciative that I came."

"He told me that the lawyers called him back early. That's a damn shame."

"I guess so," she said, looking into his eyes for some clue to what he'd learned from the detective.

"Didn't like the looks of it. It's ridiculous," he said, crossing his arms in front of him. "Anyone can see that he's broken up over the loss of his wife."

She smiled uncomfortably. "Of course." She turned back toward the horse. "Did you know her well?" she asked.

He shrugged. "Well enough, I guess."

"But you must've gotten to know her pretty well. I mean, she spent a lot of time here. And you've been working here for quite a while, haven't you?" she asked, walking out of Rosie's stall. She closed the door behind her.

"Why would you think that?" he asked, his eyes staring at her coldly.

She shrugged her shoulders as she began walking toward the barn exit. "I thought Steve mentioned something to that effect."

He shook his head as he joined her. "You must have misunderstood," he said, walking beside her. "I came here last winter. I was . . . going through a tough time. I was sick of the winter, sick of the city, sick of life. I told you I had lost my company. I needed to get away. I told him one day that I was going to quit. Move to Florida." He shrugged his shoulders as his gray-green eyes shifted their gaze back to her. "He had a different idea."

"That you move to the island."

"Leslie had been using a pilot on the mainland. Just calling when she needed a ride. Steve didn't like that arrangement. He was worried about her. Afraid she might need to get off the island for some reason and wouldn't be able to. He asked me if I'd consider the job."

"Had you met her before?"

"You sure have a lot of questions," he said, looking at her suspiciously.

Alex looked away, slightly taken aback. "I'm sorry," she said.

Roger smiled as if he was just teasing her. "Once or twice."

Alex glanced back at him. "What?"

"I'd met her once or twice before. But I didn't really know her. I wasn't too worried, though. Steve told me that I'd have my own place. Right on the beach. It sounded almost too good to be true."

"Was it?" she asked.

He turned away. "It was better than I'd hoped."

Alex was not surprised to see the forlorn expression on Roger's face. She had suspected that Roger had been infatuated with Leslie. She imagined it must have been pretty lonely for him there. Leslie had been a beautiful woman. But still, she doubted Leslie would have looked twice at a man like Roger. He may have been somewhat attractive, but he just wasn't the type of guy to set the world on fire. In addition, Leslie, from all she had heard, valued money, and Roger barely owned the hat on his head.

Alex looked around. "It is beautiful here. There's a sense of history to this place. It's just that it's so . . . isolated."

Roger began walking away, back toward the house.

"Roger," she called, stopping him. "Do you think she was murdered?"

Roger turned back slowly. He looked at her carefully. "Do you?" he asked.

She laughed nervously. "Of course not," she replied, shaking her long hair.

He gave a quick nod of his head, flashing her a smile. "Just do your job. And enjoy the weather. I have to go look in on Ollie." He dropped his smile. "Steve's meeting with his lawyers again today."

She watched him walk back. She turned toward the stables, her eyes catching a glimpse of the house where Leslie died. She needed to go there. To see it for herself.

Alex heard the door slam. Roger was in the house. He would fix Ollie breakfast, sit with him, clean up the dishes. She figured she had about half an hour.

She walked back into the barn and headed straight for Rosie's stall. "Okay, girl," she said. "We're going to go for a ride."

She led Rosie out the front of the barn, glancing back toward the house to make sure the coast was clear. She typically didn't like to ride bareback, but she didn't want to take the time to saddle Rosie up. She reached her arms around the suddenly docile horse and lifted herself up onto the animal's back. She dug her heels into the side of the horse as she held on to Rosie's mane.

"Okay, kiddo," she said in a low, soft voice as she dug her heels into the sides of the animal. "Lead the way!"

The horse took off as Alex steered her into the pine forest behind the barn. She didn't want Roger to see which way she was going. There was a thin path that eventually led to the other side of the island, not too far from the house. The horse galloped down the pine-needle-covered path, moving easily through the dense woods. Rays of sun danced through the shadowy, cool forest in front of them.

Alex held on to Rosie's mane tightly, crouching down occasionally to avoid the low swinging branches. The horse rode on automatically, as if she had been this way many times before. Alex wondered if Leslie had ridden Rosie there the day she died. Perhaps Rosie had witnessed her mistress's death.

The horse slowed at the clearing as though waiting for a signal. Alex gave Rosie's mane a yank to the right, and the horse galloped on toward the house. Alex could see the house now, looming in front of them. It stood on the edge of a cliff. Bits and pieces of plastic, once carefully secured to the windows to keep out the elements, now blew casually in the wind, barely attached.

Worried about stray nails loose on the ground, Alex stopped Rosie a safe distance from the house. She dismounted slowly, still holding on to the horse. She stood there, staring at the house for several minutes. The house was just as ominous close up as it was from a distance. It was huge. A giant conglomeration of wood, nails, and cement that contained at least ten thousand square feet. Unlike the main house, this was stark, and simple, designed with the future in mind.

She pulled herself back up onto Rosie's back and led the horse away from the house. She would have liked to look around the back, but she didn't dare leave Rosie unattended. No, she thought. She would wait. And next time, she would come on foot.

When she arrived back at the barn, Alex put Rosie in her stall and went directly to her apartment, locking herself in the bathroom. She pulled her computer out of her duffle bag and hooked it up to her cellular phone. She dialed an 800 number and logged on to the *Times* system. She watched the screen as it flashed the confirmation of her password, which just happened to be her real last name.

She checked her mail. She had received a message from Tim: "Thanks for letting me know you're okay. Would appreciate a phone call to discuss extension. In regard to the kids, here's the deal: they were riding on a boat near the Chapman estate. Claim they heard her screaming, but now the word is that the coast guard found them dealing drugs and the kids offered testimony in exchange for a light sentence. Your one and only."

Alex was getting ready for bed when she was distracted by a knock on the door. She had heard Steve return an hour earlier, and she had been expecting him. And even though she had tried to talk herself out of prepping for his visit, she had been unable to resist. Wearing only her nightshirt, she walked toward the door as she brushed her long, silky hair away from her face. She opened the door.

Roger stood in front of her. His sun-blond hair was still damp from a recent shower, combed carefully around his ears. He wore a crisp white shirt and clean jeans.

"Roger," she said, surprised.

He nodded. "Mind if I come in?" he asked.

She shook her head. "Please do," she managed. She stepped back, allowing him to enter. "How's Ollie?"

He nodded toward the house. "He's sleeping. Sound asleep. He has been for more than an hour. You wore him out today," he added with a laugh. Alex had spent the afternoon teaching Ollie to ride his pony.

She smiled. He looked at her uncomfortably.

"So . . ." she said, shrugging her shoulders. "Is there something you needed me for?"

He paused. "I was just wondering if . . . maybe you'd like to go for a walk with me?"

She glanced back toward the house. Had Steve asked Roger to come over?

"I . . . is everything all right?" she asked, worried.

He nodded. "Sure. It's just a beautiful night, that's all."

She smiled uncomfortably. This was bad. Frightening thoughts raced through her head. Roger sees Steve coming over to visit her . . . Steve sees her with Roger and thinks there's something going on . . .

She shook her head. "I'm sorry. Normally I'd love to . . . but I'm afraid that Ollie wore me out today as well."

He looked toward the house anxiously.

"Are you sure there's nothing wrong?" she asked again. She had a sneaky suspicion he wanted to tell her something. Perhaps a walk wasn't such a bad idea.

He shook his head, forcing a smile. "No. I . . . I'll see you tomorrow," he said, turning around abruptly.

"Roger . . . wait," she called out, her journalistic instincts taking over. "It will only take me a minute to change." He paused and waited at the bottom of the steps.

Alex whirled around inside her room, looking for her jeans. She pulled them on quickly, hurrying in an attempt to avoid Steve. She knew it was risky to go with Roger, but she couldn't let her feelings for Steve interfere with her common sense. Roger had some information regarding Leslie. She was sure of it.

She anxiously hopped down the stairs, taking them two at a time. She paused when she got to the bottom. The light in the dining room was out. That meant either Steve hadn't stared boxing yet, and she had plenty of time, or he wasn't planning on boxing at all . . . or he was already finished, in which case, he would be over any minute.

"Do you want to walk down to the beach?" Roger asked. She shrugged her shoulders.

"Whatever you want," she replied, attempting to appear nonchalant.

She glanced sideways at Roger as they walked in silence. He really wasn't a bad-looking man. He just looked a little weathered and rough, as if he had drunk and smoked too much his entire life—although she hadn't seen him do either since she had arrived on the island. When they were a safe distance from the house, Roger spoke. "Thanks for coming. I just wanted to talk to you . . . about Steve. That's all."

"Steve?" she said, looking at him curiously.

Roger stopped walking. "Shit—I never should've gotten you out of bed. I shouldn't even tell you this, anyway," he said.

"What is it?" she asked, stopping and facing him.

"It's just that . . . well . . . I'm kind of in a bind."

"What do you mean?"

Roger started walking again. "I like you, Alex. I don't want to see you get hurt."

She hurried to catch up with him. "Hurt? What do you mean?"

"I wasn't on the boat with you two, but I've got a pretty good sense that, well, something happened between you two. I like Steve and all that," he said insincerely, "but he's not too great with women."

She stopped walking and turned to face him. "What are you saying?"

"It's none of my business," he repeated. "But Steve was never faithful to Leslie. She told me so herself. He had a girlfriend . . . a fairly serious one. She said Steve wanted to divorce her . . . but she wouldn't give him the satisfaction. She couldn't."

Alex swallowed, trying to keep her cool. Had Steve been lying to her? "Why couldn't she?" she managed to whisper.

"Because her father had left Steve everything. If she divorced him, she wouldn't have a dime."

She nodded. "I see." Obviously, she had been wrong to think that Leslie had just dismissed Roger.

On the contrary, they had been close enough to merit her confiding in him. But why was Roger telling her this? And why did he get so choked up when he spoke about Leslie? Was Roger trying to get back at Steve by telling her lies about him?

He glanced back at her as he took her hand. "I'm sorry that I had to tell you this. He wants you here for Ollie. And I don't blame him. Ollie needs someone like you right now."

Alex's head spun with unanswered questions. "What's her name?" she asked quietly, hoping to catch Roger in his lies.

"What?"

She pulled her hand away. "This woman that he was having an affair with. What's her name?"

"Leslie never said," Roger answered, obviously trying to sound casual.

Alex nodded as she looked back toward Steve's house. "If you don't mind," she managed, not at all sure whom she was to believe about all this, "I feel like the day has finally caught up with me. Perhaps we could go to the beach another time."

Nineteen

Alex crawled into bed as her mind slowly and painfully mulled over the information she had received from Roger. She had wanted so much to believe that Steve was innocent. Had her feelings blinded her? Encouraged her to overlook inconsistencies and untruths that might have proven his guilt?

Alex glanced out the window. Clouds covered the

moon, making the night seem even blacker than usual. She wiped away something wet and salty from her mouth and realized that she had been crying. She had not wanted to believe what Roger had told her about Steve—in fact, she had been tempted to dismiss the whole conversation—but she knew, as a journalist, it was information that she must consider. But if Roger had been telling the truth about Steve's infidelity, and it was a big *if,* she knew the DA wouldn't hesitate to point to a motive for murder.

But was Roger telling the truth? He seemed pretty cagey when she'd asked him specifics about Steve's girlfriend. But why would he make it all up? Could Roger possibly be involved with Leslie's death? Was he trying to throw suspicion on Steve to cover up his own guilt?

Alex turned on her side. She had to regroup and continue her investigation. She would never be able to commit to Steve unless she had totally exonerated him of his guilt. Her caring for him may have caused her investigation to suffer a setback, but it was far from over.

Her mind was so entrenched with thoughts that she didn't hear the floorboards creak beside her bed. She opened her eyes only to see a man's shadow standing over her. She opened her mouth to scream, but the sound was blocked by a mouth that covered hers with a passionate kiss.

Steve kissed her until he could feel her body relaxing. He paused, allowing her to breathe. She pulled back, sitting up straight.

"Did you miss me?" he whispered.

"You were only gone a day," she said, fighting an urge to wipe away his kiss.

He fell beside her, his arms dangling around her in a loose hug. "What does that mean?" he asked teasingly, kissing her ear.

"How were your meetings with the lawyers?" she asked, not looking at him.

He pulled back. "We'll see," he said carefully. "I read what the boys had to say. I don't think they were anywhere near this place as they claim to be."

"Even if they were, there was nothing to hear. Right?" she asked.

"Of course not. But these kids . . . if you can call them that . . . have a long history of minor scrapes with the police. They only came forward because the police pulled them over for speeding and found some drug paraphernalia in their car. They asked for immunity from prosecution if they provided evidence of a murder."

"Are the police taking them seriously?"

"Not after my lawyers were finished with them."

"So everything's all set," she said carefully. "You don't need to go back to Miami for a while."

He shrugged his shoulders. "I wish that was true. Tell me," he said, brushing the hair away from her eyes, "did you have a nice day?"

"I guess so."

He leaned forward to kiss her again. But instead of greeting his kiss, she turned away.

"What is it?" he asked.

Alex stepped out of bed and walked over to the window. "I think we should slow things down."

He pushed himself up. "What is wrong?" he asked, surprised.

"I need some space," she said casually, silently wincing as the words came out of her mouth. She remembered how she'd felt when Tim had used that line on her years ago.

He hesitated a moment. "What's going on?"

She turned back to face him, her breasts silhouetted against the soft material of her T-shirt. "I just . . . I've always had a problem with commitment. I'm sure I'll . . . I mean, we'll be fine. I just need a little time."

He stood up and walked over to her. He put his hands on her shoulders. "That's all? Nothing else is bothering you?"

She attempted to smile as she looked at him. "No."

He pulled her chin toward him as he looked searchingly into her eyes. "We'll take it as slow as you want."

"Good," she said, backing away.

He looked at her as if he wasn't sure whether or not to believe her. "There's really nothing wrong?"

She laughed slightly. "Not with you, anyway."

He looked at her curiously. "Do you want me to leave?"

Alex nodded.

Steve hesitated, surprised. Although he had made the offer, he hadn't really expected her to accept. "Okay," he said, confused. "I . . . I'll see you later." Steve paused as if waiting for her to reconsider. He gave her a quick nod before turning and walking out of the apartment.

She watched him go, breathing a sigh of relief after the door was shut. She hadn't expected him to take it so well. She had expected him to put on a bit of a show, to act as if he did indeed really love her. She shook her head. Perhaps Roger had been telling the truth.

Alex was up with the sun. She was taking the last horse out to the run when she heard the main house door slam. She looked up. Steve was walking toward his car with a carry-on bag.

Their eyes met, and he paused. He changed directions and began walking toward her. "Good morning," he said stiffly.

"Good morning," she replied, imitating him. "Where are you going?" she asked, nodding toward the bag.

He glanced down at it. "I've got to get back to Miami."

She tried to contain her surprise.

"The weather report wasn't all that great this morning, so I thought I'd better bring an overnight bag in case I'm stuck there," he continued.

She pretended to make a face. "I hate Miami," she said.

He laughed. "I bet you do, outdoor woman that you are. I bet you hate all big cities. Actually, I'm not too fond of them myself."

"So you may be spending the night?" she asked. As soon as the words were out of her mouth, she regretted them.

He shook his head, looking at her strangely. "Not if I can help it."

"I'll look after Ollie while you're gone," she said.

"Thanks," he said, putting on his sunglasses. "I was counting on that. Roger's fixing Ollie breakfast right now. I was going to take Ollie with me . . ."

But he would just get in the way, she thought.

"But he seems to be happy here . . . for once."

She nodded.

"About last night . . ." he began.

She looked at him blankly.

He shrugged. "I missed you. I knew I had to return to Miami, but I made a special trip back here last night just to see you. I didn't want to be away from you."

She looked away.

He hesitated a second. "I don't mean to pressure you. It's just that I haven't felt this way in a long time. If ever. I just can't seem to keep my mind off you . . ." he said, moving close enough for her to smell his musky aftershave.

"I've got work to do," she said, cutting him off as she turned away. She began walking back toward the barn.

"Right," he said softly, watching her.

She disappeared inside the barn and waited until she heard his car drive away before stepping back out into the sun. She had gotten herself in a mess, and she needed to pick up speed in her investigation. If she could still call it that. If she had been treating this as a "real" investigation, she would have e-mailed Tim last night and informed him of Roger's accusations. Instead, she had decided to keep them to herself, until she could determine if they had merit.

In any case, she was glad Steve was going to be gone for a while . . . for whatever the reason.

The front door slammed, and Alex glanced up to see Ollie walking out of the house. Despite his seeming dependency on her, he didn't seem very excited to see her.

"Good morning," she said as he got closer. Ollie looked at her. "What are you doing today?" she asked, not expecting an answer.

"Ollie," Roger called, opening the door. He spotted Ollie with Alex and walked out toward them. "Hello," Roger said, nodding at Alex.

"Good morning," she replied.

"How'd you like to play hooky today?" he asked.

"What?"

"I've got to go to the mainland for some things. I thought maybe you could come, too, and help me look after Ollie."

She looked at the horses. "I've got a lot of work today . . ."

"Nothing that can't wait till tomorrow. It's supposed to storm later this afternoon. If we go now, we'll be back before it starts. You can leave the horses in the run."

"It's supposed to storm?" she asked, looking up at the sky. So Steve had been telling the truth. Perhaps he would be stuck in Miami. Still, it was hard to believe that foul weather was upon them. There was not a cloud in sight. "It's beautiful."

"Weather turns suddenly here." He nodded toward the truck. "C'mon." She thought about it for a second and realized she didn't want to be on the island alone with her thoughts.

"Sounds great," she said appreciatively.

* * *

The wind from the speedboat cooled the thick, salty air. Alex hugged Ollie to her tightly as the boat jumped over the waves, spraying them with cool sea water.

Soon they were surrounded by speedboats and sailboats. Roger slowed down as he entered a private marina.

He pulled the boat into an empty dock and jumped out, tying it to the wooden post. He offered Ollie his hands. Alex lifted Ollie up and into Roger's arms, then she stepped up onto the seat, and Roger grabbed her arm, guiding her out.

Alex looked around her. It was nice to be back in civilization again. She felt a soothing relief as she stared at the assorted people walking around and listened to the typical harbor hubbub of beeping boat horns and laughter. She glanced toward the phone booth on the corner. She was tempted to try and call Tim, but she wasn't sure she could manage with Roger and Ollie so close.

"Can we walk to the stores from here?" she asked.

He shook his head. "No. Leslie kept a car here. We never moved it. It's in the parking lot right behind the main building."

"They let you keep it here?" she asked, quickly deciding against the call. She was worried that Roger might insist she make it from the estate instead.

He smiled. "Steve pays them good money to keep it here."

She nodded. She was surprised that the police hadn't checked it out. But then again, they thought Leslie had committed suicide. Why would they rummage through her car for clues?

Roger led them around the side of the building and walked into the parking lot. It was strange to see Roger and Ollie in such a public setting. She thought that they both looked out of place, uncomfortable.

Roger stopped at a gold Mercedes convertible. "This is it," he said, opening the driver's door. "Hold on a minute," he said, crawling inside the car. "Your seat's pulled way up."

Alex looked the car over while Roger fussed around with the seat. The car couldn't have been more than a year old.

Roger unlocked the doors, and Ollie slipped into the backseat as Alex took her position in the front. There was a distinct aroma of rich, refined leather. The car even smelled expensive.

"Do you want the top down?" Roger asked. He was comfortable in this car, and it showed.

Alex shook her head. She didn't want the top down, just because she was sure that was how Leslie had liked it. She could imagine Leslie in this car with the top down, her long blond hair flowing behind her as she drove. She would wear large sunglasses and a hat of some sort to block the sun. But she had no doubt that Leslie *always* drove with the top down.

"Leslie loved this car," Roger said, downshifting as he drove out of the marina parking lot. "I've avoided using it since she died. I mentioned it to Steve the other day, but he didn't seem to have any interest in selling it. It's probably still too . . . *painful* for him."

She nodded, glancing worriedly back at Ollie. She didn't know what effect talking about his mother would have on him. But he was staring out the window passively.

"How often did she come to the mainland?" she asked.

"When I first moved here, she used to come over all the time. To play tennis and things. But she didn't come over as much in the last few months."

"Really? Why was that?"

"I think she was tired of trying to keep up an act for people. I mean, everyone around here knew her. She was so beautiful. She was noticed everywhere. She was like a movie star. It got to be an effort after a while."

"I see," she said, noting the infatuated tone of his voice.

"I have to run in here," he said, motioning to a grocery store on the right. "Do you mind waiting in the car with Ollie?" She shook her head. "I think Leslie kept her CDs under the seat if you're interested."

"Thanks," she said. She was curious about what kind of music Leslie liked.

Reaching under the seat, she found a loose CD almost immediately. She pulled it out. It was a musician she had never heard of. She popped it in, and a soothing blend of new age music began to radiate through the car. She quickly popped it out. Not exactly what she had in mind. Reaching under the seat again, her fingers grasped something else. She pulled out a square leatherbound book.

A datebook.

She opened it up, aware of a faint perfumed smell emanating from the crisp white pages. She held the book up to her nose.

Lilacs.

Alex held the book in front of her as if it was a priceless gem. She carefully flipped through the pages. Everything was written with a blue fountain pen in unusually neat, legible handwriting. She thumbed through the dates. Each date listed her activities such as "Tennis—2 P.M. Lunch at the Club—3 P.M."

She glanced back at Ollie as the excitement welled in her throat. Ollie was oblivious to her activities. He sat still, seemingly transfixed by his reflection in the shaded glass. She looked back at the book in her hands, not quite believing her find. She quickly thumbed to July thirteenth, the date Leslie died.

She was surprised at what she found. Unlike the clear, concise writing that appeared on the other pages, the handwriting on this page was almost illegible, as though it had been scribbled quickly, and in pencil. Scrawled haphazardly across the page was "Lv NY 10, 3:20, 5."

She flipped to the previous day, July twelfth. "Lv Miami 8. 510 E. Avenue—12:30" was written in blue pen in the same clear, concise handwriting that appeared throughout the book. Alex thought back to Leslie's unmade bed, the nightgown strewn haphazardly across it. The unorganized state of her bedroom made sense. Leslie would have had to leave in a hurry to catch her eight A.M. flight.

Alex closed the book. She already knew that Leslie Chapman had flown in from New York the day she died. That was a well-known, reported fact. But was her decision to visit the island on July thirteenth spontaneous? The scrawled writing in the datebook made Alex think that was indeed the case. So did the fact that Leslie had not bothered to find a matching pen. Were the times "10, 3:20, 5" flight departures from New York?

Alex focused on the address in the book, an address she had immediately committed to memory. Obviously, Leslie had had an appointment in New York the day before she died. Did that appointment have anything to do with her sudden decision to return to the island?

Alex saw Roger step out of the store, holding a large plastic bag in front of him. Alex slipped the book back under the seat.

"Find anything?" Roger asked cheerfully, opening the door.

Alex glanced at him, alarmed. Her initial reaction was that she had been discovered. She suddenly realized he was referring to the music. She shook her head, emitting a short laugh. "Some new age sounding CD. Wasn't quite what we were looking for, was it, Ollie?" she said, glancing nervously at the backseat. Ollie, as usual, ignored her.

Roger glanced back at him and shook his head. He slid into the front seat and started the car.

"Ollie," she said to the child. He didn't respond. "Maybe we should get him back," she said, shifting her gaze back to Roger.

He glanced up at the sky. "I guess so," he said. "Clouds are starting to roll in, anyway."

He drove past the parking lot and stopped at the entrance to the dock where they had left the boat.

"I'll let you guys out here. You can get Ollie on the boat while I park the car."

She glanced back at the boy. She had hoped to be able to snag the datebook and smuggle it back to the island, but there was no way she'd be able to do that with Roger staring at her. "Ollie's fine. He doesn't mind a little walk. It'll be good for him."

Roger shook his head. "We've had problems with him before. He's okay coming here, but he's a pest going back."

She looked at Ollie again. She couldn't imagine him being a pest, at any time. But still, Roger might get suspicious if she argued too much.

"C'mon, Ollie," she said, hopping out of the car and opening his door. Alex offered him her hand, and Ollie grasped it tightly as he quietly followed her back to the boat.

She was helping Ollie with his life preserver when Roger came back with the groceries. Alex finished tying on the preserver and turned back toward the front, taking her place next to Roger. "He's usually not this bad," Roger said, nodding toward Ollie. "Must've been being in Leslie's car without her."

She nodded sympathetically. It had been hard for all of them. But worth it, Alex realized as her thoughts drifted back to the datebook stashed under the seat. She would have liked to inspect the inside of Leslie's trunk. After all, if Leslie had hurried back to the island after a stay in New York, there had to be an overnight case somewhere. Unless someone had already unpacked it.

Alex realized that she might not have another opportunity to search Leslie's car, but she would have an opportunity to get back inside Leslie's bedroom. But first she wanted to visit the construction site.

"Ready to go back home, Ollie?" Roger asked.

Ollie's eyes flicked open. "Promise me," Ollie replied.

Roger laughed. "I promise you. We're on our way."

When they arrived back at the estate, Roger asked Alex, "Want to come in for some late lunch?"

"No thanks," Alex replied politely. "I've got some things to take care of before the rain hits."

"Sure," Roger said in his typical laidback manner. "Whatever."

Alex walked toward the barn until she heard Roger shut the front door. She then cut around the barn and across the arena, running quickly toward the woods. It would have been faster to take a horse with her, but she didn't want to have to worry about all of the glass and nails surrounding the construction site.

The afternoon sun was casting long shadows through the trees, fragrant with the sweet smell of pine. A needle wedged inside her sandal, and she hurriedly pulled them both off, running the rest of the way in bare feet. Only when she reached the clearing in front of the site did she stop to put them back on.

She stepped lightly and carefully toward the house, as if a wrong or heavy step might awaken the dead. She walked up the brick front steps and twisted the front door knob. Surprisingly, it wasn't locked. She slowly pushed the door open and peeked inside.

The entranceway looked like a typical construction site. Several Coke cans were scattered on the cement floor along with sawdust and nails.

Alex stepped inside carefully, leaving the door open. She walked through the dusty, half-constructed rooms, trying to form a vision of what the finished house would have looked like. It was obvious that despite the rough state of construction, quite a bit of money had already been invested. She wondered what had led to them stopping construction on the house. Was it a mere coincidence that Leslie had died only days later?

Alex stopped in front of a large winding staircase that did not yet have a railing. She stepped up onto the first step, cautiously testing it to see if it was strong enough to support her weight. Convinced that they were more durable than they looked, she began to climb the stairs, carefully stepping around the nails that were scattered around.

Alex's mind drifted back to Leslie. It was hard not to envision her walking up these very stairs. Was she distraught when she made her fatal climb . . . or drunk? Alex glanced down at the entranceway beneath her. The lack of a banister implied that Leslie had not been all that intoxicated. She would have had to have her wits about her in order to make it upstairs without breaking her neck.

But if she was going to kill herself, why do it here? Why not the other house? Unless, of course, she hadn't killed herself at all. Perhaps she had been planning to meet someone here, and that same someone had killed her.

Alex arrived at the top of the stairs and looked around her. The rooms had no doors on them yet—or walls, for that matter. But wooden beams had been constructed which clearly outlined the various rooms. She walked down what was to have been the hall, evident by the wooden posts on either side of her. She stopped at the frame of a large doorway at the end of the hall and stepped inside.

The room was outlined with the same bare wood posts that marked the other rooms. What made this one different was that the far wall facing the sea was completely open. A large balcony had been under development, but the wood flooring was all that currently existed. If Leslie wanted to kill herself, she could have simply run across the room and leaped to her death. There were no pieces of plastic over the windows, no bits of wood to hinder a fall. It was perfectly clear.

Alex walked slowly and cautiously toward the balcony under which Leslie's battered body had been found. She reached the door frame and stopped, holding on to the inside as she peered out. It was a magnificent, spectacular sight. Almost hypnotizing. The sea had grown rough in the hour since they had docked back on the island. She could see the dark, ominous rain clouds moving in toward the island. She figured she had about half an hour before it really got nasty.

Alex peered down at the floor of the balcony before focusing back on the rocks about a hundred feet below. Supposing that Leslie's death was not a suicide, and someone had murdered her, he had chosen a wise place. No one would survive a fall from a balcony like this.

Unless she was already dead by the time her body hit the rocks.

Of course, not only would an autopsy have determined if Leslie had died from wounds suffered before her fall, but a pathologist would have also been able to determine if Leslie's fatal injuries had been consistent with a forward or backward fall. If she had landed on her back, that might signify that she had been backing up, perhaps even backing away from someone. If she had landed facedown, her injuries would be consistent with a suicidal jump.

A soft wind blew through the room, causing a pencil to roll across the floor. Alex jumped nervously and looked toward the noise. She breathed a sigh of relief as she walked over to the pencil. As she bent down to pick it up, she spotted something in the corner, peeking out from a piece of plywood. The corner was dark and littered with several old Coke cans, some of which had been used as ash trays. Walking toward the littered corner, she picked up the item that had caught her attention. It was a nylon. An expensive, silky nylon, the kind that needed a garter to hold it up. It looked exactly like the stockings Alex had found in Leslie's dresser. It must have been Leslie's, but why would she have taken it off in this house? Here in this unfinished room?

The door slammed shut, and she instinctively shoved the nylon into her pocket.

"Anybody there?" she called out, only to be met with silence. She laughed. Of course no one was there. The wind had obviously blown the door shut. After all, Roger was back at the house with Ollie, and Steve was in Miami. She was just feeling jumpy.

Alex glanced back toward the balcony once more. There was another theory she had to consider. Perhaps Leslie's death had been an accident. Maybe she had spontaneously decided to see how the construction was coming along. Alex touched the nylon in her pocket. Alex could see her now, standing there, in the same spot where she was now standing. Her long blond hair blowing in the gentle breeze. She had been hot, uncomfortable from her trip. She had stopped to take off her nylons. After all, she was home now. She wanted to be comfortable. She pulled one off and dropped it on the floor as she focused on the other. The breeze picked up, and the nylon blew away from her, out toward the balcony. She paused to pick it up, but the breeze blew it even farther. It was a dare now, and she didn't think twice about venturing out onto the half-finished balcony. But something had happened. Something went wrong. She had lost her balance and . . .

Alex shivered slightly as she turned back toward the door. She was not alone.

"Steve!" she gasped.

He stood in the doorway, staring at her coldly, his dark eyes radiating the fire of betrayal. "What are you doing here?" he commanded in a throaty, hoarse voice.

She backed away. "I was out walking. The door was open. I was curious . . ."

"Curious?" he said, approaching her slowly.

She nodded, backing away fearfully toward the open balcony. "What are you doing here, anyway?" she asked, attempting to lighten the atmosphere. "I thought you might be staying in Miami . . ."

He grabbed her arms, holding her tightly. "I thought you were instructed to stay away from this place," he said, his hands gripping her arms so tightly it was impossible for her to move.

"You're hurting me," she said, causing him to release his grip immediately.

He backed away, running his fingers through his hair as he shook his head. He turned and faced the balcony, staring out at the waves crashing on the rocky surface below.

Alex glanced toward the doorway. She could make a run for it, right now, while he was distracted. But where would she run to? She was trapped on the island. Trapped by her own devices. She began slowly making her way toward the door.

Steve's voice stopped her. "Alex," he said, looking at her. His brown eyes were tired and bloodshot. "You know your nightmare? The one that makes you scream? Well, I have one, too. The only difference," he said, his voice becoming almost a whisper, "is that mine doesn't go away with daylight."

She stood still, almost holding her breath. Was he about to confess? She had to help him, guide him into his confession.

She took a few quiet, tentative steps back toward him. She knew enough from her years of reporting that she had to soothe him, to remind him that he trusted her.

"Tell me about your nightmare," she said quietly.

He turned back toward the water.

"Trust me, Steve. Tell me . . ."

He laughed. It was not a warm laugh, but a cold,

short sound that emanated his distrust. "Tell you and I'll feel better, right?" He shook his head. "I'll tell you what will make me feel better. To get rid of this house. Which I intend to do next week."

"What are you talking about?"

"I'm tearing this place down," he said softly, his voice becoming sad again. "I'm getting rid of it. I can't bear to look at it anymore."

He turned back toward her. Tears glistened in his eyes. He walked up to her and wrapped his arms around her, holding her tightly. He pulled back and looked into her eyes, as if searching for salvation. "I'm sorry if I frightened you when I came in. I was just surprised to see you here."

She pulled him to her, as though he was a child in need of comfort. "It's all right," she said, hugging him. "I understand. You need to move on . . . to put Leslie's death behind you."

He pulled away. "No. You don't understand." He turned away again, facing the water. "The next few weeks might be difficult for us, Alex. You're just going to have to trust me," he said. He looked at her again, their eyes locking. "As I've decided to trust you."

It was obvious that something had happened with the case, she realized. Something that had upset him. She thought back to the boys who had claimed they heard Leslie scream. "What happened in Miami?"

He walked toward her and took her hands in his. "They've decided that the boys' statements merit an autopsy."

"They're exhuming the body?" she said.

Steve pulled her toward him. "On Friday," he whispered.

Alex felt a pang of disbelief shoot through her. Suddenly, she didn't want a pathologist report. She wanted everyone to move on. To leave Steve and Ollie alone.

"Oh, Steve," she said sincerely. "I'm sorry."

He looked at her, brushing her hair away from her face.

"But maybe it's for the best," she continued. There was an element of falsity to her voice. "The autopsy will prove what you've said all along . . . that Leslie committed suicide. People will leave you alone," she added hopefully.

He walked toward the balcony, stopping at the doorway. The wind whipped around them, blowing their hair and causing a shrill, haunting noise to emanate through the house. "The media are vultures," he said. "They don't have a conscience. They will interpret the report as they want to interpret it. It won't make any difference. I'll be convicted by a mass jury . . . even if there isn't a trial."

"But," she said carefully, "how do you know she *wasn't* murdered?"

His body stiffened, but he did not turn back toward her. Instead, he continued to face the water. "What do you mean?"

She walked around to face him, standing in front of him with her back to the open expanse of the sea. She knew that he could push her off easily. But she also knew that he wouldn't.

"I mean, maybe she was having an affair. And the person she was having an affair with killed her. Maybe it was even a construction worker . . ."

"Stop," he ordered, focusing his cold, dark brown eyes on her. "She killed herself. She'd tried before. This time she was successful."

"How do you know?" she persisted. "There wasn't any note . . ."

Steve turned away. Alex stopped. She had just assumed there wasn't any note. If there had been, why hadn't he turned it over to the police? Why would he hold on to a piece of evidence that would exonerate him? Unless he didn't want the contents to become public.

"Steve," she said, grabbing his arm. "Was there a note?"

"Come on," he said, ignoring her. "I'll drive you back."

"Answer me," she said, practically shouting above the wind. "Was there a note?"

He turned back toward her. He shook his head.

"Why did you stop construction on this house the week before she died?" she asked.

"Why do you ask?"

"Well, it's just kind of weird," she stuttered. "A weird coincidence. Days after you stopped work on the house, Leslie killed herself . . ."

"Leslie was the one who wanted them to stop work. She wasn't happy with the design. She wanted to rework the layout of the rooms . . . at least that's what she said." He shook his head. "I think it's just what you said . . . a coincidence."

He offered Alex his hand. "C'mon. A storm is coming. I don't know how strong these beams are," he said, motioning to the supports that were holding up the makeshift roof. "We need to get back."

Twenty

It was close to midnight when the rain showers turned into a full-fledged storm. Alex jumped out of bed and attempted to close the shutters as the wind whistled around the barn. As she listened to the neighing of the spooked horses beneath her, she briefly pondered venturing into the barn to try and quiet them somehow.

She fastened the shutters as well as she could and sat back on her bed. She wished she could blame her inability to sleep on the horses, but the truth of the matter was that she didn't mind the hubbub in the barn. She wouldn't have been able to sleep tonight, anyway.

After deciding that there was really nothing she could do to soothe the animals, she crawled underneath her sheet and pulled it up around her chin. She was focused on Steve, and his behavior at the house where Leslie had died. What did he mean when he said he had a nightmare that didn't go away with daylight? Had he been on the verge of confessing to Leslie's murder? And what if he had confessed? Would she have had the strength to seek justice?

She pulled the covers over her head. She commanded herself to get some sleep. There was nothing she could do until morning. She had done everything she could this evening, including writing to Tim and informing him about the discovery of Leslie's datebook. She had given him the address she had found in the datebook and asked him to track it down for her. She had also asked him to check on the departure times of flights from New York to Miami on July thirteenth.

Alex was almost certain not only that Tim would honor her request but that the information guaranteed an extension of her stay there as well.

Her thoughts were shattered as the shutters broke free from their hold and began to bang against the outside wall, allowing the rain to blow into her room. She threw the sheet back and jumped out of bed. As she pulled the shutters against the wind, a small splinter jammed into her pinkie finger. She fastened the shutters and sucked on her finger. Immediately, the shutters popped open again, and the rain continued to blow into the room, soaking not only the nightshirt she was wearing but the bed as well.

She had had enough. She grabbed her denim dress

and slipped it over her nightshirt. She glanced in vain for an umbrella that she knew did not exist.

With a burst of energy, she opened the door and, without hesitating, plunged into the stormy elements. Within seconds, she had made her way down the slick staircase and across the muddy driveway to the temporary refuge of Steve's front door.

Alex knocked. She felt awkward, as if she were dropping in on an old boyfriend who just might have other plans for the evening. She knew she was being ridiculous. After all, Steve *was* her landlord. And her apartment was a wet mess right now.

"Alex!" Steve said, flinging open the door and helping her inside. "What's the matter?"

"I'm sorry to bother you," she said. "But my shutters won't stay closed, and the rain is blowing in . . ."

"Do you want to stay here tonight?" he said, looking at her sympathetically. She was drenched.

She paused.

Steve sighed. It was obvious that Alex didn't even want to stay in the same house with him. "Or do you want me to fix them now?"

"I'd like you to fix them," she said, trying not to think of her wet bed.

"Okay," he said, his expression tightening. "What's the matter with them?"

"The latch isn't working."

"I can hammer them shut until morning. Then I'll have Roger replace them if he needs to."

She nodded. "Okay."

"Why don't you sit down in the living room?" he said, motioning toward it. "It will take me a minute to find the hammer."

She wandered into the living room and sat down on the couch, hugging her knees to her chest. The rain storm hadn't cooled the island any, but she still felt chilled. She wondered what Steve had been doing in the dark house. She could tell by the way he was dressed that he hadn't been boxing. He was wearing his usual uniform of jeans and a rugby shirt.

She felt a hand on her head and looked up. Steve was brushing her wet hair away from her eyes with his free hand. He held the hammer in his other.

"Do you want anything to drink before we go?" he asked in a voice he usually reserved for Ollie.

She shook her head as she stood up, suddenly aware of what she must look like.

"All right," he said, smiling kindly. "We'll have to make a run for it. I can't find the damned umbrella."

She shrugged. "The rain has already done its damage."

"Easy for you to say," he said teasingly. "You've already taken a shower with your clothes on." He opened the door. "Let's go," he said, holding the door open for her against the gusts of wind that threatened to blow it shut before they even made it outside. Alex began to run back to her apartment as Steve ran on ahead of her. He was inside before she even reached the stairs.

She ran up the stairs, following him. She gasped when she entered the apartment. The situation had grown worse since she had left. Little puddles of water were on the floor, and everything within five feet of the windows was soaked. Alex glanced nervously toward the closet where she had stashed not only her computer but the nylon as well. So far, at least, the closet looked dry.

Steve shook his head as he wiped the rain drops away from his eyes.

"This place is a wreck. I'm going to nail the shutters closed, but you can't stay here tonight. Come back to the house with me. You can take a nice, long, warm bath and sleep in the same room you slept in when you had your accident."

She shook her head.

"You don't have a choice," he said, pulling a nail out of his wet jeans pocket. He nailed the shutters shut and then turned back toward her. "Grab some dry clothes. And let's go."

Back at the main house, Alex ran the tub water while she peeled off her wet clothes. She stepped into the warm water and sat down, sliding underneath the surface. She closed her eyes, attempting to relax. She quickly decided it wouldn't be possible. It made her too uncomfortable to have Steve so close. She gave up on the warm bath and stepped back out of the tub, drying herself off and slipping into her nightshirt.

She stepped into the hall and quietly made her way back to her room.

"That was quick."

Steve's voice caught her by surprise, and she inhaled sharply as she spun toward him, putting her hands over her terrified heart.

"I'm sorry," he said, grinning. He had changed into his night attire—which consisted solely of a pair of boxers. "I didn't mean to startle you."

Alex shook her head as a hint of a smile crept to her lips. "I guess I'm just a little jumpy."

She looked behind him curiously. What had he been doing at that end of the hall? There was nothing down there except Leslie's room.

He nodded as he walked up to her. "Storms can have that effect." He hesitated as he gazed sensually into her eyes. "Did the bath make you feel better?"

Alex's eyes glanced over the well-defined chest she had memorized with her mouth. She blushed, looking away.

"I hope my attire doesn't embarrass you," he said, a little surprised by her blush. "I didn't think twice about it. After all, you've seen me in much less," he added, approaching her.

"Good night," she said stiffly, rebuffing his advance as she turned away.

She walked into her room and shut the door behind her. She leaned against the door until she was satisfied that Steve had gone downstairs. She then crawled inside the hard, single bed, closed her eyes, and listened.

She soon heard the all-too-familiar sound of Steve hitting the punching bag.

Thump, thump . . . thump, thump . . .

It was a frightening sound, she decided. A sound of anger.

She sat up straight.

She couldn't sleep. She needed to find out if Steve had been in Leslie's room and, if so, what he had been doing. She crept out of bed, pausing at the door as she took a moment to question the risk. Without her handy bobby pin, she doubted she would even be able to get inside the room.

In a desperate quest for answers, Alex slowly pushed the door open and slipped into the hall, quietly making her way back toward Leslie's room.

She grabbed the handle to the door and stepped back, surprised. The door was unlocked.

She held her breath as she leaned against the door, pushing it open just far enough to slip inside. Once inside the room, Alex stood still as she pondered her next move, allowing her eyes to acclimate to the darkness. Suddenly, a flash of lightning illuminated the room.

Alex gasped.

The room had been entirely cleaned out. All of the furniture was gone. All of the pictures were gone. Nothing was left.

Alex walked over to the closet and slid open the door.

Empty. Completely empty.

"Looking for something?"

She whipped around. Steve stood behind her, his arms crossed in front of him. He had put on jeans, but his chest was still bare. He dropped his arms and began walking toward her in the dark, with only the occasional flash of lightning to mark his way.

"I heard a noise, and the door was open . . ." she began nervously.

"What is it that you're looking for?"

She shook her head, backing up against the wall. "Nothing. I just . . . I thought that maybe Ollie was in here . . ."

He grabbed her by her arms. "Don't play games with me, Alex," he whispered in her ear. He breathed in the sweet smell of her hair. "This is the second time today I've found you where you weren't supposed to be."

"I know. I'm sorry. I'm just curious by nature," she said, shrugging her shoulders.

Steve dropped his arms and took a step backward. He looked at her searchingly, as though he was determining the truthfulness of her words. "This was Leslie's room," he said finally.

"She didn't even sleep in the same room as you?" Alex asked, pretending innocence.

He shook his head. "I told you. Our marriage wasn't like that," he said, turning to leave.

"What happened to the furniture?"

He stopped. "For a month after she died, I couldn't bear to go in here." He ran his fingers through his hair as he turned toward her, his face a mask of sorrow and pain. "When we were on the boat, I had Roger clear this room out. I wanted everything gone. I couldn't stand to look at it any longer."

He glanced at her eyes. She stood in front of him, silently evaluating him. He hesitated before turning back toward the door.

"I don't understand why you didn't divorce her," she said suddenly. He stopped.

"What?" he asked, still facing the door.

"Surely it would've been best for both of you."

He turned to look at her. "Divorce isn't always the best way . . ."

"I don't understand," she said, her voice rising. "You claim you didn't even have a marriage. Was it

Ollie? Or was it the money? Or maybe you just couldn't bear to let her go . . ."

"Alex!" Steve called out angrily, interrupting her. He stood in front of her, breathing heavily as he tried to swallow his rage.

Alex put a hand to her forehead as she shook her head, embarrassed at her outburst. "I'm sorry," she said quickly. She moved toward the door. "I'm sorry," she said again.

"Wait," Steve said, stopping her. His voice had lost its edge, and he was in control once more.

She stopped walking but did not turn back toward him. She felt his hand on her arm.

"C'mon," he said, steering her toward the door. "I think we need to have a talk." He shut the door behind them as he nodded for her to follow. Alex trudged after Steve silently as he led her down the stairs and into the living room.

"Have a seat," he said, motioning toward the couch. She sat down obediently.

He picked up what looked to be the same crystal decanter she had seen in Leslie's room and poured her a glass of the gold liquid, not even bothering to ask her if she wanted it first. "Here," he said, handing her the glass before he poured himself the same.

Alex held it to her nose and took a quick whiff. Scotch.

He sat down next to her. She could see the little beads of sweat that had formed on his perfectly sculpted, hairless chest.

"I told you on the boat that Leslie and I had a long history of problems," he said. "I also told you that I wanted a divorce. But Leslie, despite her feelings about me, did not want one. She was adamant."

"But you still could've divorced her . . ."

He shook his head. His face hardened as the muscles in his jaw visibly tightened. "No. She told me that if I divorced her, she would take Ollie away from me."

Alex looked away. "But surely she couldn't take away your son."

"Maybe. Maybe not. But she could drag out the divorce, making it extremely unpleasant for everyone, especially Ollie. I wasn't willing to subject him to that. My freedom wasn't that important to me."

"Maybe she loved you," Alex said weakly, although she had a feeling it was money, not love, that motivated Leslie.

He shook his head. "Hardly. Leslie didn't know the meaning of the word." He paused. "Except with Ollie. She loved Ollie. She hated everyone and everything else. Including herself." He looked at his glass.

He sighed. "I did try and divorce her once. Before I understood exactly how much she despised me. It was last spring. I offered her a divorce. I offered to give her everything I had. The company. The houses. The money. Everything. I was willing to walk away from it all . . . with Ollie. He was all I wanted."

"And?"

"She laughed at me. She said I would never take Ollie away from her. Never. She wanted custody. Sole custody. She threatened to drag out any divorce, to bring Ollie into it . . ." His voice drifted off. He shook his head. "I couldn't do that to him."

She glanced away. So there was a reason Steve might have wanted his wife dead. It was the only way out of a bad marriage.

He reached a hand toward her, running his fingers gently along the outline of her face. "I know this is difficult for you, and I'm sorry. But I wanted to tell you the truth. I don't want there to be secrets between us. I want you to trust me. I *need* you to trust me," he said, leaning forward as he kissed her chin. He reached his hand behind her neck and drew her in toward him, kissing her hard on the lips.

She pulled back.

"Alex, I don't understand," he said tenderly. "I thought you and I had something . . ."

"Stop it," she said, brushing him away as she stood up. "I just . . . I'm having a hard time swallowing this whole divorce thing."

Steve looked at her as if he couldn't believe what he was hearing. "You don't believe me?" he asked incredulously.

Alex shook her head miserably. She dropped into the chair. "I don't know what to believe anymore," she said, shrugging her shoulders. She wanted to ask him specifically about the woman he was supposedly involved with, but she didn't dare for fear that her question would reveal that Roger had been confiding in her.

"I had a son to consider, for God's sake. And I had no intention of having him grow up without a father and going through . . . what I went through." His eyes seared into hers. "You of all people should understand that."

Alex glanced away. She found Steve's talk about family loyalty difficult to understand, but perhaps that was just because she knew nothing about family loyalty. She wouldn't recognize her own father if she bumped into him on the street.

"Alex?" She glanced up. Steve was standing in front of her, his forehead creased with concern. "Look, I know there were rumors out there about me and my supposed affairs. That was Leslie's doing. She wanted to make sure that if I were ever to leave her, the court's sympathy would be with her. She was always accusing me of having someone else." He shrugged his shoulders. "I don't know what else to say."

She nodded. "I'm just . . . tired. I think maybe I should go to bed," she said. "It's been a long day."

"I'm sorry about what I said . . . bringing up your father . . ."

"It's all right," she said quickly, standing up. "Look," she added. "I've never believed in fairy tales, and I think the idea of having a traditional family where everybody really loves each other and thrives on togetherness is a pipe dream. But I think Ollie is lucky to have a parent who cares enough about him to . . ." She paused. She looked him in the eye as she said, "To sacrifice his own happiness for him. He's luckier than a lot of other children."

He nodded. "Like the child who still haunts your dreams?" he asked quietly.

Alex turned pale as she glanced back at him. "What?"

He stood in front of her. "The child who died," he said gently. "What happened?"

"I told you I couldn't talk about it," she replied angrily.

"I might be able to help you."

"No," she said. "You don't seem to understand. I don't want to confide in you, Steve. Not you. Not anyone. Do you understand?" she pleaded. "I just want to be left alone."

"No," he said, grabbing her arm. "We belong together. I know it. I can feel it. Do you know what the chances are of you ending up here on the ranch like you did? But you did. Just when I was losing hope that I would ever have any normal type of life again, you appeared. You gave me back my hope, Alex. My dreams—not only for myself but for Ollie. I want an opportunity to do the same for you."

She shook her head. "Oh, Steve," she said weakly. "You don't understand . . ."

"*You* don't understand," he said, cutting her off. "I love you, Alex," he said, more confident with every word. "Once my personal problems are settled, I want to marry you."

She backed away. "No," she said sharply. "You don't even know me."

"I know you think way too much. I know you have nightmares that make you cry in your sleep. I know you sigh softly when I kiss you. I know you get tiny little crinkles in the corners of your eyes when you smile. I know you're smart, sweet . . ."

"Stop," she said, holding up her hand.

He took her hand and began kissing it, slowly pulling her to him. "Let me love you, Alex," he said softly. "Don't be afraid of me. I just want a chance to make you happy. Just a chance."

She grabbed both of his hands, steering them away from her body. But her eyes betrayed her. She wanted to believe him. She needed to believe him. "I'm confused."

"What's so confusing? I'm crazy about you. And you yourself told me that's what you wanted. Someone who's crazy about you and who listens to you. I love you, Alex. And all I'm asking is that you listen to me. I'm an old-fashioned guy. I don't go falling in and out of love. I just know that what I feel for you . . . is special. I want to spend the rest of my life with you. I'm just asking that you consider it."

"But what will people think?"

"Let them think anything they want. My wife was depressed. She tried to kill herself before, and she succeeded the second time. My son and I have been through a traumatic experience. He needs a mother. I want a wife."

It sounded so simple. Too simple. She turned toward the window.

He shook his head in frustration. "Why can't you believe that I love you?"

"I need some time," she said.

He put his arms around her, enveloping her in a hug. "There's no rush. We have all the time you need," he said hopefully.

She pulled back and looked up at him. "Steve. The coroner will find that she jumped out of the window. Won't they?"

He hugged her again. "Of course," he whispered in her ear.

Twenty-One

Tim handed the cab driver a twenty and jumped out of the cab, narrowly missing getting hit by a bike messenger. He swung the door shut and opened his umbrella. The past few weeks had been unusually cold and wet. He pushed his trench coat up around his neck and checked the address scribbled on the piece of envelope he had been carrying in his pocket. He looked up at the brownstone building in front of him. This was the place, 510 E. Avenue. He noticed the sign said "Dr. E. G. Mason, OB-GYN. Walk-ins accepted."

This was the place. He was surprised that Leslie Chapman, with all of her money, would go to a clinic in a shabby part of town when she could have gone to the best doctor in the city.

He jumped up the stairs, taking them two at a time. He wasn't thrilled at the prospect of trying to get a doctor to reveal confidential records. He didn't have to do this anymore in his career, and barely a day went by that he didn't appreciate that fact. But this was a favor for a friend. For more than a friend, he reminded himself. For Alex.

He had surprised himself by missing her since she had left. He still felt a certain degree of loyalty toward her. Maybe not sexual loyalty but emotional loyalty. After all, they had never really broken up. One day, she had simply moved out. They had never even had the obligatory "maybe we should see other people" speech. Although Tim had suspected that Alex felt a talk like that would have been a little ridiculous, considering he had never really stopped seeing other people, even when they lived together.

He had tried to explain to her why he was unfaithful. But, quite frankly, he couldn't explain something that he didn't understand himself. Alex had been everything he had hoped for. Beautiful, smart, independent, funny. But his sleeping with other women really didn't take away from his feeling for her. They were two different issues, as he had tried to explain to her, unsuccessfully. He knew he loved her. It wasn't that. He just couldn't see himself promising to spend the rest of his life with anybody right now. Not even her. But he would walk through fire for her. Which he had a sneaky suspicion he was just about to do.

He pushed the buzzer. "Good morning. May I help you?" a voice said.

He pulled out his press pass and flashed it at the video camera. "Good morning, ma'am," he said, noticing that he had adapted a rather folksy accent. *Knock it off,* he told himself. *This isn't Mayberry.* He cleared his throat. It had been a long time since he had done any less-than-legal undercover work, and he was rusty. Not to mention nervous. "I'm Tim Barnes, reporter for the *New York Times.* I'd like to talk to Dr. Mason, please."

"About?"

"A murder," he said, raising an eyebrow.

The buzzer sounded, and he entered the building. He walked up to the receptionist's desk as she slid the plastic panel open. She was in her early twenties, well built, with an expensive, toothy smile. "Have a seat," she said, still smiling pleasantly. "I'll see if he's available." She slid the plastic panel back in place and walked away from the window.

Tim took that opportunity to glance around the waiting room. It was plush, serene, and empty. The only lights were lamps placed in all corners.

"Sir," she said. He turned. She was standing in the

doorway. "You're in luck. Dr. Mason will see you now."

Tim was ushered into a cramped room, where a small man sat behind an enormous wood desk which seemed to dwarf both the man and the room. "Dr. Mason?" Tim asked.

The man stood up. "What can I do for you?"

"You are Dr. Mason," Tim said.

The man nodded impatiently. "And you are?"

"Tim Barnes. Reporter for the *New York Times.* I'm here to ask you a few questions about a patient of yours."

The doctor sat back down. "As I'm sure you're well aware, Mr. Barnes, there is such a thing as doctor-patient confidentiality."

Tim gave him the best patronizing smile he could manage. "I understand, Doctor. But I can assure you the patient I want to ask you some questions about is not concerned with confidentiality anymore."

"Well, then, she'll have to notify me herself."

"That will be impossible," he said, savoring the drama of the moment. "You see, she's dead."

The man's eyes narrowed. "Who's the patient?"

"Here's the situation, Doc," Tim continued. He was on a roll now. "This woman came to see you less than twenty-four hours before she was killed. I'd like to know if she found anything out at her appointment that might have upset her . . . or upset someone else."

"Who are we talking about?"

"Leslie Chapman."

"*The* Leslie Chapman?"

Tim nodded.

The doctor slid back in his plush leather chair. "I'm afraid you've been wasting my time. Leslie Chapman is not . . . rather, was not . . . a patient of mine."

Tim smiled impatiently. "We found evidence that she was here the day before she died."

"I've seen the reports of her death. And I can assure you, I haven't seen anyone who looked like Leslie Chapman."

"Do you mind if I check out your appointment book?"

"Yes. As a matter of fact, I do."

Tim slammed his fist down on the doctor's desk, startling both of them. He leaned forward. "A woman is dead, Doctor," he said dramatically. "Another woman may be soon if you don't help me. I need you to look through records and tell me who was here on Wednesday, July twelfth, at one P.M." Tim finished his outburst still leaning forward, staring angrily at the doctor.

The doctor paused. He swallowed. "I'll be back," he said finally.

Tim leaned back in his chair and smiled. If he had a cigarette, even though he didn't smoke, he'd light up.

The doctor came back a few moments later, followed by the receptionist. She held a large book in her hands. "This is my receptionist. She was working the day you say Ms. Chapman came in."

"We had several new patients that day," she said, annoyed at the inconvenience of having to look them up.

"She had an appointment at one in the afternoon."

"We had a 'Leslie Anne' at one o'clock."

Tim pulled out a photo of Leslie that he had snitched from the newsroom. "Did she look like this?"

She paused, studying the picture. "It could have been her."

"Doctor?" Tim said, showing him the picture.

"I told you, I know what Leslie Chapman looks like."

"Look at the picture," Tim ordered.

The doctor looked at it quickly. He hesitated. "It's possible," he said.

Tim kept the picture out. "Anything unusual about her visit?"

The doctor glanced at the receptionist. "Go pull her file," he said.

The doctor eyed Tim. He was obviously irritated. Tim looked down at his nails, which only seemed to irritate the doctor more.

The woman walked back into the room and handed the doctor a file. He opened it up. "Let's see . . . she might be the woman you're interested in. Didn't leave any phone numbers. No insurance. She paid in cash."

"Isn't that unusual?" Tim asked.

The doctor nodded. "Five-foot-seven. One hundred twenty-five pounds." He shut the file.

"Well? Why did she come here? Was she sick?"

The doctor shook his head. "This woman was three months pregnant."

Tim paused, allowing the information to sink in. "What did she want? An abortion?"

The doctor shook his head. "I don't think so. She said that her periods had been irregular most of her life. She just wanted confirmation that she was pregnant. It was obvious that she was."

Tim nodded. "One more thing. Did you prescribe any medication for her?"

The doctor glanced down at his notes. "Nothing."

"Are you absolutely positive?" Tim asked, leaning forward as he raised an eyebrow.

"Absolutely," the doctor answered, meeting Tim gaze directly. "By the way, do you need a picture of me for the paper?"

Tim glanced at him, confused.

The doctor shrugged his shoulders. "You know what they say: there's no such thing as bad publicity."

Tim looked away. "A picture isn't really necessary now. But thanks for the offer."

Twenty-Two

Alex opened her eyes. The good news was that she was alone. The bad news was that she was naked in Steve's bedroom. She jolted up in bed and grabbed around inside the covers for her nightgown. She put her fingers on it as Steve opened the door.

"Good morning," he said, sitting down on the edge of the bed.

"Good morning," she said, pulling the covers up.

"How are you feeling this morning?"

She shrugged her shoulders. "Fine, I guess."

"It's a great day. You'd never even know that we had a storm last night. I was thinking that maybe we could take advantage of it. Maybe have a picnic on the beach with Ollie."

She shook her head. "I've got work to do, remember?"

"I've already talked to Roger. He's bringing someone in to cover for you for the rest of the week."

She hesitated. "But I don't want anyone to cover for me."

"Come on," Steve said. "Please. I know you're scared about us moving too fast, and I'm sorry I said all that last night."

"You are?" she said, obviously not happy to hear him admit it.

"I'm not sorry about what I said. I meant what I said. But I'm sorry if I scared you. I know that you had wanted to take things slow."

She sighed. "It will take me about ten minutes to get dressed."

He smiled. "I'll get Ollie together. We'll meet you outside."

"Wait," she said. "Where's Roger?"

He shrugged his shoulders. "I don't know. Outside somewhere."

She looked toward the window, concerned.

"What's the matter?"

"I can't very well go traipsing across the yard in my nightgown. What if he sees me?"

Steve laughed. He opened his dresser drawer. "I think we can take care of that problem." He pulled out a sweatshirt and a pair of sweatpants. "Here," he said, setting them on the bed next to her. He used the moment to move closer to her, close enough to rub her chin affectionately with the back of his hand. "We'll be waiting," he said.

Alex threw his clothes on and slipped downstairs. She could hear Steve talking to Ollie as she practically ran down the stairs. She stepped outside in her bare feet. The day was as Steve had said: beautiful, warm, and sunny. She looked around for Roger. Several of the horses were already out in the fields. She started a half walk, half jog toward her apartment. She was almost at the barn when Roger stepped out of the darkness of the entrance. She squinted in the sun and gave him a quick wave.

He nodded as he waited at the foot of the stairs leading up to her apartment. He crossed his arms in front of him as he leaned against the building.

She didn't like the expression on his face. He looked unhappy. Displeased with her.

"I had to sleep at the main house last night," she announced in a loud voice. She smiled. "I was absolutely drenched last night. Steve had to nail the windows shut. My room was so wet I couldn't even sleep in there."

Roger just looked at her. "I fixed your windows this morning."

She nodded. "Thank you. Thank you so much. Well, I'll see you a little later. I've got baby-sitting duties today," she said, cutting around him so that she could run up the stairs.

He grabbed her arm. "Do you know what you're doing?"

She looked at him. His eyes radiated concern.

She shrugged off his arm. "If you dislike him so much, perhaps you should look for another job," she said.

"Or maybe transfer to another position within the company? Like you?"

Her face dropped. She stepped down closer to him. "What's that supposed to mean?"

"I mean, I know what kind of duties you've been performing. I know why you suddenly don't have time . . . why you've never really had time to do what you were hired to do."

She turned and began running up the stairs. If she stayed there much longer, she might say something she would regret. "He's got that other woman," he called out. "He wouldn't break up with her for Leslie. He's not going to do it for you."

She turned back toward him. "That's where you're wrong," she said coldly. "He asked me to marry him last night."

Alex shut the door and leaned against it. She felt she was beginning to lose her mind. She needed to make a choice. She couldn't keep playing this game both ways. Either she was going to decide to trust Steve and her own feelings of love for him, or else she had to give him up and turn against him, devoting herself to digging up enough evidence to earn her a place on the front page of the *New York Times*.

Alex opened her drawer and pulled out her swimsuit. Her decision had been made long ago.

*   *   *

The beach looked fairly unscathed from the winds the night before. Alex swung the picnic basket down onto the sand. Steve followed, carrying Ollie on his shoulders. "Excellent choice of a picnic spot," he said, smiling at her. "What do you think, sport?" he asked Ollie, playfully tugging on his legs. He lifted Ollie off his shoulders and stood him on the sand. Ollie stared back up at him, as if he couldn't make up his mind whether he was glad to be down or not.

"Who packed this picnic lunch?" Alex asked with a smile.

"I did," Steve said, playfully indignant.

Alex grinned and opened up. There were three peanut butter and jelly sandwiches and a bag of potato chips along with three cans of apple juice.

"I haven't eaten this well since fifth grade," she said.

He smiled. "I like to cook," he said teasingly.

She shook her head as she laughed. "It's obvious."

Steve pulled off his backpack and pulled out a large beach blanket.

"Here, sport," he said. "Come sit on this." He laid the blanket down on the sand. He looked up at Alex. "Are you going to go for a swim?"

"In a little bit," she said, taking off her T-shirt. "I like to get nice and hot first," she said innocently.

"Ahem," he said, winking as he cleared his throat. He motioned toward Ollie.

"From the sun," she added, kicking off her shorts. She was wearing her yellow tank suit for a change. She had always liked it, but it was a little more revealing than her blue one.

"Oh," he said, pretending surprise as he admired the way the yellow tank showed off her tan. "Well, I'm ready for a swim," he said, pulling off the white T-shirt he had been wearing with his black bathing trunks. "Ollie?"

Ollie sat on the blanket, staring down at the woven pattern on the blanket. Alex saw the mischief drain from Steve as he looked at Ollie. "Ollie?" he said again, holding out his hand. Ollie ignored him, lost in his own world. Steve bent down next to him. He traced his finger along the pattern on the blanket. He followed the pattern to Ollie's feet and ran his finger up his leg, playfully nipping him in the nose. Ollie looked at him.

"Let's go for a swim, son," he said, somewhat tired. He picked Ollie up. "You don't know what you're going to be missing," he called back to Alex. Alex smiled, stretching out on the blanket.

She watched him play with Ollie, dipping the child's feet in the water and then quickly lifting him up, holding him over his head. Seeing him with Ollie made her even more convinced she had made the right decision. This man was not a murderer. He was a loyal, devoted father who would never have killed the mother of his child. She had to believe in him. She *did* believe in him.

That was not the problem. The problem was more complicated, simply because it was not in her control. It had to do with emotions and feelings of betrayal, the feelings that Steve was bound to have when she informed him that she was not the woman he had thought her to be. She could see it now: *The good news is, yes, I'll marry you. But the bad news is, I'm a reporter who came here to destroy you. Sorry about that!* Would he forgive her? Or would he refuse ever to trust her again? Maybe even send her packing without listening to her explanation?

She swallowed back her anxiety. If Steve did indeed love her as he said he did, then he would have to accept the truth . . . and her. If not, well, she would have to go back to New York and try to see if she could salvage any part of what would be an extremely battered career.

Steve swung Ollie up onto his shoulders as he waded back out of the water. "I think he's had enough," he said, putting Ollie down beside her. "Will you watch him for me? I'm going to swim some laps."

"Across the Caribbean and back?" She smiled. Nothing like a good joke to loosen things up, she thought sarcastically.

He gave her a small laugh as though he appreciated the effort.

"Sure," she said, putting her arm around Ollie protectively. She drew a line in the sand. "Want to make sandcastles?"

Ollie looked at her. She smiled at him before glancing back toward Steve. Steve ran toward the water, his muscles contracting as if he was racing to battle. He had the body of a twenty-year-old lifeguard. As he dived into the cool water, Alex stood up. "C'mon, Ollie. Let's move closer to the water. It's cooler there."

Ollie took her hand, and they walked toward the moist part of the sand. She sat down at the tide line and motioned for Ollie to sit next to her. She scooped up a pile of sand and patted it into a small hill. Ollie watched her quietly. She kept going until, finally, she had several small hills. The water suddenly came in, smoothing out her hills in a single stroke. Ollie let out a cry, startling her.

"It's okay," she said.

Ollie cried again, putting his hands over the areas where her poorly created castles had been.

She moved to put her arms around him, and he cried out again. "Steve!" she yelled, looking toward Steve. But Steve had seen the commotion, and he was already on his way in.

He rushed out of the water. Ollie was banging on the sand now, crying harder.

"I was making sandcastles. The water washed them away," she explained quickly.

Steve picked Ollie up.

"Look, Ollie," she said, scooping the sand into a

pile again. "It's all part of the game. We can make new ones." She looked worriedly at Steve.

"I'm sorry," she said. "I thought he would enjoy . . ."

"It's not your fault. He'll be all right. He was just surprised." He pulled back, looking at his son. Ollie shook his head and wrapped his arms tightly around Steve's neck, nestling his head in his shoulder.

Then Steve did something strange. He smiled. "Shhh," he said, comforting his son. "Dad's here. It's okay," he said. He brought Ollie back to the blanket and laid him down. Ollie looked up at him. "Are you hungry, sport?"

Ollie gave him a slight nod. Steve smiled. "Let's eat!"

Half an hour later, they had moved to the shade, and Ollie was taking a little nap at the foot of a large palm tree. "Why did you smile?" Alex asked.

"When?" he asked.

"When Ollie was upset."

He smiled again, as though deep in thought. "He hugged me," Steve said softly. Alex thought back. She had been so uptight about Ollie being upset that although she had seen him hug his father, she hadn't thought twice about it.

"Yes," she said, thinking. "Yes, he did." She grabbed his hand and squeezed it.

"He even answered me when I asked him if he wanted some lunch," he said, caressing her fingers. "It's because of you."

She shook her head. "That's not true. I've seen you with him. You're so good with him. So patient."

He looked toward the water. He shook his head. "I don't know."

"What do you mean?"

He turned his back to her as he walked away. "I mean, you were right. Before, when you told me that Ollie needs special help. As soon as I can, I plan to get him some professional help. I had hoped he would just snap out of this, but it doesn't seem like it's going to happen."

Alex nodded. "Will you take him back to New York?"

He shrugged his shoulders. "Maybe London."

She looked at him, surprised. "What about your business?"

"It's in capable hands. I may even sell it. I don't intend to go back."

She paused for a moment. Was this the same man she had read about? The man who had risked and ignored everything and everyone for his career? "Why not?"

"I don't like what it did to me," he said. "This whole tragedy has really forced me to reevaluate what I want from life." He turned back toward her. "The kind of person I want to be. The kind of person I want to be with," he said, staring her in the eyes.

She glanced away. It was the opening she needed. "Steve," she began. "I want to tell you something." She paused as she looked at him. "I'm not who you think I am."

Steve laughed. "C'mon, Alex. Like I told you last night, I know you better than you think. I see the way you look at Ollie. I can see the love in your eyes. You're so patient with him. So kind. I see the way you are with the horses. The way you tamed Rosie. The way you tamed me."

He leaned in closer to her, his lips almost brushing against her mouth. "I think you know the power you have over me. I want you with me. I want you by my side during the day and in my arms at night." He kissed her, slowly and deeply.

She pulled away. "Oh, Steve," she said sadly. "There's something I need to tell you. About . . . me. My past . . ."

He paused, waiting for her to continue.

She looked away. "Is it about Lennie?" he asked quietly, encouraging her.

She shook her head. "No. Although, once I tell you this, I'll be able to tell you about what really happened with Lennie."

He nodded slowly. With a slight laugh, he said, "This is sounding serious."

Alex took a deep breath, summoning her courage. She blurted out, "I'm a reporter, Steve. I came here to get a story about you. To find out if you really did kill your wife."

The smile faded from Steve's lips. His brows furrowed in confusion as her confession began to register.

"I love you, Steve. You have to believe me. I really do. I'm telling you the truth because I want to stay with you. I want to marry you . . ."

His stare stopped her cold.

"I'm sorry," she offered.

He glanced away, his eyes settling on Ollie. "What have you reported so far?" he asked in a distant, empty tone.

"Nothing," she said. "I haven't given them any story."

His gaze shifted back toward her. "Why are you telling me this now?" he asked suspiciously.

"Because," she said desperately, "I love you."

Steve stood up and began walking toward his son.

Alex jumped up and grabbed his arm. "Say something."

He didn't have to. The disappointment and disbelief were obvious in his eyes. She dropped his arm. "Don't walk away, Steve."

"Congratulations, Alex," he said angrily. "You did an excellent job. You won over your subject and encouraged him to confide in you. A brilliant job."

"Don't do this," she managed weakly.

"What is your name, anyway? Or would you rather not tell me?"

"My name *is* Alex. Alexandra. My last name is Webster. Alexandra Webster. I was brought up in Grosse Pointe, Michigan. I've been a reporter ever since I graduated from college. I work for the *New York Times*. They didn't even want to send me here, but I needed a good story. An important story. I was covering a story about kids who were drug runners . . ." She rambled.

"I know the rest. I've read your stories," he said angrily. "Alex Webster, star reporter. Expert at invading privacy and disturbing lives."

She bit her lower lip. She understood why he was angry. She had expected it. But she hadn't expected him to walk away from her. From them.

"I know this seems terrible, but you have to believe me when I tell you that I wouldn't hurt you or Ollie. You have my word . . ."

"Your word?" Although he had interrupted her, it was not with anger. Instead, he spoke with an air of defeat, as if every word only served to remind him of her betrayal. "That doesn't mean much anymore, does it?"

Alex stood still as Steve picked up his sleeping son. Without so much as a glance in her direction, he began walking toward the road, carrying Ollie in his arms.

Twenty-Three

Alex dropped down in the sand and covered her face with her hands. It had gone even worse than she had expected. Still, she couldn't blame Steve for his reaction. She had only hoped, somewhat naively, that true love would conquer all.

She sighed as she picked her head up. She looked into the shimmering blue water in front of her as she pondered her next move.

She had no intention of simply leaving the island and running back to New York. Instead of withdrawing, she was going to fight to win Steve's trust once more. Somehow, she needed to prove herself worthy of his love.

Alex glanced back toward the path. If only she could prove to Steve that she did indeed believe in him, that she wanted to help him. Of course, if she was able to convince the public of his innocence, she would be able to give Steve and Ollie a chance to return to a life free from doubt and persecution.

But to achieve that, she needed concrete proof that Steve Chapman did not murder his wife.

Alex grabbed the picnic basket and began a slow jog back to her apartment. She had a lot of work to do. And she had to move fast. She wouldn't be surprised if Steve asked her to leave the island by the end of the day.

Back at her apartment, Alex pulled out her cellular phone and plugged in her computer. It was a relief not to worry about who might walk in and find her at her computer. There weren't any secrets anymore.

As she listened for the familiar sound of the computer accessing the system, she pulled the nylon out of an envelope she had stashed in her closet and set it on the table.

She looked at the screen. She had a message from Tim.

She opened the mail and read it slowly, taking in the information as though she was trying to memorize it word for word. She hit delete and looked up from the screen.

Leslie had been pregnant.

Alex leaned back in her chair as she carefully evaluated the impact this information had on the case.

If Steve had been telling her the truth when he admitted that he and Leslie had not been intimate for years, then the baby could not have been his. Alex frowned. If the police found out, they could use this to implicate Steve. She could already envision the headlines: "Jealous husband kills wife over infidelity."

But Alex disagreed. In fact, as far as she was concerned, Leslie's pregnancy helped prove his innocence. If Steve had wanted a divorce, he could have used her pregnancy to prove infidelity and sway the court in his favor, allowing him to win custody of Ollie.

Alex went over the facts in her mind. One: Leslie flies to New York for a doctor's appointment. Two: She finds out that she's pregnant. Three: She makes plans to return to Rye Island immediately. Four: She dies shortly after her return to the island.

Alex turned off her computer and folded her phone. She hesitated. Something was bothering her. If Leslie's pregnancy was enough to drive her to commit suicide, why not do it in New York? Why take the trouble to fly back to the island? Had her pregnancy been just one of several factors that inspired her to take her own life? Had she argued with Steve and flown back to the island in a fit of anger, taking her own life as soon as she arrived?

Alex shook her head. She was missing something. She was sure of it.

Alex paused. She picked up the nylon and ran her fingers over the silky netting. *Okay,* she thought. *Go over what you know one more time.* One: She finds out she's pregnant.

What do women typically do when they find out they're pregnant?

Tell the father.

And where was the father? Alex paused. The answer was right in front of her: On the island. As he still was.

Roger.

She felt her breath tighten as she realized she had ignored the obvious. Of course, she thought. Leslie had been having an affair with Roger. And when she found out she was pregnant, she rushed back to tell him.

But there was a problem with that theory. Leslie Chapman, by all accounts, liked money. She married Steve to get her inheritance. She refused to divorce him because she was afraid she wouldn't get enough money. Why would she excitedly rush back to share news that might encourage Steve to divorce her?

Alex shook her head. She just couldn't believe that a woman like Leslie would run off into the sunset with a man like Roger and have babies.

But perhaps Leslie had no intention of divorcing Steve. Maybe she had planned to raise the child as a Chapman. Or, more likely, she had planned to terminate the pregnancy. And when she shared her plan with Roger, he killed her.

But, of course, Alex reminded herself, the entire theory was blown apart by the fact that Roger had an alibi. Roger was flying on a trip from the Bahamas when Leslie died and didn't even arrive on the island until after Steve had discovered the body.

Alex glanced toward the window. She was not only jumping to some pretty big conclusions, she was giving herself a headache.

Alex stuffed the nylon back into the envelope and stashed it with her computer in the back of her closet. She checked her watch. She needed to stick to the facts. And she had to hurry. She had just enough time to shower and take some aspirin before she paid Roger a surprise visit.

Alex had seen Roger's cabin from the road, but she had never gotten close to it before. From the outside, the entire house looked to be the size of one big room. The white paint had begun to peel away years ago, and an old air-conditioning unit was sticking out of the front window. Weeds covered the sides and the front of the building.

She smoothed out the wrinkles of her crisp pink linen sundress and stepped up to the door. She knocked lightly.

Roger opened the door, wearing only a T-shirt and jeans. "Well, hello," he said, looking at her curiously.

"Can I come in?" she asked.

He held the door open, and she walked inside, aware that his eyes were taking in her every curve.

"Looks like someone needs to invest in a little Coppertone."

"Did I get burnt?" she asked, glancing at her arms. They didn't look burnt to her.

"I'd say no more than third degree."

"More good news," she said.

"More? What was the first piece? The intended nuptials?"

She hesitated, ignoring his barb. "So this is where you live," she said, nonchalantly changing the subject.

"Yes. It's my vacation villa in the sun," he said. "I assure you the brochure made it look a lot more spacious."

She smiled, appreciating his attempt at humor. The house was even more dismal inside than out. A small bed was shoved into a corner of the room. A kitchenette was in the far corner, along with a small refrigerator which she guessed contained only beer. To the right of that was a small kitchen table and two chairs. There was a door off to the right, which she guessed led to the bathroom.

"You'd never guess this was a church," she said.

He just looked at her. "Why are you here?" he asked. "To inquire about renting this place for the wedding?"

She glanced at him. Obviously, he hadn't spoken with Steve yet. "I want to talk to you. About Leslie."

The muscles in his jaw tightened. He motioned to the chairs. "Have a seat."

She sat down quietly.

"Does Steve know you're here?"

She shook her head.

Roger laughed. "That's a good thing. He wouldn't like it."

"Because of Leslie?"

The smile faded from Roger's face. "Because he doesn't like me."

"That's not true," she said. "He trusts you with Ollie. He fired everyone else but you. He must've liked you."

"What did you want to ask me?" he asked, irritated.

"I want to be certain that I'm making the right decision about marrying Steve," Alex said nonchalantly. "I mean, I've heard the gossip surrounding Leslie's death."

"I see," he said, with a hint of a smile. "And that's the only reason you're interested."

She looked away demurely. "Of course."

His hand shot across the table, and he grabbed her arm, digging his fingers into it. "Look at me," he said carefully.

She yanked her arm back. "What's the matter with you?"

He laughed. "I know who you are, Alex. I know who you really are, Miss Webster."

She stood up. She couldn't say his revelation surprised her. "How did you find out?"

He smiled at her sheepishly. "The detective. When he had some trouble tracking you down, I told him that there was a chance you might have been a reporter or something. The rest was easy, just a few phone calls. At least, that's what he charged me for. And he told me to give you a tip. In the future, you might want to think about changing your first name, too."

"Tell him thanks for the free advice," she said, irritated. "Why didn't you tell Steve?" she asked indignantly.

"Because I want him convicted of murder," he said slowly and deliberately.

She paused for a moment, unsure of whether he was making some sort of bad joke. From the intent way he was looking at her, she guessed he was sincere.

"And," she said, slowly sitting back down, "why is that?"

"Because I know he killed her. And I want him to pay for it."

"Those are pretty strong words," she said, keeping her cool. "Do you have proof?"

"Not exactly. But there's something that you should know. Leslie and I were . . . well . . ."

"Having an affair," she said, finishing his sentence.

He looked toward the window, with an expression that said his thoughts were far away. "Yes," he said finally.

"Okay," Alex said, gathering her thoughts. "Let's start at the beginning. How did you meet her?"

He looked at her. "Steve arranged it. He knew that I'd been having trouble. My company went bust. He offered to pay off all my debts. Take the company off my hands. Said he'd give me a well-paying job. All I had to do was fly his wife on and off the island. He'd set me up in a little place," he said, motioning around him.

"And you began an affair with her."

"Hey, I looked at it as part of my job," he said.

Alex paused. "You expect me to believe that Steve hired you to sleep with his wife?"

"When Ollie was in school, Leslie would leave him in New York with Steve. She'd be on the island all by herself. I think Steve liked having her gone. Out of his hair. Maybe he wanted her to be unfaithful, too, so he could divorce her and get the kid. I don't know," he said, shrugging his shoulders.

"So you think he wanted his wife to sleep with you," she said, shaking her head.

Roger threw back his head and laughed. "I thought you were supposed to be smart. A good reporter. Don't you see?" he said, fixing his gaze on her. "He knew I had a reputation for L and L . . . liquor and ladies. He chose me for her."

Alex eyed him carefully. She couldn't imagine Steve

273

would allow anyone who had a reputation for being a drinker to fly his planes. "But why would he do that? Did she need fixing up?"

"Of course not. She was beautiful and sexy. Steve never appreciated her. Not like I did. He didn't want to have to deal with her at all. So he sent me down to entertain her when she visited. And to keep an eye on Ollie."

"And so you did."

He nodded. "Yep," he said, standing up. "Want a beer?"

She shook her head. Roger opened the refrigerator, and Alex peeked over his shoulder, glancing inside. She had guessed wrong. A half-eaten loaf of bread was wedged in between the cans. Roger took out a beer and held it up to his cheek. "Feels good. Sure you don't want one?"

She nodded. "I'm sure." She waited until he had sat back down again before continuing. "So what happened?"

"She wasn't happy out here all alone with the kid. She kept to herself for a while . . . but, well, she was a very attractive woman. Things just happened."

"Did Steve know?"

"Of course. Like I told you, that's what he wanted. But then things got complicated."

"What do you mean?"

"Leslie and I fell in love. It surprised the hell out of both of us. She was talking about leaving Steve. She loved me that much."

"Did she tell Steve?"

He nodded. "He told her if she left him, he wouldn't give her a cent. And he'd make sure he ruined her."

"But that doesn't make any sense. You just said that he wanted nothing to do with her . . ."

"It was all about control," he said, slamming his fist on the table.

"But surely a judge . . ."

"Steve Chapman is a powerful man. He went crazy. He threatened her, telling her that he would expose her as a silly, frivolous woman, who had been unfaithful since the day they married. A woman who was so unstable that she had to be confined to a mental institution."

"Was she?"

"Was she what?"

"Unstable."

"Whatever she was, he made her that way. He turned her father against her, got the old man to leave him all the money. He hated her, but he was obsessed with her. He controlled everything. Still does."

"Did you pick her up from the airport the day she died?"

He looked at her, surprised. "What?" he said, momentarily confused.

"She was in New York. The day before she died."

"I know," he said, sitting down. "I talked to her Wednesday night."

"You called her in New York?"

He nodded.

"Was Steve there?"

He shook his head. "He was hardly ever home."

Alex hesitated. "What did you talk about?"

"She said she hated it there . . . in New York. Ollie was driving her crazy. She wasn't feeling well."

Alex paused. "Was she close to Ollie? Good to him?"

"Sure, he was her son." He looked at her. "What are you trying to imply?" he asked suspiciously.

She pursed her lips. "What else did she say?"

"She said it was a mistake to go back there. She didn't want to stay. She said she was taking Ollie and leaving Steve for good. She wanted me to pick her up the next day in Miami, but I couldn't. Steve had asked me to fly some executives to the Bahamas for him."

"So you think Steve followed her here?"

Roger nodded.

"So neither of them had planned to be on the island that weekend?" she asked, remembering Steve's statement that he had come to the island for a long-planned family weekend.

"No. Not at all. In fact, they were supposed to be in New York. But, like I said, she was only there a day. She couldn't stand being away from me, and Steve knew it. Just like he knew she was coming back here to be with me. That I had won. He couldn't stand to lose her. Especially to me," he said bitterly.

She hesitated, thinking. "Let's get back to the executive Bahamas trip. Was that usual? Asking you to fly some executives around?"

He looked up at her. "He had never asked me to do that before."

"If you weren't available to pick her up, how would Leslie get back to the island?"

"She and Ollie were going to take a cab to the ferry. We made plans to meet at about five. At the house that was being built. But I didn't make it till after six. By then it was too late. She was already dead."

"Why did you plan to meet at the construction site?"

He shrugged his shoulders. "Because Ollie stayed away from there. And he was coming back with her."

Alex stood up. A picture on Roger's dresser had caught her eye. She walked over to the dresser and picked it up. It was a picture of Leslie in front of the horse, the same picture she had seen in Leslie's room. The room that Roger had been forced to clear out.

"That was the horse that Leslie had before Rosie," Roger said wistfully. "She loved that horse more than she . . . she had to put it down last year."

Roger looked at the picture with a hint of pleasure, as if envisioning Leslie made him feel a little better. Alex studied his reaction. He must have hated Steve for making him clear out her room. Hated him enough to . . . She thought back to finding the datebook under the seat of Leslie's car. Hadn't he just told her that Leslie hadn't driven that car the day she died? "You put that datebook under the seat, didn't you?" she said, uttering the words almost as soon as she thought them. "You wanted me to find it."

He nodded.

"Where is it now?" she asked.

"It's in Steve's desk drawer. I had to put it back where I got it."

She shook her head. She was beginning to feel nauseated. "So you knew about the doctor."

He furrowed his brow. "What doctor?"

She cursed herself immediately, realizing her slip. There hadn't been any mention of a doctor in Leslie's book. Only an address. "I don't know," she said, shaking her head. "I was hoping you could tell me." She avoided his eyes. She couldn't look at him. She glanced at her watch. "I should be getting back."

Roger jumped up and grabbed her arm. "Don't lie to me," he said, pleading. "Please. What doctor?"

Alex was frustrated that she had let such an important piece of information slip right out. Damn! Now she had no choice but to tell him the truth. "She went to a gynecologist the day before she died."

He nodded, encouraging her to continue.

"She was pregnant."

Roger didn't respond. He just looked at her.

Alex pulled her arm away but continued to stand beside him. "You knew that, didn't you?"

"We were going to get married," he said softly. "She was the best thing that ever happened to me."

"Why didn't you tell this to the police?" she asked.

"It wouldn't matter," he said angrily. "He'd get off. I had to stay here and wait. Wait for him to slip. Prove his guilt."

The bitter, hard tone of his voice was enough to send shivers down her spine. Alex closed the door, not bothering to tell him that not only did she disagree with him, but she intended to help Steve do just the opposite.

By ten o'clock that night, Alex had not yet heard from Steve. Viewing this as a positive sign, she decided that she would wait until morning to ask for his forgiveness once again. Twenty minutes later, however, she had changed her mind. Alex walked over to her closet and pulled out the envelope containing the nylon. Realizing her dress was without pockets, she held the envelope in one hand as if it was a clutch purse.

She had to see Steve tonight. In the morning, he would be rushing off to New York for the autopsy and would be understandably preoccupied. She needed to talk to him one more time.

Alex walked over to the dark house. She opened the front door without knocking. "Steve?" she said in a loud whisper.

She walked around to his office. Steve was sitting behind his desk as if waiting for her.

He glanced up at her as she walked in.

"Steve," she said. "I want to talk to you."

He sighed. "I don't think there's anything to say."

"Just listen to what I have to say. I'm not asking you to forgive me. I'm just asking you to hear me out."

He nodded. "Go ahead."

Alex sat down in a chair facing the desk. She held the envelope in her hands, feeling the edges with her fingers. She took a breath and began. "I first heard about you a year ago. I mean, naturally, I knew who you were before that, but about a year ago your company took over my cousin's firm, and he . . . well, let's just say he didn't handle it all that well. My family—or, rather, my mother—asked me to investigate you."

"So this is a vendetta?" he said with disbelief.

"No! Not at all. I barely knew my cousin. It's just that, well, I started compiling a file on you." She took another deep breath. "Shortly after that, I wrote a story on kids who were drug runners. One of my sources, a little boy named Lennie Kosix, was killed," she said, looking away as her eyes filled with tears at the mention of Lennie's name. "He may have been killed because a dealer recognized him as my source." Her watery blue eyes focused back on Steve. "The managing editor of the paper demoted me to the Living Arts section. I thought that my coming here, investigating you, would prove that I was ready to be an investigative journalist again. You have to understand. I had nothing when I left. I needed this story . . ."

"So your career's in the crapper, and you're selling me out to get back on your feet."

"No! I wouldn't do that."

"Wouldn't you?" he asked with disbelief. "I suppose you're too ethical for that?"

"Steve, you've got to believe me. I wouldn't hurt either you or Ollie."

"Pretending to be somebody you're not . . . pretending to care when you don't . . . and you don't want to hurt us? What the hell am I supposed to tell Ollie? How could you do this to a child?"

"But I do care about Ollie. I don't want to hurt Ollie . . . or you. I just want us to go back to the way things were. I don't want to write anything about you at all."

"The way things were? I was in love with Alex Rowe. Alex Webster means nothing to me."

Alex hesitated. This was going worse than she had expected. "Look, I know how you must be feeling right now," she said, trying to stay calm. "I don't blame you. I just . . . want you to give me another chance."

"What else have you found, Alex?" he said as if he hadn't heard anything she had been saying. "Have you been going through my desk when I wasn't around?

Looking through phone bills? Interrogating my staff, my friends? I know how you people operate."

"Please, Steve," she said, looking into his eyes. "You *know* me. I know that you know what I'm saying is true. I'm sorry I didn't tell you earlier. I was torn between you and my career. I guess I knew that I couldn't have both. But I've made up my mind." She leaned forward. "It's you I want, Steve. You and Ollie."

"And what if I told you that I didn't want to go back to the way we were? What if I told you that I was sending you back to New York and I never wanted to see you again in my life? What would you do then?"

"There's no story, Steve," she said quietly. She resignedly leaned back against the chair. "You're innocent. And if you sent me back tonight, I'd simply return to the Living Arts section."

"You wouldn't tell them I was innocent?"

"It wouldn't matter. Because I don't have any proof." Alex paused. "If you let me stay, however," she said hopefully, "I can help prove your innocence. I can help you return to a normal life."

He shook his head. "No thanks."

She leaned forward in her chair. She wasn't giving up this easily. "Did you know that Leslie was pregnant?"

Steve sat motionless, stunned. "What?"

"She was three months pregnant when she died."

"How . . . how do you know that?"

"I found her datebook in her car. It had the address of a doctor's office in it. She went to the doctor the day before she died, Steve."

"Let me guess," he said angrily. "After you 'found' this datebook, you went and talked to this doctor?"

Alex shrugged her shoulders guiltily. "I, ah, well, I had someone check out the address and talk to the doctor."

Steve sank into his chair. He shook his head. "Oh

280

my God," he mumbled. "How could you do this to us, Alex?"

"Look, Steve. I'm sorry. But it's information that would've come out sooner or later." Alex glanced away. It *was* possible. However, it was also unlikely. "Roger knew she was pregnant," she said, her eyes focusing back on Steve.

"Roger?"

She nodded. "They were having an affair."

He eyed her suspiciously.

She looked at him curiously as she began to understand why he wasn't all that surprised at learning about Leslie's indiscretion with Roger. "But you already knew that, didn't you?"

"So tell me, Alex," he said tiredly, not bothering to answer her question. "Is Leslie's supposed pregnancy public knowledge over at the *Times* now?"

She shook her head. "No. The reporter who conducted the interview is extremely discreet."

"Right," he said sarcastically. "A discreet reporter."

Alex shamefully lowered her head. He did have a point.

Steve ran his fingers through his hair. "So, does Alex Webster, investigative journalist, think my wife's pregnancy ties in with her death? Do you think the news made her want to kill herself?"

She shrugged, unfazed by his anger. "I'm saying that it certainly is a possibility. It's also a possibility that she was murdered."

"By who? Roger? The supposed father of the supposed baby?"

"It's a possibility, Steve."

"He wasn't even on the island when she was killed," he said, frustrated. "He was flying some business associates from Nassau to Miami. The only people on the island were Leslie and . . . Ollie."

She stood up, holding the envelope out toward him. "What's that?" Steve asked, nodding toward the envelope.

Alex handed it to him. "I found this on the floor of the master bedroom in the house where Leslie died."

Steve opened the envelope slowly. He pulled out the nylon. "A stocking?" he asked, confused.

Alex nodded. "Why would she take off only one stocking before she killed herself?"

The anger burned in Steve's eyes. "What are you suggesting? That I killed her? Is that what you're insinuating?"

"No!"

"Who else knows about this nylon?"

"No one," Alex said.

Steve looked at her curiously. "Why didn't you tell anyone about it?"

"Because I know that they would've questioned why a woman would take off one nylon before she killed herself. Just like I did."

Leaving the stocking in the middle of his desk, he stood up and faced the window. He crossed his powerful arms in front of him as he spoke. "I think you should leave."

Alex swallowed. "Leave you alone? Do you mean tonight? Or that you want me to leave permanently?"

"I want you off the island, Alex. Tomorrow morning. I'd take you tonight if I could. But, since it's rather late, Roger will have to take you in the morning."

Alex nodded. Without saying another word, she turned and left the room.

Steve dropped back into his chair and twirled it around to face the door.

How could he have allowed himself to be so foolish as to fall in love with a reporter? To have allowed himself to be so blind at a time when he was fighting for control over his life?

How could he, such an intensely private man, have let down his guard with a woman he barely knew? Even proposing marriage to her?

He shook his head. She had played him for a fool, and he had performed the part beautifully.

He stood up and walked over to the window as he crossed his arms in front of him. He looked up at her apartment. The light was on, and he could catch a glimpse of her every now and then as she moved around the small room. She was packing. She wasn't wasting any time.

Steve felt a ball of pain well in his throat as he forced himself to turn away. He had made the right decision. She had to leave. Didn't she?

He glanced back at the stocking on his desk. Had she given him the stocking as a peace offering? He picked it up and clenched it in his hand as he closed his eyes.

Perhaps, he thought, he needed to slow down . . . to think things over for a while. Put himself in her shoes. She had been doing her job, and when she began to care about him, she had made a decision not to hurt either him or Ollie. Even though that decision had cost her her entire career.

Perhaps, he realized, he should be thanking her right now instead of sending her away.

Alex was zipping her duffle when Steve knocked lightly on her door. "Alex? I need to talk to you."

Alex glanced toward the door. She assumed he was coming to throw some more accusations her way. And she couldn't say she blamed him.

She opened the door. "I'm packed."

He nodded. "Look," he said, leaning in the doorway. "I'm sorry about what I said back there. I just . . . I guess I was a little surprised."

Alex shook her head, discouraged. "I don't blame you, Steve. I really don't. If I were you, I'd probably never want to see me again."

"Well, that's why I'm here. I'm not sure I want you to go."

"What are you saying?" she asked hopefully.

"You seem to think the autopsy is not going to prove my innocence. I hope you're wrong. In fact, I hope it will put this issue to rest once and for all."

Alex bit her lower lip as she looked away.

Steve was watching her carefully. "But if it doesn't . . ."

"If it doesn't, I can help you."

He paused as he stared deep into her eyes. "Do you think I killed my wife?" he asked quietly.

"No," she said sincerely. "But the autopsy results might not prove your innocence. They might be inconclusive. Or they might find something that they think would give you a motive for murder."

"Like?"

"The pregnancy. They might think that you murdered her because you had conclusive proof that she had been having an affair."

Steve shook his head as he leaned against the door.

"Tell me about Roger. Why did you keep him on when you fired everybody else?"

His forehead wrinkled in frustration. "I told you, Alex. Roger didn't kill Leslie, either. He wasn't even on the island. He had the helicopter. I would've seen it. And besides that, he's not a killer. He never would have killed Leslie."

"Because she was the mother of his child?"

Steve shifted his eyes away from her uncomfortably.

"You knew about their affair, didn't you?"

Steve sat down on her bed. He took a deep breath. "I suspected it, but . . . I've known Roger for a long time," he began. "We grew up in the same neighborhood. He used to be a boxer, too, but he never turned pro. He's had a tough life. A few unfortunate breaks. He's also been loyal to me. When Leslie was . . . killed, Roger was one of the few people who stood by me."

Because he wanted to hang you himself, she thought. "What do you mean, he's had a tough life?"

He paused. "He hurt his arm when he was eighteen.

284

It ruined his boxing career. He kind of went crazy for a while."

"What do you mean?"

"I mean he's got a record."

She raised her eyebrows, not hiding her surprise. "What?"

"I'm only telling you this because you offered to help, and I'm sure, with your considerable resources, you'd find out sooner or later. He's perfectly harmless," he added, offhandedly. "But when he was younger, he was thrown in jail for a while. It screwed up his chances of ever going to a good school. Getting a good job."

"So you helped him out?"

"He was a pilot. Even had his own charter business for a while. He ran into some money problems, so he came to work for me."

Alex sat down on the edge of the couch. She was stunned. Why didn't Roger tell her about his record? "What did he do that landed him in prison?"

"The official charge was assault. It was basically a bar fight that got out of hand."

"How did you feel about him being . . . involved with Leslie?"

"If he was, he has my sympathy. But I doubt it was anything serious. Leslie preferred the young, handsome, tennis pro type." He said the last statement without a hint of bitterness, as though it was simply a fact.

"According to Roger, they were going to get married."

He focused his brown eyes back on her. "He told you that?" he asked with disbelief.

"Not only that. He thinks you killed her."

"What?"

"He was in love with Leslie, Steve. And he thinks you murdered her."

Steve looked as if he had been struck. "I'm sorry,"

Alex offered. "But I think you should know. I wouldn't trust him. He's out to nail you."

"If that's true, why hasn't he gone to the police?"

"Because he wants evidence."

"No," he said, shaking his head. "I don't believe it."

"He told me, Steve. This afternoon. And not only that. He's known who I was since we were on the boat. If he was on your side, why didn't he tell you who I was?"

Steve stopped. It was hard to believe that his most trusted aide, his most trusted friend, had betrayed him.

"Not only that," Alex continued. "He told me that you were having an affair when Leslie died. That you were planning on marrying this woman."

"What?" Steve asked, shocked. "What woman?"

"He said she was married," Alex continued calmly. "He didn't tell me her name."

"It's bullshit." Steve focused his brown eyes on Alex. "Surely you didn't believe him."

Alex shrugged her shoulders. "Not now. But when he first told me . . ."

"That's when you said you needed space," Steve said, thinking back. It was all making sense now.

Alex nodded.

Steve shook his head. "Why is he doing this?" he said softly.

"Well," Alex sighed, "either he really believes that you killed her and he's trying to punish you, or he knows that you didn't and he's trying to frame you."

"Well, if he does believe I killed her, he'll get his evidence," he said evenly. "Tomorrow. Along with everybody else."

"And what if the autopsy shows that she was murdered?"

His bloodshot eyes focused on her. "Look," he said, shaking his head. "If I had wanted to give an interview, I would've given one long ago. My privacy is very important to me."

286

"I respect that. I'm not going to betray your confidence, Steve. I promise you."

He walked over to the door. He stopped with his hand on the knob and turned back toward her. "Thanks for not reporting everything you've discovered. Every hunch you have."

"I told you, Steve. I'm not going to be writing any story that you don't approve of."

He nodded as he looked away. "About you leaving. About us. I . . . I've got a lot to think about. Maybe you could stay here at least until after the autopsy. We'll talk more when I get back."

"Sure," she said, trying to contain her joy at her reprieve. "That sounds like a good idea."

He nodded. "I'll see you when I get back."

"Steve," she said, stopping him. "I know you're innocent. I'll do whatever I can to help you. I still feel like we're in this together."

He nodded as a brief, sad smile flashed over his lips. "Welcome to my nightmare, Miss Alexandra Webster."

At seven o'clock in the morning, Steve was knocking on her door. Alex, who was down in the barn, heard the knocking and ran out.

"I'm down here," she said from the bottom of the steps. Steve turned around, almost embarrassed. He was dressed in an expensive-looking back suit with a trench coat folded over his arm. His thick brown hair was slicked back away from his face, emphasizing his rather square jaw.

"I'm sorry to bother you," he said, "but I have to leave if I'm going to catch my flight, and I can't find Ollie anywhere. I was planning on taking him with me, but . . ."

"I'll watch him. I'd like to." She was flattered that he trusted her enough to watch his son. And she noted he had not asked Roger. Perhaps her warnings about him were beginning to sink in.

"Thanks," he said, nodding as he bounded down the stairs. He stopped in front of her. "I think he'd rather stay here with you, anyway."

"Good morning," Roger said, suddenly appearing behind Steve. Neither one had heard him walk up.

Alex pulled back, embarrassed, even though Roger had certainly not interrupted anything.

Roger shot Steve an icy glare. "You flying yourself today?"

Alex thought she could see a muscle tighten in Steve's jaw as he nodded. "Just to Miami. I'm flying commercial from there." He glanced at his watch. "I better get going." Just then, Ollie burst out of the woods and ran toward his father, flinging his arms around him.

"There you are," Steve said, visibly relieved. "I was worried about you." He bent down to look Ollie in the eyes. "I have to go to New York today. Do you want to come with me or stay with Alex?

Ollie looked worriedly from Steve to Roger and then finally to Alex. He walked over to Alex and took her hand.

Steve nodded. "That's what I thought." He glanced up at Alex. "You don't mind?"

She shook her head. "Not at all."

"Thanks." Steve climbed into his car.

"Good luck," Alex called out as he started the engine. Steve gave the three of them a quick nod before driving away.

"Come on, Ollie," Alex said, ushering the child back into the house as soon as Steve's car had disappeared. "I'll fix you some breakfast."

Roger followed her in, shutting the door behind them. "I need to talk to you," he hissed at Alex.

Alex gave him an icy stare, motioning toward Ollie. "Not now," she said clearly and concisely.

"Why not?" Roger demanded.

Alex looked at Ollie. "Go on in the kitchen. I'll be

there in a few minutes." Ollie shot Roger a worried glance before turning away.

She waited until Ollie was at the opposite end of the house before she began to speak. "Are you crazy?" she said angrily. "Talking like that in front of Ollie?"

"What difference does it make?" he said coolly. "It's not like he's going to tell his father. The kid doesn't talk. He's not right. As far as I'm concerned, Leslie's death has put him over the edge."

"I disagree. I think he's a very bright little boy," she said.

"So what's the deal?" Roger said, changing the subject. "You and Steve kiss and make up?" he asked testily.

Alex didn't want to antagonize Roger. She wanted him to trust her so that he would continue to confide in her—or lie to her, as the case may be. "I want to talk to you . . ." Alex began.

"And I want to talk to you," he spat. "I couldn't sleep all night. All I could think of was that Steve had not only killed the woman I loved, but he had murdered my child as well."

Alex took a step back, speechless.

"And I come here and see you staring into his eyes like there's no tomorrow."

She sat down on the second to last step of the stairway. She shook her head. "Roger, I know you're upset . . ."

"I thought you were a reporter," he said, disgusted. He opened the door to leave.

"Why didn't you tell me about your record?" Alex asked calmly.

He glanced back at her. "Is that what Steve told you? That I had a record?"

"Don't lie to me," she said. "It will be easy enough to check."

He shut the door. He leaned back against it, like a schoolboy who's been caught stealing pencils. "That's another reason I couldn't go to the police. They'd never believe me. I wouldn't stand a chance against Steve. They'd want to pin this on me."

"And why didn't you tell me that you and Steve grew up together?"

He shrugged. "What difference does it make?"

"I need to have all the facts," she said testily. "You've got to be honest with me."

Roger looked down at the floor. Alex sighed. "Look . . . I know how you feel. But there's still a chance that Steve didn't kill Leslie. I know it's hard for you to be objective . . ."

Roger laughed. "Objective?" he said, almost taunting her with the word. "Interesting word. Are you *objective?*"

"I've been trained to think objectively . . ."

"Don't give me that bullshit, Miss Webster," he said, walking toward her. "You may have been objective when you first arrived here, but you're sure not anymore."

Alex shifted her gaze away from him. He shook his head. "You don't want him to be guilty, do you?"

"Of course not," she replied quickly, looking back at him. "Who would? He's got a child, for God's sake . . ."

"What about my child?" Roger shouted. Alex jumped up and looked worriedly down the hall. She wondered if Ollie had heard him.

She glanced back angrily at Roger. "Calm down. Let's wait to hear what the results of the autopsy are before we start getting hysterical," she ordered.

Roger glared at her as stepped outside, slamming the door behind him.

Alex sat back down on the stairs and rested her head in her hands.

There was nothing more to be done until they had the results of the autopsy. If it was proven that Leslie had committed suicide, perhaps Roger could have some peace.

If, however, the results were inconclusive . . .

Alex stood up and glanced down the hall again. Little Ollie. If only he would talk. If only he could tell her what he saw that day.

She began to walk slowly toward the kitchen, as if every step was her last. The only thing to do right now was to wait. To wait and to pray.

Twenty-Four

"**S**teve! Over here," Jay said. Although it was only the middle of September, New York City had been suffering from an unseasonably cold and rainy fall. Jay had taken precautions. His face was covered with a wool scarf, and his briefcase was tucked under his arm so he could stick his hands in his pockets.

Steve nodded toward his lawyer, relieved that he was in the right place. In an effort to avoid the media, Jay had arranged for them to enter the New York medical examiner's office through the back door. Even if a few reporters were staked out in back, they would have had a difficult time recognizing Steve. His trench coat collar was pulled up around his ears, and dark sunglasses shaded his handsome eyes. Jay grabbed the door and opened it, motioning for Steve to enter. Steve glanced at him, shaking his head at Jay's scarf. "For God's sake, Jay. It's not *that* cold. You *are* a Southern boy."

"You got that right. And this Southern boy is about to freeze his butt off waiting for you," Jay said, following him inside the well-lit, sterile-looking hall.

Steve slipped off his glasses. "Sorry. My flight was delayed."

But Jay wasn't paying attention. He was busy scrutinizing the room numbers above the doors as he unwrapped his scarf.

"You do know where you're going, don't you?" Steve asked. "I'd hate to walk into the wrong room." He tried to ignore the distinct unpleasant odor that emanated through the building. It reminded him a little too vividly of high school biology.

"You and me both, pal," Jay replied as he began walking purposefully down the hall.

Jay paused as they reached the end of the hall. He pulled a paper out of his pocket and checked the number written on it. "This way," he said, pointing toward the right.

Steve shot him a look that said he'd better be right.

"So," Jay said. "Nervous?"

Steve paused. He wondered how much of the truth his lawyer really suspected. "I wouldn't say I'm nervous," he replied carefully. "I'm emotionally drained. Upset and disturbed that my wife was not allowed to rest in peace . . ."

"Hey," Jay said quietly. "There's no media here, remember? And I'm sure as hell not going to quote you."

Steve sighed. "Sorry," he said. "This whole thing has been devastating. Just when I think I'm moving on with my life . . ."

"Speaking of which," Jay said, "how's the girl?"

"The *girl?*" Steve asked.

"Don't play dumb."

"You mean Ollie's nanny?"

"None other."

"For starters, she's not a girl. She's a very intelligent woman."

"I'm sure," he said sarcastically.

Steve started getting annoyed. He didn't like the

way Jay was referring to Alex. "You don't know her. She would surprise you."

"Just like you?" Jay said, leading him up a flight of stairs.

"What's that supposed to mean?"

"I thought I told you to lie low for a while."

"I am lying low," Steve said, following Jay down another long hall.

"I meant figuratively."

Steve shook his head. "I couldn't break it off with her. I . . . need her. I can't explain it," he added quickly.

"Well, I'm sure we'll get good news today, and you can officially move on with your life."

"And what if it's not good news?" Steve asked, keeping his gaze focused on the end of the hall.

"Then it becomes my problem," Jay replied smoothly. "And I'm very good at solving problems."

Steve pursed his lips. He would have the strength to handle whatever happened today. He had to think of Ollie. And Alex. She claimed to love him, but would she have the courage to stand by him if he was branded a murderer?

"Okay," Jay said as they reached the end of the hall. "The waiting area is right through there." He pointed toward a large glass door off to the right. He checked his watch. "We're a little late. Ralph is probably here already," he said, referring to Ralph Adams, the district attorney's prosecutor assigned to the case.

"I'm sure he's licking his chops right now," Steve said wryly.

"He's not a bad guy," Jay insisted. "And he could've treated you much worse. He didn't even think there was a case. That's why he didn't want an autopsy."

"*Didn't* is the key word."

"He's responding to public pressure. The media had a heyday about those two kids who claimed they heard Leslie screaming."

"Those 'kids' are drug dealers. They were offered a deal for their testimony."

"We all know that. But just to make sure everyone is happy, they're going to check her to make sure."

Jay opened the glass door. A stout, bespectacled, balding man stood in the corner wearing a three-piece suit with a bow tie. He nodded at them as he stood up from the plastic chair. "Jay. Steve," he said, shaking their hands consecutively. "Did you guys have trouble making it through the cluster of vultures waiting outside?"

Jay shook his head. "We came in through the back."

"Any word yet?" Steve asked.

Ralph shook his head. He looked at his watch. "I'm a little surprised. They even called and told me to get here early. They said they got the body here sooner than they expected. They've had it for about three hours."

Jay glanced away, worried.

Steve caught his expression. "Is that usual?" he asked.

A woman in a white lab coat appeared at the door. "Mr. Adams?" she said.

Ralph nodded. "Yes?"

"Please follow me," she said.

Steve glanced at Jay as he moved toward the door in an attempt to follow Ralph. Jay shot out an arm, holding him back.

"Ralph," Jay asked calmly, still holding on to Steve. "Do me a favor and give us the results before you talk to anyone else."

Ralph glanced at Steve. Pain and misery were evident in Steve's eyes. It was hard to believe the man standing before him was the same champion boxer Ralph had idolized during high school. And he had not been alone. Every young man had wanted to be Steve Chapman. And now, with the whole world speculating on his guilt, Ralph didn't blame him for being upset. "Sure, Jay," he said.

The glass door swung shut as Steve angrily shrugged off Jay's hand.

"We couldn't seem too anxious," Jay said.

Steve turned away. He ran his fingers through his hair. "Too anxious?" he said angrily. "We're talking about my wife, for God's sake. I have a right to know."

"And you will." Jay crossed his arms in front of him. "Look, I know this is rough, but we're lucky they even told us about this. Sometimes a prosecutor will go to the grand jury and the whole ugly thing is done behind the client's back."

Steve leaned against the wall. All his life, he was always considered so strong. So tough. Invincible. He certainly didn't feel that way now.

If he didn't have Ollie, he wouldn't care as much. But if he was in prison, who would take care of his son?

He had so much time to make up for with Ollie. So much to make up for in life. He just wanted a chance.

Fifteen minutes went by. Fifteen turned slowly into twenty, and twenty turned even more slowly into twenty-five.

After twenty-six minutes, Jay stood up, intent on investigating the delay. "I think I'm going to go stretch my legs," he said, moving toward the door.

"Yeah, right," Steve said. He knew exactly where his attorney was heading. "I'm going with you."

They didn't have to. Ralph Adams had appeared at the door. He was holding a legal notepad.

Steve and Jay were silent as Ralph opened the door. "Okay," Ralph said. "They had a little bit of difficulty with the body because of the amount of time that it had been . . ."

"Give us the basics," Jay commanded, no longer following his own advice.

Ralph looked down at his notes. "The official cause

of death was severe head trauma. More importantly," he said, looking toward Steve, "her injuries were consistent with a forward fall, or a suicide jump."

Steve breathed a deep sigh of relief as he closed his eyes.

"What the hell took so long in there?" Jay asked. "Exchanging recipes?"

"Actually," Ralph said, glancing at Steve again, "they found something rather surprising." He hesitated. "Steve . . . how did your wife feel about children?"

Steve took a step forward. "Why?"

"I don't know how to tell you this," Ralph began, "but your wife was pregnant. At least three months."

Steve looked at Jay and nodded. "We were expecting our second child," he said calmly. He was glad Alex had prepared him.

Jay's mouth dropped in surprise.

"You didn't know?" Ralph asked.

"No, I didn't," Jay said, his eyes focused on Steve.

"Well, if she wasn't happy about this pregnancy, that could explain why she killed herself. She also may not have been feeling that well . . . all those hormones. You know how women get."

Steve stared at a wad of gum stuck on the floor. He couldn't breathe.

"Thanks for your help, Ralph," Jay said, putting a hand on Steve's shoulder. "I think we need to get Steve out of here. I take it the case is officially closed?"

Ralph nodded. "It would look that way," he said.

Steve looked up at him. "Thank you," he managed.

Twenty-Five

Because there was no TV on the island, Alex kept within earshot of the radio and the phone all day, waiting for news. She did her best to entertain Ollie, but by the early afternoon, the stress and the heat had begun to wear on her. She resorted to sitting on the patio, fanning herself with her book as she watched Ollie stare at the water. By nightfall, there was still no word.

She put Ollie to bed at nine and sat down in the library, underneath the big rotating fan. She wasn't surprised that she hadn't seen Roger after their altercation. She had made him angry, and she suspected he would avoid her until the results were in.

She checked her watch. Why hadn't Steve called? Perhaps he couldn't. Perhaps the results were so incriminating they had arrested him on the spot.

She walked over to the bar and poured herself a glass of Chardonnay. She opened up the wood blinds as far as they would go, as if to encourage the wisp of air flowing through the room. She stood at the window, admiring the stillness of the night. She could hear the crickets above the background of the water splashing against the shoreline. She looked toward the black, starry sky, as if she might recognize Steve's plane overhead.

The shrill ring of the phone snapped her out of her almost hypnotic state.

"Hello?" she said, not hesitating to answer.

There was a pause. "Are you alone?" She closed

her eyes as she felt disappointment overwhelm her. It was Tim.

"Why are you calling me?" she asked. "You know better than that."

"I know he's in New York. I guessed you'd be staying at his house."

"How do you know he's still in New York?" she asked. "Have you heard anything?"

"Sorry," he said. "Not a word."

She sat down on the couch. She put the glass of wine up to her forehead, as if it would cool her.

"Your mother called me today."

Alex felt a twinge of guilt at the mention of her mother. She had been meaning to write to her, but she hadn't had a chance. "My mother? Why? Is something wrong?"

"She was worried about you. She thought she would've heard from you by now."

"What did you tell her?"

"The truth. That I was worried about you myself."

"Oh God," she moaned, panicking. "How could you? You know my mother. She'll get a few cocktails in her, and she'll start calling her friends back in the States, telling them how Steve's holding me prisoner here."

"Is he?" he asked sarcastically. "What are you doing at the main house? Or have you officially moved in?"

"Don't start, Tim," she said.

"Start what? I'm curious about how the investigation is progressing. I've been doing my part. Have you been doing yours?"

She was silent.

"I have to admit that I thought I would have heard from you by now," he said. "Especially after I put my neck on the line with that doctor."

"I'm sorry, Tim," she said. "I did get your message about Leslie. But I didn't have time to write back yesterday."

"Or today?"

"I've been busy. Steve left me here with Ollie . . ."

"How sweet," he said, his words dripping with sarcasm.

"I really do appreciate what you did," she said quickly.

"So does her pregnancy tie in?"

"No," she said.

"No?" he repeated, surprised. "Don't you think it's a coincidence . . ."

"No," she interrupted.

Tim was silent. "Well," he said, a lethal edge oozing from his voice. "Perhaps you'd be interested to hear that I also checked on those departure times. You were right. The times you gave me were the departure times of flights from New York to Miami."

"I thought so."

"When are you going to tell me what the hell is going on?" Tim said angrily.

She hesitated. "Tim . . . I, well, there's no other way to tell you this. I've decided to shelve the investigation."

There was silence on the other end as her words sank in. *"You what?"*

"There's no story. You were right all along."

"Let me get this straight. Before the autopsy results are even in, you've made the decision, all by your little self, that after all the time we've invested in this story, you're going to pull out."

"It's not going to happen, Tim. There is no story."

"I see," he said. He didn't believe her. "So you're coming back to New York. Tomorrow, right?" he asked, testing her.

"No," she said.

"Alex, what're you doing?"

"I'm sorry, Tim. What I'm trying to say is . . . I quit. Thanks for everything . . ."

"C'mon, Alex! You can't be serious!"

"I'm sorry, Tim. Good-bye." She put the phone

down and sat on the couch. She closed her eyes and leaned against the cushions.

Dear God, she prayed silently. *Please give me the strength to accept those things I can't change and the courage to change those things I can . . .*

"Alex?"

Alex opened her bloodshot eyes.

Steve stood in the doorway.

"I didn't hear you come in . . ."

"You were sleeping." he said, walking over to the couch. "How's Ollie?"

She sat up. "He's fine. Perfectly fine," she replied quickly. "What happened?"

He sat down next to her. "Her injuries were consistent with a suicide."

Alex closed her eyes as a rush of relief flowed through her. She sighed deeply.

"I'm sorry I didn't call you. I wanted to tell you in person."

"I was so worried," she said quietly.

"We both were," he said, brushing her hair away from her eyes. "It was pretty tense there for a while. The autopsy took longer than they thought. It was the thought of Ollie that kept me going. Ollie and . . . you."

She gave him a weak smile. He leaned in and kissed her softly. He pulled back. "I was thinking about what happened yesterday."

"And?" she asked nervously.

"I wish that we had met under different circumstances, but we can't change who we are. Either one of us. The bottom line is . . . I love you. And I don't want to lose you," he said. "I'd like us to start fresh . . . together." He leaned forward, running his fingers through her tousled hair. "Let's get away from here. Get on the boat and travel. Maybe even go back to the Bahamas again." He paused, staring into her eyes as he waited for her response. "We have to move on, my love. Both of us. We need to put the past behind us."

She gave him a weak, grateful smile. "When do we leave?" she asked, leaning forward and kissing him.

Roger stood at the window, staring in at the happy couple. He hadn't planned to spy on them. He had seen Steve drive in and had walked to the house because he was anxious to hear the results of the autopsy. But he had seen them in the library from the drive, and he hadn't been able to resist his urge to eavesdrop on what looked like a very charming scene. But as their bodies melded together, Roger stood back from the window, unable to watch anymore. He turned and, with a quiet sigh, began walking the lonely path back to his dumpy cottage. Unfortunately for them both, it wasn't over for him.

Twenty-Six

Tim rolled his stiff office chair away from his desk. He looked through the glass walls that separated his office from the rest of the newsroom. The official deadline for tomorrow's news had been more than an hour ago, and the reporters still at their desks were either frantically finishing up last-minute stories or tidying up their desks, readying for the next day.

Without bothering to get up, he continued to roll his chair over to the credenza against his only solid wall. He picked up a bootlegged copy of the autopsy and thumbed through it. He had been unable to confirm reports that the prosecution was officially dropping its case against Chapman . . . not that they had ever bothered to charge him officially. His inability to confirm reports meant one of two things. Either they weren't talking until they called a press conference, or they hadn't decided whether they were going to press charges yet.

He thumbed through the copy, his mind quickly tabulating and evaluating the facts. Severe head trauma. Injuries consistent with a suicide jump. Why hadn't they announced that they were dropping the charges? He looked at the report again, searching for a clue that he might have missed.

Despite what the authorities had planned, Tim no longer had any intention of dropping the investigation. He didn't believe Alex when she said that there was no case. He took her resignation as a sign of just the opposite. He was convinced that she had found out that Steve Chapman was guilty and didn't have the guts to turn him in.

As he scanned the report in front of him, a small detail, practically overlooked in the report, seemed to take on quite a bit of significance.

Leslie Chapman had been wearing only one nylon when her body was found.

He leaned back in his chair. The importance of the nylon was negligible. It might just mean that it had slid off when the police rescued her body from the tide. Or it might mean that she had taken it off herself. But why would she have taken it off?

"Hey, Tim!"

Tim glanced up. It was Tina Hagen, the young reporter who had recently been promoted to the crime beat. He smiled at her. In certain respects, she reminded him of Alex. At least how Alex used to be, when she first started. The same brilliance. The same devotion and excitement for her job. "I'm running out to grab some dinner. You want anything?"

Tim shook his head. "Let me ask you something,"

he said. "Let's say you're wearing a pair of fancy nylons. The sexy kind . . ."

"Wait a minute," she interrupted. "Is this a come-on?"

"There are laws against that," he said, showing her the file he had in his hand. "It's related to the Chapman death." She looked at him as if she wasn't quite sure she believed him.

"You know what kind I mean?" he continued.

"The kind with the garter?"

He nodded. "Right. After you put them on, why would you take them off?"

"You don't have to take them off to go the bathroom, if that's what you're getting at."

"So you only take them off when you want your legs to be naked."

She shrugged. "Not exactly. If you wear them over your underwear, like most women, you have to take them off to get your underwear off."

Like when you want to have sex, Tim thought. Leslie Chapman had been meeting someone the night she died. She had either slept with him or had been planning to. He was sure of it. And either that person killed her, or someone else found out about it and killed her for her indiscretion. And who would have reason to be jealous? Her husband.

Tina hesitated, waiting for him to make some lewd comment. He didn't. "Anything else?" she asked.

He leaned forward and smiled. "How would you like to cover the Chapman case?"

Twenty-Seven

"This little guy went to market . . . and this little guy went to, ah, town . . . and this, wow," he said, teasing her as he tugged on her big toe. "This is one big guy . . . he went to . . . he had to get his own island 'cause he wouldn't fit anywhere else."

"Okay, okay," Alex said, giggling. Steve was down on the end of the bed, gently tugging on her toes. He picked her feet up and kissed them.

They had been awake for about an hour, lying in bed and cuddling close together, talking about everything and nothing at all.

Steve pulled himself up beside her, and she nestled her head inside his arm. She ran her fingers over his sleek, muscular arm, squeezing his pectoral muscle. "That's some muscle," she said, impressed.

"Why, thank you," he replied, laughing.

He leaned over her, playfully pinning her down on the bed. He gazed down on her. "So, Miss Webster? Where do we go from here?"

She grinned. "Where do you want to go?"

"Somewhere with Ollie . . . and you." He fell back down beside her. "Like I said last night, I want to get off this island. As soon as we can."

She nodded as she pushed herself up on one arm, facing him. "I agree."

"And then what?" he said.

She shrugged her shoulders. "I don't care."

He paused. "What about the paper?"

She glanced up at him and smiled. "I quit. Last

304

night. I told them that there was no story and I was quitting."

He ran his finger around her chin. "Are you okay with that?" he asked, concerned. "I know how much your career means to you."

She grabbed his finger and held on to it. "I'm ready for a change."

"Oh, really," he said as she pulled his fingers inside her mouth. He swallowed as she bit down on them gently. "And what kind of change might that be?" he asked, every word an effort.

"Give me some ideas," she said, taking his fingers out of her mouth and running her tongue up the inside of his arm.

"Ah . . . well," he said, watching her carefully. "You could marry me, for starters."

She stopped as she looked at him. "That sounds like an excellent idea."

He smiled as he grabbed her, pulling her on top of him.

"Promise me?" Ollie said, standing in the doorway.

Alex jumped off Steve and frantically pulled the covers up to her chin.

"Hey, sport," Steve said cheerfully. "Did you miss me yesterday?" Ollie didn't respond. "Go on downstairs. I'll be there in a minute, and we'll have some breakfast, okay?"

Ollie shut the door behind him. Steve looked down at Alex and smiled. "We better hurry up and make this legal."

Alex nodded. "I agree."

Steve took her hand and kissed it. "How do you want your eggs?"

Alex shook her head. "You should know by now that I'm not a breakfast kind of gal."

"Suit yourself," he said, jumping up and pulling on his boxers. He glanced around the room. "You haven't seen a pair of jeans floating around here, have you?"

Alex pointed to the chair. He followed her finger. "Right where I left them," he said, cheerfully putting them on. He bent over her and kissed her forehead. "I'll see you downstairs."

"I'm right behind you."

But only ten minutes later, when Alex arrived in the kitchen, Steve's mood had changed, and Ollie was nowhere in sight.

"Where's Ollie?"

Steve nodded toward the door as he slipped on his shoes. "He's outside."

She put a hand on his back. "What's the matter?"

"I told him we were leaving the island," Steve said worriedly. "That we were free to go wherever we wanted. That he could go back to school soon."

"And?"

"I'm not really sure what upset him, but he just pushed me away. Literally. He pushed me away and ran crying out the door. I'm going to look for him."

"I'll help," she offered, following him outside into the humid and cloudy day.

Steve shook his head. "No. No, that's all right. I'll find him. I'll catch up with you later," he said, obviously preoccupied.

Alex glanced toward the barn. She wanted to help him look for Ollie, but she was careful not to overstep her bounds. She decided to focus her maternal instincts on feeding the horses instead.

She opened the door to the barn and stepped inside. For the first time that day, she thought about Roger. She wondered if he knew about the results of the autopsy. She suspected that he did and hoped that he would have enough sense to trust the results. As angry as he was, as much as he wanted someone to atone for his lover's death, he had to let it go. Steve had not killed Leslie.

Alex grabbed a pail of feed and lugged it over to Rosie's stall.

"You're late."

306

Alex whipped around, startled. Roger stood in the entrance to the barn, his face a dark shadow. "You scared me," she said, putting her hand to her heart.

He walked through the dark barn, approaching her slowly. If he was trying to make her nervous, it was working. "Good morning," she said, as cheerfully as she could muster.

"I wouldn't say so. Looks like we're in for a hell of a storm."

"Are they calling for rain?"

He nodded as he leaned against a neighboring stall. He focused his attention on Alex. "I've been looking for you. I just wanted to tell you . . . I'm sorry about yesterday. I got a little carried away."

"Don't worry about it," she said, encouraged. She opened the door to Rosie's stall and slid the feed in. "I'm sure you heard, but it's over. Finally and officially. Leslie's death has been ruled a suicide."

He nodded. He pushed his cowboy hat back off his face as he watched her.

She smiled at him pleasantly, even though the way he was staring at her was giving her the creeps.

"So that's it?" he said finally.

Uh, oh, Alex thought. *Here we go.* "I just told you what they said . . ." Alex began, still not facing him.

"It proves nothing," Roger said, walking toward her. He jammed his hands into the pockets of his well-worn jeans. "She was pushed. From behind."

"No," Alex said. "She was depressed. It's just as Steve said."

"We were in love. She was not depressed. I'm telling you she didn't kill herself."

"Maybe she didn't mean to. Maybe she just fell off. Accidents happen."

"Not this time," he said.

Alex shook her head as she started to walk away.

"Tell me you're not going to give up," he said, grabbing her arm.

"I can't make that promise, Roger. I'm sorry."

Roger dropped her arm.

"Look, Roger," she continued reasonably. "They have no reason to press charges. The autopsy results point to suicide. She had a history of mental illness, and she tried to kill herself twice before, once in front of a zillion witnesses. There is no case!"

"There's something you don't know. Something that might change your mind." He ran his tongue over his chapped lower lip. "The day she was killed, I was with her," he said quietly.

She leaned forward slightly, as if she hadn't heard him correctly. "What?"

"I was with her . . . right before it happened," he said, his face twisting with sorrow. "I lied to you before. I couldn't tell the police I was there. They would've thought that I killed her. Don't you see?"

Alex gave him a look that reflected her disbelief. "That's not possible. Steve said that you arrived on the island *after* she was killed. You couldn't have been here already. He would've seen your helicopter."

Roger shook his head. "I flew back early that morning from the Bahamas. I parked the helicopter in a field by the marina and took the boat back here, putting it away in the boathouse. After Steve got here, I drove the boat back to the mainland and flew back to the airport, hopped back in the jet, and went to pick up the boys in the Bahamas."

Not only did that all sound extremely complicated, but Alex doubted Roger would have had enough time to make two trips to the Bahamas.

As if he knew what she was thinking, he said, "It takes a half hour to fly from the Bahamas to Miami. It takes ten minutes by helicopter to fly from Miami to the marina. Fifteen minutes to get to the island by boat. We're talking about one hour. If you don't believe me, check with the airports and confirm the flight records."

Alex's blue eyes shifted uncomfortably to the floor.

"I was here," he repeated. "We had planned to

meet at the house that Steve was building. Leslie liked to meet there because Ollie knew he wasn't allowed near there. Steve had told him it was too dangerous, and the kid listened to him. It made it the ideal meeting spot for us. And besides," he said, a slight smile forming on his lips as he remembered, "she used to like the fact that we were making love in what was to be Steve's grand master bedroom."

Alex swallowed. "You were . . ."

"We had just finished making love. We were getting dressed . . ."

The silk stocking. Leslie had taken her stockings off for her encounter with Roger.

"We heard a noise . . . someone opening the front door. She whispered for me to get out of there. I slipped down the back staircase and out the back door. I left her there . . . I never saw her again."

Alex shook her head. "No," she said weakly. "I don't believe you. Why didn't you tell me this before?"

He turned away. "I was afraid you'd think that I killed her."

She leaned against the side of the barn door. "Why didn't you tell the police?" she asked, almost thinking aloud.

"Because they would've suspected *me* of murder. And I didn't kill her. *He* did." Roger sighed, shaking his head. "The police never would've believed me. An ex-con. Did time for assault." He shrugged his shoulders helplessly "And even if they did," he added, "Steve would've gotten his high-priced attorneys to get him off."

"Look," she said. "I'm sorry. But you should've told the police. And even if you did hear the door open, there's no proof that it was Steve. It could've been the wind," she said, grasping at straws. "Or Ollie."

"I thought you were interested in finding the truth, but you don't care about that anymore, do you? You're in love with him," he said. He began laughing.

"Stop it, Roger."

"You don't want to believe he killed Leslie. Because you want to love him. You think you're just going to ride off into the sunset now that this whole nasty business is over with," he said, suddenly serious again. "Well, you can forget it. I told you. He doesn't love you. He already has a girlfriend. She comes first. She has for years. Just stand in line, sweetheart. Wait your turn."

"That's enough!" Alex turned and began to walk briskly out of the barn.

"Alex," Roger called out. "He's a liar."

Alex shut the door to her apartment. The air inside her room was so thick she was sure she could see it. She turned on the fan as she took a couple of deep breaths to calm herself. As soon as she showered and changed, she would find Steve and insist that he have Roger leave the island immediately.

She ran her fingers through her hair as she walked over to her closet. She didn't believe Roger's story. There were too many holes in it. If he really had been with Leslie, then he should have told the police.

She heard a noise and stopped. She looked toward her closet. She opened the door slowly.

"Hello, Ollie."

Ollie was rocking back and forth with his little blond head tucked into his knees. "Promise me," he whispered.

Alex dropped down beside him. She wrapped her arms around him in a loose hug. "Shhhh. It's okay," she whispered quietly.

He looked up at her. "Promise me you won't tell anyone . . ."

"What?" she asked, stunned.

"Promise me you won't tell anyone you killed Mommy. Promise me you won't tell anyone you killed Mommy . . ."

It took Alex a moment to realize what he was say-

310

ing. Had *he* killed his mother? "What are you saying, Ollie?"

Ollie pushed her away as he began to speak even more loudly. "Promise me you'll never tell anyone promise me you'll never tell people that you pushed Mommy you can never tell people Ollie you were never there understand promise me promise me."

"Ollie!" Steve was in the doorway. Having searched all the other obvious hiding places, he had suddenly realized that Ollie was probably in Alex's closet, which seemed to have become his new favorite hiding spot. He rushed over and held his child in his arms. Ollie opened his eyes and began breathing heavily, as though exhausted. "Ollie, it's all right. I was wrong. You didn't kill her. My God, Ollie, I'm sorry. I'm sorry."

Alex sat still as her mind quickly began to put everything together. Steve had arrived at the island. He had found Ollie . . . by his wife's body? Or in the house, where she had jumped? Even if he did find him in the house, why did he think that Ollie had killed her?

Steve picked Ollie up and carried him toward the door. Alex jumped up, grabbing the door for him. She followed them back to the house and waited downstairs while Steve comforted his son and coaxed him into taking a nap.

When Ollie was settled, Steve walked back into the den and sat down behind his desk. His face had lost all the earlier expression of joy and was now tired and drawn. He rested his forehead in his hands.

"You thought Ollie killed her," Alex said quietly. "That's why you've isolated yourselves out here. You've been protecting him."

Steve glanced away. He ran a hand over his tired eyes.

Alex stood up and walked over to him. She put her hand on his shoulder as a show of support. "But why? Why did you think he killed her?"

He sighed. "We weren't supposed to go to the island that weekend. I got a call from Leslie early that

311

afternoon announcing that she had left the city and returned to the island with Ollie. She was hysterical . . . and drunk. She said that Ollie had somehow gotten trapped in the trunk of her car, and she couldn't get him out. I told her to call the sheriff, and in the meantime I would leave immediately and get here as soon as I could. When I got here, the trunk was open in Leslie's car. I began screaming for them . . . I couldn't find them anywhere. When I finally made it to the construction site, I found Ollie sitting on the balcony in the master bedroom, rocking back and forth. He wouldn't tell me what happened. He was in shock. It was then that I noticed Leslie's body on the rocks below.

"I didn't know what to think," he continued. "I knew Leslie had been drinking. I thought that maybe she had locked Ollie inside the trunk of her car as some sort of punishment . . . or maybe just to keep him out of her way."

"It's over now, Steve. Ollie didn't push her. She committed suicide. It's all over."

Steve shook his head. "I wish that was true." He grabbed a piece of paper and handed it to her. It was a fax. A copy of a story from that morning's *New York Times*. Alex read the name of the reporter. Tina Hagen. One of Tim's young protégés. Alex began to read as she walked back over to the couch and sat down.

The article described the autopsy results the previous day, but instead of referring to them as the definitive end to all suspicion, it mentioned the missing nylon, the uncertainty of the medical examiner, and the lack of any suicide note. The article also claimed that the investigation was far from over.

She glanced up at Steve when she was finished. "I didn't have anything to do with this."

He nodded. "I know you didn't." He shook his head. "But somebody at the *Times* is certainly after me."

Yeah. Tim. And it was her fault.

And the article wasn't the only problem they had. "There's something else you should be aware of," she began.

"This doesn't sound good," he said.

"It's not. Roger told me this morning that he was on the island with Leslie the day she died. He flew back from the Bahamas earlier in the day so that he could rendezvous with her before you arrived. You didn't see the helicopter because he claims he took the boat from the marina."

"What?" Steve asked, confused. "But he didn't fly those guys back to Miami until four."

Alex nodded. "He claimed he flew back to the Bahamas and picked them up."

Steve nodded. "So?"

"So he's saying that he and Leslie were having a . . . rendezvous in the house that was being built when they heard the door open. He claims he crept out the back way. He's convinced it was you he heard. That you killed her."

He sighed. "The stocking. She hadn't finished getting dressed."

Alex nodded silently. They both knew what the implications were. Why would Leslie kill herself before she even finished getting dressed?

"Maybe she slipped, Steve . . ."

"Oh my God," he said quietly. It was as if he couldn't even hear her.

"Maybe she was bending down to pick up her stocking, and she just fell . . ."

"Is Roger going to the police?"

Alex shook her head. "I don't think so. We can handle this, Steve. Regardless of what really happened."

"So what does he want? Money?"

"Don't give him any money. Just get him off the island. Fast. If he wants to go to the police, let him. He doesn't have a case, and he knows it. He's just spinning his wheels."

"But he could make things difficult for . . . us."

"Listen to me, Steve," Alex said authoritatively. "The sooner he leaves, the better."

As Steve nodded, a roll of thunder sounded in the distance. The storm was getting closer.

That night, Alex made dinner for the three of them. It was the first time she had cooked for them since she had set foot on the island. She had to make do with what was in the refrigerator, so she settled on spaghetti with meat sauce. It wasn't the most exciting dish in the world, but she hadn't cooked in a long time, and it was a definite step in the right direction. None of them appeared to be in a very good mood, but Steve made a valiant effort to keep the conversation light.

Alex's mood had been dampened by the fact that because of inclement weather, Roger was still on the island. Steve hadn't given her many details about their conversation, but she had the feeling it had been fairly heated. According to Steve, Roger had already packed by the time Steve arrived at his house. Apparently, Roger was as anxious to be rid of them as they were to be rid of him.

After dinner, Alex offered to clean up while Steve tucked Ollie in. She was drying the last plate when she felt Steve's strong arms wrap around her. "Excellent timing," she said, waving toward the dry plates. "I'm finished."

"Already?" he said, nibbling her ear. "I'm just getting started."

Alex twisted around so that she was facing him. She wrapped her arms around his neck. "You seem to be in a good mood."

"I am now," he said, brushing some hair away from her face. He grinned at her. "Guess what Ollie just said?"

She smiled. "He talked to you?" Despite the child's

outburst earlier that afternoon, he had continued his usual silence for the remainder of the day.

Steve nodded. "I turned off the light, and he said, 'Good night, Dad.' "

She breathed a sigh of relief as she flung her arms around him. "That's great news!"

The thunder crashed as the lights flickered. Steve pulled her to him as he glanced out the window. "It's getting pretty bad out there."

Alex nodded as she followed his gaze. Heavy raindrops were beginning to splash on the blinds. "I hope the horses don't get spooked."

"There's nothing to be afraid of," Steve said, running his fingers through her hair. "I promise you."

"I'm not afraid," she said, pulling back as her eyes settled on his. "I have very good instincts."

"Is that so?" he asked, teasing her.

She nodded. "Yes. And they're telling me that everything is going to be all right."

Steve pulled out her shirt and slid his hands against her naked back. "And what," he asked, reaching toward the back of her bra, "are they telling you now?"

"That I'm in serious, serious trouble," she murmured.

"I would say so . . ." he said, unsnapping the clasp on her bra. His hands grazed her hardened nipples. "There's no turning back now," he whispered, as he leaned over to kiss her neck.

"I'm not going anywhere without you," she said, closing her eyes.

"Well, I'm going upstairs," he said, taking her hand.

"Then it would appear that I am, too," she said. Alex was so focused on Steve that she didn't even notice he had taken the unusual step of locking the front door. In fact, both were so carried away with their passion that neither bothered to look out the front window as they walked past. If they had, they might have noticed the small light shining inside Alex's otherwise dark apartment.

Twenty-Eight

Roger calmly plugged in Alex's computer and made himself a cup of coffee as he waited for it to go on-line. He had suspected that stealing Alex's computer would be easy. And he had not been disappointed. What he had been concerned about, however, was deciphering her code and getting into the *Times* e-mail system. But she hadn't been nearly as clever as he had given her credit for. Last name, first initial. And there he was.

He pulled up the old messages, those received and sent. He read each one intently, taking his time. When he was finished, he hit the button to send a reply message. He then began typing very carefully: "You've got to help me. I have proof that Steve killed his wife, and he knows it. I'm in trouble. Send help immediately. Hurry."

When Roger was confident that the message had been sent, he picked up a brick from the building where Leslie had been murdered and smashed it into the computer. His gaze shifted from the remains of the computer to the syringe on his dresser that he had carefully filled with horse tranquilizer. It was enough to paralyze a strong man for at least thirty minutes, but not enough to kill him. After all, he didn't want Steve dead. He wanted him to suffer.

The first thing Steve did when he woke was to go downstairs and turn on the radio. A frown appeared on his lips as he listened to the dismal weather report.

Roger would not be able to leave today, that much was certain. A bad tropical storm that was going to bring hurricane-like winds was heading toward the island, and they didn't have much time. He glanced around the room. The library was the safest place to ride out the storm. But they still had a lot of work to do to make it even safer. That included boarding up the windows and bringing in jugs of water and food.

"Good morning," Alex said cheerfully from the doorway.

Steve smiled as he stood to greet her. "How did you sleep?"

"Wonderful," she said, kissing his chin.

But Steve was all business this morning. He nodded toward the gloomy-looking sky outside the window as he said, "We need to get busy. Will you go check on Ollie? I'm going to start boarding up the windows."

"It's going to be that bad?"

"According to the radio."

"Oh boy," she said, making a face. She had never been through a hurricane before, or even a tropical storm. "I'll go get Ollie. Where is he?"

"Still sleeping."

Alex shook her head. "I just checked in his room. He's not there."

Steve's forehead creased with worry. "Are you sure?"

Alex nodded. Steve left the room and bounded up the stairs. "Ollie?" Alex followed right behind him. When they were convinced the floor was empty, they ran downstairs, calling and checking in closets.

"Don't panic," Alex said carefully. "He's got to be around here somewhere. I'll go check my apartment."

Steve nodded. "I'll start looking around the grounds."

As Steve hurried down toward the water, Alex made her way toward her apartment, sliding through the mud as she ran. She opened the door to her apartment, all the while calling Ollie's name. She pulled open her closet door, half expecting to see Ollie inside. "Ollie?" she said to the empty closet.

"Did you find him?" Steve was behind her, breathing heavily as he took a moment to catch his breath.

Alex shook her head. "I'm going to search the barn," he said. "You go back in the house and stay there. The wind is picking up. It's not safe to be outside in this."

"Let me help you," she said, grabbing a windbreaker out of her closet. "I'll start boarding up the windows."

"I'd feel better if you stay inside. I don't want to worry about you, too."

Alex nodded as she tried to flash a reassuring smile. She had no intention of staying inside the house. She followed Steve into the misting rain and waited until he had slipped inside the barn before veering toward the woods.

"Ollie?" Steve stepped inside the dark barn. Despite the threatening storm, the horses seemed to be fairly quiet this morning.

Leaving the door open, Steve walked rapidly through the barn, checking each and every stall just to make sure his son was not somehow tucked inside.

"Ollie, are you here?"

"No, Steve, he's not." Roger stood in the entrance to the barn. He turned his back to Steve as he slid the door shut.

"What?" Steve asked, confused.

"I said," Roger repeated calmly, "he's not here."

Steve began to walk toward him slowly. Every muscle in his body tightened as he prepared himself for a fight.

"How do you know?" he managed.

Roger leaned back against the barn door. "Because he's in the trunk of your car, where I put him. He likes it in there."

Steve lunged at Roger, but Roger was ready for

him, his fingers looped through a set of brass knuckles. Roger punched Steve in the stomach, and Steve bent over, gasping for air. "You don't quite have what it takes anymore, do you, Steve? Pity. You used to be such a good fighter. Guess you've just gotten old and lazy."

Before Roger could move out of the way, Steve jumped to his feet, hurtling a punch that sent Roger spinning backward. Roger landed against the side of the barn. "You shouldn't have done that," he said, massaging in his sore jaw. His right hand slipped into his pocket. He let go of the brass knuckles as he fingered the syringe.

Steve grabbed him by his lapels and picked him up off the ground as he banged Roger up against the side of the barn once more. "Why are you doing this?" Steve asked through clenched teeth.

Roger yanked the syringe out of his pocket and, before Steve could respond, jammed the needle into his neck. Surprised, Steve let go of Roger as he yanked the needle out.

"What did you do?" Steve asked as a strange numbness shot through him, making him feel heavy and lethargic.

Roger ignored Steve as he brushed himself off.

"Roger," Steve said, dropping to his knees. "I can't move . . ."

Roger shook his head as he leaned over, putting his hands on his knees. He pulled the syringe out of Steve's lifeless hands and slipped it back into his pocket. "No, Steve," he said, as if talking to a child. "You've been given a good shot of horse tranquilizer."

Steve tried to shake his head. "What?"

Roger crossed his arms as if disgusted by him. "Don't worry, it's not fatal. It'll wear off eventually. In time for you to pay for your sins."

Steve looked at him. He had no idea what he was talking about. "You don't get it, do you?" Roger said.

He paused, watching Steve's eyes blink heavily. "I've watched you the past few months with more hatred than I ever thought possible. You were going to walk, Steve. Right off into the sunset with that new little girlfriend of yours and your deaf, dumb, and blind kid. As if Leslie had never even mattered. And then it occurred to me that it wasn't really doing me any good to just sit around feeling sorry for myself. I needed to take action. I had hoped that I could persuade Alex to help me. But you fixed that, too, didn't you? Steve, Steve. Always so charming. So good with the ladies."

Steve's body gave into the poison that was running through his veins, and he fell over on the floor. "I didn't kill her," he said with considerable effort.

Roger walked over to him. He put his boot on Steve's chest as he leaned over him. "You may not have pushed her off that balcony, my dear old friend, but you killed her just the same," Roger said, rolling up his sleeves.

"And I can't let you get away with it," he said. "And now I'm afraid I have to punish you. You see, I'm going to recreate Leslie's murder. Only this time, you're going to kill Alex."

Alex pulled her hood up over her head as she walked into the heavily wooded area. She couldn't stand the thought of Ollie alone in this weather. "Ollie!" she screamed as loudly as she could. Originally, she had planned on checking the beach, but as she came up to the path that led there, she suddenly realized where Ollie might hide: the house where Leslie had died.

The rain splashed against her face as she ventured through the pine forest. She walked at a fast clip, despite the fact that her wet, dirty tennis shoes provided little protection against the muddy, slippery mess that had previously been a path.

She followed the path out of the woods and into the clearing in front of the construction site. Alex paused as soon as she saw the half-built house, quickly remembering what Steve had said about the unstable supports.

If Ollie *was* hiding inside, she needed to get him out fast.

"Ollie?" she called out, approaching the house. The front door, which had always been locked, was banging open. Alex fought back a creeping sense of fear as she bravely made her way toward the house. She looked around the mud for footprints . . . any sign that Ollie had been this way.

She walked up the curving stairs and grabbed the door. "Ollie?" she said, leaning inside the house. She stepped inside, gingerly shutting the door behind her. She glanced around the empty shell. She knew that before she looked around the first floor, she needed to check the room where Leslie had jumped to her death.

She ran up the stairs and made her way through the barren hall, stopping at the entrance to Leslie's room. "Ollie?" she asked hopefully, looking around her.

She walked through the center of the room, her eyes focused on the tumultuous sea before her. The view from the unprotected balcony was frightening. Black, ominous clouds stormed toward the house as ten-foot waves crashed toward the shore. She looked away, glancing quickly around the room.

She paused as the front door slammed shut. She ran into the hall. "Steve?" she asked hopefully.

Roger peeked around the corner of the staircase. "Just me," he said.

The smile faded from Alex's face. "Oh. I'm looking for Ollie."

Roger nodded as he hopped up the stairs, taking two at a time. "Yeah, I know. I just saw Steve. He told me to find you. When you weren't at the house, I had a feeling you'd be here."

"Did he find Ollie?"

Roger shook his head, "Afraid not." He glanced around the room that was drenched in memories. He and Leslie had often made love in this very room, *Beautiful Leslie.* So full of life. He had never met a woman like her before, and he knew he never would again. He would have died for her. And now he would kill for her. It had nothing to do with Alex. It was just that justice needed to be served. "Did you check beneath the balcony?" he asked matter-of-factly.

The blood drained from Alex's face. "What?" she asked quietly. Had she misunderstood him, or was he calmly insinuating that Ollie had jumped to his death?

"Maybe he jumped," Roger said with an eerily calm voice. "Just like his mother."

Roger walked out onto the balcony, not threatened by the intimidating wind. He put his hands on his hips as he glanced beneath him. He turned back toward Alex and nodded. "Like mother, like son."

Alex stared at him. It took a second for his statement to sink in.

"Come see for yourself," Roger said, motioning toward the balcony.

Alex's breath tightened. First Lennie, then Ollie. Two deaths. Two deaths she caused. "No," she mouthed, although she was slowly walking toward the open space. She stopped in the doorway to the balcony. The wind whipped through her sheer windbreaker, blowing her wet hair back from her face.

She shook her head. She couldn't bear to look below her. "I can't."

Roger walked back to her as he looped his arm around her shoulders, pretending to comfort her. "He must've jumped because of you. Because you were trying to take the place of his mother," he said into her ear, in a low, almost soothing voice.

Alex shook her head as she held her hands to her ears.

"His little body is so perfect down on the rocks. But he won't be there for long. He's going to get swept out to sea. You've got to see him, Alex. To say good-bye," he said, steering her gently to the ledge.

"No," she screamed, breaking away and running back into the room.

"He's with his mother," Roger said, almost beginning to convince himself. "Isn't that nice? They can both be together," he continued, approaching her slowly.

It was the look in his eyes that tipped Alex off. Roger was lying. "Let's go get Steve. He can help," she said, inching her way slowly toward the door.

Roger shook his head. "Steve's . . . busy. He can't help. I'm afraid it's just you and me," he said.

Alex swallowed. She knew she was in trouble. She could sense the hostility seething beneath Roger's calm and cool exterior. Her only and best hope was that she could outrun him. She turned and dashed into the hall, but Roger was too quick for her. He grabbed her by the arm and threw her back into the room.

"Did you kill Ollie?" she whispered, backing away.

He shook his head. "No," he replied. "I never laid a hand on that child. I would never harm Leslie's child. Now or ever. I've locked him in the trunk. Just like I did before." He paused, his crazy eyes resting on her face.

"And Steve?" she whispered.

"Unfortunately, Steve's a different story."

"No," Alex murmured, shaking her head.

"You see, he destroyed something I loved. And he didn't even get in any trouble for it. Nothing," he said. "And now I have to go to a lot of trouble to make sure that justice is served. I didn't kill him. That would be too easy. I want him to suffer."

"He didn't kill her, Roger. You've got to believe me . . ."

"Oh, I believe you. I know he didn't kill her."

Alex looked at him as everything began to crystallize.

He nodded. "Steve didn't push her off that balcony, sweetheart. I did."

"You . . . ?" Alex began. Her voice drifted off.

Roger shook his head. "I pushed her off the balcony, but Steve killed her."

Alex didn't have time to feel fear. Because in that moment, her investigative brain was putting together all the pieces of the puzzle that had evaded her. Although Leslie had not been expecting Roger, he was on the island when she arrived, waiting for her. When she went inside the house, he locked Ollie in Leslie's trunk to keep him out of the way. When Leslie realized her son was trapped in her car, she called Steve and told him to come to the island—just as Roger knew she would. After she placed the call to Steve, Roger had taken her to the construction site . . . and . . . then what? Had he raped her? Or had she tried to seduce him in an attempt to save herself?

"He destroyed her," Roger was saying. "You see, I made her happy. But she knew that we couldn't be together. That's what she told me the night before she died. She said that she was going to come to the island to have a romantic weekend with Steve. She was going to destroy my child . . . just so she could stay with Steve."

"That was very ingenious of you, Roger," Alex said as calmly as she could manage. "Making it look like suicide. You really did put Steve through hell, you know."

He shook his head. "He hasn't suffered."

"So what's your plan this time? If you kill me now, what makes you think the police won't go after you?"

" 'Cause you've already sent a note to your paper, telling them that you know Steve killed Leslie, and now . . ." he said, standing in front of her, "now he's after you."

Without hesitating, Alex picked up her knee and knocked him in the groin.

As he knelt over in pain, she ran toward the door. Furious, Roger picked himself up and grabbed her just as she started down the stairs. He threw her up against the wall. "That was stupid, Alex."

She bit down on his hand, drawing blood. As a stunned Roger pulled back, she broke out of his grasp and ran down the hall. He grabbed her arm and yanked her toward him.

"Roger, don't." She tried to reason with him. "You're not a killer. Let me bring Steve to justice. Let me do it."

He shook his head. "It's too late," he said, twisting her arms behind her.

"C'mon now, Roger, think about this." "She tried again." "They're going to know that message you sent wasn't from me. I've been in contact with them all along. They know about you. I already told them Steve was innocent."

Roger shook his head. "It won't work, Alex," he said. He hoisted her to her feet and shoved her into the room. "I'm sorry, Alex," he said, almost tenderly. He tightened his grip on her arms as he pushed her toward the balcony.

"AHHHH!" A strange, loud, gurgled scream pierced the room.

Ollie stood in the doorway.

"Promise me!" Ollie screamed, closing his eyes. He began talking very fast, screaming the words in one breath, as if they were burned in his memory. "Please Roger don't please you're hurting me I love you I'll do anything you want don't kill me I want to be with you I love you what are you doing don't stop please Roger stop you're scaring me stop help me please somebody help ROGERRRRRRR . . ."

Ollie opened his eyes and stared straight at his mother's killer. Roger loosened his grip on Alex.

"You were there," Roger whispered to Ollie, his voice just loud enough for Alex to hear. "You were there," he said, his voice rising in pain and rage. He dropped his hold on Alex and walked calmly toward Ollie.

"Ollie, run!" Alex commanded with all her might.

But Ollie stood completely motionless, as if he hadn't heard her.

"You should've stayed in the trunk!" Roger said, hitting Ollie across the face and knocking him to the ground. Alex lunged at Roger, but he threw her off easily. "You should've never opened your mouth, kid," he said, raising his hand to hit him again. But he never got a chance. Alex had picked up a long, narrow piece of wood and with all her strength hit him broadside in the back. He shouted in pain as he lurched forward.

"Run, Ollie!" she yelled. But still Ollie refused to move.

Roger picked himself up and turned to face Alex.

"Don't come near me," Alex threatened Roger, holding the piece of wood like a baseball bat. He made a move for her, and she swung the wood. Roger jumped out of the way and grabbed it, twisting it away from her and throwing it to the ground. He grabbed her, twisting her hair and shoving her toward the balcony. "Roger," she said, holding out her hands to stop him as she tried to reason. "It's me. It's Alex." Roger slapped her hard, knocking her to the ground. She fell on her back, her head hanging off the balcony. "Please," she said.

"Let her go!" Steve stood in the doorway. "Kill me instead, Roger. You didn't do a very good job of even slowing me down, did you?"

Alex glanced around her. She really hoped Steve knew what he was doing. One push would send her off the edge.

"Goddamn," Roger said at the sight of Steve.

"C'mon . . ." Steve said, coaxing him back into the room. His shirt was pulled out, and his voice was slightly slurred. He was dragging the right side of his body as if he had had several cocktails too many.

"You always wanted to take me on. You even beat me once . . . one time, when we were kids. Remember? Take me on, Roger . . . see if you can."

Roger stood still, weighing his options.

"I bet you can't win, Roger. I bet I can take you even when I'm half drugged."

Roger took the bet. He reached inside his pocket for his brass knuckles.

Alex bolted from behind him. Grabbing Ollie's hand, she pulled him into the hall.

Roger's first swing missed Steve completely. So did his second.

"Looks like you're a little out of shape there, my friend," Steve said as he drove his right fist into Roger's stomach and his left fist flew against Roger's chin.

Roger dived into Steve, the mere force of his body pushing him onto the balcony. As the two men struggled, they rolled precariously close to the edge. Steve jumped on top of Roger and pinned him to the floor. "You put Ollie in the trunk so that you could kill Leslie, didn't you?"

Roger tried to take a swing, his brass knuckles wedged in his hand. Steve swiped them away, knocking them out of his hand and over the edge of the balcony. A crash of thunder caused the whole building to shake.

"C'mon," Steve said, twisting Roger's arms behind his back as he stood him up and walked him back into the room "We're going back to the house. As soon as it clears up, you're going to the police."

Roger suddenly did a backward kick that caught Steve by surprise, hitting him in the gut. As Steve loosened his grip, Roger twisted away and backed up onto the balcony.

"What are you doing?" Steve called out.

Roger stood on the edge of the balcony. The wind whipped his blond, matted hair back away from his forehead. "C'mon, Roger," Steve said, his hands outstretched. "C'mon inside."

Roger shook his head, tears welling in his eyes. "Now you've killed us both," he said resignedly.

Steve watched in horror as the tormented man took

a backward jump off the balcony, silently falling to his death.

"Steve?" Alex called from the hallway.

Steve turned around slowly as Alex made her way toward him. Ollie was behind her, his arms around her legs.

"Did he . . ." she said, her voice drifting off.

He nodded. Another crash of thunder roared over them. "C'mon," he said, wrapping his arms around Ollie and Alex. "Let's get out of here."

Twenty-Nine

Tim stepped through the mud. His expensive Gucci shoes were going to be totally trashed. Had he known that he was going to be spending the night tramping around a swamp in Florida, he never would have worn them, but unfortunately he didn't find that out until he arrived at his office and turned on his computer.

He pushed his glasses back up on his nose and looked around. Fortunately for this small island, the storm had not turned into a hurricane, although the wind and torrential downpours had been pretty vicious. His eyes focused on the ten uniformed men huddled together in front of the barn. He had called the police as soon as he received Alex's message, and although they had assured them they would do what they could, he knew they would be limited because of the storm. He himself had been unable to catch a flight to Miami until this evening.

It was almost midnight, but the Chapman estate was lit up like Christmas. Five more men in police uniform were standing around talking in the front of the building. Tim glanced around. *Where in the hell did all of these cops come from, anyway?* By boat, he realized. Like him. Or by helicopter, he thought. Unlike him. He took off his damp jacket and whipped it over his shoulder. A portly uniformed man broke away from the huddle at the barn and walked up to him. "Identification, please."

Tim pulled his identification out of his pocket. "Tim Barnes. *New York Times.*"

"You're a long way from home, aren't you?" The portly sheriff asked.

"How's Alex?" he said worriedly.

"I don't know how you managed to get out here, but we're not talking to the press . . ."

"I'm a close friend of Alex . . ." He paused, not sure whether to use her real name or her alibi. "Of the woman who was on the island. I'm the guy who called the police and told them that she had sent me a message that she was in trouble."

"Oh, yeah" the sheriff said, as though his memory was suddenly coming back. "She's okay. Follow me. I'll take you to her."

Tim followed him into the house. He saw Alex sitting on the couch, holding an ice pack to her mouth. "Alex," he called out. She was hurt. He pushed the sheriff out of the way as he rushed over to her. "Did he try to kill you?" he asked. "I warned you. I told you not to do this," he continued, dropping down to his knees in front of her.

"Tim," she said. He hugged her. She pulled back. "What are you doing here?" she asked.

"I got your message."

Alex paused, trying to remember. "I don't understand."

"You said that you had proof that Steve killed his wife. That he was trying to kill you, too."

"Oh, yeah" she said, nodding. Tim was referring

to the message Roger had told her about. "I didn't send that."

Tim turned toward the sheriff. "How bad was that hit on the head?"

"There's nothing wrong with my memory, Tim," she said, irritated. "I didn't send that message. Roger stole my computer. It must have been him."

"Roger?" he said, surprised. "The pilot?"

She nodded. "He took my computer and sent you that message. He tried to kill me," she said, wearily awaiting his lecture.

Tim stared at her, registering her story. "Really," he said finally, as though he wasn't sure whether or not to believe her. He looked toward the corner of the room, where Steve was standing talking to some policemen. "Alex," he said, smiling politely at the sheriff. "I want to take you back to Miami with me. Tonight."

Alex shook her head. "I'm not going back to the *Times,* Tim. I quit. Remember?"

Tim looked at her, his frown deepening. "There's something I need to talk to you about. In private." He glanced at the sheriffs name tag. "Do you mind if I borrow her for a few minutes . . . Sheriff Mulney?"

The sheriff shrugged his shoulders. "Not at all," he said, wandering away.

"Thanks," Tim muttered under his breath. He focused back on Alex. "Where can we talk?"

Alex sighed. She knew that Tim would not give up until she acquiesced. With a great deal of effort, she managed to stand up. He led her out of the room.

"Where to?" he asked, grabbing her arm to assist her. She motioned toward the dining room.

"In there," she said.

They went inside the room and shut the door. "What happened?" he asked in a low voice.

"I told you. Roger was nuts. He drugged Steve with some sort of horse tranquilizer, and then he tried to kill me. His plan was to kill me and have Steve take the fall. Just like he tried to do with Leslie. But fortunately for me," Alex continued, "Steve is in such great shape the tranquilizer didn't last as long as Roger thought it would. Steve saved my life," she said. "I could've died."

"You don't say," Tim said sarcastically. "Sounds like a hell of a story."

"I'd say so."

"What happened to your lip?" he asked, peering at her disapprovingly.

She touched her hand to her tender lip. She winced. "Roger hit me."

Tim nodded as he paused, pursing his lips. "It makes you look funny." He looked around him. "Interesting room," he said, his gaze focused on the heavy bag dangling in the middle of the room.

"What is it, Alex? Did he tell you that he loved you or something? That's it, isn't it? Protecting your man in the name of love?"

"I'm telling you the truth," she said defensively. "Leslie and Roger had been having an affair. When she tried to break it off with him, he killed her."

Tim nodded. "Where's this kid you're so fond of?"

Alex looked at him curiously. "Ollie? He's sleeping."

Tim paused, staring at her. "Where was he through all this?"

"Roger locked him in the trunk of the car. That's where he was when Leslie was killed, too."

Tim hesitated. "I guess I should tell you that I didn't come all this way just to bring you back."

"What are you talking about?"

His eyes focused on her coldly. "I came here for a story."

Alex met his gaze directly. "Go ahead and write it," she said coolly. "I'd be happy to give you some quotes."

"I'm sure you would," he said. "But no thanks. I'm here for the truth."

"I came here for the truth, as you'll remember. And I found it."

Tim was looking at her.

"Tim, please," she said. "I care for you, I really do. But I could never live with you again. And I don't think you'd want me to, anyway."

He swallowed. "Dick said he'll take you back. Your old job. Your old salary."

Alex could feel her face turn red. "How nice of him. But I don't want to come back."

"I thought that was the whole reason you had taken this . . . case on," he said, emphasizing the word *case,* "because you wanted to return to investigative reporting."

She paused. "Well, I changed my mind."

He sighed as he glanced down at the floor. "What you just said about you and me living together . . . well, you were wrong," he said with finality. He looked away. "I wanted you to marry me," he said quickly.

Alex sighed. She shook her head and smiled. "You've never been a very good liar."

"Yeah, well, you should know that I haven't just been sitting around, either. Conchita and I have been seeing each other."

Alex didn't miss a beat. "I'm happy for you," she said. "Conchita is a great woman. You're a lucky guy." She stopped short of saying that Chita, however, was not so fortunate.

"Goddammit, Alex," he said, realizing that she couldn't be persuaded by jealousy. "Have you lost your mind? Do you know what you're doing? The man is a murderer. A murderer . . ."

"Stop it," she said.

"He's using you!"

Alex slapped him. He held his hand to his cheek, staring at her as if she had gone insane.

She stepped back, shocked by her behavior. "I'm sorry," she said. "It's just . . . I'm tired and . . ."

Steve entered the room. "Oh," he said, pretending surprise at seeing them in there. "I'm sorry. I heard voices . . ."

"That's all right," Alex said, focusing back on Tim. "Tim was just leaving."

Tim glanced at Steve before looking back at Alex. "So that's it?" he asked. "Your mind is made up?"

Alex nodded silently.

Tim turned toward the door. "Congratulations," he said coldly to Steve. Tim paused in the doorway as he glanced back toward Alex. "Keep in touch?" he asked.

She gave him a little smile and nodded. He shook his head as he walked out of the room.

Steve looked at Alex. "Who was that?" he asked.

She looked toward the closed door. "My old . . . coworker. He's dating a friend of mine."

He looked at her curiously.

"And," she continued nonchalantly, "well, we . . . I mean, Tim and I, lived together for a while."

"Hmm," Steve said, glancing back toward the door. "And he came to try and talk you into coming back to him?"

"Not exactly. Roger sent some message, pretending it was from me, stating that I was afraid for my life and needed him here immediately."

The sheriff poked his head in the door. "We found him," he said almost cheerfully, referring to the discovery of Roger's body. "We were fortunate. The waves just threw him up beside the house . . . or, rather, what used to be the house." The supports in the house had given way during the storm, causing it to crumple as though it was made of cards.

Steve glanced at Alex. "Excuse me," he said, looking at her as he followed the sheriff out of the room.

Alex waited for Steve to leave before wandering into the hall and over to the library. She curled up in a ball on the couch. She slid down, resting her head on the pillows.

Thirty

Alex awoke to the sound of a door shutting. She shook herself awake as she glanced at her watch for the time, momentarily forgetting that it had been smashed in the altercation with Roger. She pushed herself up on the couch and looked toward the hall. Steve stood in the entrance to the room, resting his weary body against the frame of the door.

He crossed his arms in front of him as he flashed her a weak smile. "They're gone."

She nodded. "What time is it?" She yawned.

"Almost dawn."

"You must be exhausted," she said sympathetically. She patted the couch. "Come sit down."

He sat down beside her and casually dropped his arm around her, pulling her into his arms. She rested her head on his shoulder. "Has the drug worn off?"

"I guess so," he said, opening and closing a fist. "I still feel a little numb."

"Are you sure you don't want to go to a doctor?"

"I'm sure," he said absentmindedly.

She looked up at him. He was staring at the wall, his expression blank.

"Thinking about Leslie?"

He nodded, snapping out of his trance. "And Roger. I'm having a tough time believing that he killed her. That he tried to kill you."

"Leslie wanted to break it off with him. The thought of her staying with you and getting rid of her pregnancy was too much for him. So he killed her. He was always jealous of you. He just lost it."

"And then he tried to pin it on me."

"I think he did that to ease his guilt. Part of him really believed that you were ultimately responsible. It's the only way he could live with himself."

"Thank God he didn't know that Ollie had seen the whole thing."

"Maybe that's why Ollie didn't speak. He was afraid Roger would kill him, too."

Steve shrugged his shoulders. "Maybe. But I think a large part of it was just shock and terror." Steve paused. He shook his head. "Poor kid. How did he manage to get out of the trunk?"

"Most trunks are made to lock people out, not in," Alex said matter-of-factly.

"Is that so, Miss Reporter?" he asked, teasing her. She laughed.

"There's a sound we haven't heard too much around here lately," he said, outlining her lips with his index finger.

"Not enough, that's for sure."

He squeezed her tightly. "I don't know how I would've made it through without you."

"And now that you've made it through?" she asked.

"I don't know how I could ever be without you." He shook his head. "I thought I was going to lose you . . ." he began.

"You didn't."

"No," he said, staring into her eyes. "I could never lose you," he said, cupping her face in his hands. He paused. "Alex, where do you want to go from here?"

"Home," she said, not hesitating.

"Home?"

"Back to New York. Where we'll be surrounded by people. Where Ollie can get help. Where we all can return to life."

"Return to life?"

"You know what I mean. I've had enough of private

islands. *Real* life. I feel like I've been running for the past year. Ever since Lennie died. And I'm tired of running."

He gave her a little squeeze. "You haven't been screaming in your sleep anymore."

She shook her head. "No. A part of me will always miss Lennie, but . . ." Her voice drifted off.

"Are you going to return to the paper?"

Alex shook her head. "No chance. I'd like to do some sort of job where I can help children, instead of just writing about them. I'd like to help children like Lennie get the chance in life that Lennie never got. Be a social worker or something."

Steve smiled. "I love you, Alex Webster." He picked up her hand and held it to his cheek. "This home that you have in mind. Is there room for a man and his son?"

She shrugged. "There's definitely room, but I'm afraid there's only one room. A social worker's salary in New York City doesn't go very far."

Steve nodded. "I see. Well, let's assume for a minute that I'll take care of the home."

"In that case, there's even room for a boxing bag."

He raised an eyebrow as he glanced down at her. "Hmm. I'm no expert by any means, but it sounds like true love."

"That," she said, nibbling his chin, "is definite."

Epilogue

"**A**lex!"

Alex turned around as she pulled her wool hat down around her ears. The robust, athletic little boy with blond hair was ice skating toward her so fast that she doubted he would be able to stop in time. She was right. The child flung his arms around her, nearly knocking her off her feet.

"Where's Dad?" Ollie asked, looking up at her. He had started speaking shortly after Roger's death, and although he was quiet and shy in the beginning, time had healed his resilient soul. Now, just a year after their return from Rye Island, he sounded and looked just like any other healthy eight-year-old boy. He had even embraced athletics and was particularly fond of those sports occurring in the winter and fall. He had practically begged Alex to take him to the Rockefeller Center skating rink this afternoon.

"He should be here any minute. Where's your hat?"

"I left it on the bench."

Alex glanced across the ice rink. "On the bench?"

"I couldn't wear it," he said, shrugging his shoulders as if the statement was self-explanatory.

"Why?" Alex asked slowly, trying to follow.

" 'Cause Renee is here," he said, motioning over his shoulder to a cute and perky ten-year-old brunette.

Oh, of course, Alex thought. If you were trying to impress the chicks, you didn't wear a hat. She smiled. No wonder Ollie had been so anxious to go skating this afternoon. He had returned to being a normal little boy in no time.

"Hey, sport! What happened to your hat?" Steve called out to Ollie as he approached the rink.

Alex turned toward her handsome husband. He was wearing jeans and a down jacket . . . and was quite obviously hatless himself. He came up to the duo and gave them a joint squeeze. Alex smiled. "He's not wearing a hat because he's trying to impress a girl," she whispered. She ran her fingers through Steve's thick, curly hair. "What's your excuse?"

"Yeah," Ollie said gleefully. "What's your excuse?" He laughed mischievously as he pushed himself off Alex and back onto the rink.

"Are we in adolescence yet?" Steve whispered in her ear, keeping an eye on Ollie.

"Not quite."

Steve nodded with a twinkle in his eye. "Can't wait."

Alex laughed. Despite his pretend consternation, she knew Steve was thrilled that his son was behaving like any normal child his age.

"How's everything at the club?" she asked, referring to the recreation center that she and Steve had built for disadvantaged youths. Steve had followed his heart, selling his company and investing his talent and money in the community where he had grown up.

Steve nodded. "Everything is going along fine. By the way, your mother called. I knew it was her because she asked to speak to an Alexandra Webster Chapman, as though I might have forgotten your name."

Alex laughed. "Maybe she didn't know it was you."

Steve smiled as he kissed her forehead. "She knew all right."

Alex shook her head and sighed. Her mother had refused to come to their wedding, stating that she could never accept Steve as a son-in-law. But over the past year, she had slowly begun to warm to him, even agreeing to visit them. Alex had picked her up at the airport that morning, and although she insisted on staying at the Plaza Hotel, Alex viewed her trip as a step toward getting their mother-daughter relationship back on track. "She'll come around. Did she say what time she wanted to go to dinner?"

Steve nodded. "Not only did she say what time, but she also said where. I think she wants me to try and buy her affection."

"It's going to be expensive," Alex warned, smiling.

"I could guess that from the restaurant she chose." Renee, Ollie's dream girl, sped past them, with Ollie in hot pursuit.

"Oh, to be young again," Steve said, feigning wistfulness

Alex shook her head. "No thanks. I'm happy to be right where I am . . ." She glanced up at him as she continued, "Here in the middle of civilization . . . with my family."

Steve smiled as he looped his arms around her waist. "Have I ever told you that I love you, Mrs. Chapman?"

Alex smiled, deeply content. "Yes, you have. But I promise you I'll never get tired of hearing how much."

"Dad?" Ollie was standing in front of them. "Can Renee come over for dinner?"

Steve shook his head. "We're meeting Alex's mother tonight for dinner. Remember?"

Alex offered, "You can have Renee over tomorrow. We can get videos and make popcorn."

Ollie grinned. "Promise me?"

Alex smiled as she and Steve exchanged a knowing glance. How different those words sounded now. They both answered Ollie in unison: "We promise."